> ## "The first thing I'm buying is the biggest, softest feather bed to be found. That's what you deserve."

Hanna snickered as he set her on the porch. "My, I have married well, haven't I? I have a husband who places my comfort above all else—"

She barely had time to complete the teasing comment before Cale clutched her hand and nearly dragged her up the steps in his haste for privacy. A blush exploded on her cheeks when the stage owner—a wiry little man with frizzy gray hair—glanced up from where he sat, warming himself by the fire. He grinned wryly as his gaze bounced back and forth between her and Cale.

Hanna decided she didn't care if the proprietor knew why they were in an all-fired rush to reach their room. If her legs had been longer, *she'd* have been the one tugging Cale up the steps.

**Praise for Carol Finch's previous title**

**Call of the White Wolf**
"The wholesome goodness of the characters…
will touch your heart and soul."
—*Rendezvous*

"A love story that aims straight for the heart
and never misses."
—*Romantic Times*

# CAROL FINCH

# BOUNTY HUNTER'S BRIDE

## HARLEQUIN®

TORONTO • NEW YORK • LONDON
AMSTERDAM • PARIS • SYDNEY • HAMBURG
STOCKHOLM • ATHENS • TOKYO • MILAN • MADRID
PRAGUE • WARSAW • BUDAPEST • AUCKLAND

ISBN 0-373-29235-X

BOUNTY HUNTER'S BRIDE

Copyright © 2002 by Connie Feddersen

This edition published by arrangement with Harlequin Books S.A.

® and TM are trademarks of the publisher. Trademarks indicated with ® are registered in the United States Patent and Trademark Office, the Canadian Trade Marks Office and in other countries.

Visit us at www.eHarlequin.com

Printed in U.S.A.

Please address questions and book requests to:
Harlequin Reader Service
U.S.: 3010 Walden Ave., P.O. Box 1325, Buffalo, NY 14269
Canadian: P.O. Box 609, Fort Erie, Ont. L2A 5X3

This book is dedicated to my husband,
Ed, and our children—Kurt, Jill, Christie, Jeff and Jon.
And to our grandchildren,
Livia, Blake, Kennedy and Brooklynn.
Hugs and kisses!

# Chapter One

*Fort Smith, 1870s*

"Oh, my God, what have I done?" Hanna Malloy whispered apprehensively as she stepped off the steamboat that had transported her upriver from New Orleans. She stared at the gloomy, overcast sky, which promised another spring rain shower at any moment and listened to the drone of insects that swarmed near the river. In dismay, she surveyed the muddy frontier outpost of Fort Smith. *This* was her salvation? *This* was the answer to her prayers and her reward for six months of careful planning to seize control of her future? What in heaven's name could she have been thinking!

"Want some help with them bags, missy?"

Hanna stepped away from the foul-smelling miscreant who'd approached her while she was lost in thought. The shaggy-haired man with beady gray eyes flashed her a smile that was missing two front teeth.

"Thank you for your kind offer of assistance, but I can manage on my own," she replied.

The short, pudgy brute eyed her carpetbags covetously, glanced this way and that, then lumbered off. Hanna had the unmistakable feeling that if there hadn't been dozens of river boatmen, cowboys fresh from trail drives, gamblers and railroad workers bustling around her, the man would've snatched her bags and taken off at a dead run.

Hanna gulped and glanced uneasily around her. She wasn't in the best of company at the moment. Indeed, in all her twenty years of existence, she'd never been in such bad company without the protection of a chaperon.

A sense of panic and disillusionment very nearly overwhelmed Hanna. For moral support and a sense of comfort, she clasped the golden locket—a childhood gift from her mother—that hung around her neck. Inhaling a bracing breath, she strode past the abandoned, stone-walled garrison that had been built on a sandstone bluff overlooking the Arkansas River.

"Oh, Lord," Hanna muttered as she hiked toward the frontier town set a mere hundred yards from the eastern border of infamous Indian Territory—where thieves and murderers were reported to run rampant. There were no paved avenues, no luxurious hotels, no fashionable boutiques and no lights to illuminate the mud-caked streets. There were, however, Hanna noted, amazed, a string of thirty saloons, a newspaper office, one bank and several shops that provided basic necessities. Dozens of wagons, hacks and saddle horses waited beside the uneven boardwalks.

She'd planned and schemed, hoarded her monthly allowance and used the funds her departed mother had set aside for her wedding trousseau for *this?* Sweet merciful heavens! Even in her modest-priced lavender gown Hanna looked overdressed and out of place in comparison to the few women she passed on the street.

Hanna squared her shoulders, hitched up the hem of her dress and marched determinedly forward. She had to remind herself—repeatedly—why she'd turned her back on her aristocratic lifestyle, sacrificed all the opulent luxuries in New Orleans and left her father's handpicked groom at the altar. She, who had what most women aspired to, had climbed out the window of a church filled to capacity, and made a mad dash to the riverboat that would deliver her to the precious freedom she'd craved—dreamed of—for years. For the sake of independence, she'd have to learn to adjust and accept life on different terms than what was familiar.

Hanna stepped onto the uneven boardwalk in front of a saloon to avoid the heavily rutted mud street. Tinkling piano music, masculine laughter and the smell of cigar smoke greeted her as she passed one tavern after another, to reach one of the ramshackle hotels in the offensive frontier town.

When a drunken ruffian stumbled from one of the saloons and rammed her broadside, Hanna clamped her arms around a rough-hewn post to prevent herself from being catapulted into the mud. Her carpetbags swung crazily from her fingertips.

"Well, what have we here?" the man slurred, licking his lips and leering at her through bloodshot eyes.

Thunder boomed overhead, signaling impending doom and threatening Hanna's firm resolve. If she had any sense at all she'd reverse direction and hightail it back to the river to catch the next steamboat to New Orleans and the familiarity of life as she knew it. The thrill of reaching her personal promised land had been dashed, replaced with disillusionment and uncertainty.

"Why don't you 'n me find us a room and git better 'quainted?" the drunkard suggested, in what she presumed to be his most seductive voice. It fell miserably short of the mark.

Hanna shivered with repulsion and pushed herself away from the splintered post. "Excuse me, sir," she said stiffly. "I'm on my way to meet my fiancé." That was a half-truth, probably one of many she'd have to tell before she got where she was going.

Before the scruffy-looking man could grab her arm, Hanna sailed off at a fast clip, praying she could reach a hotel before she was waylaid again. Even in her haste she noted she was attracting entirely too much attention from the men who milled about on the boardwalks. Sweet mercy! The ratio of men to women in this town must be so lopsided that males salivated at the mere sight of a female, Hanna decided. She made a mental note to purchase another gown that downplayed her femininity the first chance she got. All this unwanted attention was making her nervous and spoiling her attempt to maintain a low profile.

The last thing she wanted was to find a string of men trailing behind her. She'd endured quite enough of men and their hidden agendas—not to mention their more obvious intentions toward her person. Because of her wealth and position in New Orleans society, she'd dealt with more than her share of gold diggers and opportunists who were anxious to attach themselves to her family's fortune. And her father, damn him, had paraded a string of handpicked suitors past her, then finally delivered his ultimatum when she kept stalling and found fault with every one.

The thought of her domineering father stiffened her resolve and brought her chin up to a determined angle. Despite the crash of thunder and the sudden downpour that formed a curtain of rain along the overhang of the porch roof, Hanna assured herself that she had what she wanted. Now *she* was in control of her life and her destiny.

The sacrifices she'd made to reach Fort Smith, the hardships she might face during her exodus, were worth every trial and tribulation. At long last she was free of her father's control. He was *not* making another decision for her, *not* dictating to her ever again. This was her declaration of independence from Walter Malloy, the powerful, influential shipping magnate who believed that his only daughter was a pawn to be played to his advantage.

Walter believed that money could buy anything and that every man had his price. During the steamboat ride upriver, Hanna had made a pact with herself that she would turn her father's cold-blooded philosophy on him, to ensure she broke his control over her forevermore. She'd abandoned all attempts to please him, to earn his love and respect. She had spent years trying to gain his attention and approval, but he seemed loath to spend more than a few moments looking in her direction before turning away. In his eyes she would never be the beloved son he'd lost to illness.

Therefore, Hanna had left her life of sophistication, refinement and elegance behind, to find herself a husband. *Her* idea of the perfect mate, not her father's. Hanna had mentally listed her qualifications for an ideal husband. He would be an intimidating man himself—not one easily cowed by her father's booming commands, nor easily swayed by bribes, which bent so many people to her father's fierce will.

Hanna glanced up to note the wooden sign that indicated she'd reached a hotel. If she were in New Orleans she wouldn't have set foot inside such a shabby establishment. But this wasn't New Orleans and she wanted nothing more than to take refuge from the rain and the crowd of men that swaggered along behind her. She was tired of being ogled, and weary from her journey. Not to mention the emotional turmoil she'd undergone after her father announced that she would wed *whom* he decreed, *when* he decreed and *where*.

The thought sent frissons of frustration undulating through her. Hanna definitely needed a secluded place to rest, to unwind, to regroup before she reviewed her checklist for the husband she hoped to acquire quickly and expediently. After she caught her breath, she would inquire around this muddy, backward frontier town to locate a man who'd agree to share his name, for a substantial price. Hanna would be her father's daughter, use his own tactics, for the first and last time.

After a brief wedding ceremony, the groom could go his way and she would go her own way—west. She'd heard it said that out West a woman wasn't as restricted by social expectations as in the East. Out West was where free-spirited individuals migrated, to live by their own rules and establish new lives for themselves.

Surely somewhere in this outpost of three thousand souls she could find one man who was intimidating and strong-willed enough to withstand her father. A man who didn't stay in one place long enough for Walter Malloy to track him down and offer him scads of money to have the marriage annulled, before dragging his daughter home to wed that stuffy, pompous aristocrat he had chosen.

Hanna winced, remembering her confrontation with her father. He'd boomed at her in that deep, foghornlike voice, shouting that Hanna had rejected the very last suitor, and that she would become Mrs. Louis Beauchamp—of the highly prestigious Beauchamps who could trace their family lineage back to the titled gentry of France. The merger of two wealthy shipping magnates would ensure a monopoly the likes of which New Orleans had never seen.

In outraged fury, Hanna had refused, insisting that if Walter was so immensely fond of Louis Beauchamp—of the highly respected Beauchamps—then *he* should marry the man.

That had been a mistake of gigantic proportions. Walter's face had turned the color of raw liver and he'd bellowed that there *would* be a wedding and a merger and Hanna *would* accept his decisions, like the dutiful, grateful daughter she was supposed to be.

From that day forward, a chaperon—Rutherford J. Wiley—was assigned to her each time she left their sprawling plantation on the Mississippi or ventured from their elegant town house in New Orleans. According to Walter, Hanna would have no opportunity whatsoever to defy his decree.

Or so he thought, she mused, smiling triumphantly as she made a beeline toward the registration desk of the hotel. She'd taken advantage of the only window of opportunity her father had left open to her the past few months. The *window* in the room where she was to dress in her wedding gown before Walter walked her down the aisle to become the bride of Louis Beauchamp—of the proud and pompous Beauchamps. That window had been her salvation. Hanna had been prepared for that moment of opportunity, had planned for it, right down to the last detail.

She imagined that her father had cursed several blue streaks when he'd realized she'd escaped. She would've liked to see the look on his face when he realized she'd defied him and fled the city posthaste. If she knew her father—and she knew him well—he would spare no expense in hiring the most qualified detectives—the Pinkertons, no doubt—to haul her home.

But it would be too late. She'd have a husband and she'd be long gone by the time Walter discovered where she was and what she'd done to counter his insufferable dictates.

"May I help you, miss?"

Jostled from her thoughts, Hanna glanced up to see a bewhiskered and bespectacled man with a shiny bald head staring at her. "Yes, sir. I would like a room, please. Your best," she added, certain the *best* Fort Smith had to offer would fall miserably short of the luxuries to which she'd grown accustomed.

The proprietor—James Jensen, according to an engraved wooden nameplate on the counter—smiled kindly at her. "I'm sorry, miss. I'm afraid second best is all I have to offer. Our most spacious suite was rented an hour ago to a man who's become legendary in these parts. He's one of Judge Parker's most effective and most reliable, ya see.'' James leaned forward confidentially. ''By nature and profession, he's not a man folks want to cross. But he and his dog saved my life one dark winter night when four bloodthirsty hooligans dragged me into the alley to pistol-whip me and steal the money I was taking to the bank. Now we have a standing agreement. When he's in town he receives the best accommodations I have to offer. Free of charge.''

Hanna was intrigued. The reputation of Judge Isaac Parker—the Hanging Judge, as he'd been dubbed—was known far and wide. This living legend who rode for Parker might be exactly the kind of man she was looking for.

''He's a deputy marshal?'' she asked hopefully.

James smiled wryly. ''When necessary. Bounty hunter mostly, though. You might say he's the judge's last resort when all civilized methods of law and order fail. This gun-fighter takes the most difficult cases and deals with the worst desperadoes who hide out in Indian Territory. 'Course, being a half-breed Cherokee, he knows every inch of that seventy-four thousand square mile territory, every secluded haunt where outlaws like to hole up with their ill-gotten gains.''

''So, you're saying this accomplished bounty hunter, and sometimes deputy marshal, is in and out of town frequently?'' she asked with growing interest.

''Mostly out,'' James reported as he turned the registration book so she could sign her name. ''He's only in town once a month or so to deliver prisoners, testify at trials and collect his rewards.''

In other words, this legendary tracker and shootist was sent out to apprehend the most vicious, barbaric criminals who preyed on society. He risked his life on a daily basis for sizable rewards.

Anticipation sizzled through Hanna. From the sound of it, luck was on her side. Within an hour of reaching Fort

Smith she had a prime candidate for a husband. He was more or less a gun for hire who provided a necessary service. If he were accustomed to dealing with deadly killers on a regular basis he wouldn't bat an eyelash at confronting her blustering father. Walter Malloy would be no more intimidating to this fearless gunfighter than a buzzing mosquito.

"Most of the deputy marshals ride across Indian Territory in groups of two to four, pulling a wagon that serves as mobile headquarters, office, kitchen and jail," James added. "But not Cale Elliot. He and his dog travel alone, and that's the way he likes it."

Cale Elliot, she mused as she signed a fictitious name on the register to throw her father's detectives off her trail. And they *would* come looking for her; she didn't doubt that for a minute. By then, Hanna would have a wedding ring on her finger and a marriage license in hand.

When she'd originally devised her scheme to escape her father's control, she had considered seeking out a condemned convict for a husband. But it didn't take her long to realize she needed a live body. If she were a widow her father could easily tote her back to New Orleans to wed Louis Beauchamp. No, Hanna needed a real live husband, and this half-breed bounty hunter sounded as if he fit the bill perfectly. She could be wed immediately and disappear before her father tracked her down.

"Here ya go, Miss…" James glanced down at her signature "…Rawlins. Turn right at the top of the stairs. Your room is two doors down on the left."

"Is my room near the bounty hunter's?" she asked eagerly.

Assuming Hanna was hoping for nearby protection, James smiled, then glanced over her head to note the raft of men who were hovering in the doorway to cast their eyes on the attractive new arrival. "He'll be right across the hall from you. He's not one for idle chitchat, but if trouble arises, he's the man you'll want on your side.''

Mrs. Cale Elliot, she mused. That had a nice ring to it....

A worrisome thought furrowed her brows. What if Mr. Elliot was already married? Perhaps he had a wife who lived in the Cherokee Nation.

Don't go borrowing complications, she chastised herself as she accepted the key from James. Hanna decided to approach Mr. Elliot with her proposition as soon as she had time to freshen up. If he was married he might be able to recommend another deputy marshal who would suit her purposes just as well.

''You won't have to walk far to enjoy a fine meal,'' James informed her, nodding his bald head toward the adjoining restaurant. ''My wife and her sister are fine cooks. Best in town, in fact. You've come to the right place for a clean, tidy room and mouthwatering meals.''

''Thank you, sir. I'm sure the room will be splendid and the meals exceptional,'' Hanna replied as she hoisted up her satchels, then headed for the steps.

''I'll call one of the servants to carry your bags,'' James offered.

''No need for that. I'll manage on my own.'' From now on Hanna intended to be self-reliant. It was her luggage, after all, and she'd carry it herself.

She could feel male eyes boring into her back as she climbed the creaking staircase. For once the tiresome attention of men didn't annoy her. She was too preoccupied with the prospect of locating a suitable husband. She had important matters on her mind and was one step closer to the protection granted by marriage, to enjoying independence, freedom and living her life how and where she chose. Soon she'd have the opportunity to explore her hidden talents, to discover what she excelled at, rather than being stifled by her father's demands and expectations.

Did she have a knack for writing? A talent for painting? Could she become a noted clothing designer and seamstress? An actress or singer? The possibilities shimmered before her like a pot of gold at the end of her personal rainbow.

She'd head west to find herself, to find her own niche. Without her family's well-known name to raise eyebrows and attract the attention of opportunists itching to latch on to an heiress, she could be herself for once in her life. Hanna doubted she'd discover love somewhere beyond the notorious Indian Territory. As far as she could tell, love didn't exist. It was a whimsical notion and she obviously didn't possess lovable qualities. If she had, her own father would have cared deeply for her. But no matter what, she would not become a trophy wife, the window dressing for Louis Beauchamp—a man who thought and behaved like a younger version of her father. A man who wanted her only for her looks, social prestige and wealth, not for the person she was inside.

Hanna halted on the landing to catch her breath, and took note of the sign that read No Animals Allowed. She hiked up the second set of steps and veered right. She sincerely hoped her quest for the perfect husband took her no farther than across the hall.

After the ceremony she would wire the family lawyer to announce she'd met the necessary requirements to take control of the trust fund her mother had bequeathed to her—money her father and Louis Beauchamp couldn't touch or control. She'd take a stagecoach to cross Indian Territory, then Texas—and beyond. She wouldn't look back. Instead she'd look forward, with great anticipation, to her freedom and her future.

Cale Elliot draped his saddlebags over the back of a chair, then picked up the whiskey bottle from the table. James Jensen never failed to have a room ready and wait-

ing when news arrived that he and his prisoners had returned to Fort Smith. After he had saved James from a
vicious beating, the man had become his instant and stead-
fast friend. Which was a good thing, because Cale didn't
have many of them. His line of work alienated folks on
both sides of the law, and his tumbleweed lifestyle provoked wary speculation rather than friendship.

Cale tossed down a drink, feeling the whiskey burn from
his gullet to his empty belly. Since this was a private cele-
bration of sorts, Cale helped himself to another gulp. After
five frustrating years of posing questions and following
leads, he'd learned the whereabouts of the man who'd
killed his half brother and sister-in-law. Cale had finally
stumbled onto the vital information, and feelings of long-
awaited revenge roiled inside him.

Although Joe Horton had dropped out of sight in Kan-
sas, Arkansas and Indian Territory, he'd apparently resur-
faced in Texas, using the assumed name of Otis Pryor. One
of the fugitives Cale had interrogated during the trek back
to Fort Smith had supplied the information in exchange for
leniency. Of course, Cale would've offered the outlaw the
moon to entice him to spill his guts about Otis Pryor. And
indeed, Cale would have a word with Judge Parker before
Wilbur Burton went on trial, as promised. But Cale's
"word" wouldn't be a kind one. The ruthless son of a
bitch had murdered two elderly Cherokees and stolen their
livestock. The only message Cale intended to give the
judge was that justice damn well better prevail.

Cale set the bottle down with a soft thunk, then scrubbed
his hand over his bearded jaw. He desperately needed a
hot, soaking bath and two days of uninterrupted sleep. The
three cutthroats he'd hauled to justice had done their
damnedest to outrun him and the best tracking dog west
of the Mississippi—maybe even the best in these entire
United States. Cale and Skeet had run themselves ragged

for three weeks, searching for clues and questioning witnesses about the crimes of murder and robbery.

It had taken a hair-raising firefight and a knock-down-drag-out brawl to convince the fugitives to surrender. In the end, Cale had manacled his prisoners and delivered them to the jail in one piece—more or less. But he'd come damn close to having his head blown off by the blast of a sawed-off shotgun. His own bullets had been aimed to slow down his assailants, not kill them outright. Judge Parker preferred to have criminals brought to trial. Sometimes Cale had little choice and was forced to return with his fugitives jackknifed over the backs of horses. But he had no intention of showing any mercy when he encountered Otis Pryor. An eye for an eye, he mused bitterly.

Unfortunately, the scuttlebutt was that Otis had surrounded himself with a small army of hired guns and had forced out the previous owners of a ranch with death threats. He'd used the money he'd stolen from Cale's half brother, Gray Cloud, and several other hapless victims to stock his ranch with stolen cattle and horses, and regularly sent out his gang of thieves to steal more livestock to increase the herds.

Cale couldn't storm the fortress with pistols blazing. No, he had to devise an ingenious scheme to avenge the deaths that had taken all that was left of his family. For years, Cale had been fighting other men's battles for them, righting wrongs that had gone too long unpunished. Now it was *his* turn, *his* time to seek personal justice. But first he needed an effective plan to infiltrate Otis Pryor's stronghold and sneak past the corrupt law officers that were in that bastard's pocket.

Skeet's quiet growl put Cale's senses on high alert. The dog had been catching a nap under the table. Suddenly, Skeet laid back his ears and bared his teeth. Cale reflexively slid his Colt from its holster and inched silently toward the door to pounce on whoever thought to pounce on him unaware.

This wouldn't be the first time someone tried to sneak up and blow him to kingdom come. That adage about outlaws being thick as thieves was right on the mark. Cale had lost track of the number of times some hooligan tried to bushwhack him for jailing a fellow gang member. He couldn't recall the number of death threats against him.

In fact, less than a year earlier, a vengeful gang member had broken down the door of this very room and tried to shoot Cale while he was lounging in his tub. Cale couldn't even enjoy a leisurely bath without some spiteful son of a bitch attacking with a pistol or dagger.

When Skeet bolted to his feet, prepared to bound toward the door, Cale signaled for the burly beast to hold his ground. Cale positioned himself beside the door and listened to the faint rap. Before the unwanted visitor had time to react, Cale jerked open the door, wrapped his arm diagonally across the intruder's chest and rammed the pistol barrel beneath his chin.

Only it wasn't a man; it was a woman.

"What do you think you're doing?" she squawked in surprise.

"What the hell...?" Cale croaked as he appraised the shapely bundle of womanly curves and soft flesh that he held clamped in his arms.

## Chapter Two

Cale was so shocked by the unexpected sight and feel of the female pressed up against him that he stood immobilized, his arm crushed to her heaving bosom, his pistol still crammed against her throat. He couldn't say he'd been surprised often in his thirty-two years of hard living. But the woman's unexpected arrival at his door sure 'nuff stunned the hell out of him.

Her fresh clean scent infiltrated his nostrils, and he had to try hard not to breathe her in. The feel of her lush body clasped familiarly to his was a vivid reminder that he hadn't been with a woman since he couldn't remember when.

He would have predicted that this refined, delicate-looking female would keel over and faint dead away—or at the very least, wail, whimper and beg for release. But she didn't. The lady obviously had a stronger constitution than he would have presumed. He liked that about her, among other things—like the way she felt in his arms. But she was either amazingly courageous for coming here, or incredibly foolish. He didn't know which.

Although the woman looked as harmless as a fly, he didn't release her. She could be the distraction that preceded the springing of a trap. Some sneaky weasel could be lurking in the hall, waiting to blow Cale to smithereens.

"Skeet," Cale whispered, then angled his head toward the partially opened door.

The dog trotted across the room and cut around the corner so sharply that he slammed into the woman's legs before searching out trouble in the hall. A moment later he returned to sniff at the woman's skirts.

No doubt Skeet was as unfamiliar with the perfumed scent of a citified woman as Cale was. Usually Cale's reputation and profession worked as effectively as repellent to send decent women running in the opposite direction— often screaming. He was, after all, a hired gun, the circling vulture of Judge Parker's brand of justice, and a half-breed to boot. Although the Cherokee had been labeled as one of the five *civilized* tribes in Indian Territory, most folks regarded all Indians—himself included—as heathens to be avoided and confined to reservations.

Which made it all the more baffling as to why this lovely, obviously well-bred woman was here.

"Whaddaya want, lady?" Cale growled menacingly.

She appeared so badly shaken that he figured he'd scared the wits clean out of her. Well, good. If she didn't have more sense than to come knocking on the door of a man of his reputation, she needed a good scaring.

"I—I…have a p-proposition for you, sir," she panted.

Thick Louisiana accent, he noted. He wondered if this little Southern belle realized she was way out of her league when dealing with him. If she didn't know it yet, she would soon. Even he knew it was taboo for gently bred ladies of quality to consort with men like him. If she wanted to keep her reputation intact she needed to get the hell away from him—fast.

When it finally dawned on Cale what she'd said he glanced down into her pale face—and nearly drowned in the depths of the most remarkable violet eyes he'd ever seen. A thick fan of curly lashes framed those spellbinding pools, which sparkled as if lit from within. Her peaches-and-cream skin was blotched with color—an outward manifestation of the fear that was streaming through her. 'Course, he could feel her heartbeat hammering like a tom-tom against his forearm, so there was no question that he'd frightened her badly.

"Proposition?" he echoed. "What the hell kind of proposition?"

She gulped audibly and tried to force a smile, but he noticed the expression wobbled on the corners of her Cupid's-bow lips. And damn, what a sweet, inviting, sensuous mouth she had, too. He was tempted to steal a taste while he had the chance. For sure, this was likely the one time in his life he'd ever be this close to sophisticated feminine perfection.

This little bundle of lavender satin and lace had it all—the delicate skin and bone structure, the curvaceous body, the beguiling face and a coil of silver-blond hair that reminded Cale of trapped moonbeams. His rough handling had caused one side of her coiffure to come unwound, leaving two thick, curly strands dangling on his shoulder—just close enough for him to get a whiff of their clean scent.

Why had the personification of every man's sweetest dream rapped on *his* door, offering *him* a proposition? What the hell was this? Some kind of cruel joke? Hadn't he been ridiculed because of his mixed heritage often enough without *her* showing up to remind him of who and what he was?

Suspicion clouded Cale's mind again. He wondered if some spiteful renegade who wanted to launch him to hell had paid her to set him up. "Skeet, guard the door," he ordered gruffly.

With ears laid back and an unwelcoming snarl, the dog obeyed instantly, sinking down on his haunches in the hallway. Cale kicked the door shut with the heel of his boot. When he shifted to pat the woman down, ensuring that she wasn't packing hardware, she squawked in offended dignity.

"Now see here, sir! There is no call to manhandle me! I only came for a chat. Any fool can see I'm not the slightest threat to you."

"Where're you from, princess?" he asked as he slid his hand beneath the hem of her gown to check for stashed weapons in her soft kid boots. Again she squealed indignantly when his hand touched her leg. He ignored her and completed his search. When he was assured she was hiding nothing but her seductively curvaceous body, he dropped the pistol still trained on her and slid it into its holster.

She made a big production of fluffing the wrinkles— caused by his manhandling—from the sleeve of her gown. Then she looked down that pert little nose at him. "I swear, I've never met a more suspicious man. Do you greet all your guests with a gun to the chin and a swift frisk?" she asked with a huff.

"I don't usually have guests, only intruders," he reported as he motioned for her to take a chair at the table. "I asked where you hail from."

"N'Awlins, though I don't see that it matters," she said snippily.

"Figured as much. That drawl is unmistakable."

Hanna took a seat, noting Cale Elliot didn't do her the courtesy of pulling out her chair the way most gentlemen would. But what did she expect? This rough-edged bounty hunter knew nothing about polished manners and etiquette. Not that she held it against him. She'd had her fill of haughty aristocrats who showered her with effusive flattery and fawned over her in hopes of drawing the interest of a wealthy shipping heiress.

When Cale straddled a chair—backward—and stared warily at her from beneath his furrowed brow, she realized this was a novel experience for her. *He* was a novel experience. This brawny bounty hunter, who dressed in worn buckskin, was absolutely nothing like the stuffy gentlemen her father had tossed in her path since she'd blossomed into a woman. There was a wild, dynamic presence about this man that intrigued her.

Eyes as dark as midnight, surrounded by a hedge of coal-black lashes, bore into her, as if searching out the hidden secrets in her soul. A leather band at the base of his neck anchored his long glossy hair—hair as black and shiny as a raven's wings. He looked as if he hadn't been within a mile of a razor in weeks. His dark beard and mustache gave him a most formidable appearance.

Hanna was certain that even her father might be just a tad intimidated by this ominous-looking creature. She knew for a fact that Cale Elliot was a solid, muscular six-foot-two and two hundred plus pounds, because she'd been plastered up against his rock-solid body. He was hard-edged, tough and suspicious. Not to mention that only God knew how much blood he had on his hands. This, she predicted, was the last man on earth her father would want her to marry—which was one more reason why Cale Elliot was positively perfect for her.

"Are you married?" she blurted out, then bit her lip and cursed her lack of finesse.

Two black eyebrows shot up to his hairline. "What the hell kind of question is that?" he said, then snorted.

"A straightforward one," she replied, marshaling her nerve and her resolve. "Are you married or not?"

"No. Are you?" he retorted in the same gruff tone he'd employed since the moment he yanked her up against him and jammed his pistol to her throat.

"Not yet, but I plan to be very soon," she replied resolutely.

Cale frowned, bemused. "Why are we having this conversation and who *are* you?"

Hanna overlooked his rude manner and defiantly ignored his question. With each passing second she became increasingly confident that this was the man she needed to ensure her independence from her father. Cale Elliot was hard as nails, formidable and abrupt. His reputation and occupation warned most people away. Most people, but not Hanna Malloy. She'd marry him on the spot if there were a clergyman or justice of the peace present.

"All right, Miz N'Awlins," he drawled, mocking her Southern accent. "What's this business about a proposition? I've had a long three weeks and I'm ready for a bath, a nap and a hearty meal. You're keeping me from them. What the hell do you want with me?"

Hanna lifted her chin and met his piercing stare. Fleetingly she wondered if the devil himself had eyes this deep and black and penetrating.

"Well? Spit it out," he snapped impatiently. "Your time's almost up. I don't like conversations that last more than a minute."

Hanna flinched at his razor-sharp tone. She had to get up her nerve all over again. Since Cale Elliot apparently preferred straightforward and right-to-the-point dialogue, she'd accommodate him.

"I want to marry you," she told him flat out. "I have five thousand dollars in cash as incentive to convince you to accept."

Cale reared back so abruptly that he very nearly launched himself off his chair. His obsidian eyes shot open in stunned surprise and his bewhiskered jaw dropped to his broad chest. "Wha'd you say?" he choked out.

His shocked expression provoked her amused smile. If nothing else, she had Cale's undivided attention. "You heard me, Mr. Elliot. I want a husband and I want one now. I want that husband to be *you.*"

He just stared at her as if she had Spanish moss dangling from her earlobes. Well, she mused, she supposed they were even now. He looked as stunned as she'd felt when he'd rammed a pistol beneath her chin and clamped her against his brick wall of a chest.

When Cale finally recovered from his shock, his gaze narrowed dubiously. This had to be a setup, he decided. Unfortunately, he was too rattled to figure out what the hell was going on. Why would this enchanting, sophisticated female propose to him? To distract and confuse him? Someone had obviously put her up to it. No decent woman in her right mind would want to attach herself to the stigma that followed him like a looming shadow.

He had a dozen strikes against him, and she looked to be all that was gentle and refined in this world. She could have her pick of beaus, and she claimed she wanted to marry *him?* There was definitely a catch, he decided. Was she a ruined woman who desperately needed a name for her unborn babe? Was she intent on punishing an unfaithful suitor by taking a husband far below her social status?

Another thought, of a dark and violent nature, bombarded Cale. If this lovely creature had been set upon by some lusting, abusive bastard, who'd left her with child the same way—

Cale jerked upright, refusing to let bitter memories of the past intrude and distract him. It was true that he was rough around the edges, had very little formal education and no sophistication whatsoever, but if there was one thing his Cherokee mother had taught him it was never to misuse a woman to satisfy his own needs. He had never forced himself on a woman and he didn't hold with men who did.

"Well, Mr. Elliot?" she prompted when he lingered so long in thought. "I'll pay you half the money now and half after the ceremony. Do we have a bargain?"

"First off," he said, settling his forearms on the back of the chair, "don't call me *Mistah* Elliot or *suh*," he ordered, mimicking her drawl. "The name's Cale, pure and simple. Secondly, why do you want to marry me? It's obviously not because of my refined manners, my dashing good looks and endearing charm.''

He watched her astutely as she folded her hands in her lap, squared her shoulders and lifted her amethyst gaze. Cale steeled himself against the hypnotic lure of her eyes, her elegantly formed features. He felt as if reality had somehow been suspended, leaving him drifting in a world so remote from the daily rigors of staying alive that he could scarcely conceive of it.

*He* was sharing conversation with this astoundingly beautiful woman? In *his* room? That in itself was scandalous. Her reputation would be in shambles if anyone saw her arrive or exit.

He watched her draw a deep breath that caused her full breasts to strain against the dainty bodice of her gown. Her delicate brows drew together, as if she were carefully choosing her words.

"I'm offering no illusions, Mr.—Cale," she quickly corrected. "I wish to take your name in a marriage of convenience. The union will not be consummated, of course. There will simply be an exchange of cash for possession of the marriage certificate. I've no intention of restricting or altering your life, nor mine. After the ceremony you are free to go your way and I will go mine."

Well, he thought, so much for that titillating fantasy of having this lovely vision naked in his bed. He should've known she wouldn't be the slightest bit inclined to cuddle up with the likes of him.

"If there comes a time when you meet a woman you wish to marry, you need only to contact me and I'll tend to the divorce proceedings quickly. In essence, I'm simply asking you to put your signature beside mine on the dotted line. You'll be well paid for your assistance."

Cale studied her for a long, pensive moment, trying to figure her angle. He wondered which scenario fit her situation. The jilted Southern belle out for revenge? The ruined lover trying to save face? The abused woman who'd come to fear intimacy because of a nightmarish assault, and who sought protection with his name and reputation?

"What do you get out of this marriage of convenience?" he asked curiously.

He watched her squirm beneath his piercing scrutiny, but eventually she composed herself and flashed him a smile that did funny things to his pulse. He tried not to become distracted, but damn, she was so pretty that her beauty kept sidetracking him. Forcefully, he concentrated on her reply.

"I want the freedom to go where I please, do as I please," she declared with noticeable determination. "I want the freedom to answer to no one but myself for the first time in my life. I am sick to death of being stifled and controlled and maneuvered by men who see me as nothing but a pawn. I want to discover who I can be in the West."

He cocked a brow at that. Little Miss I-Wanna-Be-Independent didn't have a clue what dangers she'd face while traveling across Indian Territory to reach the land of milk and honey she envisioned. Well, the fact was that the milk was curdled and the honey came with dozens of bee stings. She'd have to wise up and toughen up considerably before she could handle herself in places where law and order didn't prevail the way they did in *N'Awlins*. It went without saying that she was naive and obliviously unaware of the difficulties she'd encounter on the road to her much-sought-after freedom.

Life beyond Indian Territory was brutal. Life anywhere was a bitch, and you just had to learn to deal with it.

Because of his background and line of work, he'd become jaded and cynical. He dealt with liars, cheats, thieves and killers on a day-to-day basis. He'd brought in dozens of criminals who would drop a man in his tracks, just to seize possession of his fancy boots, his fast horse or his pocket change.

The prospect of turning this unsuspecting female loose in dangerous territory made Cale cringe.

His thoughts scattered like buckshot when she doubled at the waist to lift the hem of her skirt. Curiously, he watched her wrestle with her cream-colored petticoats. She straightened in her chair and laid a roll of money—that had been inconspicuously hidden inside the hem of her petticoats—on the table between them.

"Here's half of the easiest money you'll ever make, Mr.—Cale." She stared him squarely in the eye. "Do we have a deal?"

"You're running from someone or something," he guessed accurately.

He noticed her telltale flinch before she composed herself and flashed him a distracting smile. Cale was an expert at reading faces, and he noticed the guarded expression in her eyes. He could almost hear the cogs of her brain cranking, as she tried to decide how much of the truth to tell. He figured white lies and half-truths were all he'd likely hear from her.

"I am on the run, in a manner of speaking, but not from the law. Only from an intolerable situation."

"Are you with child?" he asked bluntly.

Her face flooded with so much color he wondered if she'd go up in flames. She shook her head vigorously, causing a few more tendrils of silver-blond hair to cascade over her shoulder. "No, I'm not," she assured him in a strangled voice.

Judging by her reaction to his probing personal question he suspected she was as pure as the driven snow. Damn, he and this pixielike female were polar opposites. Cale had been purged of purity and cured of naiveté years ago. He'd seen the worst that one human could inflict on another. He'd been cursed frequently and fluently. He'd been to hell and back so many times that the devil himself had nothing new to teach him.

Impatiently, she rose to her feet, then reached for the money on the table. She pivoted to modestly tuck the roll into her bodice, then wheeled back to face him. "If you aren't interested in my bargain, perhaps you could refer me to one of your acquaintances who might be agreeable."

Cale stood up, sighed, then stared at her for another long moment. "I'll think about it," he said, stalling. "I need a bath and a sleep. I'll meet you downstairs in the restaurant for supper in two hours. Surely you can wait that long to get yourself hitched."

She smiled faintly as she turned toward the door. Cale's betraying gaze dropped to the graceful sway of her hips— hips that he'd touched familiarly while searching for concealed weapons. No wedding night, she'd said. No more than a chaste kiss to seal their hasty union at the ceremony. That didn't sound like much fun.

Well, hell, even the best of men—and he was the *furthest* thing from the best of men—would object to being denied one night in this woman's arms. After all, he'd be legally entitled, wouldn't he? He'd rather spend one night with her and opt to let her keep her wad of money.

Always on alert, Cale reflexively grabbed his six-gun when she halted abruptly, then lurched toward him. He was definitely cynical and mistrusting, he mused. He didn't even trust this vision of refined beauty not to double-cross him. But then, life had taught him to trust no one but himself if he wanted to live to see another sunrise.

Her violet-eyed gaze dropped to his hand, which now held a pistol pointed at her chest. She lifted her face and her wry smile indicated that she understood his instinctive need to be leery and alert at all times.

"I suppose, like you, I'll have to learn to be less trusting and more attentive if I'm to survive in the West."

"You've got that right, *sugah,*" he said, mocking her

magnolia blossom accent. "I can guaran-damn-tee that honorable men are few and far between where you're going. You could use a crash course in survival. No offense, Miz *N'Awlins,* but you're about as green as they come."

"No offense taken, sir," she replied. "And while we're being honest with one another, you should know that you are still my first choice as a husband. I prefer not to go hunting for second best—" Her voice dried up when she opened the door and was met by Skeet's menacing snarl.

"Come," Cale ordered quietly.

The oversize dog cast Hanna a wary glance, then trotted forward. When she made the crucial mistake of reaching down to pet Skeet's broad head the dog snapped at the air a mere inch below her outstretched fingers. She jerked back her hand to ensure she still had five fingers attached. Again she'd surprised Cale. Most folks he encountered gave Skeet a wide berth and never tried to befriend him. Obviously, she was a kind, caring soul, despite whatever situation had put her on the run and provoked her to tell him little white lies.

"A word of warning," Cale cautioned as he snapped his fingers, signaling the dog to heel. "Never, ever, make sudden moves toward Skeet. He's in the same line of work I am and he's damn good at it. Better than I am, in fact."

She stared at Skeet, then glanced at Cale. "I could have sworn I saw a sign posted on the steps that said No Animals Allowed."

Cale nodded. "You did. But Skeet has special privileges. I did a small favor for James Jensen. Now Skeet and I have the best hotel accommodations. Skeet may be banned from the restaurant, but he has the run of this suite."

She smiled slyly at him. "That is the boiled-down version of the story James conveyed to me. Saving a man's life and ensuring that he wasn't parted from his hard-earned money constitutes far more than a *small* favor, Mr. Elliot.''

When she turned to go, Cale called after her. "Oh, by the way, *if* I agree to your bargain, I want *six* grand and there *will* be a wedding night.'' He waited for her reaction, curious to see just how determined she was to get herself a husband. Determined enough to pry another thousand from her purse and come willingly to their marriage bed, if he so requested?

Cale watched another blush suffuse her cheeks, saw her eyes flare with temper and her fists knot in the folds of her gown. Better that Little Miss N'Awlins know here and now that he couldn't be charmed or cajoled into doing anything he didn't want to do, especially when he knew she wasn't being completely honest with him.

"Well?" he asked, battling an amused grin as he watched her stiffen like cured mortar and glare daggers at him. "You never did tell me your name. Seems that if I *do* decide to wed you I oughta know what to call you.''

"I'll consider your request," she said tightly. "We can hammer out the details over supper.''

Five would get him ten that she was going to spend the next two hours trying to figure out how to convince him that he didn't really want a wedding night and that five grand was more than plenty for the use of his worthless name.

And speaking of names... "Who are you?" he asked again.

"Sarah Rawlins," she said, then turned and left.

Cale scowled at the closed door. He'd bet his last silver dollar that he still hadn't learned that mysterious woman's true name. Again he wondered what she was running from and how soon the past would catch up with her. It always did—somehow or other. That was the gospel according to Cale Elliot.

He drew in a deep breath and muttered when the alluring

scent of her perfume filled his senses. It clung to his clothing, teasing him, tormenting him. Just like the vision of that woman with secrets in her eyes.

Muttering at the sudden, whimsical image of him and Sarah Rawlins—or whoever she really was—rolling around naked on his bed, Cale stalked to the door to flag down a maid and request water for a bath. Considering that dainty female's affect on his male body, he could use a cold bath, but his screaming muscles needed relief. He'd spent too many days in the saddle. Too many nights on the ground, sleeping with one eye open and one hand clamped over his Colt.

He'd spent three weeks on constant alert, expecting to be bushwhacked at every bend of the road, from every overhanging sandstone cliff, from the shadows of every cave where outlaws lurked, armed to the teeth. Cale desperately needed to soak in a tub, relax and ponder Sarah's proposition.

Hell, he thought, if she really was determined to marry someone, it might as well be him. It wasn't as if he had any other potential prospects beating down his door. But all the same, a man was entitled to a wedding night for the use of his name—especially when his new wife looked, smelled and felt as tempting as Sarah Rawlins.

Her offer of money didn't persuade or impress him, because money wasn't a motivation for him. He'd been stockpiling cash in Fort Smith's bank for years and had money to burn. What he didn't have was a wife and the titillating trimmings of a wedding night. He wanted that violet-eyed beauty to come willingly into his arms, wanted to know what it was like to touch purity and refinement.

And secretly wished her innocence and good breeding might somehow rub off on him.

Cale waited impatiently while a troop of young boys filed into his room to fill the tub with steaming water. When he had the place to himself once again, he stripped off his clothes, sank into the tub and sighed contentedly. Ah, there was nothing better than a long-awaited bath…unless it was one uninterrupted night in the arms of an alluring woman who'd sought him out with an intriguing proposition.

# Chapter Three

Hanna stood in the middle of her cramped room, which contained nothing but crude necessities—a narrow, lumpy bed, washstand, lantern and small towel. Grumbling, she plopped down on the bed. Her perfect, would-be husband had turned out to be as demanding as her father. Furthermore, Cale Elliot was an unscrupulous scoundrel. He wanted a wedding night and six grand, did he? Hanna silently fumed over the fact that a man had manipulated her again. It was the story of her life.

On second thought, she supposed she shouldn't be surprised by Cale's counteroffer. Expecting any man to blithely agree to a wedding without the night that customarily followed was asking a bit much. As for the extra thousand dollars, Hanna would be more than compensated when her trust fund was released to her. That really wasn't the issue here.

Spending the night with Cale Elliot was. The mere prospect of the unknown caused uneasy sensations to ripple through her.

Hanna glanced across the room to stare in the mirror that hung above the washstand. She pulled the pins from her hair and shook her head to send curls streaming down her back. Although Cale Elliot was as rough around the edges as a man could probably get, and they had nothing in common, there was something about those intense dark eyes and that bronzed face that intrigued her. Not enough, of course, to agree to going to bed with him, unless all other possibilities of gaining his assistance were exhausted. To Hanna, intimacy was just one more way for a man to control and dominate a woman. According to her married friends, lust was much more enjoyable for a man, and it was a woman's duty to tolerate her husband's physical desires. It seemed blasted unfair, but there you had it. That was marriage for you.

Hanna called up Cale's mental image as she stretched out on her bed to rest. Despite her irritation at him, there was a wild nobility, an aura of dynamic power about Cale that she envied. Although he would make a most inappropriate husband if they were brushing shoulders with the upper crust of society, undeniably, there was something about the man that appealed to her. She was at a complete loss to explain or define her reaction to him. The fact that she *had* reacted to him on some basic level disturbed her.

Surely she couldn't be attracted to Cale Elliot. He looked too rugged for her tastes, and she naturally assumed from his appearance that there would be nothing gentle or enjoyable about his embrace. He certainly hadn't showed any tendencies toward tenderness when he'd clutched her to him, then searched her for weapons as impersonally as he might search a criminal.

The question was how determined was she to marry? Determined enough to sacrifice her innocence to a stranger who would take what he wanted from her and likely give nothing in return?

The thought caused Hanna to shiver, and she reflexively reached out to flip the thin bedspread over her shoulders. She lay there for a moment, asking herself just how much she was willing to sacrifice for her long-awaited freedom. She'd come this far. She'd given up all that was familiar and comfortable, but she was *not* returning to her father's home to marry Louis Beauchamp, no matter how many French titles his uppity ancestors had flaunted.

Hanna drifted off to sleep, knowing that she would meet Cale Elliot's stipulations, as distasteful as subjecting herself to his lusty pleasures would undoubtedly be. It was only one night, she consoled herself. She could endure that sort of physical torture for one night, couldn't she? After all, nothing worth having came without a price, did it? This was the price she had to pay to call her life her own.

Her freedom and independence were worth it.

Walter Malloy stormed to the far end of his elegantly furnished study, wheeled around, then stalked back in the direction he'd come. Curse that devious daughter of his! He'd thought he'd finally got that willful girl under his thumb and convinced her to wed the man of his choice. Walter had found the perfect social match, but Hanna had defied him.

When Walter had stood at the church a few days earlier, staring in disbelief at the open window and realizing Hanna had fled, he'd vowed all manners of punishment when he located his runaway daughter. He would never forget the humiliation and embarrassment he'd suffered when he was forced to enter the sanctuary and announce to the guests that the wedding had to be postponed.

Walter scowled sourly and pivoted to wear another path on the imported Aubusson carpet. He'd been left to deal with Louis Beauchamp's outrage and indignation. Even Walter had gotten sick of hearing how the entire lineage of Beauchamps had never been left at the altar, and that Hanna's deceit ranked right up there with high treason.

Gad, what a disaster! By the time Louis had finished ranting and raving about the potential shipping monopoly being null and void if Hanna didn't return to voice a public apology and follow through with the wedding, Walter was in the throes of a full-blown headache—and it hadn't let up yet!

The quiet rap at the door prompted him to lurch around and glare at the agent he'd sent to locate Hanna. "Did you find that ungrateful child of mine?" he boomed.

Rutherford J. Wiley stepped inside and closed the door behind him. "No, sir, I'm afraid not. Miz Hanna seems to have vanished into thin air. I checked the train depot, shipping yard and riverboat depot, but her name didn't appear on any of the passenger lists."

"Well, of course not, you dolt!" Walter bellowed. "You think she'd traipse off, dragging her real name behind her?"

The agent shrank as Walter's buglelike voice ricocheted off the walls. "Of course not, sir."

Walter's stubby arm shot toward the door, as if the feather-brained hireling didn't have enough sense to know where it was. "Wire the Pinkertons immediately," he barked. "Give them my daughter's description. Instruct them to name their price, and I'll double it. I want every available detective on this case and I want them now!"

"Yes, sir, at once, sir." Rutherford spun on his heels and scurried through the foyer posthaste.

"Hell and damnation," Walter muttered as he resumed his restless pacing. He'd lost his only son, the child who was to become the heir to the vast fortune Walter and his wife, Clarissa, had amassed. Now his wife was gone and he was consumed with such grief that there were times Walter swore constant work was all that kept him from losing his mind. He was left with a daughter whose appearance reminded him so much of his beloved Clarissa that staring too long at Hanna caused his heart to squeeze painfully in his chest.

Now even Hanna had abandoned him, and Walter had the raging Louis Beauchamp breathing down his neck, vowing all sorts of revenge if the missing bride didn't turn up within the month.

Walter threw himself into his chair to brood. When he got his hands on Hanna, he swore he'd never let her out of his sight for a minute until she'd been delivered into Louis's hands and had spoken her wedding vows. Then she'd be Louis's headache, and Walter would gladly relinquish his responsibility.

Other men had dutiful daughters who honored and respected their fathers' wishes. Why was he stuck with an unruly misfit who'd been taught her place but refused to remain in it?

Cale waited until he heard the quiet click of the door across the hall before he gathered various weapons and tucked them into his boots, at the small of his back and inside the sleeve of his buckskin shirt. Then he strapped the double holsters around his waist and tied the wicked-looking Bowie knife to his thigh. He'd armed himself to the teeth for so long that he felt naked without the feel of cold steel resting against his skin.

When he was sure Sarah—or whatever her real name was—had made it to the staircase, he opened the door and stepped into the hall. Cale had no intention of damaging the woman's reputation further, if they didn't reach an agreement. Escorting Sarah downstairs would send gossip flying. Cale was too well known in town, and she was so stunningly attractive that he suspected she drew considerable attention and speculation without unnecessarily linking her name to his.

Cale halted at the head of the steps and watched Sarah descend to the lobby. Sure 'nuff, she was already the object of scads of male attention. A throng of men congregated at the door and huddled inside the foyer to feast their lusty eyes on her. Cale gnashed his teeth, surprised by the sudden possessiveness that gnawed at him. He knew exactly what this gaggle of men was thinking. Hell, he could practically hear their collective speculations ringing in his ears. They wondered, as he did, how this ravishingly attractive female would look in the altogether.

When Sarah stepped into the restaurant and disappeared from sight, hungry male gazes lingered on the empty space she'd occupied, and whimsical sighs caused a warm draft to whisper through the lobby. Hell. A woman as bewitching as Sarah was definitely trouble, Cale mused as he descended the steps. He'd be asking for a barrel of it if he instigated the clever plan that had been buzzing around in his head since he awoke from his nap.

Cale wanted nothing more than to apprehend Otis Pryor, shut down that bastard's illegal operation and seek personal revenge. The perfect solution to infiltrating Pryor's stronghold in Cromwell, Texas, had hit him like a bolt from the blue. It was an ingenious cover—if he could convince Sarah to participate in the sting. In hopes of gaining her cooperation, Cale had devised a tempting incentive while he dressed for supper.

His thoughts trailed off when he entered the restaurant to see Sarah seated in the middle of the busy establishment, awaiting his arrival. Another unfamiliar sensation spiked through him as he strode forward. Despite all the male gazes focused on her, she was staring directly at him, as if he was the most important individual in the room.

Cale took a seat across from her and nodded a greeting when she forced a smile. He could tell she was apprehensive after the live grenade he'd dropped in her lap before she exited his room earlier. Judging by the look in her eyes and the pinched expression around her mouth, she'd reached a decision. He doubted she was comfortable with it, but she was determined to meet his demands, in exchange for his name on the marriage license.

"I took the liberty of ordering a steak for you. My compliments," she said, doing a damn fine job of holding on to her composure.

"No, my compliments," he contradicted as he leaned his elbows on the table and met her gaze directly. "That is, if you've decided to accept my terms."

She tensed up and sucked in a deep breath that drew his betraying gaze to the rising swell of her breasts. After a moment her gaze dropped to the tabletop and she fiddled with the silverware. "Yes, I will agree to your terms, sir."

Relief washed through Cale. If she was *that* determined to see this match made, even if it meant sacrificing something as personal and irreplaceable as her innocence, then he felt certain he could convince her to meet his new terms.

"The rules have changed slightly since we last spoke," he announced.

Her chin came up and her entrancing eyes narrowed warily. "I cannot fathom what other personal sacrifices you expect me to make, other than the one I've already agreed to, sir," she said through clenched teeth. "It doesn't get more personal than *that!*"

There was spunk, spirit and a hint of temper behind her words, he noted. He liked that. Women without backbone bored him to tears. This little lady could be pushed around a bit, but she refused to be shoved.

"First off, Miz Magnolia, I told you to drop that *suh* business," he said, emphasizing her drawling accent. "Secondly, you can keep your money *and* forgo the wedding night."

Her delicately arched brows shot up like exclamation marks and her jaw dropped. She stared at him in wide-eyed dismay. "Am I to understand that you *won't* marry me then?"

Her voice rose steadily, drawing the attention of the other patrons in the restaurant. All eyes zeroed in on them, as if they were specimens under a microscope. Cale swore under his breath when the room became dead silent. Well, hell. So much for keeping rumors and speculations to a minimum.

Cale draped his arm over the back of the chair and twisted sideways to address the attentive crowd. "My fiancée," he announced, gesturing toward his flush-faced companion. Several startled gasps broke the silence. "Does anybody here have a problem with that?"

Dozens of curious gazes swung to Sarah. Cale said, "Go ahead. Tell 'em, Miz Magnolia. Then maybe we can all get on with supper."

Her face turned crimson, but he had to give her high marks when she tilted her head to a proud angle and tossed her very radiant—and very convincing—smile around the room. "It's true that Mr. Elliot and I plan to marry very soon."

More dead silence. Cale knew what the onlookers were thinking—the same thing he'd thought when she'd proposed to him. Why would a lady of obvious quality and refinement want to hitch herself to an unsociable half-breed gunfighter when she could take her pick from the cream of the aristocratic crop?

To Cale's amazement, Sarah defended him when the crowd of inquisitive patrons glanced distastefully at him. "Cale Elliot is my perfect match," she declared with absolute certainty. "I am honored and proud to become his wife. In fact, there isn't another man on the face of this earth who would suit me better."

Cale slumped back in his chair, as stunned as the rest of the owl-eyed patrons. She didn't have to go *that* far. Why had she?

Suddenly, folks were staring at him, as if trying to determine what hidden qualities she saw in him that they'd obviously overlooked. It made him squirm uncomfortably to be the subject of such deliberate concentration.

Hanna smiled in amusement when the big, brawny

bounty hunter shifted awkwardly in his chair. Her glowing accolades had unsettled him. Apparently he wasn't accustomed to having his praises sung.

Although Hanna had no idea what new stipulations he'd decided to place on the bargaining table, her opinion of him had escalated the moment he'd announced he wasn't forcing her to share a wedding bed and that no money would exchange hands. No matter what he asked, she'd agree, she decided instantly. Well, short of shooting someone for him, that is.

"Now that we've cleared the hurdle of announcing our engagement, what are these new stipulations?" she asked. "I..."

Her voice evaporated when the buxom waitress set two platters of steaks, fresh bread, beans and fried potatoes on the table. Hanna glanced at Cale, anxiously awaiting his reply.

He leaned forward, his whiskered face set in a serious expression. "I want you to pretend to be my loving wife for a month."

Hanna frowned dubiously. Maybe she'd been too hasty in complimenting him in front of the crowd. Had she just agreed to forgo *one* night of unwanted intimacy for an entire *month* of it? "I don't understand what you're implying."

Cale sighed audibly. "Look, Miz Magnolia—"

"The name is Sarah Rawlins," she corrected tersely.

"No, it isn't. I'm not as ignorant as I look. And until you trust me enough to divulge your real name it's gonna be Miz Magnolia, so you better get used to it."

"Very well, Mr. Elliot," she drawled excessively. "Now about these new terms." So as not to appear overly apprehensive, she plucked up her knife and fork and began whittling away at the thick steak.

"Here's the deal," he began, glancing around to ensure he wasn't overheard. "I need a cover to track down my half brother's killer. I recently learned that Otis Pryor has established a stronghold in Texas and he's paid off the local authorities. If I ride in as a deputy marshal I'll probably get my head blown off before I can serve a warrant for Pryor and his army of ruffians.''

Good gad! He *did* want her to shoot someone for him. Hanna gaped at him in astonishment, her fork poised inches from her open mouth. "You want me to kill him when he least expects it?" she chirped.

Cale camouflaged a bark of laughter behind a cough. Nonetheless, he drew considerable attention. "Hell, no. I plan to establish myself as a shopkeeper. I figure that with my knowledge of weapons I can pass myself off as a gunsmith, change my appearance and polish my manners so Pryor won't be suspicious of my arrival in town. That's where you come in.'' He paused to take a bite of juicy steak.

"Go on," she encouraged him. "What's to be my role in this scheme?''

"You travel with me across Indian Territory with the wagonload of weapons to stock the store. During our journey I'll teach you the skills you'll need to survive in the West.''

Hanna smiled agreeably. "I find no fault with that. I'm aware that I have a lot to learn if I'm to become as self-sufficient and capable as you.''

"In exchange for my expertise, I want your expertise," he insisted.

She frowned, befuddled. "I have no expertise. Heavens, I've never been allowed to explore my potential talents.''

Cale smiled at her and she felt a peculiar flutter in her chest. The man was almost attractive when he smiled, even with all that facial hair concealing his features. "You have more skills than you can imagine," he said. "You possess the social graces and refinement I lack when it comes to fitting into society. I *need* to learn to fit in.''

The way he said it touched her heart. She, because of her wealth and the prestige of her family name, had been automatically accepted. But Cale's background and occupation made him a social pariah. It wasn't fair, but Hanna had learned long ago that life wasn't necessarily fair.

"I'll teach you to be a capable survivor if you'll teach me to be a gentleman," he continued. "Plus I'll be your personal bodyguard during the trek through the wildest country you've ever encountered." He stared at her grimly. "I won't lie to you, Miz Magnolia. The journey through Indian Territory won't be a Sunday stroll through the park. We'll be traveling through rugged terrain. We'll encounter bears, mountain lions and poisonous snakes— the worst of them being the two-legged variety. We'll be camping out in the open most nights, subjected to inclement weather and possible attack. But you have my vow that I'll protect you with my life, if you agree to this charade."

Hanna swallowed uneasily. He wasn't painting a pretty picture here. Perhaps she'd been too hasty when she decided to head west to claim her independence. Maybe she should've lost herself in the bustling crowds of Philadelphia, Boston or New York.

Yet this man claimed he'd take a bullet for her, if need be. Hanna had never experienced that brand of protective loyalty and devotion. Where she came from, her physical appearance—which she had nothing whatsoever to do with—elegant wardrobe, social status and wealth, drew empty pledges that were quickly given and hastily forgotten when an easier target and better opportunity arose.

Hanna's respect for Cale rose another notch. She had the instinctive feeling that she'd finally met a man she could trust not to betray her or forsake her. They would both benefit from this bargain. She'd have a private chaperon, a tutor and bodyguard to accompany her to Texas. He would benefit from her social skills and her charade as his wife while he investigated his brother's death. Although Cale hadn't offered the gory details surrounding his brother's demise, this was vitally important to him—as important as her need for freedom.

Cale wanted to ensure justice was served. Hanna didn't blame him. She knew how much it hurt to lose a loved one, having lost her mother and brother—the two people in this world who actually cared about her. Having endured the heart-wrenching emotion of personal loss, Hanna had vowed never to let anyone close enough to subject herself to that kind of anguish again.

In Cale's case, it must be a hundred times worse, knowing his brother's murderer was running loose, preying on other innocent victims.

Cale stared at her solemnly, intently. "Furthermore, I agree to release you from our bargain the minute I apprehend Otis Pryor. You'll be free to go your own way. I don't need your money because I've stockpiled my own savings in the local bank."

"My offer still stands," she insisted. "If you intend to buy inventory for your store and rent space, you might need the extra funds. We'll both need a suitable wardrobe to play this charade. I brought along only a few changes of clothes in my satchels."

He nodded pensively. "Good point, Miz Magnolia. I hadn't considered those details. So…do we have a bargain or not?"

Hanna peered at the sinewy hulk of man sitting across from her. She'd have to wait another month or two to enjoy her freedom, but it lessened the load that weighed down her conscience. This symbiotic liaison would be equally beneficial, and she hadn't had to resort to her father's manipulative methods to get her way.

She still wasn't quite clear on exactly what Cale meant by "portraying the loving wife," but she'd heard it whispered by her friends that feigning headaches, various illnesses and monthly feminine conditions worked effectively in holding amorous husbands at bay. Surely Cale wouldn't want to upset her by forcing unwanted intimacy on her, since he desperately needed her cooperation in this masquerade to avenge his brother's death.

Why, she could drop the entire charade at any moment, she realized. Then where would he be? For once she *had* the power to control the situation. He needed her, she realized, with an unfamiliar sense of pride and gratification. She'd been used before, plenty of times. Men perceived her only as a means to obtain wealth, as a prestigious trophy to drape on their arms. She'd never really been needed for a higher purpose.

My, that was something, wasn't it? This self-sufficient, highly skilled gunfighter *needed* her, as much as she needed him. Hanna was firmly convinced now that fate was smiling down on her. Furthermore, if she succeeded in transforming Cale into a gentleman, she wouldn't have to fret about her illogical attraction to him evolving into deep attachment. She, after all, disliked polished gentlemen, and she'd become immune to their practiced charm. The way she saw it, her bargain with Cale placed her in a no-lose situation. The man and this arrangement were positively perfect.

"Very well," she said decisively. "We have a bargain. The sooner we're married the better. In addition, you've mastered your first social skill, sir."

"Yeah? What's that?" he asked curiously.

"You managed to conduct a civilized conversation that lasted more than a minute."

She smiled and he smiled back. Another unfamiliar sensation flooded her chest when his onyx eyes sparkled with amusement. It was as if they'd just formed an unlikely bond and cleared another hurdle in their negotiations. The expression of relief that settled on his rugged features must surely have mirrored her own sentiments. The bargain was set. Excitement and anticipation sizzled through Hanna.

She was one step closer to casting off the yoke of her father's domination and embracing her promising future.

All she had to do was fight her way through an infestation of outlaws and renegades in the wild, untamed territory that was known as the Armageddon of the West. She'd do her part to aid in the capture of a notorious murderer and his army of ruthless desperadoes.

And then she'd be home free....

Good gad! What was she getting herself into?

# Chapter Four

Hanna awoke the next morning teeming with excitement and anticipation. She was anxious to gather supplies that would aid in her quest to discover her hidden talents. With a tidy roll of cash stashed in her reticule, she opened the hotel room door, then smiled in greeting when Cale's door opened a moment later.

"Good morning," she said cheerfully. To her dismay his penetrating gaze drifted over her pale blue gown and lingered on the gold locket around her neck. She thought she looked passable in her simple gown, but apparently he disagreed.

"Take Skeet with you," he said without preamble as he clutched her arm to assist her down the steps.

"That isn't necessary," she insisted. "I'm only going to pick up a few gowns and supplies at the general store."

"Skeet, guard," Cale ordered the menacing-looking dog, which reminded Hanna more of a wolf than a domesticated canine. "I'll purchase the buckboard and trail rations for the trip while you're shopping. I'm due to testify in court this afternoon, so I'll speak with Judge Parker about the ceremony."

Another surge of excitement washed through her as she descended the steps. Considering Cale's swift efficiency, she might be wed within a few days—making her untouchable to her father. The prospect filled her with elation and she smiled.

"You look mighty pleased with yourself, Miz Magnolia," Cale noted, studying her intently. "Any particular reason why?"

It was on the tip of her tongue to reveal her true identity and the reason for her excitement, but caution bade her to bide her time. She'd tell Cale everything he wanted to know *after* she had the marriage license in hand.

"I'm eager for our wedding." It was the truth—sort of.

"Eager to marry me?" He scoffed. "I doubt it."

Hanna halted abruptly on the landing. "Now, see here, Mr. Elliot, I will not have you putting yourself down in my presence. I don't care what anyone in this town—or this entire country, for that matter—thinks. You are the perfect husband and I want you to be *mine!*"

Cale blinked in surprise when she emphatically defended his worthiness for the second time. Damn, if this mere wisp of a female didn't make him feel good about himself.

He stared at her uplifted chin, then his traitorous gaze drifted over the scooped-neck bodice of her gown and the trim indentation of her waist. She was such a tempting morsel—which was why he insisted on sending Skeet along as a bodyguard.

The woman didn't seem to have a clue how much trouble she could get into just tramping down the streets of this rowdy town. If any man tried to lay a hand on her, Skeet would make him back off—or risk losing a few fingers.

"I'll meet you back here for lunch," Cale instructed as he escorted her down the last flight of steps. "In the meantime, pay attention to your surroundings. Got it?"

When she laid her hand on his arm and smiled up at him, Cale steadied himself against the baffling sensations her touch evoked. Her skin was as smooth as alabaster and his was as rough as alligator hide. That was just another reminder of the polar differences between them. And if she didn't stop reaching out and touching him unexpectedly he wouldn't be able to keep his mind on business.

Bottom line—this woman's touch affected him. She affected him. Keeping his vow to bypass a wedding night was going to be torture, pure and simple.

Of course, Miz Rawlins from N'Awlins had a noticeable effect on all men, Cale decided as he stared at the male crowd that hovered by the door—with their tongues hanging out and their leers directed at his future bride.

"It's so sweet of you to fret about me," she said, totally oblivious to the gaggle of men gawking at her.

"I'm a long way from sweet," he snorted. "No one has ever used that word to describe me before."

"Then they obviously don't know what a fine man you are," she insisted. "But I can take care of myself. Truly."

That, he thought, remained to be seen. Cale placed his hand possessively on the small of her back to guide her through the raft of men staring at her as if they'd never seen a woman before. Certainly not one as refined and bewitching as this one.

He inwardly groaned when they stepped outside to find another congregation of men waiting to feast their eyes on the newest arrival. Apparently the news of Sarah Rawlins's heart-stopping good looks had spread through Fort Smith like wildfire. Hell, it'd be a full-time job watching over her. Cale was definitely going to dress her in oversize buckskins and a hat to disguise her gender during their trek through Indian Territory.

When they parted company, Skeet trailed at her heels. Cale watched a dozen male gazes follow the hypnotic sway of her hips. Possessiveness slammed him broadside again, but he told himself to get past it. This wouldn't be a true marriage, after all. It wasn't a marriage of convenience, either, because there would be nothing remotely convenient about having Sarah underfoot. She'd be an invitation for trouble and the worst personal temptation imaginable if Cale didn't make her look like a boy—from a distance. Up close, there was no question that she was all woman.

Adding suitable clothing for Sarah to his own list of purchases, Cale strode off to the blacksmith's shop to modify a wagon with a false bottom to conceal his shipment of weapons. No way was he going to advertise the fact that he was hauling enough guns and ammunition to equip a small army. He wanted to project the appearance of two travelers laden down with household supplies. That in itself was temptation enough for the swarm of thieves that lurked in Indian Territory.

Cale sighed in frustration as he strode into the livery stable. He had the unmistakable feeling that, despite all the experience he had under his belt, wedding Sarah and toting her across rough country was going to be the most difficult task he'd ever undertaken. And even though she kept insisting that he was perfect for her, Cale didn't believe it. He'd never believe it, because he knew who and what he was—and so did everyone else around these parts.

He suspected she'd lose most of her cheery idealism after their rugged trek to Texas. Miz Magnolia didn't know it yet, but she was on a collision course with reality. A damn shame, that, he mused. He wished the world was as rosy, noble and embracing as she wanted to think it was.

Hanna scurried around the general store like an enthusiastic child on a limitless shopping spree. Already she'd grabbed two sensible gowns off the rack, gathered art supplies, knitting needles, yarn, two bolts of fabric, parchment and charcoal pencils—in order to pursue her quest for her hidden talents. When she discovered her potential—whatever it might be—she was going to be prepared.

"Anything else, miss?" the shopkeeper questioned as he eyed her copious purchases curiously.

Hanna was certain the proprietor considered her frivolous and eccentric, but for the first time in living memory she didn't have to explain herself to her father or anyone else. "No, this will be all," she said most politely.

Hanna handed over the cash after the frizzy-haired man totaled her expenses. She scooped up the armload of packages and spun toward the door. Skeet waited just outside, and she swore the wolflike creature scowled in displeasure at her for separating him from his beloved master.

Honestly, there was no need for Cale's precaution, she mused as she strode down the uneven boardwalk, leaving Skeet to sniff at whatever had caught his attention. No one was going to molest her right here in broad day—

Her thoughts scattered like buckshot when an unseen fist clamped around her elbow and forcefully jerked her into the alley. Before Hanna could let out a shriek, a grimy hand curled around her nose and mouth, cutting off her air supply. Terror pulsed through her veins when she glanced sideways and recognized the scruffy ruffian who had approached her on the docks. Hanna kicked and squirmed when the man wrapped an arm across her chest and dragged her deeper into the shadows.

Where was that blasted dog when she needed him? Moments earlier he'd only been a few steps behind her. Well, Hanna decided, it was time to prove she could fend for herself. She dropped her packages and bit a chunk out of the man's finger. Simultaneously, she kicked her heel against his shin. Her abductor howled and cursed foully, but he refused to remove his hand from her mouth, so she bit down even harder on his finger.

"Argh!" Her captor yelped as he shoved her roughly against the side of the building. Trash barrels tumbled, and Hanna hit the dirt with a dull thump as he heaved her away from him.

Her breath gushed out in a whoosh as her head and spine slammed against the clapboard walls. She tried to scream before he pounced at her, but he'd knocked the breath clean out of her. No sound escaped her lips except a feeble whimper. And then he was upon her, backhanding her before he jerked her to her unsteady feet.

Finally Hanna managed to gather her wits and expel a bloodcurdling scream with Skeet's name attached to it. The inhuman snarl from behind her gave her hope, but the burly brute had ripped the bodice of her gown and left it gaping before the wolf dog lit into him with teeth bared.

Suddenly it was her captor who was squealing like a stuck pig, fending off a vicious attack. Hanna, clutching her torn gown, braced herself against the wall and screamed for all she was worth. In fiendish horror she watched the dog—which she suddenly loved dearly—make short shrift of her abusive attacker.

As Hanna pressed a shaky hand to her stinging cheeks, she swore she'd never again be so naive and trusting when Cale warned her of potential danger. She'd probably gotten exactly what she deserved for not paying attention, but she was ever so glad Cale had insisted on sending along Skeet.

Cale jerked to attention when he heard a piercing shriek in the distance. He dropped the piece of lumber and dashed from the livery. Sarah was in serious trouble. The second shriek put him in a dead run, and he accidentally knocked bodies out of his way as he tore off down the street.

It had been years since Cale had dealt with the sensations of panic and fear. He'd mastered those emotions, but fear for someone other than himself was totally unfamiliar. He didn't like the feeling that had his pulse hammering like hailstones, his gut twisting into a tight knot.

When he heard a vicious growl and a wail of pain, he elbowed through the crowd of onlookers and dashed through the trash-strewn alley. His legs suddenly refused to move when his gaze landed on Sarah, whose flawless face now boasted a red welt and whose delicate gown had been ripped from neck to waist.

Cale was still standing there, immobilized, when Sarah spotted him. She dashed toward him like a homing pigeon going to roost. She cuddled against his chest, and his arms reflexively closed around her. He felt her quaking fear vibrating through every fiber of his being.

"Call off Skeet," she croaked.

"Not in this life," Cale growled as he watched Skeet pin his victim to the dirt, his powerful jaws resting threateningly against the man's jugular. Any heathen who laid his filthy hands on Sarah deserved to be chewed to bitesize pieces.

"Skeet, stop!" Hanna demanded as she huddled against Cale.

Amazingly, the dog unclamped his jaws and stood over the man, with his sharp teeth mere inches from his throat. Bemused, Cale arched a brow. It was the first time Skeet had obeyed a command from anyone but him. Must've had something to do with the fact that Sarah had tucked the uneaten portion of her supper steak in her purse and left it for Skeet the previous night, Cale decided.

"Somebody get the town marshal," he ordered. *"Now!"*

Bodies scattered while Skeet stood guard, refusing to let the miscreant gain his feet and run for his life.

"Damn it, woman, didn't I tell you to pay attention?" Cale snapped angrily.

Sarah nodded her tousled head, but refused to look up at him. He didn't blame her. He was feeling positively murderous and probably looked it.

"I'm sorry. I didn't think—"

"Obviously not," he interrupted sharply. This was a good time to teach her a valuable lesson that she damn well better not forget. "You don't trust anyone if you want to survive. You presume nothing. You remain on constant alert. Have I made myself clear?''

She jerked back slightly and glared up at him. When he saw the red welt on her cheek at close range and noticed the extent of the damage to the gown she clutched modestly to her chest, the damnedest thing happened. The vicious fury drained right out of him. Just like that. Poof! Suddenly it didn't matter that this naive innocent hadn't applied every precautionary measure that had become second nature to him. All that mattered was that she was alive and in one piece—more or less.

''Well, hell,'' Cale muttered as he noticed the unshed tears glistening in those mystifying violet eyes. He slid his arm beneath her knees and scooped her into his arms.

''Put me down! I—''

''Clam up, Magnolia,'' he interrupted as he carried her through the crowd of onlookers. ''Skeet, stay.''

Without another word Cale strode toward the hotel, and he didn't break stride until he reached his room. Propriety be damned, he decided. He was going to deposit Sarah in his bedroom, and nobody better mess with her again or he'd go on a shooting spree the likes of which this town had never seen!

It dawned on Cale that he'd gone a little crazy, was feeling off balance and out of control. But he didn't care. Any man who would abuse a woman deserved to be poisoned, shot, stabbed and hanged in short order. It had been a sensitive issue with him since his— Well, for a long time. 'Nuff said.

Cale laid Sarah gently on his bed, then forced himself to look away when his gaze dropped to the exposed swell of her breasts. She clutched at the tattered bodice and her face turned the same color as the welt on her cheek. Cale wheeled around to grab a towel, then dipped it in water.

''Here, Magnolia,'' he said as he sank down on the edge

of the bed. "Hold this to your cheek. I'll fetch you another dress."

"Th—thank you," she stammered shakily. "I—I'm really sorry I've inconvenienced you."

Well, there was another first, he realized as he stalked across the hall to retrieve the lavender gown that was draped over the end of her bed. No one had ever apologized for inconveniencing him and scaring him half to death before. He snatched up the garment and quickly reversed direction.

"Put this on while I retrieve Skeet." He jerked his pistol from its holster and his knife from its sheath on his thigh. He laid both weapons beside her. "Anybody comes through that door besides me, you shoot 'em, and stab 'em a couple of times for good measure. I'll be right back."

She stared at the weapons with rounded eyes, then peered up at him.

"And don't tell me you can't or won't shoot," he demanded gruffly. "You'll do what you have to do to protect yourself and that's that."

Cale wheeled around and marched out the door. Once he was in the hall, he sucked in a deep, steadying breath, and told himself to calm down. It was easier said than done. In the last quarter of an hour something had shifted and resettled inside him. He couldn't put a name to it. Wasn't sure he wanted to.

Hell and damnation, his brief association with the mysterious Miz Magnolia was altering his life in ways he hadn't anticipated. He couldn't deal with her without being affected by her. Furthermore, he'd only had to worry about protecting his own hide for years. Now he was saddled with an incompetent female who naturally attracted trouble and didn't know how to handle it effectively.

He had to be capable enough to protect her, as well as himself. Yep, he decided on his way down the steps. He definitely had to teach that helpless female several self-defense maneuvers or he wouldn't be able to sleep at night, wondering who'd be waiting to molest her when she struck off on her own in the West.

His life had suddenly become complicated, he realized, as he hiked off down the street to collect his dog and ensure that Sarah's attacker was carted off to jail.

Hanna levered herself onto a wobbly elbow, then pushed upright to shed her torn gown. The delighted anticipation of gathering supplies had been ruined by the unexpected attack. But what disturbed her most was the way she'd flung herself into Cale's arms the instant he arrived on the scene of disaster. For some reason she was embarrassed to have a man as capable and self-reliant as Cale Elliot witness her incompetence. Why that should matter so much Hanna didn't know. But it did matter—a lot.

When Cale came through the door with Skeet on his heels and his arms laden with packages, Hanna braced herself for another scathing lecture. To her amazement Cale didn't light into her. He simply struck a rigid pose beside the bed, stared down at her with those eyes that were the color of the sky between midnight and dawn, and said, "I made arrangements for your meal to be brought up to you. If you'll meet me at the courthouse after supper the judge can perform the ceremony."

"Today? Really?" she squeaked in amazement.

He nodded briskly. "That's what you want, isn't it?"

That was exactly what Hanna wanted. She just hadn't expected to have her whim met so quickly. But then she reminded herself that she was going to marry a man who was expedient efficiency at its finest. It was a trait she greatly admired. Someday she hoped the same could be said about her.

She stared quizzically at Cale when he reached out, as if to brush a recalcitrant strand of hair away from her face. He apparently changed his mind at the last moment, and his hand dropped to his side. The near gesture spoke of tenderness and comfort that she hadn't expected from him.

Cale stared at the air over her head. "Maybe you should catch a nap, Magnolia. I'll leave Skeet here to accompany you to the courthouse."

When he pivoted on his heel, Hanna stared at his broad muscular back. "Thank you."

"For what?"

"For not raking me over live coals for my stupidity," she murmured.

He glanced over his shoulder, making her squirm beneath that probing gaze that never failed to unnerve her. "Who ordinarily rakes you over live coals?"

He was prying again, and she couldn't bring herself to tell him who she was just yet. "I'll answer all your questions later," she promised.

"After the deed is done?"

She tried to smile, but the puffy welt on her cheek made it a mite painful. "Precisely. When I marry you my troubles will be over."

"And mine will have just begun," he murmured on his way out the door.

Cale was decidedly uncomfortable with the emotions this dainty female aroused in him. This morning she'd touched his hand and insisted he was an honorable, worthy man—despite what the rest of the world thought of him. Then she'd scared him witless when she was attacked and mauled. Then he'd almost made the crucial mistake of touching her consolingly a moment earlier, as if there was an affectionate bond between them.

Hell, who was he kidding? He was just a means to her mysterious end, and he'd bargained to make her a means to his personal brand of justice. *Don't get sentimentally attached,* Cale cautioned himself as he set off to tend his errands. His association with Miz Magnolia would last only a month—two at the most. He'd exchange survival skills for polished etiquette, and she'd go her way while he went his. End of story.

He had to quell these fits and starts of lust that kept lambasting him at unexpected moments. A deal was a deal, after all. Having her come running to him for comfort and protection had been hard on his blood pressure—and certain parts of his anatomy. She might be his wife after supper, but she was still off-limits, he reminded himself sternly. And if he had a brain in his head he wouldn't let himself forget that, no matter how much he wanted to touch and taste and hold.

*In name only,* he mused in frustration. Helluva deal he'd made, wasn't it?

Hanna awakened with a jolt and glanced apprehensively around the room, trying to orient herself to her surroundings. The instant she saw Skeet napping beneath the table, the unnerving incident in the alley came back in a rush.

Rolling off the bed, she knelt in front of the wolflike dog, which bared his teeth at her. "I know you don't like me, Skeet, but I didn't thank you properly for saving me."

Although Cale had warned her not to make any sudden moves toward Skeet, she tried a new approach. She held out her hand, palm up, in front of his snout. The dog growled softly but didn't snap. Hanna took that as a sign of progress. She didn't try to touch Skeet, just left her hand dangling in midair until he took a cautious sniff.

After a moment she pushed to her feet and walked across the hall to retrieve the wedding gown she'd stuffed in one of her satchels.

Hanna dressed for her second wedding in less than a week. For certain, she was more enthused and eager than she'd been at the first one. Although she knew she didn't mean anything to Cale, she wanted to look her very best. She'd chosen a gown with a low-cut neckline that buttoned down the front—to facilitate a quick change before she escaped through the church window and boarded the steamboat.

She tugged at the swooping neckline, but it didn't help much. One gulping breath and her breasts would spill from the lacy confines. Well, she'd just have to remember not to breathe deeply until she shed this gown.

Once she had her hair pinned atop her head in a fashionable coiffure, she assessed herself in the mirror. She'd likely be overdressed to marry a man who preferred buckskins and moccasins. But he was doing her a tremendous favor, and she intended to acknowledge it by dressing like a proper bride.

Hanna was dismayed to note the welt on her cheek had turned black-and-blue. She dabbed on some powder to hide the bruise as best she could. Shoulders squared, head held at a determined angle, she marched toward the door, then yelped when Skeet sprinted past her, knocking her off balance. She braced her hand on the wall to steady herself, then opened the door.

Skeet padded into the hall, glanced this way and that, then stared up at her as if to say the coast was clear. Hanna smiled on her way down the hall, remembering the lazy, worthless hound her father kept around as a prestige symbol. That purebred creature couldn't hold a candle to Skeet. Just as she couldn't hold a candle to Cale.

The discomforting thought caused Hanna to grimace. She *would* prove herself worthy and competent, she promised fiercely. She was *not* getting by in life on her looks, even if her father insisted that was all she needed to do. She was going to count for something—as soon as she had the opportunity to discover what she was good at.

"Miss Rawlins, you look enchanting," James Jensen said as she descended the steps.

Hanna smiled gratefully as the hotel proprietor came around the counter to position himself between her and the crowd of men who loitered in the lobby.

"I must say, I didn't quite believe the rumors flying around the restaurant last night, but despite what anyone says, you've chosen a fine man. The best, in fact," James assured her.

"I couldn't agree with you more," Hanna replied.

"Er…even if this *is* rather sudden," James murmured, "Um, all the same…"

She knew the hotel proprietor was dying of curiosity, fishing for an explanation for this whirlwind wedding. But Hanna was hesitant to confide the story to anyone. She simply smiled sweetly at James.

"I think you should know that a well-dressed, distinguished looking man named Richard Sykes, from the Pinkerton Detective Agency, questioned me two hours ago about a young lady who fit your description."

The color drained from her face. Blast it! Her father hadn't wasted a moment in sending out the troops. But then, she'd anticipated that. She just hadn't expected to have Pinkerton bloodhounds on her trail *this* quickly.

James patted her clammy hand and veered down the hall. "Not to worry, my dear. I pleaded ignorance, but I doubt your secret will be safe for long." He glanced pointedly at the crowd of men. "Cale left the buckboard by the back exit. There's a young lad waiting in the alley to take you to the courthouse."

Nodding appreciatively, Hanna exited and climbed into the wagon. Skeet hopped on to the wagon bed behind her. Apparently Cale was aware of the situation and wanted to transport her to the ceremony as discreetly as possible. She had the uneasy feeling he'd be full of questions when the ceremony ended—if he waited that long to demand answers.

An apprehensive sensation settled in the pit of her stomach while she was whisked down the alley at a hasty clip. For all she knew the agent could be watching for her, waiting to pounce. If the Pinkerton agent interrupted the wedding, her hopes of freedom would be dashed.

With a quick murmur of thanks, Hanna bounded from the buckboard and the young boy drove away. She moved swiftly toward the courthouse. Leaving Skeet to wait outside, she asked directions to Judge Parker's chambers, then breathed a sigh of relief when she closed the door behind her. Now, if only Cale and the judge would show up so she could see this deed done quickly!

Hanna lurched around when the door swung open with a whine and an authoritative giant of a man with a tawny mustache, thick goatee and piercing blue eyes strode toward her. She smiled cordially as she extended her hand. "I'm marrying Cale Elliot," she announced.

The judge's stern expression softened and he chuckled as he took her hand. "So I've been told. Come with me, Miss Rawlins, and we'll get the license in order before my deputy arrives."

While the judge turned his back and thumbed through the desk drawer for the necessary legal papers, Hanna heard the door creak open again. She glanced over her shoulder to see a well-dressed gentleman wearing a fashionable bowler hat hovering in the shadowed alcove by the door.

Hanna panicked. The Pinkerton agent! Damnation, he'd found her before the ceremony could be concluded!

Her heart hammered frantically in her chest as she darted a sideways glance toward the window. That had been her escape route once before, and it might have to be again. Confound it! Where was Cale when she needed him?

While Judge Parker was preoccupied, Hanna inched closer to the window, keeping her back turned to the unidentified man. The click of footsteps crossing the judge's chambers echoed like a death knell, causing another wave of anxiety to swamp her. The footfalls rang in her ears, bringing captivity one step closer.

Hanna fidgeted with the locket around her neck, seeking the comfort the object usually brought. She didn't dare turn around and alert the Pinkerton agent that she was aware he was stalking her. All she had was the element of surprise on her side, and she wasn't about to give that up.

The closer he came, the faster her heart pounded in her chest, making it difficult to draw breath. Hanna stared desperately at the latch on the window, trying to calculate the amount of time it would take to lift the sash, jump through, and make a mad dash for cover.

The hair on the back of her neck stood on end when the footsteps halted close behind her. *Now!* the voice of survival screamed at her.

Hanna launched herself at the window, but a steely hand shot out to manacle her wrist, dragging her backward while she stared helplessly at her porthole of freedom. Hell and damnation, she'd been inches away from escape and now she'd be dragged back to her irate father and that stuffy Louis Beauchamp!

God help her!

# Chapter Five

"Going somewhere, Miz Magnolia?"

Hanna lurched around at the sound of the familiar voice. Her jaw dropped and her eyes popped as she surveyed the new and improved version of the bounty hunter she'd met the previous day. Gone were the worn buckskins and assortment of visible weapons. Cale's shaggy mane had been neatly trimmed. He'd shaved off the dark beard and mustache that had concealed the square line of his jaw, the dimple in his chin and the high cheekbones that denoted his Indian heritage. Sweet merciful heavens! She'd never imagined Cale Elliot to be so breathtakingly handsome, and she was sorely disappointed in herself for gaping at him in rapt fascination.

For years she had scorned her shallow suitors for focusing on her outward appearance and inherited wealth. Now here she was—the world's worst hypocrite—practically drooling over Cale's powerful masculine physique wrapped in expensive finery. The sheer beauty of his face mesmerized her.

"Thank God!" In relief Hanna threw herself into his arms and held on for dear life. She was getting married after all, not being captured and dragged back to her father and unwanted fiancé. "I thought you were—" She slammed her mouth shut so fast she nearly snipped off the end of her tongue. "That is to say, you look positively dashing."

Cale glanced over her blond head and smiled reassuringly at Judge Parker, who stared inquisitively at Sarah's peculiar behavior. Cale knew exactly what she'd thought when he strode up behind her. He'd seen her stiffen, glance speculatively at the window. Her body language had told him that she hadn't recognized him and that she was preparing to make a hasty departure via the window.

After James Jensen informed Cale that a Pinkerton agent was snooping around town, Cale had made arrangements to have Sarah driven discreetly to the courthouse. What he didn't know was *why* the agent was trailing her. Being suspicious by nature and by habit, he couldn't help but wonder whom she'd murdered and if the stash of money she carried was stolen.

Yet there was a decided innocence about Sarah—or whoever she really was, and he intended to find that out very soon. An innocence that made it hard for him to believe she was capable of murder and mayhem. Although he suspected she'd fed him white lies and half-truths up to this point, Cale was more than a little stunned to realize he trusted Little Miz Magnolia's honor and integrity. And that was saying something, because Cale had learned years ago not to put faith in anyone but himself.

When Sarah withdrew and stared happily at him, Cale forgot to breathe. His gaze fell to the revealing décolleté that displayed her creamy breasts to their best advantage. He tried to swallow—and couldn't. To say this woman was beautiful had to be the understatement of the century. Despite the unsightly bruise on her cheek—and he'd like to mutilate and murder the heathen who'd put it there—she was every man's secret fantasy come true.

And she wanted to marry *him?* The question ripped through his mind for the dozenth time. *Why?*

Cale figured a gentleman should gush compliments when he beheld such a vision of ravishing beauty, but his tongue seemed to be stuck to the roof of his mouth. He simply stood there, drinking in every inch of her luscious swells and curves, itching to run his fingers over her satiny skin.

Judge Parker cleared his throat and arched a brow as he stared at Cale in wry amusement. "You indicated expedience," he prompted his tongue-tied deputy marshal. "Shall we get on with it?"

"Yes," Sarah insisted as she clutched Cale's hand and pivoted to face the judge.

She looked so fiercely determined that Cale had to bite back a grin. Never in his wildest dreams had he envisioned such a sophisticated beauty practically champing at the bit to get herself hitched to him.

"Please don't back out on me because a Pinkerton agent is looking for me," she whispered. "There is nothing illegal or immoral about wanting this marriage to take place. I need the protection of your name, and I will be happy to explain why later. But, please, not now, okay? Can we continue the ceremony?"

The judge dutifully rattled off the words to legally bind them together. All the while, questions swirled in Cale's mind. What was she running from that had a Pinkerton agent snooping around town? Cale promised himself that he'd have answers before the night was out. It was easier to be prepared for trouble if you knew what form it took and what to expect rather than wandering blindly into a catastrophe.

He glanced up, startled, when Sarah gouged him in the ribs.

"Do you take this woman?" Judge Parker prompted a second time.

"I do," he said, and nodded.

"And do you—" The judge frowned at the name she

had written on the piece of paper she handed to him, then gaped at her. "Hanna *Malloy?*"

"*Malloy?*" Cale crowed in disbelief as he stared at his soon-to-be bride. "Good grief!" The well-known, disgustingly wealthy shipping entrepreneur from New Orleans was her father? Even *Cale* had heard of the dynasty that could practically buy and sell the whole blessed country!

The beseeching look Hanna Malloy flashed him caused his breath to gush from his lungs. She stared at him as if all her hopes and dreams were pinned on him, as if he held the answer to all her prayers, the key to her future.

Well, hell. What man could peer into those incredible amethyst eyes, fringed with long thick lashes, and turn her down? Not even him. He wasn't *that* hard-hearted.

"Okay, go on, Judge," he said with a gusty breath.

"*Do* you, Hanna?" the judge asked, still looking a little bewildered.

"I do." She sagged in relief and her knees wobbled when the judge finally pronounced them man and wife. Now all that was left was a hasty kiss and the signatures on the license. In a few more moments all would be said and done, and she would be virtually untouchable by her father. Walter Malloy could shout and rant and rave for all he was worth, but he couldn't undo this marriage. She had her freedom at long last.

"Kiss your bride, son," the judge said, smiling.

Hanna tilted her face upward, expecting a chaste kiss—and found herself practically bent over backward as Cale's full lips took possession. She sizzled. She burned. She nearly melted in a puddle while he kissed her as if there was no tomorrow and they were sharing their last dying breath.

Astounded, tingling with unprecedented sensations that channeled in every direction at once, Hanna found herself kissing him back with the same fanatic enthusiasm he directed toward her. Heavens, it was like breathing fire, as if every ounce of sense she'd spent two decades cultivating was being sucked right out of her body, leaving her functioning on nothing but pure desire.

And then, just as suddenly as he'd grabbed her, he propped her upright. He clamped an arm around her waist when she staggered clumsily, then he reached out to shake hands with the judge.

"We'll need witnesses," Judge Parker declared as he strode toward the door. "I'll be right back."

In openmouthed amazement Hanna stared at her handsome new husband, whose dignified clothes were no more than a civilized veneer concealing the sensual wild man who'd just kissed her senseless.

"That's what you get for not telling me who you are," Cale muttered at her. "And damn it, who'd you kill to send a *Pinkerton* chasing after you?"

"I didn't kill anyone," she squeaked. "Honestly."

Cale's head was still spinning like a windmill after that mind-boggling, heart-stopping kiss. Furthermore, he couldn't believe he'd married a shipping heiress. For criminey sake, what could Hanna have been thinking?

He was still scowling at her and trying to recover from his sudden lust attack when James Jensen and his wife trooped in to sign their names on the three copies of the licenses that Hanna requested. She confiscated the documents before the ink had time to dry and tucked them in her reticule. While she graciously thanked the Jensens and the judge for their assistance, Cale towed her toward the door. *Now* he was going to get answers, and he'd better get the whole truth from Miz Magnolia or she was going to see him at his absolute worst.

"I can see that you're irritated," she murmured as he whisked her out the door and practically dragged her toward the nearest alley.

"Irritated?" he said, and snorted. "Lady, you don't know the half of it! Hanna *Malloy,* for God's sake!"

With Skeet at his heels, Cale bustled Hanna down the back alleys, past the buckboard and his saddle horse, which had been returned to the back exit of the hotel, as he'd requested. He half expected the Pinkerton agent to be standing guard at his hotel door. To his vast relief, no one was in sight.

"I think we should leave immediately," Hanna insisted, staring apprehensively at the stairway. "Once we're en route, I promise to tell you everything you want to know."

Cale stared at her long and hard, but he couldn't work up much contempt for her deception when she gazed pleadingly at him with that colorful bruise on her cheek. Nor with her full breasts all but spilling from that neckline, driving him crazy.

"Fine. We'll leave." He barreled through the door to retrieve the buckskin clothes he'd purchased for her. "You're wearing these. We don't need more trouble than we already have breathing down our necks, *Hanna,*" he emphasized resentfully.

Cale tugged off the cravat that had been strangling him for the past hour, then shed his expensive jacket. Hanna opened her mouth to retaliate against his snide tone, but when he hurriedly unbuttoned his shirt and cast it aside, her eyes widened and her jaw dropped again. It dawned on him that she probably wasn't in the habit of watching a man undress in her presence.

"Oh, pardon me, Princess Malloy. I suppose the wealthy, pampered heiress of Louisiana's most noted shipping magnate isn't accustomed to changing clothes with a man in the same room." He waved his hand toward the adjoining door. "You can change in there, and be quick about it."

She stared at him for a long silent moment, assuring him that he was definitely the first half-naked man she'd ever seen. For some reason that pleased him immensely, even though he was aggravated with her. Her gaze zeroed in on the bronzed expanse of his chest, then her eyes leaped to his face and she blushed profusely. Hanna took off like a flying carpet, the garments clutched to her bosom.

Cale sighed audibly as he peeled off his breeches, then grabbed his buckskins. He didn't have the time or inclination to indulge his new wife's delicate sensibilities at the moment. He was as frustrated as all get-out and impatient to leave town before trouble came knocking on his door. Plus the kiss he'd delivered to Hanna in the judge's chambers left him smoldering like live coals. He'd been determined to enjoy that kiss, since he'd promised to bypass the usual wedding night that came with marriage. But he really hadn't expected Hanna to reciprocate so enthusiastically when his mouth came down possessively on hers.

Man, she'd nearly burned him to a crisp when she'd kissed him back. His body was still simmering, and forbidden need played hell with his disposition—which had taken a turn for the worse when he discovered who she was.

He was fastening his assortment of weapons in place when the door to the adjoining room banged open and Hanna stepped into view, looking laughably transformed in baggy clothes that downplayed her feminine assets. There was a pinched expression on her face and a violet fire in her eyes as she walked straight up to him and tilted her chin to meet his gaze.

"I thought you were different," she said with a huff, startling the hell out of him. "You seemed to like me well enough yesterday and this morning, when I was Sarah Rawlins. But the moment you discovered my identity *you* changed. *I* did not. I am exactly the same person I have always been and I'll thank you to remember that."

Apparently, she'd recovered her composure while changing clothes and had gathered a full head of steam. He didn't know why she was so sensitive all of a sudden, but she definitely had a bee in her bonnet. Well, tough, so did he.

"You aren't the same person anymore," he retorted. "Now you're my lawfully wedded wife and you might as well know right off that I'm not a man who appreciates convenient lies and surprises of gigantic proportions."

His rejoinder seemed to have taken some of the starch out of her, for she said, "Fair enough. I'm sorry I snapped at you, but I've spent half my life watching that same astonished reaction from men when they discover my identity. I don't like it. I have no control over where I come from and I do not want my name to define who I am. Which is exactly why Hanna *Elliot* is heading out West, where the boundaries of gender and society aren't so strict and the name *Malloy* won't hang over my head like a curse."

Cale didn't claim to be a genius, but he was smart enough to realize Hanna was hypersensitive about her heritage. Why? He didn't know. There was a lot he didn't know about her—yet.

When a brisk rap sounded on the door, Cale's hand reflexively dropped to the pistol on his hip. Skeet bounded onto all fours, ears laid back, teeth bared.

"Deputy Marshal Elliot, I'd like a word with you. My name is Richard Sykes and I'm from the Pinkerton Detective Agency."

Hanna froze to the spot, her alarmed gaze shooting to Cale. He gave her silent instructions to gather the last of her belongings and pitch them out the window. Hanna hurriedly obeyed, then flung her leg over the windowsill.

"C'mon, Elliot, I know you're in there," called the impatient voice in the hall.

"Go away. I'm on my honeymoon," Cale called back

as he rolled up his fashionable clothes and stuffed them in his saddlebag.

"That's what I want to talk to you about. *That* and your new bride. Her father and fiancé want her back immediately. There will be an extremely generous reward for annulling your marriage and turning Miss Malloy over to me."

Hanna's frantic gaze flew to Cale. His expression revealed nothing of his thoughts. He simply motioned her out the window, across the roof and down to the waiting buckboard. Hanna didn't know if he wanted her to make a fast getaway or simply wanted her out of earshot while he bargained with the detective.

Twisting around, she planted both feet on the roof and then made the crucial mistake of looking over the edge. She clamped a shaky hand on the eave, willing herself to move, but her feet refused to cooperate.

This was a fine time to discover she had a strong aversion to heights. Damnation, what other weaknesses would she discover about herself when she was on a quest to find her strengths and her hidden talents?

Hanna dragged in a fortifying breath and tried to figure out how to contort her quaking body so she could latch on to the beam that supported the narrow roof above the back exit of the hotel. Before she found the nerve to ease over the edge—where a fourteen-foot drop waited—a hand clamped over her mouth.

Curse it! Cale had betrayed her for money! She twisted sideways, expecting to see the Pinkerton agent. To her everlasting relief, Cale's grim face hovered above hers. He tossed her satchels and his saddlebags into the buckboard below, then leaned as close to her as her own shadow.

"Wrap yourself around me, Miz Mags. We'll tackle this together," he murmured in her ear.

Hanna was so relieved to know he hadn't betrayed her and that she didn't have to face her newfound fear alone that she gladly flung her arms around his neck and wrapped her legs around his hips.

A lopsided smile quirked Cale's lips and one black brow arched as she pressed herself against him like a second skin. "That didn't take much convincing," he whispered, amused.

"I just discovered I don't deal well with excessive heights," she said, her face buried against his chest. "I've never climbed off a roof before."

"I'd have thought differently, since you've been living in the Malloy ivory tower," he replied smartly. "Fiancé, huh?" He sank down on the edge of the roof to grope for a foothold. "I wondered where you got that fancy wedding dress on such short notice. Left him at the altar, did you?"

"Yes, he was totally unsuitable for me, but I couldn't convince my father of that…oh, God!"

Hanna hung on for dear life when Cale slithered like a snake to ease over the eave and latch on to the supporting beam. Above them an irritated bellow rang out, followed by Skeet's loud bark. Hanna winced uncomfortably when her back scraped against the sharp edge of the beam and Cale shimmied downward, dragging her along with him.

Then he hooked his arm around her waist, swung her sideways and dropped her in the back of the wagon. Skeet commenced barking viciously when the detective slammed against the door, determined to gain entrance.

In a flash, Cale dropped down beside Hanna, grabbed her by the collar of her shirt and hoisted her onto the seat. He snatched up the reins and snapped them over the horses' rumps.

Hanna grabbed Cale's arm to prevent herself from somersaulting into the wagon bed when the team lunged forward into a gallop.

"You can't leave Skeet," Hanna insisted as they careened around the corner of the alley at breakneck speed.

"Skeet and I have had to part company before. Several

times, in fact. He's holding the detective at bay. He'll find us. Here, put on this cap and hunch your shoulders so you don't look more like a female than you already do,'' he ordered.

Hanna pulled the dingy cap down around her ears and slouched in the seat. By the time they reached the river's edge the ferry, loaded with wagons and horses, was preparing to leave. Despite a startled protest, Cale drove the wagon onto the barge, forcing the other horses and wagons to shift to provide room for the extra vehicle.

"One hurdle down," Cale remarked as he stepped over the seat to rearrange and secure the last of their belongings. "So, whaddya think, Mags? Having fun yet?"

Oddly enough she was having a grand adventure, and adrenaline was shooting through her like fireworks. She stared across the river toward Indian Territory. Maybe danger was waiting at every turn. Maybe the West wasn't her long-awaited promised land. But she felt free and alive and anxious to accept the challenges awaiting her.

Life was no longer a tedious string of stuffy soirees, pandering suitors in quest of her inheritance, and parental demands and ultimatums. She was her own woman, with her entire future ahead of her.

Hanna breathed in a gulp of the muggy air that hung above the river and told herself the world had never looked or smelled better. She owed Cale a tremendous debt and she vowed to do whatever she could to keep her end of their bargain.

Her respect for him had increased by leaps and bounds, knowing as she did that he'd turned down a sizable bribe when he refused to hand her over to the Pinkerton agent. She wanted to hug the stuffing out of Cale for delivering her across the river, but she figured she'd raise a few eyebrows, since he'd implied she was to portray a scruffy urchin. She kept her face downcast, refusing to meet anyone's gaze, while the barge moved toward the dock on the far side of the river.

In a matter of minutes Cale drove off the ferry, and he wasted no time urging the team of horses to a thundering gallop. Hanna held on by her fingernails as the buckboard bounced over the ruts in the road. She knew Cale wanted answers, but he seemed intent on putting a safe distance between them and the detective. She couldn't fathom how Skeet was going to catch up when Cale was making tracks in such fiendish haste. But knowing the dog was so utterly devoted to Cale, she predicted Skeet would wade through hell or high water—or both—to be reunited with his beloved master.

And so she stopped fretting about the animal and held on while Cale raced over the rugged terrain that was so unlike the delta she'd once called home. They rode for hours over a road so rough that it rattled her teeth, winding deeper into the foothills and dense forest. She expected Cale to call a halt when the sun dipped behind the rising mountains, but he picked his way through the darkness, keeping a relentless pace, remaining on constant alert.

Hanna tried to remain awake, but it had been a physically and emotionally exhausting day. It wore her out just thinking of everything that had happened since she'd awakened this morning. Heavens, she'd never squeezed so much living into so few hours. And to think this was probably standard routine for this bounty hunter who was now her lawfully wedded husband.

On that thought her eyes drifted shut and she slumped against Cale's sturdy shoulder. It didn't escape her notice that this was the first time in her life that she had placed her trust in a man—and he hadn't disappointed her.

Cale winced as he came awake to see the first rays of dawn spilling across the morning sky. He had a crick in his neck and an unidentified weight was bearing down on him, making him stiff and sore. He glanced down to see a mop of blond hair draped over his chest and a slender arm curled around his shoulder.

When Cale had gently laid Hanna on the pallet and stretched out beside her to ward off the damp evening chill, he hadn't expected her to crawl all over him. It was kind of nice, actually—though, admittedly, a bit uncomfortable.

Carefully, so as not to wake Hanna, he ran his fingers through the platinum tendrils, marveling at their silky texture. *His wife.* Cale still couldn't wrap his mind around that astounding concept. Having been raised in one culture and living in another—one that bore more contrasts than similarities—Cale wasn't sure what he was supposed to feel or how he was supposed to approach this temporary marriage.

He was a man accustomed to operating on analytical logic, reflex and instinct. He'd never allowed emotion to enter the equation. But since he'd met this sometimes amusing and sometimes exasperating Southern belle, a need to protect, as well as unprecedented feelings of possessiveness, had hounded him. He didn't know how to deal with the tenderness that kept creeping up on him—like now, at this very moment.

This five-foot-nothing female disturbed his routine and distracted his thoughts. She aroused him, and he knew he had to learn to deal with *that* because consummating this marriage wasn't part of the bargain. Which was why he intended to set the swiftest pace possible across the territory. He'd be his old self again when they reached Texas, and he could focus his energy and his thoughts on bringing Otis Pryor to justice.

When Hanna squirmed and sighed, her breath whispered against his neck like a lover's caress. Cale gritted his teeth when his body hardened and another jolt of forbidden hunger ran through him. He needed to get up and get moving, and he was about to do just that when those dusky lashes fluttered and he found himself staring into those beguiling violet eyes. Then she smiled drowsily at him and another bolt of desire shot straight to his loins.

Damn, this woman set off so many unfamiliar emotions and intense sensations inside him that he didn't know how to deal with them all at once.

"Mornin'," Hanna drawled huskily.

He couldn't help but smile back at her. "Mornin', Magnolia Blossom."

She sighed again, nuzzled against his chest, then must've realized where she was and who she was sprawled over. Her eyes shot open and she dug the heel of her hand into his solar plexus in her haste to lever herself off him. Her face flooded with color as she shrank back.

"I…" She raked the tangled tresses from her flushed face. "Sorry. I hadn't realized I was using you for a pillow."

He shrugged casually, although there was nothing casual about the hungry need hammering at his body. He was still hard and achy, and he figured he was going to have to get used to that condition if he kept constant company with Hanna.

Cale rolled agilely to his feet and turned his back to conceal the noticeable bulge below his waistband. "We need to grab a bite of trail rations and head south," he said, his discomfort making him abrupt. "We'll probably have a Pinkerton on our tail. As if we don't have enough trouble to deal with in this neck of the woods."

Hanna watched Cale methodically break camp and hitch the team of horses to the wagon. It disturbed her that she'd cuddled up to Cale in sleep like a trusting child. But then, she had begun to trust and rely on him after he'd refused to deliver her to the detective.

Despite Cale's reputation in society, he was an honorable man. He'd made a bargain with her and it looked as if he intended to keep it. She reminded herself that he was motivated by a driving need to avenge his brother and sister-in-law's deaths. It wasn't so much a growing attachment to her, but a need to have her play a role that would gain him access to his enemy's camp. She'd just have to learn to curb this unexpected fascination for this man who was now her husband.

Furthermore, she owed Cale an explanation. She'd give it, she decided, after she saw to her needs and she and Cale were underway.

"The creek's that way, through that line of trees to the west," Cale said, as if he'd read her mind.

Hanna blushed. She'd never spent so much uninterrupted time in male company and had never discussed bodily functions. She'd better get used to that because she and Cale would be living in each other's pockets for the next month, she reminded herself.

Hurriedly, Hanna strode toward the canopy of blackjack trees and fought her way through the dense underbrush. After seeing to her needs, she sidestepped down the steep embankment to wash her hands and face in the creek. She heard the quiet snarl before she located its source. A mangy black bear and her cubs lurked on the opposite side of the narrow creek.

Hanna shrieked in alarm when the mother bear bounded through the water, headed straight toward her. Hanna was up the embankment, bursting through the underbrush in no time flat. The air left her lungs in a pained whoosh when she ran headlong into Cale, who was racing toward the creek to respond to her cry of alarm.

Hanna bounced off Cale's broad chest and landed with a thud in the bushes. Before she could catch her breath he yanked her to her feet and shoved her behind him. Pistol cocked and aimed, he stood with his weight balanced on the balls of his feet, prepared to take the brunt of attack in an effort to protect her from harm.

Another corner of her heart caved in as she marveled at

this man's fearlessness, his unerring capabilities. She wanted to be like him. She wanted to face her fears and conquer them one by one. Instead, she'd squawked like a plucked chicken, turned tail and raced toward Cale for assistance.

When an attack didn't come, Cale said, "What the hell was that about?"

"Mother bear with her cubs," Hanna explained, then dragged in a steadying breath. "She came after me."

Cale pivoted, grabbed her elbow and swiftly zigzagged through the underbrush. "Lesson number one—always expect trouble," he lectured. "Lesson number two—watering holes are the favorite haunts of man and beast. Screaming only incites alarm, so keep your trap shut. There's no telling who or what is in the area, so don't invite more unwanted guests than necessary."

"I'll try to remember that."

Cale stopped abruptly and lurched around. His eyes blazed, black and fierce, prompting her to back up a step. "No," he said through gritted teeth. "You won't *try* to remember. You *will* remember. We're traveling through criminal-infested territory and you just made a tactical mistake that a lot of folks make. The *dead* ones," he added emphatically. "There *are* no allowances for mistakes out here in the wilderness. Always assume the worst. Always anticipate trouble and you'll never be surprised or disappointed." He wheeled around and towed her toward the camp.

Hanna frowned curiously when she took time to survey the heap of supplies and rations in the wagon bed. "I thought you were purchasing weapons and ammunition," she said as he scooped her up and set her on the wooden seat.

"I did." Cale tied his pinto gelding behind the wagon, then bounded up to the seat. "I had the blacksmith build a false bottom in the bed to conceal the arsenal. No sense inviting thieves to swipe our stockpile of weapons.'' He snapped the reins and the horses trotted forward. "Now, you were going to tell me why an heiress, who probably had everything most females could possibly want at her fingertips, and a fiancé waiting at the altar, decided to take an assumed name and marry a half-breed. Spit it out, Magnolia, and don't leave out any details.''

"We really need to work on your gentlemanly tact," she said. "'Spit it out' suggests ridding oneself of foul-tasting food.''

He shot her a sideways glance, his thick brows bunched over his onyx eyes. Clearly, he was in no mood for a discussion of manners. "Let's hear it," he demanded curtly. "You've stalled long enough."

# Chapter Six

Hanna drew a deep breath and gathered her thoughts as Cale followed the barely passable trail that wound deeper into the tree-choked mountains. She knew she owed Cale an explanation, but it hurt to admit aloud that she was nothing more to her father than a gambit and a pawn, and that braving the dangers of the wilderness was preferable to the gilded cage where she'd lived for the past few years.

"The reason I'm heading west is because my father doesn't love me and he can't quite forgive the fact that I'm the heir who survived when he lost his son to illness."

Cale noted the torment and bitterness in her voice, but he didn't interrupt to soothe or console her. He wanted the facts, though he couldn't quite believe Walter Malloy had no affection for this breathtakingly beautiful and sharp-witted woman.

"My father has dedicated his life to making money. He measures worthiness by profits and accumulated wealth," Hanna explained. "That's why only the best known detectives were sent to track me down. You could have named your own price to turn me over to them and you would have walked away with a small fortune."

Cale believed it. The agent who'd talked to him through

the hotel door had assured him that he'd be set for life if he handed over Hanna.

"My father can barely abide the sight of me. He strongly disapproves of the fact that I have a mind of my own and that I want to be mistress of my own fate. I refused the offers of several suitors who came with my father's stamp of approval. He finally lost all patience and ordered me to wed Louis Beauchamp. He never left me alone until I was at the church, preparing for the ceremony."

"Beauchamp." Cale frowned pensively. "The name rings a bell."

"As well it should. His family is also involved in shipping and distribution, second only to the high and mighty Malloys," she muttered resentfully. "It was to be a merger of historical proportions. A monopoly that would grant control of Louisiana ports to our combined families."

"So you cut and ran the first chance you got," Cale said as he guided the horses down a steep embankment to ford a creek.

"Actually, I climbed out the church window and boarded a steamboat." She smiled for the first time since she began the tale. "I knew my father would spare no expense in tracking me down. I needed a husband who couldn't be intimidated or tempted by his money."

Cale was flattered to learn that Hanna had selected him for the very reasons most folks avoided him. His less than respectable reputation in society, for one. Secondly, his ferocity and practiced skills in facing off against dangerous odds. *She* defended him when others scorned him and avoided association with him.

Although her strong motivation for wanting to marry him had nothing whatsoever to do with love and affection, she did respect and admire him. She wasn't afraid to say so, either. My, wasn't that something?

In turn, Cale had come to admire her determination. He

doubted there were many women who would turn their backs on fabulous wealth and a privileged life. Hanna Malloy—correction, *Elliot*—was to become her own woman, to make her own choices and live with the consequences. Her decision to make her own place in the world was as fierce and unwavering as his need to track down the man who'd taken what was left of his family.

Perhaps they were a mismatched pair, but they shared driving goals and ambitions. 'Course, Hanna had one hell of a lot to learn if she was going to survive in the wilds. She'd had two near brushes with calamity in two days, and conditions were going to deteriorate rapidly during this journey.

Cale wasn't a pessimist but a realist, and he knew trouble waited around every bend of the road. Hanna was his responsibility, because he was dragging her cross-country by wagon when she might've been safer on a stagecoach. Although meeting up with robbers—who'd pick her clean like buzzards—was certainly within the realm of possibility in these parts. After all, Indian Territory was a haven for criminals and this particular area was as thick with thieves as it was thick with trees.

"Oh, my God!" Hanna's abrupt shout caused Cale to stomp on the brake, nearly catapulting them both over the backs of the horses, which were wading knee deep in the creek.

Cale snaked out a hand to jerk Hanna back in place, and then he glanced around to determine what she was yapping about. His tension drained away and an affectionate smile pursed his lips when Skeet bounded onto the back of the wagon, not looking the least bit concerned about aiding in Cale's hurried escape from town. However, the dog looked happy to be reunited with his master.

"I was worried about you," Hanna cooed as she reached back to caress the dog's neck.

Cale blinked in surprise when Skeet didn't object to

Hanna's touch. The dog never allowed anyone to pet him but Cale. When had these two formed a bond?

He watched in amazement as Hanna scooted sideways and patted the empty space that resulted. Skeet slapped his mud-caked paws on the seat, then hopped forward. Hanna gently slid her arm around the dog's thick shoulders and gave him a hug. Still the animal didn't growl in objection.

Cale's first instinct was to protest the fact that Hanna was turning Skeet into a pet. The last thing he needed was for the beast to go soft on him. On the other hand, he had major difficulty scolding Hanna for demonstrating her affection for his partner, a dog that had held the detective at bay while they made their escape.

The woman was definitely leaving her mark on Cale and Skeet both. Maybe it wasn't such a bad thing to enjoy the tender side of life—temporarily, of course. As long as he didn't get too attached, Cale reminded himself sensibly. For sure, it would be better all around if Hanna toughened up and he and Skeet didn't soften up too much.

Emotions were a hazard in Cale's line of work, and he refused to let himself forget that. He knew there was a bullet out there with his name on it. That was the reality of wading around in this criminal-infested territory. All Cale asked of whatever deities truly ruled the universe was that he would live long enough to see Otis Pryor pay for the deaths he'd committed.

"Now you know why I crave freedom and independence and want to experience life to its fullest," Hanna said, breaking into his thoughts. "How is it that you chose this profession? I'm also curious about your upbringing."

Well, that was another first. No one had ever cared to ask how he came to be or why he rode for Parker. Cale had never shared his life story with anyone. Not that it was much of a story, but he was a private man who'd never been inclined to open up and let anyone close. Losing his half brother had slammed the door on any emotions that

Cale harbored beneath the hardened shell required to perform his duties. He dealt with the worst criminals that society had to offer. He kept to himself, didn't give anyone the chance to betray him, to double-cross him. He didn't let anyone behind the barrier that separated him from the rest of the world.

"Well, spit it out," she said teasingly.

The smile she tossed at him, the sight of her sitting on the seat with her arm draped over Skeet's back, hit him right where he lived. Cale heard himself chuckle. It was a rusty sound, he had to admit.

"My bad manners must be rubbing off on you, Miz Magnolia."

She shrugged, dragging his attention to the lacings that covered her breasts. He could see a teasing hint of cleavage, reminding him that Hanna was every inch a woman, no matter what he dressed her in.

A woman off-limits and far beyond his social status.

"I'm half-Cherokee," he said as he focused on the thick trees that lined the narrow path. "A bastard, in fact." He didn't know why he'd added that. Maybe to remind her— and himself—that their backgrounds were poles apart. She didn't flinch or recoil in disgust, just stared at him with those sparkling violet eyes that tempted him to lose himself in forbidden dreams.

"You don't know who your father was?" she asked.

He nodded jerkily. "He was one of the soldiers who drove our tribe from their homeland and into confinement before they were marched down the Trail of Tears to Indian Territory. He was supposed to be guarding our people. Instead, he attacked a young maiden barely fourteen years old."

Cale scowled when Hanna's eyes glistened with unshed tears. He didn't want to upset her with this unpleasant tale. He didn't like remembering it, much less speaking of it. But once he began, he couldn't seem to stop, as if the anger and frustration that had bubbled beneath the surface like lava had finally boiled out.

"My people were driven by troops, at the point of bayonets, into stockade camps. Thirteen thousand people were taken on foot on the eight-hundred-mile journey to Indian Territory in the dead of winter. Despite sickness and grief, they were herded from their homeland like animals," Cale muttered bitterly.

"Although a third of our tribe died en route, my grandparents included, my mother, Nakwisi, survived the hardships of the journey. She was taken in by the clan of the warrior she was to marry when she came of age," Cale informed her. "The Cherokee lost so many that even halfbreeds were welcome and wanted. But then, most Indian cultures focus more on offspring and their potential contribution to the tribe than whites do, especially with children of mixed heritage. I didn't really understand what it meant to be an outcast until the whites taught me."

Hanna's heart bled for Cale. In comparison to his mother's plight, Hanna felt spoiled and peevish for straining against the confines and limitations set by her domineering father.

"I believe my mother cared for me," Cale continued as they rode beneath branches that shaded the trail. "But the older I became, the more she withdrew and avoided contact with me. Then my stepfather came to me one day when I was eight and told me that I was to move my belongings to the lodge of a family that had lost their son to illness."

"But why?" Hanna asked, tormented that Cale had been foisted off with little regard to the needs of a young, impressionable child.

Cale glanced at her, his face a mask that revealed no emotion. "Because my mother looked at me and saw the man who'd attacked her. The older I got, the more pronounced the likeness was. By then my half brother, Gray

Cloud, was a toddler who needed her affection. He was the rightful son, and I evoked too many painful memories for my mother.''

Hanna's heart twisted in her chest. In a way, she and Cale shared similar backgrounds. They'd both grown up knowing they weren't wanted. But his life had been harsh, while she'd had everything she needed. Except the one thing she wanted most—her father's love.

Cale hadn't grown up knowing what it was like to be loved, either.

"I was allowed to associate with Gray Cloud," Cale explained. "We trained together, keeping the old ways of our tribe alive. Although we were under the watchful eyes of the soldiers at the reservation, we learned the ways of warriors. We were chosen to ride with the Cherokee police force, known as the Lighthorsemen.

"Eventually my brother married and built a home on the land the government allotted to him and to me. It was our long-range plan to work the land together. Since I was of mixed heritage and had gained a reputation with white law officials, I was offered a job as a deputy marshal and bounty hunter to rid the territory of invading whites.''

"I don't understand," Hanna interjected. "I thought you were already working with Cherokee law enforcement.''

He nodded his dark head. "The Lighthorsemen handle disputes and crimes among the tribe. Judge Parker has jurisdiction over white criminals who prey on Indians and upon each other. I took another name, accepted the job and turned to bounty hunting, because the better pay allowed me to help my brother and his wife establish our farm.''

Hanna was quick to note the change in his expression, the way his fists clenched on the reins. The memory of losing his family still tormented him, though he tried not to let it show. Truly, it amazed her how quickly she had learned to read his moods and expressions. She'd become exceptionally attentive toward Cale in a short amount of time. That astounded her. But she could almost feel the pain radiating from him as he stared into the distance, on constant alert.

"We had saved a sizable nest egg for improvements and had acquired a large number of livestock," Cale told her. "Then a gang of thieves descended into the valley, to rustle our cattle, horses and sheep, and steal money...."

There was a long pause that tore at Hanna's heart.

"I found my brother dead, apparently trying to save his wife from assault."

The words dropped like stones, and Hanna couldn't prevent herself from sliding toward Cale to wrap her arms around his neck, forcing Skeet to exchange positions with her. "I'm so very sorry. I know how it feels to lose someone who means the world to you."

Cale squirmed uneasily, uncomfortable with Hanna's compassion, uncomfortable with the fact that he'd told her the grim story he'd never shared with another living soul. He'd never had a confidante before, but he had to admit it was a relief to vent his grief rather than keeping it buried inside.

His thoughts scattered as he rounded the bend and came upon a small grassy clearing. Cale stamped hard on the brake and reflexively reached for his shotgun. Two men lay sprawled on the ground, facedown, unmoving.

"Wait," he murmured when Hanna tried to vault from the wagon to help. She glanced questioningly at him and he gestured toward the supposed victims of attack. "This could be a trap. Never trust what you think you see."

"Lesson number three," she murmured as she waited for him to climb down. "Tell me something, Cale? Is there anything in life that you *can* see and believe?"

"Death, maybe," he murmured, distracted. "But sometimes it sneaks up on your blind side when you aren't looking. So I guess you can't trust it, either."

He handed Hanna the shotgun, though she wasn't sure she could use it. With both pistols drawn, Cale led the way. Hanna watched him scan the area, pausing to listen for any sound that might alert him to unseen trouble. She tried to emulate his actions, but figured it would take her years of constant practice before she could equal his expertise.

"Skeet," Cale called quietly.

The dog bounded from the wagon to scout the perimeter, and Hanna realized what Cale meant about the animal's abilities in the wild. Skeet became eyes in the back of Cale's head when necessity demanded, an extra set of ears tuned to trouble.

Once Skeet circled the clearing, he came to heel, as if to assure Cale the coast was clear. Only then did Cale approach the downed men. He shoved his boot against the older man's shoulder, sending him rolling over in the grass.

Hanna sank to her knees when she saw the bloody wound on the man's chest. Her stomach rolled and she had to force herself not to look away.

"Dead."

Cale's voice was so matter-of-fact, so completely devoid of emotion, that she winced. It dawned on her that this was the world where Cale resided, and that emotional detachment was what kept him from losing his composure. Unfortunately, she didn't have his experience, and the emotional shock of stumbling over a dead body made her light-headed. Those dizzying sensations intensified when Cale walked over to determine the condition of the younger man.

"Hanna, go back to the wagon. *Now,*" he ordered abruptly.

Her gaze shot to the blond-haired man and she gasped at his disfigured face. She clambered to her feet when her stomach flip-flopped. She was going to be sick.

No, she wasn't! she commanded herself. Maybe she had lived in an ivory tower most of her life, but she had to learn to cope with bleak reality—the reality of Cale's existence. This was part of her learning process, thoroughly distasteful though it was.

"Damn it, I said—"

"No." Hanna met his dark, glittering gaze with staunch determination. "I'll be damned if I'm going to leave you standing here alone with the scent of death all around you. I'll help you bury them."

"Who said anything about burying them? They haven't been dead very long, which means we need to get the hell out of here before we find ourselves in the same condition. Whoever did this can't be far away. I'd just as soon not happen onto them while I have you in tow. I promised to keep you alive."

"Nevertheless, it's our Christian duty to see these men properly buried," she maintained.

"Hell, woman, if trouble doesn't find you then you seem determined to go out and flag it down." He gestured toward the unfortunate victims. "These men look to be as bad as the bastards who shot them. I wouldn't be surprised if there are warrants out for *their* arrest," Cale snorted. "If we hang around here we might be digging our own graves."

"I'm still not leaving them for the buzzards," Hanna insisted. "It seems to me that it makes little difference who we are or how fortunate we might be in life. It's what we can do to relieve the plight of others that counts."

"Look, you can be Florence Nightingale or the first female pope for all I care, but we aren't taking time to dig graves," he snapped. "Don't forget there's a detective looking for you, and I suspect he isn't too far behind us. Let him do the digging.... Damn it, Hanna!"

Exasperated, Cale watched Hanna march determinedly to the wagon to retrieve the shovel he'd purchased to toss dirt on campfires. With her shoulders squared, her head held at a stubborn angle, she walked toward the nearby creek to find a place where digging wasn't so difficult.

She glanced at him, her violet eyes glittering. "Don't try to change who I am and what I stand for, Cale. My father already tried and failed."

"And don't try to change who I am and what I stand for," he countered. "Ordinarily, it's my duty to transport renegades such as these to Judge Parker for identification. But *not* while I have you in tow. You're costing us valuable time we don't have."

Despite his comments, she started digging. Damn it, the woman wouldn't back down from the devil himself. Which was obvious, because Cale felt like the very devil at the moment and she wasn't backing down.

Cale scowled in frustration. "Well, fine, if you want to wear yourself out behind a spade, then so be it. You'll run out of steam before long, and then we can hit the trail again."

To his amazement, Hanna refused to buckle to exhaustion. She just kept right on digging until Cale's conscience started beating him black-and-blue.

"Here, gimme that." He scowled at her as he jerked the shovel from her blistered hands. "And keep your distance from the bodies. Go fill the canteens or something."

"No, I said I'd—"

Her voice fizzled out when he glared murderously at her. She might as well get acquainted with his bad side, he decided. He gave her that don't-cross-me-or-you'll-be-damn-sorry glower that had made many a man back down.

Surprise, surprise. Little Miz Magnolia Blossom just hitched her chin a notch higher and matched him stare for stare. It dawned on him that his care and concern for her had backfired in his face. She trusted him not to hurt her—therefore she wasn't the least bit afraid of him. Well, damn.

Muttering sourly, Cale relinquished the spade. "Okay, have it your way, but don't come crying to me when those blisters break open."

He was halfway across the clearing before he realized he'd given in to her. Hell's jingling bells, he couldn't make a habit of that. Plus he knew what it took to stay alive in this area, because this was his stomping ground. Dillydallying over tenderhearted tendencies wasn't it!

While he again sent Skeet to scout the perimeter of the clearing for trouble, Cale reminded himself that Hanna was going to have to learn to ignore a few of those Good Samaritan virtues if she wanted to endure in the West. She'd never make it farther than the Indian Territory if she planned to say grace over every hapless victim she left resting in peace.

It took two hours of valuable daylight to tend to the chore. Cale knew they'd have to make up for lost time by taking the rugged shortcut over the mountain pass. It would enable him to compensate for the delay, but it was ten miles of the roughest trail this side of the Rockies.

Cale glanced toward the towering peak to the south and resigned himself to a long uphill walk, with the horses and wagon trailing behind them.

"She did *what?* Has she lost her mind?" Walter Malloy bellowed at the Pinkerton agent seated in front of his desk.

The somber-faced detective nodded, then looked down at the telegram he'd received from his associate. "According to Agent Richard Sykes, your daughter married a half-breed bounty hunter who rides for Judge Isaac Parker. The man is the law's last defense against the worst criminal elements in Indian Territory." Agent Dixon looked up. "I've heard of Cale Elliot. Not the kind of man I'd envision as your daughter's husband. But he is definitely a legend in his own time when it comes to law enforcement."

Walter swore under his breath, then paced the length of his office. He couldn't believe that willful child of his had gone to such drastic extremes to defy his dictates. When Louis Beauchamp heard about this... Walter stopped pacing abruptly. No, Louis was not going to hear about this. The Pinkertons would track down his infuriatingly rebellious daughter and he'd have the marriage annulled so she could wed Louis and get that ranting Frenchman off his back.

Blast and be damned! How could one woman cause so much trouble? Clarissa would never have behaved so outlandishly. She had been all that was dignified, refined and soft-spoken. For years Walter had tried to mold Hanna to fit the memory of his beloved Clarissa. Tried and failed, again and again.

"I want that gun-toting heathen found and I want my daughter back, no matter what the cost," Walter snapped. "I'm paying the agency a fortune and I've offered astronomical rewards for information. I expect results!"

Agent Dixon surged from the chair. "We'll have three agents on their trail within the week," he promised.

"*Three?*" Walter hooted. "In a *week?* No, I think not. I want *six* detectives out there in *three days!*"

"Sir, we're only human and our horses do not come equipped with wings," Dixon pointed out.

"They would if your daughter was traipsing across that godforsaken territory with some half-breed of a bounty hunter as her husband. I expect telegrams delivered daily, reporting your progress."

"Sir, telegraph offices are few and far between in the territory," the agent explained. "We will, however, keep you abreast of our search and recovery mission."

When Dixon tipped his hat politely and exited, Walter sneered after him. He hated situations he couldn't control, hated the fact that Hanna was purposely tormenting him.

Why couldn't it have been his son who'd survived instead—

Walter smothered the thought before he even completed it. Angry though he was with Hanna, as much as she'd frustrated him the past few years, she was still the living—if tormenting—memory of Clarissa.

Muttering, Walter slopped brandy into his glass and gulped it down in two swallows. Hanna had married a savage? A hired gunslinger? My God! It was simply too incredible to fathom.

Walter plunked himself down at his desk and stared at the portrait of his wife and son that hung above the mantel. They were together in heaven, he mused. He was stuck here in hell, trying to track down his belligerent daughter, who had proved beyond question that she would do anything—even wed an undesirable—to rebel against his wishes.

He swiped his hand over his balding head and swore colorfully. If he weren't every bit as stubborn as Hanna, he would wash his hands of her and call off the search. But she was like him, he realized grimly. Pure, fierce determination flowed through her veins. This was a battle of wills, and he was not going to lose. He would have her back under his control and she could take her frustration out on her stuffy fiancé.

The thought of turning Hanna loose on Louis Beauchamp brought a smile to Walter's lips. If nothing else, Louis deserved to be married to Hanna. Let *him* try to control that feisty female and see how far *he* got.

# Chapter Seven

Hanna voiced no complaints when Cale announced they would have to walk over the steep mountain pass and carry as many supplies as possible to ensure the team of horses didn't give out. Gasping for breath, she paused to readjust the load slung over her shoulder. Her blistered fingers burned as she clamped them around the gunnysack of supplies she'd bought to help her explore her talents.

Her legs wobbled slightly, but she told herself she was building the needed stamina to meet the rigorous challenges of her new life. Plus she'd seen to it that the unfortunate victims had a decent burial. Although Cale was aggravated with her for delaying their journey, she simply could not, in good conscience, turn her back on her fellow man, even if of the criminal element.

Despite screaming muscles, Hanna trudged ever upward, assuring herself that descending from the pass would be easier. In the meantime she envied Cale's strength and endurance, for he made the feat of turning himself into a beast of burden look easy. She would have pointed out that he had a few tenderhearted tendencies himself for taking the horses into consideration and lightening their load, but she didn't think he wanted to hear it. Wisely, Hanna kept the thought to herself.

"We'll stop for a rest here before we descend the trail," Cale announced as he topped the mountain.

A rest. Praise the Lord! Hanna mused as she huffed and puffed up the towering ridge. She swung her gaze across the panoramic landscape of tree-covered mountains, admiring the natural beauty of her surroundings. This was indeed a rugged, untamed land. It tested one's endurance, but was gloriously spectacular.

Her attention shifted to the brawny man beside her and she studied his masculine profile while he panned the area, ever watchful and attuned to the prospect of trouble. Life hadn't been particularly kind to Cale, but he had made the best of it, taking it in stride and finding his niche. She intended to do the same—with Cale as her example and inspiration.

Hanna tried to conjure up one man of her acquaintance who could compare to Cale's rugged good looks, his amazing skills and his self-reliance. There simply wasn't one. Cale was in a league of his own—tough, hardened and relentless.

He also had a broad and magnificently muscular chest. Now that she'd seen it, she found herself wanting to brush her hand over all that bronzed skin and feel the leashed power and strength beneath her fingertips.

The betraying thought, which came out of nowhere, made her blush. Ever since she'd laid eyes on Cale's half-nude body the most incredible thoughts and wicked speculations had been darting around in her mind, distracting her. She definitely needed to keep her focus on the arduous task of staying alive in this unforgiving wilderness.

"What the hell's in all those packages you're carrying?" Cale asked as he glanced at the sack on her back.

"My future talents," she declared as she stood beside him on top of the world.

He frowned, bemused. "Come again?"

"Artist supplies, writing tablets, thread, yarn and fabric,'' she replied. ''Once I have the opportunity to discover my hidden talent I plan to master it.''

''Damn, Magnolia, whatcha gonna do if it turns out you can't paint, knit, write or sew?''

The question took the wind out of her sails, but not for long. She tilted her chin up and said, ''Then I'll find something else that I'm good at and I will excel at that.''

Cale dropped the pack from his shoulders, gave her a pointed stare and said, ''Maybe you could be a preacher. You certainly said enough words over those two outlaws to talk them clear to heaven. When my time comes you can leave off with 'It's been nice knowin' ya.'''

''Rest assured,'' she called after him as he disappeared into the bushes, ''that I'll talk myself purple over you, but you won't be around to tell me I've already said plenty.''

Which was exactly what he'd said that afternoon before he'd swung into the wagon and gestured impatiently for her to climb aboard.

Wearily, Hanna plunked down on the ground to grab the canteen to quench her thirst and give her weary legs a rest. She sighed and closed her eyes. Ah, what she wouldn't give for a fifteen-minute nap.

Cale emerged from the underbrush and scowled when he saw Hanna sprawled in the grass, her arms outflung, her blistered palms lending testimony to the fact that she was too dainty and delicate to endure the hardships of the wilds. He should not have draggged her through this exhausting ordeal. She'd never make it on her own, and *he* would be saying prayers over *her*.

The unpleasant prospect made him grimace. Well, he wasn't going to think about that. He'd just teach Hanna everything he could in the short time they had together. Then he'd hope like hell that she'd found a civilized place to set up camp in the West to paint and write and stitch—

or whatever hidden talent she discovered in her quest to find herself and feed her soul.

Cale hunkered down beside Hanna and stared at her for a long moment. Damn but she was extraordinarily beautiful, even in those ill-fitting buckskins. Even with an unsightly bruise, a few scratches, smudges and blisters.

She had taken his breath away when he'd seen her in that form-fitting wedding gown, her hair glowing around her enchanting face like moonbeams. Her sense of wonder and enjoyment touched him because, through her eyes, he was seeing this ruggedly spectacular terrain as if for the first time. But till his dying day, he swore, the image of Hanna standing toe to toe with him in that clearing, determined to see to those two renegades' last rites, would stick in his mind. Despite the traumatic and unpleasant incident, Hanna had done what she believed was right. He admired her for it—in a frustrated sort of way.

Hanna was velvet over a core of steel. She had grit and style and character…and he wanted to lean down to kiss her so badly he ached. Those lush lips practically begged for his kiss. It probably would have been better if he hadn't discovered how sweet she tasted, how wildly she responded, how good she felt in his arms. But he'd hauled off and kissed her at the ceremony, and now he wanted a steady diet of her ripe, dewy mouth.

Come to think of it, why shouldn't he kiss her again if he felt like it? True, he'd agreed to forgo the wedding night, but he hadn't agreed to not kiss her. And so he leaned down to brush his mouth over hers in the slightest whisper of a kiss—and heard a snarl so close to his ear that he reflexively jerked away.

To his astonished disbelief Skeet bared his teeth—at *him!* With his ears laid back and his hair bristling down his spine, the dog stood guard beside Hanna's outflung hand, warning Cale to back off. Cale was totally dumbfounded by Skeet's protective instincts toward Hanna. This was the thanks he got for saving the mutt from certain death a couple of times? For keeping him fed?

Damn dog had turned traitor. Which only went to prove that if you ever depended on anyone but yourself, you were doomed to disappointment.

When Hanna's thick lashes swept up, glancing curiously at Skeet, then at him, Cale grabbed her wrist and hoisted her to her feet. "Time to move," he declared. "I want to be camped by the river by sunset."

Cale muttered under his breath when she frowned at his clipped tone. She didn't have a clue that wanting her—constantly—was starting to eat away at him. She was oblivious to the fact that his turncoat dog had been suckered in by the sound of her soft voice and her demonstrations of affection. Well, when the going got tough—and it would, it always did—they'd see who Skeet came running to.

Cale scooped up the sack of supplies, grabbed the horses' reins and hiked downhill, leaving Hanna to follow behind him.

"Did I do something else to annoy you?" she asked as she fell into step. "If this is about that catnap, I didn't intend to fall asleep."

"No, that's not the problem," he mumbled, without glancing in her direction.

It wasn't about the nap. Ah, if only it were that simple. The problem was that she lived, she breathed and she made him want her—badly. He couldn't afford this kind of tormenting distraction. Never in his miserable life had he had so much trouble paying attention to his surroundings.

Remaining on constant alert had been second nature until he traipsed across this territory with Hanna as his companion. He couldn't keep his mind off of her, and the never-ending battle with forbidden longing was making him cranky. He wasn't accustomed to dealing with his emotions. Until now. Until Hanna. Now he had to make a

conscious effort to keep his eyes off her and scout for
trouble.

Damn good thing he concentrated on paying attention,
too, he decided five minutes later. The coiling snake that
Hanna disturbed—when she wandered off the beaten path
to pluck up a colorful wildflower that caught her eye—
would've given her a nasty bite. Cale's knife cleared the
leather sheath and swished through the air before he barely
had time to register the need to act.

Horrified, Hanna leaped sideways when she saw the
knife hurtling toward her. She didn't realize its target until
the six-foot-long snake curled around the blade that pinned
it to the ground so it couldn't strike her.

Cale tramped over to dispose of the snake and retrieve
his dagger. He glared into Hanna's peaked face. "And
don't even start with me about a proper burial, Miz Bleeding Heart," he muttered. "Maybe you're all-fired eager to
experience life, but some things you really don't need to
experience to know they're painful and unpleasant. Next
time watch what the hell you're doing. Got it?"

Scared speechless, she nodded and gulped.

"Good," he said before he turned on his heels and
stalked off.

Hanna listened carefully as Cale gave her instructions
on the proper method of placing a circle of stones around
the campfire to hold a skillet, and then listed various ways
of preventing a fire from spreading rapidly to torch the
tree-covered mountains. She silently marveled at all the
survival skills he'd acquired, plus his ability to snare supper without firing a single shot.

Time and again Cale emphasized the importance of becoming attuned to their surroundings, to seek oneness with
nature. While he'd taught her to clean the wild turkey that
was roasting over the fire, he'd told her to watch the flight
of birds, which could lead her to water holes and also alert

her to the presence of unwanted intruders. He insisted that it was important to pick your battles, if at all possible, because there were some you couldn't win if you were playing by your foes' rules. Play to your strengths and use the element of surprise to your advantage, he'd said emphatically.

The instructions he'd given Hanna over supper left her head spinning, but she tried to absorb every tidbit of knowledge he imparted.

After she'd washed the utensils and plates and packed them away—according to Cale, you always had your belongings in proper order in case you needed to make a hasty departure—Hanna dug out a charcoal pencil and tablet from her sack. She was ready to try her hand at a landscape sketch of the mountains. She worked industriously while Skeet lay beside her, his broad head resting on her thigh. Cale sat across the camp, cleaning his Colts and sharpening his dagger.

Hanna could imagine herself setting up her easel somewhere in the Rockies—they were reported to boast some of the most awe-inspiring views Mother Nature offered—and committing the panoramic scenery to canvas.

"Well, what do you think?" she asked, holding up the sketch for his perusal.

Like a powerful panther, Cale rose to his feet and strode up beside her. He angled the tablet toward the campfire to take a closer look. Impatiently she watched him glance at her, scan the shadowy mountains silhouetted in the last rays of sunset, then stare at her sketch.

"Well?" she prompted when he remained silent.

"Well, what?" he asked.

"Do you think I have a potential talent for art? Keep in mind, of course, that it's almost dark, so the shading needs some more work."

"I'm keeping that in mind," Cale mumbled as he handed the tablet back to her. "Um, it's real nice."

When he glanced away Hanna frowned. "*Real nice?* That's a bit vague. I'm asking for your honest opinion here. It's been my experience that I can count on you to tell me the truth without sugarcoating it. I want to know exactly what you think of the drawing."

Cale squirmed uneasily. He didn't want to hurt her feelings, when it was evident that she was bound and determined to pinpoint and perfect her hidden talents. But a perception of height and depth were seriously lacking in the sketch. Cale never claimed to be an authority on art, but he figured a drawing of a mountain ought to at least *look* like a mountain.

"Tell me the truth!" she demanded impatiently.

"It's…not very good," he said reluctantly.

Her hopeful expression vanished.

"Maybe with some practice and training," he added, wanting to make her feel better.

"What's wrong with the drawing?" she asked, getting all huffy and defensive.

"It's one-dimensional, for starters," he said.

She bent her head over the sketch in profound concentration and worked quickly with her charcoal pencil. "Does this help?" she asked, holding the paper up to him.

Cale inwardly winced as he studied the drawing. It was worse, not better. "Um…no."

Frustrated, she slammed down the tablet and vaulted to her feet. When she glared at him he flung up his arms in supplication and said, "Hey, you asked for honesty."

"Fine, thank you very much." She wheeled toward the tree-lined river. "I'm going to bathe. Surely I can do that right."

"Keep an eye peeled for trouble," he called after her.

"Damn," Cale muttered under his breath. He'd already been testy with Hanna most of the afternoon. Now he'd trounced on her feelings when she'd set out on her first voyage of self-discovery. Given the mood he'd put her in, he sincerely hoped she wasn't so self-absorbed in disappointment that she didn't remain on constant alert.

Maybe he'd better follow her to make sure she didn't get herself in trouble. He ambled after her, keeping his distance. He knew Hanna desperately wanted to become self-reliant, but she was a helpless tenderfoot and she needed a keeper and protector. He just didn't have to let her know he was standing watch, but he would be close at hand to intervene if she encountered trouble.

While the full moon beamed down on Hanna's pale blond head, Cale dogged her steps. He made a mental note to teach her to ease through the underbrush rather than thrash about noisily. Part of the present problem, he suspected, was that she was half-mad at him for hurting her feelings and was venting her frustration by slapping at the bushes.

His thoughts trailed off as he watched Hanna halt on the sandy shore to peel off her buckskin shirt. Moonlight reflected off the glistening river and her porcelain skin. Cale sank down in the underbrush before he fell down. Sweet mercy! Maybe this wasn't such a good idea. He'd already been tormented to the extreme by erotic fantasies. Watching her undress wasn't helping.

Although all he could see was that glorious tangle of silver-blond hair that tumbled down her bare back, his body clenched and hardened painfully. Breathing became a tedious chore. When she turned sideways to toss her shirt over a nearby bush, Cale's riveting gaze settled on the full mounds of her breasts.

Aw, damn. He'd never be able to glance at her again without this tormenting vision dancing in his head. He was pretty sure the glorious sight of Hanna had been branded on his eyeballs. He should back away. Now. This very second. Should but couldn't. He'd practically grown roots and became immovable. He just hunkered there, feasting his appreciative gaze on her satiny skin and tantalizing curves, wishing he could caress what his hungry eyes beheld.

And then she dropped her breeches and stood on the shore like some sea siren paying homage to the moon above—arms outstretched, head tilted upward, as if reveling in unhindered freedom.

Cale's runaway heart thudded against his ribs so hard that he swore it would crack bone. He tried to gulp air and found none forthcoming. So much for his good deed of keeping vigil for Hanna's protection! No good deed, it seemed, went unpunished. He was suffering the worst torments of the damned—seeing and having not—while Hanna ambled naked into the river. Ripples fanned away from her like waves of mercury.

He swore he was about to have a seizure when she sank into the water, then surged upward, regaining her footing. Water droplets, like star-studded diamonds, glistened on her skin. She was facing him, a smile of pure, unadulterated pleasure on her face. He wanted to be the one who evoked that look from her. He wanted to take her on a voyage of sensual self-discovery and teach her things that had nothing whatsoever to do with survival in the wilds and everything to do with wild ecstasy.

Cale practically melted into a puddle of molten desire when he heard Hanna's carefree laughter wafting on the breeze. She giggled; she splashed; she sent up a geyser of water that caught in the moonlight, giving the scene before him a mystical quality. Exactly like a fantasy. Only he was on the outside looking in, wanting to share this moment of obvious pleasure with her.

When Hanna lay back in the water, her breasts peeking at him above the shimmering surface, Cale was attacked by a fit of pure lust. His body tingled with need so intense he was shaking with it. He had to get out of here—pronto. He had to scan the area to ensure her safety, then he *definitely* had to get the hell out of here—now!

Either that or strip off his clothes and join her in the river. No, damn it! He'd made a promise and he'd vowed not to break it. Hanna trusted him, depended on him. As much as he wanted her—and there were no words to adequately describe how much he wanted her—he had to keep his distance.

Although it took every ounce of willpower he possessed, Cale rose silently to his feet, swayed on wobbly knees and reached out to brace his hand against a spindly tree. While Hanna swirled around, submerged, then burst to the surface, he inched backward until he could no longer see her. Not that it helped. He could still visualize her, and the sound of her laughter pulsated through him.

When she burst into song Cale chuckled quietly. He was sorry to say that singing wasn't her strong suit, either. Even with his limited knowledge of music he knew Hanna was slightly off-key.

Cale waited an eternity for her to splash ashore, until it dawned on him that she sounded farther away than she should have been. He frowned, wondering what was going on down there, but was reluctant to venture closer for fear of being assailed by another tormenting lust attack.

He could hear Hanna talking to herself, and it registered in his muddled mind that she'd become disoriented and couldn't see well enough in the dark to locate her clothes. It was an easy mistake for a tenderfoot to make in the descending night, along a river lined with overhanging tree limbs. Hanna couldn't rely on the position of the moon to lead her back to her point of entry in the river. The moon was barely visible through the trees and it had shifted in the night sky.

This region of the mountain range was impossibly dense, with very few trails leading through it. Cale had come upon lost travelers often enough to know it posed a problem. The prospect of tramping down to retrieve Hanna's discarded clothing and overtaking her before she became hopelessly lost tormented him. Considering the aroused condition he was in, it would be better if Hanna found her way back to camp without depending on him.

"Cale!" The canopy of trees muffled her voice, but his body was in such a state of alert that she might as well have been shouting at him.

"I'm coming," he called, and scowled.

He thrashed through the bushes, signaling his arrival. Surely that would give her time to conceal herself in the underbrush. He reached out to snatch her clothes on his way down the beach.

"Where are you, Magnolia?"

"Over here!"

He glanced to the right, to see her head rising from a spindly bush.

"I got turned around," she mumbled in exasperation.

"Next time try tying a string to your wrist and securing it to a tree," he suggested, more sharply than he intended. "Damnation, Mags, I've lost count of how many times I've had to save your fanny today."

"I'm sorry to be so much trouble. I seem to be one huge disappointment and inconvenience after another, even to myself."

Cale stomped closer, then hurled her clothes at the bush that served as her dressing screen. "I told you to pay attention, didn't I?" he scolded her. "Didn't I tell you this trek wasn't a Sunday stroll in the park?"

"Yes," she said, properly humbled. "I said I was sorry."

Cale turned his back when she reached for her clothes. "Being sorry won't keep you alive. You let yourself get distracted, and wham. Trouble is staring you in the face before you can blink. Mark your trail so you don't get lost again."

He sensed her presence as she ambled up behind him. She sank down to pull on the clunky boots he'd purchased for her, and he shot her an agitated frown. "And stop thrashing, Magnolia. You're supposed to snake through the bushes, not slap them out of your way. It makes too much racket."

"Anything else?" she said smartly. "I can't wait to begin your lessons on behaving like a gentleman so I can criticize every move you make, Oh Great Wizard of the Wilderness. We'll see how you function when you're out of your element."

"At least I'll likely be alive to take instruction," he countered as he led the way back to camp. "You, Magnolia Blossom, might not be around to give it, because you'll have perished in one disaster or another—"

When Cale's voice dried up and he stopped, dead still, on the edge of camp, Hanna slammed into his back. She peered around him to determine what had happened. If she hadn't been alarmed to see two shadowy figures lurking by the trees, with Winchester rifles trained on Cale, she would have smirked at him.

*Semper paratus,* was he? By all rights he should be eating crow right now. Always ready, my eye! she mused.

"Well, well, got the drop on the legendary bounty hunter, did we?" called a taunting voice from the darkness.

"What's-a-matter, Big Chief? Get distracted?" said a second teasing voice. "Now there's a first. Glad I was on hand to see it."

Hanna sensed the change that came over Cale. He'd gone from alert and braced for trouble to casually relaxed in the time it took to hiccup. Still, she wondered how he felt about the nickname that referred to his Indian heritage. Apparently he knew the intruders, for he grabbed her hand and tugged her toward the campfire.

Two tall lean men, armed to the teeth, stepped closer to the fire. Their faces, which boasted several days' growth of whiskers, split in amused grins.

"Frank Laramie came riding into camp yesterday to tell

us that you'd gotten hitched. I nearly fell over when I heard the news." The man gestured toward his companion. "Same went for Julius." His teasing gaze swung to Hanna. "So you must be the bride. Deputy Marshal Pierce Hayden at your service, ma'am. This here's Julius Tanner."

Cale felt the nip of possessiveness when Pierce and Julius gave Hanna a thorough once-over and smiled in masculine appreciation. "This is Hanna. *My wife*," he stated.

Pierce arched an amused brow at the emphatic tone of Cale's voice. "Easy there, Big Chief. We just spotted your camp and decided to check it out. None of our business what you two were doing at the river," he said, then grinned impishly before turning his attention back to Hanna. "The marshals have gotten in the habit of calling Elliot the last man standing. Wonder if that still applies."

When Julius snickered, Cale flashed his colleagues a warning frown—not that it did any good. They seemed delighted to have caught him off guard, and wanted to rub it in his face. It was damn embarrassing, and he held Hanna personally accountable for his lapse in observing caution.

"Perhaps you would like some coffee and roast turkey," Hanna offered as she ambled to the wagon to retrieve the food and utensils.

Cale muttered under his breath at his lack of hospitality. For certain, he had a lot to learn about proper etiquette before he could pass himself off as a gentleman shopkeeper in Texas.

"Thanks, don't mind if we do. My stomach has been growling for hours." Julius sank down cross-legged by the fire and smiled gratefully when Hanna handed him a tin cup. "We've been tracking the Markham gang," he reported as he leaned out to retrieve the coffeepot that dangled above the fire. "Robbed a bank in Tulsey Town. Stole a herd of horses from a Chickasaw farmer and headed south. I'd watch my back if I were you, Elliot. These boys are nasty pieces of business.''

Cale nodded grimly. Just what he needed while he had the Great Distraction underfoot.

"Came across a couple of grave sites a ways back," Pierce commented before he sipped the steaming coffee. "Must not have been your doing. Ain't your style. You carry 'em back, draped over their horses."

"That was Hanna's doing," Cale explained, tossing her a sour glance. "She insisted on it. We didn't see any horses or supplies anywhere in sight, just empty holsters and ammunition belts. They looked like bad seed to me."

"Probably clashed with the Markhams," Julius muttered. "We have bench warrants for two other murderers and rustlers. Dark hair? One of 'em in his mid-thirties? The other one a dozen years older? Skinny as a rail?"

Cale nodded affirmatively. The description fit the victims perfectly. He sent Hanna a telling glance.

"Yup," Pierce interjected. "Definitely bad seed. That makes a total of six deaths attributed to the Markhams. There's two brothers and a couple of young, trigger-happy renegades-in-training, from what we've heard from the few witnesses who were left alive."

"We'd be obliged if we could bunk down in your camp for the night," Julius said as he finished off his coffee. "It's a long ride back to the base camp and our chuckwagon."

Cale knew most of the marshals worked in pairs or groups, and ventured off to scout the area where crimes had been reported. He'd never cared for that practice himself, but tonight he was grateful to have these two deputies underfoot.

After seeing Hanna disrobe and bathe, he definitely needed chaperons to ensure he didn't give in to temptation.

"Of course you're more than welcome to share our camp," Hanna said generously.

"Thank you, ma'am," Pierce murmured as his gaze slid over her for the forty-eleventh time.

"Always glad to be of help, sir." Hanna strode off to grab her bedroll and toss another snack to Skeet—who hadn't put up a fuss about the intruders because he'd known who they were.

Julius leaned closer, grinning wryly. "That woman is pure heaven to look at," he murmured. "You're one lucky son of a bitch, Elliot. But it was kinda sudden, wasn't it?"

Cale knew the deputies were fishing for information, but he wasn't offering details. "Yeah, kinda." 'Nuff said.

Pierce grinned wickedly. "Sorry to cramp your style, this being your honeymoon and all. You planning on making your wife your partner and taking her with you on all your forays?"

Now there was a prospect that gave him the willies. Hanna would probably shoot him by accident and then be set upon by a bunch of vicious bastards like the Markham gang. "Nope. Not hardly," he replied. "We'll be in Texas for a few weeks before I resume my duties for Parker."

"Glad to hear that you're going to tuck her away where she'll be safe. Sure would hate to see a fine-looking woman like that fall prey to the vermin that infest these parts. You take good care of that pretty lady, Elliot," Julius insisted.

"Plan to." Cale gestured toward the west side of camp. "Pick your spot. My wife and I will bed down east of the campfire. We'll be leaving at first light."

Pierce nodded his bushy brown head. "We might meet up with you again if you're headed toward Bennigan's Trading Post to restock your supplies."

Cale shrugged noncommittally. He preferred to avoid the post if possible. There was a woman named Millie at Bennigan's that he'd just as soon Hanna not encounter.

"We were told the Markhams have a hideout down near that pile of rock called Stonewall Peak, so we'll head-quarter at the trading post for a few days,'' Julius explained. ''Well, congratulations, Chief.'' He winked and grinned broadly. ''You've done mighty well for yourself with that new wife.''

While the deputies rolled out their pallets, Cale shoveled dirt on the fire. He stretched out beside Hanna, because that's where his associates expected him to sleep. Cale would have preferred to bed down a safe distance from her, considering the turmoil his male body had undergone during that bathing incident.

Cale lay there for what seemed like hours, aching to roll sideways and cuddle Hanna close, longing to caress every inch of her luscious body. But he was pretty sure he wouldn't have been able to stop after a few kisses and caresses. He wanted to feel her silky flesh beneath his hands, his body. He wanted to bury himself deep inside her and ease this maddening craving that was burning him alive.

Not that she'd offered to accommodate him, he mused as he counted a skyful of stars. He scowled when the stars reminded him of water droplets dancing on her flawless skin.

Cale inwardly groaned and his body clenched when Hanna snuggled up against him the same way she'd done the previous night. Cale lay there with his eyes squeezed shut, his body rigid all over, praying to all known deities that this wouldn't be the longest night of his life.

Turned out it was.

# Chapter Eight

Hanna awoke to find herself cuddled up next to Cale, her bent leg draped over his thigh, her arm flung across his chest as if it belonged there. She quickly recoiled into her own space. She decided their close association and her hopeless admiration for his expertise—not to mention this growing attraction she was helpless to control—was becoming progressively worse.

She stole a peek at Cale and noticed he was studying her from beneath that thick hedge of sooty lashes. She wondered if he'd become aware of her subconscious need to be near him. She wondered if he noticed her staring at him and fantasizing about him bending her over backward and kissing her again, so she'd have an excuse to reacquaint herself with those tantalizing sensations she'd experienced at their wedding.

Knowing Cale was an honorable man—despite society's misconception of him—she doubted he'd make any romantic advances. No, she mused as she tossed him a sleepy smile. If there was going to be any more kissing, she predicted she'd have to be the one to instigate it.

However, Cale had told her—repeatedly—to pay attention to what was going on around her. She couldn't do that if she kept dwelling on kissing him again, and speculating about what went on between married couples—behind closed doors. Even if reports indicated that passion wasn't all that pleasurable for a woman, Hanna was becoming insatiably curious. She knew for a fact that when Cale kissed her the most incredible feelings and sensations bombarded her. She had an idea that these riveting tingles and sudden hot flashes that assailed her were the direct result of her physical attraction to him.

These feelings were getting steadily worse and more intense. Take last night, for instance. While they were at the river she'd wondered what he'd do if she stepped from the bushes in the altogether and let him touch her, kiss her. It would have been outrageously brazen, but she'd been tempted to test his reaction.

The mere prospect sent a flood of heat across her cheeks and made her body burn from the inside out. She glanced over to note that Cale had cocked a thick brow and was staring curiously at her. Honest and straightforward as he usually was, she was surprised he didn't ask her why her face suddenly turned the color of raspberries.

Flustered, Hanna rolled away, then scurried off to tend to her needs. She was relieved to see Skeet trailing behind her to ensure she didn't get lost or run into trouble again.

When she returned to camp, Cale had the fire going and the coffeepot simmering. The deputies were in the process of rolling up their pallets and gathering their belongings. Both men smiled in greeting as Hanna and Skeet approached.

While Cale and the other deputies discussed the criminals they were trying to track down, Hanna wadded up the sketch she'd drawn the previous night and tossed it into the fire. One potential talent down, but several more to go, she told herself encouragingly.

Perhaps charcoal wasn't her medium. Maybe she'd be better with oil paint and canvas. She wasn't going to give up on art just yet. After all, she was just a novice. Even the da Vincis and Michelangelos of the world had to start somewhere, she rationalized.

After she'd said a polite farewell to Julius and Pierce, Cale surprised her by suggesting that she mount his pinto gelding. The prospect delighted her because her father had frowned on women riding sidesaddle—or otherwise. According to Walter Malloy, proper ladies rode in style—in carriages. They did not clamber atop a horse, with their skirts and petticoats billowing around them. After all, Clarissa had never sat a horse, and Hanna wasn't allowed to, either.

Mile after mile, Hanna rode the well-behaved mount, following the wagon. Cale hadn't been the least bit talkative, and she suspected that, being a loner for years, he'd grown tired of her chatter, her observations and her incessant questions. She'd give Cale his own space—since he seemed to want it. In the meantime she'd talk herself down from the dangerous emotional cliff she found herself teetering on—the cliff that left her longing for more from this *in*convenient marriage of convenience.

The fact was that she liked her husband—to startling extremes. That was a problem she hadn't anticipated. She was attracted to Cale—excessively attracted to him. Maybe it was time to begin her campaign to transform him into a gentleman—the exact kind of man she was immune to.

Hanna was mentally analyzing how to quell this unwanted attachment to Cale when she heard gunfire break out in the valley to the west. Before she realized it Cale had bounded from the wagon and was beside her horse, jerking her swiftly from the saddle. He shoved the shotgun into the sheath that was strapped over the pinto's shoulder, then handed Hanna the pistol he carried on his left hip.

"Take the wagon to the group of trees near the creek. There," he said, gesturing east. "Stay put until I come back for you."

"But—"

"No argument. Just do it," he growled as he vaulted into the saddle, then threaded his way downhill, blazing his own trail through the trees. "Skeet!"

The dog bounded off the wagon seat, cast one last glance at Hanna, then raced after Cale. Hanna scampered to the wagon to take up the reins.

The volley of bullets and faint puffs of smoke rising from the valley floor made the team of horses sidestep skittishly. Hanna cooed softly at them as she flapped the reins, urging them forward. It was the first time Cale had entrusted this task to her and she had no intention of letting the team run away with her. Cale had enough trouble awaiting him in the valley without adding her incompetence to the mix.

Hanna kept telling herself that when it came to handling danger he was incredibly capable, and he had a formidable reputation to prove it. But that didn't stop her from worrying about him while she listened to the crack of rifles and unidentified shouts in the distance.

She was definitely worried about Cale's safety and welfare. And it wasn't because she required a live body to hold her father at bay. It was because she cared about Cale more than she even wanted to admit. So he had better not get himself shot, because the thought of him suffering pain made her stomach tangle in a nervous knot and her heart start pounding like a hammer.

Cale swore under his breath as he appraised the situation before him. Choctaw Tom—a crusty old Indian farmer who eked out a living by raising sheep and a few head of cattle—was pinned down near his one-room log cabin, holding off the renegades who poured firepower down on him. Worse, Cale recognized Julius's and Pierce's mounts tethered at the hitching post by the cabin.

Near as Cale could tell, the deputies had likely stopped to question Choctaw Tom about sightings of the outlaw gang. No doubt the Markhams had been lying in wait. Julius Tanner was sprawled in the grass, unmoving. Pierce Hayden had tucked himself behind the water trough, which now boasted several leaks. He was exchanging a volley of bullets with the outlaws, who had the advantage of dense trees for their protection.

"Skeet." Cale gestured toward the renegade who was firing rapidly from the cover of blackjack trees to the west. The dog trotted off to even the odds for Cale.

Shotgun in hand, Cale dismounted, then made his way quietly toward the renegade to his left. The bandit was on his knees, firing at Choctaw Tom, then quickly reloading his rifle. With the silence of a shadow Cale stalked the unsuspecting bushwhacker. Cale was upon the man before he knew what hit him. Using the butt of the shotgun like a club, Cale laid the hombre out cold, then pulled the lacings from his own buckskin shirt to bind the unconscious man's wrists and ankles.

Cale fired off several shots over Choctaw Tom's head so the unconscious outlaw's cohorts wouldn't realize one of their men was down. Swiftly, Cale crept through the underbrush toward the second bushwhacker. In the distance he heard a vicious snarl and a pained yelp. Good, Skeet was disarming one of the men who was keeping Pierce pinned down behind the trough.

Moving quickly, Cale rushed the second bandit. The scraggly haired man went down like a felled tree when the butt of the shotgun connected with the back of his skull. Using the bandit's leather belt, Cale bound his wrists, then jerked off the man's breeches to make improvised restraints for his ankles.

Cale cursed himself soundly when he found himself making a mental note to tell Hanna that improvising was essential for survival. He had his hands full at the moment without letting thoughts of her intrude into his mind.

He confiscated the second outlaw's rifle and shot it off

a couple of times for good measure, then he sneaked stealthily toward the third outlaw. By now, Cale predicted, the man had realized he was in trouble and he'd be scrambling toward his horse. Cale approached the tethered animal, pulled out his dagger and slashed the cinch. If the renegade tried to bound onto his mount to make a quick getaway he'd find himself upended the moment he tossed his leg over the saddle.

When Cale heard a thrashing in the bushes, he hunkered down and waited for the bandit to come to him. Sure 'nuff, the outlaw barreled through the trees and made a beeline for his horse. He stuffed his booted foot in the stirrup, then squawked in surprise when he and the saddle somersaulted to the ground.

When the outlaw rolled like an overturned beetle, Cale raised the butt of the shotgun to put the man down—and keep him there temporarily. Groaning, the renegade slumped in the grass. Using the man's belt and breeches, Cale repeated the procedure of binding up his captive.

Three down and one to go, Cale mused as he headed toward the sound of yelps and snarls in the distance. As usual, Skeet had been thorough. The long-haired desperado was a mass of bites and had passed out moments before Cale arrived on the scene. He hurriedly restrained the last outlaw, then called out to Pierce that the situation was in hand.

"Damn, Chief, am I glad to see you," Pierce said with a gusty sigh of relief. He rose from behind the water trough and strode over to examine Julius, who had taken a bullet in the thigh. "You okay, partner?"

"Been better," Julius muttered, grimacing. "Hurts like hell, if you must know. Sure could use a drink."

"Minute." Choctaw Tom scuttled into his cabin and returned a few moments later with a jug of homemade whiskey.

Julius took a swallow, then tipped up the jug to guzzle

several more. He wiped his mouth on the sleeve of his shirt, then squinted up at Cale. "Sure could use some of that Indian magic of yours right about now, Chief. Where's that miracle poultice that everybody raves about?"

"In the wagon with Hanna," Cale replied. "Pierce, if you'll wrap a tourniquet around Julius's leg, I'll fetch Hanna and be back as soon as I can."

Cale bounded onto the nearest horse and thundered off, zigzagging through the trees at a breakneck clip. To his surprise, when he arrived at the grove of trees Hanna rushed toward him, a look of concern etching her pretty features.

"Thank God you're all right! I was worried sick," she said as she flung herself against his chest the moment he dismounted.

Her enthusiastic greeting touched and amused him. He'd never received such a warm reception from anyone. He was flattered and uncomfortable at once. Plus he didn't know how to deal with the myriad of feelings she evoked in him.

"Why were you worried about me?" he asked. "Because your father could retrieve you if you were recently widowed? Or because you need me to lead you through this wilderness?"

The half-teasing questions earned Cale a disgruntled frown. "Cale Elliot, for an exceptionally bright and competent man, sometimes you can be incredibly dense," she snapped, swatting at his shoulder. "I care about you. Haven't you figured that out yet?"

Cale swallowed a grin as Hanna clambered onto the wagon seat, crossed her arms over her chest and hitched her aristocratic nose in the air.

He tied the horse to the back of the wagon, then hopped onto the seat to grab the reins. "I care about you, too, Magnolia Blossom," he admitted quietly.

The smile she gave him nearly turned him to mush. Cale

scowled when a warm, fuzzy feeling fizzed through him. He'd better watch it or she'd turn him into a tenderhearted softy. Then where would he be? Riding around, tracking down desperadoes and fretting about how *they* might feel about being apprehended? No, he couldn't be at the mercy of his emotions or the next thing he knew he'd be dead. And sure enough, Hanna would be a widow, once again susceptible to her domineering father's control.

Cale didn't know Walt Malloy from Adam, but he disliked the man, sight unseen, for stifling this woman who had such an intense craving to soak up every facet of life like a sponge.

No, by damned, Cale would do whatever necessary to ensure Hanna realized her dreams of freedom and independence!

Hanna climbed down from the wagon the instant Cale applied the brake. She was at Julius's side in a flash to inspect his injury. During the short jaunt to Choctaw Tom's cabin, Cale had given her the boiled-down version of the firefight, and she was amazed that he had managed to thwart the ambush singlehandedly. Then she realized she shouldn't have been surprised, because Cale's abilities were legendary.

She felt an odd sense of pride when Pierce knelt beside her and murmured, "We might've teased your husband unmercifully for letting us get the drop on him yesterday, but when it comes to getting the job done, Cale Elliot can cut it. Sometimes when I see him in action, I turn green with envy."

"That makes two of us," Hanna whispered back.

"Go on inside, ma'am," Julius insisted sluggishly. "You don't need to see a grown man cry when your husband removes this confounded bullet. Besides, these breeches have to come off and I'm not planning to do that in mixed company."

"Come," Choctaw Tom insisted as he grabbed her by the elbow. "You can help most by fetching a bucket of water from the spring while I tear strips of cloth for a bandage."

Hanna scooped up the bucket and followed the aged Indian's directions to the spring. This time she marked her path to ensure she didn't embarrass herself by getting lost. She was on her way back to the shack when she heard Julius's howl of pain and a string of loud curses that practically turned the air blue.

When Hanna stepped into the sun-dappled clearing she saw Cale hunkered over Julius, performing primitive surgery. Was there anything this man didn't know how to do? she wondered as she approached. His wide-ranging skills never ceased to astound and inspire her. This was definitely the man she wanted by her side when the going got tough. Out here in the wild, that seemed to be an everyday occurrence.

Hanna realized she'd contracted a bad case of hero worship these past few days. That, heaped on top of this hopeless physical attraction, left her wondering how she was supposed to resist the charms of her lawfully wedded husband. The more time she spent with Cale the more tempted she was to test these newfound tingles of desire that he aroused in her.

Her wandering thoughts scattered like a covey of quail when Julius bellowed in anguish and cursed Cale with every panted breath. She strode up beside Cale, noting he'd covered Julius's private parts with a patchwork quilt so she wouldn't be embarrassed and uncomfortable.

Another thoughtful gesture on his part, she mused as she sank down on her haunches beside him.

"You okay with this?" Cale asked. When she nodded determinedly, he gestured toward the bucket. "Rinse off the wound so I can see what I'm doing."

Hanna dipped up the water, telling herself not to flinch or grimace or faint at the sight of more blood.

When she swayed slightly, Cale cast her a somber glance. "Are you sure you're okay, Magnolia?"

She swallowed and nodded again. She could do this. She *would* do this, she promised herself fiercely.

"Well, *I'm* not okay, if anybody around here cares," Julius muttered grouchily. "That hurts like hell blazing! You about done poking around down there, Chief?"

"Got it," Cale said a moment later. "Mags, hand me that tin of poultice." He glanced over his shoulder at the other deputy. "Pierce, take Choctaw Tom and Skeet with you to bring in the renegades I left tied up in the trees. We'll finish up here and bandage the wound."

Hanna noticed everyone wheeled like soldiers on parade to obey Cale's request. It was that simple. When Cale said do something, they did it without question. She, however, had a problem with obeying his commands without question. She smiled, wondering if that fact was lost on Cale.

Apparently not, because he flashed her a pointed glance and said, "See how that's done? Try it sometime, Magnolia."

There was a hint of a smile on his lips when he said it, and Hanna grinned playfully in response. "Being your wife, I'm excluded," she declared saucily.

"Really? I could've sworn the judge said something about honoring and obeying. Must've misunderstood."

"Must've," she replied, eyes twinkling. "He was talking about *you*."

"You two lovebirds can cut the chitchat," Julius said irritably. "Just patch me up. We've got prisoners to haul off, and I can't do it while I'm bleeding all over the place—ouch! What's in that poultice? It burns like fire!"

Hanna snatched up the strips of fabric Choctaw Tom had retrieved for bandages, then wrapped them around the deputy's leg. To her dismay she wondered how it would feel to have her hands on *Cale's* bare leg, touching his naked body all over.

"Something wrong, Magnolia?" Cale asked as he studied her intently. "Your face is flushed."

Hanna forced a smile. "I'm fine." But when her gaze strayed to Cale's gaping shirt, which was missing its lacings, her eyes lingered on the broad expanse of his exposed chest. Her gaze shot back to his face and she had the sinking feeling that he knew what she was thinking and was amused by her inability to keep her eyes off him.

They stared at one another for a long moment before Julius broke the spell. "You two go make sheep eyes at each other someplace else. And hurry up with those bandages!"

Hanna snapped to attention to complete her task, but she couldn't get her mind off the way those dark, penetrating eyes had bored into her. She could feel the sparks—the inner heat of suppressed desire radiating through her body. Yes, she definitely had feelings for Cale.

She wondered if she had the nerve to actually do something about it.

Cale rose to his feet and stepped away while Hanna secured the bandage. Damnation! His gnawing hunger for her was getting progressively worse. The self-control he'd always taken for granted was starting to fail him. He'd stared into those mystifying amethyst eyes, watching them sparkle with sensual speculation, and he'd wanted to kiss her so badly he could almost taste her. He was very much afraid that if she offered him the slightest hint of invitation he'd be ready to take more than she probably planned to offer. Being with her, wanting her the way he did, was frustrating the hell out of him.

He sighed in relief when Pierce emerged from the trees with the four bandits jackknifed over their saddle horses. Two spare mounts—ones that Cale suspected had been stolen from the men that he and Hanna had come upon earlier—trailed behind the deputy. For once Cale appreciated the companionship of other lawmen. Right now he needed a buffer to prevent him from filling his hands with Hanna. Every time he glanced in her direction his fantasies became more erotic, and he couldn't seem to control them.

"If you don't mind the company, Julius and I will ride along with you to Bennigan's Trading Post," Pierce said as he dismounted. He cut a quick glance at his injured partner. "It would be best if Julius rode in your wagon bed. He thinks he's a tough old bird, but if gangrene sets in he'll be one leg short of a pair."

Cale nodded agreeably. The inn and trading post, which had been established on the site of a previous military compound, included a sturdy stockade where marshals regularly jailed their prisoners before transporting them to the base camp, loaded them in the jail wagon and returned to Fort Smith. Considering how vicious and bloodthirsty the Markham gang were, Cale knew the more guards watching over the prisoners the better. He preferred not to expose Hanna to the ruthless desperadoes, but Julius needed assistance and required time to recuperate from his injury.

Once Cale and Pierce had their captives secured to their horses, they loaded Julius gently into the wagon. Choctaw Tom donated another jug of whiskey to the patient to ease his pain. Before the entourage set off, Julius was singing drunkenly and sipping the potent liquor as if it was going out of style.

Another jolt of protectiveness zapped through Cale as he watched the beady-eyed captives leer at Hanna. He'd warned her to keep her distance from the prisoners, but that didn't prevent the men from undressing her with their eyes.

Not for the first time Cale scolded himself for dragging Hanna across dangerous country, facing evils a sophisticated heiress shouldn't have to encounter. But he had to admit that his wife was made of sturdier stuff than he'd predicted. Thus far she'd done what needed to be done, distasteful as it sometimes was. If nothing else, she was building character, gaining confidence in her abilities and meeting all sorts of challenges.

Grimly, Cale reminded himself that she still needed scads of experience if she was to follow her dream of adventure in the West. Unfortunately, the better he got to know her the better he liked her. When she struck off on her own he figured he'd spend his spare time wondering where she was and how she was faring while she chased her rainbows.

Damn, for a loner he was quickly growing accustomed to her presence, her smile, her occasional bursts of temper. To *her*. When she went her own way to find herself, to explore her hidden talents, Cale was very much afraid he'd miss her like crazy.

# Chapter Nine

Hanna sighed in relief when she saw the crude stone-and-timber structure nestled in a fertile valley between two towering mountain peaks. Although the rough ride had left her body humming like a tuning fork, she'd adjusted after several days of traveling over the rugged terrain. She could only imagine how uncomfortable the trip must have been for Julius Tanner. But, considering how much whiskey he'd imbibed before he finally passed out, she presumed he wouldn't remember the pain and discomfort caused by bouncing over the trail.

When the wagon rolled to a halt, Hanna climbed down to absently massage her rump. Pensively, she surveyed the two-story building that served as a trading post, telegraph office, stage station and inn. Corrals encircled a gigantic wooden barn. Mules and horses grazed on the weeds and grass in the corrals, and chickens and turkeys pecked in the yard surrounding the lodge.

"Why don't you go inside while Pierce and I lock up the prisoners?" Cale suggested. "We'll bring Julius in a few minutes, then send a telegram that can be delivered to the base camp, giving notification of the Markhams' capture."

"Cale! You're back!"

Hanna glanced sideways to see an attractive brunette, wearing a scoop-necked calico gown that showcased her full bosom, bound off the porch and fly at Cale. She flung her arms around his neck and practically kissed his lips off. Hanna had the unshakable feeling that the buxom female was more intimately acquainted with Cale than she was.

When Cale cast her an uncomfortable glance and tried to set the woman a respectable distance away from him, Hanna's presumption was confirmed. She was pretty sure this top-heavy brunette was in the habit of providing sexual gratification during Cale's forays into Indian Territory.

Hanna couldn't hear what the woman whispered in Cale's ear, but she suspected it was an invitation he didn't ordinarily refuse. Jealousy took a vicious bite before Hanna had time to remind herself that she hadn't asked or expected intimacy and fidelity from Cale. True, they were legally wed, but she was the one who had insisted on a marriage in name only.

Even more baffling to Hanna was the woman's apparent eagerness to entertain Cale in the most intimate manner imaginable. Could it be that some women didn't find the sexual act distasteful? Did they actually enjoy what Hanna had heard whispered in drawing rooms and at soirees to be painful and unpleasant?

"Millie," Cale said, steering the fawning female toward her, "I'd like to introduce you to my wife. Mag...er, Hanna Elliot. This is Millie Roberts."

"*Your wife?*" Millie hooted in disbelief. Her goggle-eyed gaze swept over Hanna's less than flattering attire, then leaped to Cale. "You must be joking!"

"No," he replied, then glanced uneasily at Hanna. "Millie works at the post as a maid and waitress."

Hanna didn't believe for one minute that Cale had mentioned *all* the duties this woman performed, but she nodded politely to Millie, just the same. "I'm pleased to make your acquaintance, Millie."

Millie, apparently, wasn't all that pleased to make Hanna's acquaintance. She glared mutinously at the hand of friendship Hanna extended to her, flung up her pert nose, then stalked off with her blue calico skirts swishing around her.

Cale shifted awkwardly from one foot to the other. "Um…Millie is a little high-strung. Sorry about that."

Although jealousy and possessiveness gnawed at Hanna, it soothed her feminine pride that Cale hadn't tried to flaunt his *friend* in her face. Her previous suitors had tried that tactic on occasion, hoping to draw a commitment from her, but Hanna had never cared enough to be jealous before. The fact that Cale seemed concerned that he might have made her uncomfortable made her want to hug him— except that he'd already been thoroughly hugged by Millie.

"Tell Elmer Linden, the proprietor, to prepare a room for us…." Cale's voice trailed off as he glanced inquiringly at her. "Unless you prefer a room of your own."

"No," Hanna said hastily. "One room will be fine."

After all, they were married. Renting two rooms would likely raise questions and encourage Millie. Hanna doubted Millie would need much encouragement, especially if Cale had a room of his own.

Cale stared at Hanna with those dark, piercing eyes. "You sure, Magnolia? I can bunk in the barn with the excuse that I'm keeping a sharp eye on the prisoners."

She met his unblinking gaze head-on. "No, the arrangements of one room will be fine. I can always take a long walk this evening while you and Millie—"

His hand shot out like a striking snake to grasp her arm. "I don't want Millie."

Hanna smiled faintly. "It's all right, Cale. I'm not so naive that I don't know what is going on. Plus I've made no demands on you, so I have no right to be offended by

Millie's behavior.'' She couldn't quite meet his gaze as she added, "What you do with your spare time is your own business, and I have no say in the matter."

"We have a bargain and I intend to keep it. Embarrassing you wasn't part of our arrangement. I'll deal with Millie," he told her. "I'd planned to bypass the trading post, but Julius's injury and apprehending criminals made that impossible. I'm sorry if I've made you uncomfortable."

His comment soothed her smarting pride and touched her heart. He hadn't planned to stop here at all? He'd intended to spare her the awkward situation? For that, she could kiss him. And so she did, if for no other reason than to assure Millie—who was spying on them through the window—that she *did* harbor a certain affection for her husband.

Cale's dark brows shot up to his hairline when Hanna planted an impulsive kiss on his lips and pressed familiarly against him. Desire shot through him like an arrow, putting his overly sensitive male body in an immediate state of arousal. Images of Hanna naked beside the river instantly leaped to mind—proof positive that he would never forget how she'd looked, short of being stricken with amnesia. When the erotic image tangled with the remembered pleasure of being thoroughly kissed by her, Cale had to bite back a tormented groan.

If he wasn't mistaken—judging by this impromptu display of affection—his new bride was a mite possessive herself, despite her noble claim that she had no right to be. Well, wasn't that something? Cale was glad to know he wasn't the only one around here who was suffering occasional bouts of possessiveness. Of course, just because Hanna felt the need to stake her claim—for Millie's benefit—didn't mean that she wanted to do more than kiss him or sleep by his side as she'd done during their journey.

Hanna stepped back, looking as dazed as he felt. When

she strode off to locate Elmer, Cale pivoted to see Pierce Hayden staring at him in amusement.

"Interesting situation, Chief," Pierce said, his green eyes twinkling mischievously. "Knowing Millie's feisty temperament, she won't take the news of your recent marriage sitting down. She's had her eye on you since her husband took off a few years back."

Cale scowled. Sure, he and Millie had shared some good times when he passed through the area. And certainly, he could use some relief, because being with Hanna, and doing nothing about it, was making him a little crazy. But he'd rather suffer sexual deprivation than humiliate Hanna. What she thought and how she felt mattered to him, whether it should or not.

"C'mon, lover boy," Pierce said teasingly, "let's get these prisoners in the stockade so we can settle Julius into a room. He needs something in his belly besides that rotgut Choctaw Tom gave him."

Willfully, Cale tossed aside his problems with Hanna and Millie and strode off to ensure the prisoners were secured for the night.

Hanna smiled politely at the burly proprietor, who had hands the size of hams and fingers like link sausages. Although rugged and rawboned, Elmer Linden was quick with a smile—unlike Millie, who hovered by the window, glaring daggers at Hanna.

"You married Cale, didja?" Elmer asked as he grabbed a room key. "When did that happen?"

"About a week ago." Give or take, Hanna silently tacked on. She gave Elmer her best smile. "Encountering outlaws interrupted our honeymoon."

Behind her, Millie gave an unladylike snort. Making her irritation known, she whipped around and stalked toward the kitchen.

Elmer raised a bushy brow at Millie's theatrical departure, then glanced down at Hanna. "Well, congratulations, Mrs. Elliot."

"Thank you, Elmer," she replied with a smile.

"Your room is at the far end of the hall. I'll have a bath readied for you. Mama will be serving supper in about an hour, when the stage rolls in with its passengers."

"I was hoping to send off a telegram," Hanna commented as she glanced toward the small office behind the counter.

Elmer motioned for her to follow him. Within a few minutes Hanna had sent off instructions for Benjamin Caldwell, her mother's lawyer, to forward her trust fund to the bank in Cromwell, Texas.

That accomplished, Hanna strode back outside to check on Julius, who was still dozing in the back of the wagon. She retrieved the luggage, then returned to the inn. By the time supper was served, Hanna planned to look more presentable than she did now. If she found herself in competition with Millie for Cale's attention she would at least don a dress and try to look the part of a dignified and respectable wife.

Her arms laden with Cale's saddlebags and her satchels, Hanna climbed the steps. She encountered the disgruntled Millie Roberts at the head of the stairs and reflexively braced a hand on the banister—in case Millie had it in mind to send her tumbling down to land in a broken heap.

"You won't last a month in this rough-and-tumble territory. Despite the shabby clothes, you have the look and sound of a tenderfoot. And you can drop that pretentious Southern drawl," Millie muttered as she looked her up and down with obvious disapproval. "Plus, you aren't woman enough to satisfy Cale. I am, so don't think I won't sleep with him this time, *and* the next time he rides through here without you trailing behind him like a puppy."

Hanna wished she hadn't been raised a lady, so she could smack Millie right between the eyes. Was she going to let this bloodsucking leech sink her teeth into Cale? Not a chance, she decided.

"The Southern drawl is for real," Hanna insisted. "And Cale will be entirely too busy with *me* to spare time for *you*." Head held high, she veered around the fuming brunette.

"We'll just see about that, won't we?" the woman said with a challenging smirk.

Millie, it seemed, was determined to humiliate her every chance she got, and Hanna vowed not to let that happen. It dawned on her halfway down the hall that, although she'd dealt with jealous rivals before, she'd been too disinterested in her suitors to put up a fight. Fighting for Cale, however, was another matter entirely. He was her tutor, her guide, her confidant and her husband. Even if she really didn't have a rightful claim on his affection and his fidelity, she couldn't tolerate the thought of Cale and Millie naked, in each other's arms.

Hanna muttered under her breath when the distasteful image of her husband and his former lover rolling around on a bed, kissing each other as if there was no tomorrow, bombarded her. Angrily, she shoved open the door to the cramped quarters that contained no more than a narrow bed, small tub and crude nightstand. She was again reminded of all the luxuries that she'd sacrificed when she set off on her exodus to the West. As honeymoon suites went, this one provided basic necessities—and nothing else.

Well, she was going to make the best of her shabby accommodations. Furthermore, she was going to dress to assure Millie that, although Hanna might not be woman enough to satisfy a man like Cale Elliot, she could look and act the part of a lady when she felt like it.

To that end, she peeled off her buckskins and sank into the cold water Millie had spitefully drawn for her bath. In an hour, when she'd dressed and ventured downstairs,

Hanna would look decent enough to draw Cale's attention, she promised herself resolutely.

Maybe she was exhibiting symptoms of vanity, but she was not about to let that snippy Millie Roberts upstage her in Cale's eyes. He was her husband, blast it all. And blast this bargain while she was at it! Hadn't she claimed that she wanted to experience every facet of life? Well, maybe it was high time to discover how it felt to actually *be* a woman.

Hanna told herself, right there and then, that when it came to changing her status of innocence, she wanted no man except Cale to do the honors. He could do everything else expertly. Why not that, too?

Better her than Millie in Cale's sinewy arms, Hanna decided as she shivered through her cold bath. That spiteful woman better keep her distance from Hanna's husband or she'd be dreadfully sorry!

Cale inwardly sighed when he ambled into the barn to pen up his pinto gelding, and found Millie waiting to pounce on him. The woman was all over him like a flea on a dog. In the past he'd been all in favor of her amorous attention, but now he considered her an awkward inconvenience. Damn, what a difference a few days with Hanna underfoot made in his life.

"She's not what you need and you know it," Millie whispered as she pressed her ample bosom against his chest and locked her hands behind his neck. "I'm what you need, Cale. Why would you wed a woman who is so wrong for you?" She shimmied provocatively against him. "Not that it matters if that prissy wife of yours is primping upstairs. I still want you."

There had been a time when Millie's sensual advances interested him. Now, when he stared down at her, he saw another face superimposed—a face surrounded by tendrils the color of moonbeams, with eyes like polished amethysts. Appeasing his needs with this woman, while he craved another, didn't seem like a satisfying solution.

Cale unclenched Millie's hands from his neck and stepped away. "Look, Millie, I don't want to hurt you, but I won't see Hanna hurt, either. I made a pledge to her and I plan to honor it."

"You men are such idiotic fools," Millie said scornfully. "You always overlook a woman you *need* to dawdle with a woman you *think* you want. You'll realize soon enough that you've made a disastrous mistake. You'll be knocking on my door before the night is out. You know I can give you what a man like you needs. *She* can't. My door will be unlocked and I'll be waiting for you."

She gave him a hasty peck on the lips and tossed him a provocative glance. She also made a point of brushing her breasts against his arm before she turned around and sauntered outside—swaying her well-rounded hips.

Cale released the frustrated breath he'd been holding. It was bound to be a long, exasperating evening, he predicted as he led his horse to the stall.

When he exited the barn, Pierce was leaning leisurely against the wagon, grinning playfully. "Wish I had your problems, Chief."

"So do I," Cale muttered.

"Good, then I pick Hanna. You can have Millie," Pierce declared.

Grumbling at the tormenting deputy, Cale strode over to hook one arm beneath Julius's back and the other beneath his knees. Forming a makeshift chair, Cale and Pierce hoisted their comrade from the wagon bed and carried him into the trading post.

With considerable effort they maneuvered his limp body up the stairs and settled him in his room. Julius roused long enough to curse his throbbing leg, then demanded more whiskey.

"You need decent food in your belly," Cale insisted. "Opal Linden promised to bring up a tray herself."

"Just lie back and relax, partner," Pierce added. "Let the Big Chief's powerful poultice work its magic."

Mumbling, Julius levered himself into a more comfortable position. "Damn outlaws, anyway. I'd like to whack the one who shot me over the head with a crowbar a couple of times."

While Pierce strode off to gather their saddlebags, Cale inspected the wound. For sure, the deputy needed to stay off his leg for a few days. That would leave Pierce to stand guard over the prisoners. Cale was torn between the need to lend an extra hand with the captives and the urge to whisk Hanna away from potential trouble with Millie, who'd made it crystal clear that she was anxious to provide all the sexual gratification he needed. Not to mention the possibility of a Pinkerton on their tail.

Cale was the first to admit that he had experience galore when it came to tracking and capturing criminals who ran rampant in Indian Territory. But dealing with a spiteful former lover and a new wife—who was giving him fits and didn't even know it—was an unprecedented situation for him.

Should he devote his full attention to Hanna in order to discourage Millie? Cale didn't have a clue how to proceed. Maybe he'd be better off if he bedded down outside the stockade with Skeet and avoided a potential confrontation.

That sounded cowardly to him. Although Cale didn't invite trouble, he'd never walked away from it, either. Needing time alone, he decided to head down to the creek, take a bath, then wolf down supper—and show no preference to one woman or the other. *Then* maybe he'd relieve Pierce from guard duty. Surely Millie wouldn't come in search of him if there were four outlaws lurking behind the walls of the stockade and they could overhear every word she said.

That was the best plan Cale could conjure up, so he decided to go with it. He'd pull guard duty later, and Hanna would have the room to herself. Millie could leave her door unlocked the whole livelong night, but Cale wasn't going to accept the invitation.

He'd developed a forbidden fascination for one particular blonde—the one he'd seen swimming naked in the moonlight, luring him to her like a siren. If he couldn't have what he'd begun to crave obsessively then he'd damn well do without.

No matter what, he wasn't going to hurt or mortify Hanna, he promised himself as he strode toward the creek. A deal was a deal. He had enough willpower to curb his lusts, no matter how often Millie threw herself at him.

As he peeled off his clothes and walked into the water, Hanna's bewitching image rose above him. That was all it took to assure Cale that settling for a substitute for the woman he wanted was a waste of time.

Hanna became seriously concerned when Cale didn't arrive at the door to escort her downstairs to supper. Was he with Millie? Were they doing things together that were beyond her own scope of experience? She'd given Cale the go-ahead and was now kicking herself repeatedly for that.

Muttering at her reflection in the mirror, Hanna double-checked her appearance. She couldn't recall being hounded by such a driving need to look her best. Tonight it seemed imperative that she make Cale sit up and take notice, to make him proud to call her his wife.

This is nonsense, Hanna scolded herself. Wasn't she the self-same person who claimed that appearance wasn't everything?

Hanna found herself pacing apprehensively from wall to wall, while Skeet watched her with ears pricked and his broad head resting on his oversize paws. She forced herself to stop pacing because it was one of her father's habits and she wanted to be nothing like him.

Well, she told herself resolutely, there was naught else to do but tramp downstairs to determine if Millie was perched on Cale's lap, hand-feeding supper to him. Marshaling her pride, Hanna headed for the door, dressed in the fanciest gown she'd found in Fort Smith. Her objective was to draw Cale's undivided attention—provided he was in the dining room, not tumbling around in the hay with Millie.

"Let's go, Skeet," she said as she opened the door.

The dog's claws clicked against the floorboards as he trotted toward the door. As was his habit, Skeet went through the door first to scout for trouble. Hanna inhaled a bracing breath, tugged at the plunging neckline—this time to show more cleavage rather than conceal it—then strode off. She was not going to throw a tantrum if, in fact, Millie was draped all over Cale like English ivy. Hanna would rely on her pride, poise and dignity to carry her through the evening.

Before she rounded the corner to the steps she heard various conversations in progress below her. The stage passengers had arrived and the dining room was filled to capacity. She noticed a young woman and her small daughter, plus three respectably dressed gentlemen, who'd obviously arrived by stage. There were other patrons as well, but most of the other men were dressed like farmers and laborers, not travelers.

Hanna had progressed halfway down the steps when all conversation died into silence. She glanced across the crowded room, noting all eyes—most of them male—had turned toward her. But her only concern was for that one pair of dark, penetrating eyes that belonged to Cale. He was sitting in the corner—alone. His gaze was gliding over the exposed swells of her breasts like an invisible caress. His attention shifted to the indentation of her waist and then to the flare of the frilly blue satin skirt that covered her hips. When his attention darted to the other men in the dining hall, so did hers.

"Oh, my God!" Hanna whispered when cold, hard reality slapped her in the face. Her father's hurtful words came back to her in a deflating whoosh. He'd told her time and again that the only thing a woman needed to be good at—that which Hanna excelled at—was capturing male attention. He'd also told her that she should use her arresting looks to snare men who could benefit her already lofty position in life.

A sense of panic nearly overwhelmed her, prompting her to clasp the gold locket nestled between her breasts. What if Walter Malloy was actually right? What if all she had going for her was her God-given looks and her ability to draw men's gazes?

The demoralizing thought caused a sheen of tears to mist her eyes. What if she was no more than an attractive trophy, possessing no talents or assets aside from superficial beauty? Frustration held Hanna immobilized on the staircase, hovering there like a colorful but useless butterfly.

Dear Lord, was her life about nothing more than attracting male attention? Was this all there was? All she could ever hope to be? And worse, wasn't she using her looks to lure in Cale before Millie Roberts wrapped him in her seductive arms?

That humiliating epiphany caused Hanna to sway on shaky legs. She flung out a hand to grasp the banister before her knees buckled and she cartwheeled down the steps—which would please Millie to the extreme, no doubt.

Cale frowned, bemused, while he watched an indecipherable display of emotions chase each other across Hanna's enchanting face. Something had suddenly disturbed her during her descent to the dining hall. Although she looked like a heaven-sent vision of beauty and had captured everyone's attention, the sparkle had gone out of her eyes. Though sunlight shimmered through the window, giving her a mystical appearance and spotlighting her feminine assets—and she had more than her fair share, to be sure—he noticed her smile falter and her shoulders slump dejectedly.

Cale couldn't be sure, but he had the odd feeling that she was about to break down and cry. Why? He couldn't imagine. The nip of possessiveness that had been tormenting him for several moments vanished instantly. All that concerned him was discovering what had upset Hanna.

The fact that he was highly sensitive to the changes in her mood didn't escape him. That wasn't good, but there you had it. He could read Hanna like a thermometer, and he wasn't sure how and when that had happened. All he knew was that he had the fierce urge to retrieve her from the steps and shield her from those appreciative male gazes. He wanted to bustle her to the corner table so he could have her all to himself and find out what made her look so sad and disheartened.

Maybe she felt awkward because she knew she looked hopelessly out of place in this roomful of backwoodsmen and travelers waiting to feast on Opal Linden's fabulous meals. He knew how it felt to be out of his element and he wanted to spare Hanna those uncomfortable feelings if he could.

Suddenly Cale was on his feet, zigzagging between the tables to reach her. Hanna was staring at him with what looked to be an expression of disappointment and guilt. Guilt? Couldn't be. What did she have to be guilty about? Except that she was so damned gorgeous that all the men were practically drooling as they savored her heart-stopping beauty.

"C'mon, Mags," he murmured as he reached for her hand. "Let's eat. I'm starved."

The comment seemed to snap her from her doldrums, though he didn't know why. It was as if he'd come up with the right thing to say and hadn't even been trying.

"You didn't notice?" she asked. Those luminous violet eyes searched his, as if his reply was crucial to her.

"Didn't notice what?" What the hell was she talking about?

"You didn't notice that I dressed specifically to draw your attention?"

She seemed so intent and serious that he couldn't help but smile in flattered amusement. "You did? Why's that, Magnolia Blossom?"

She looked flustered and perturbed at once. "Well, because…" Her voice fizzled out and she stared earnestly at him as he drew her down the steps, then escorted her across the room. "Cale, tell me true," she murmured. "Do you see more in me than the way I look in a dress?" She gestured absently toward the roomful of men, who continued to stare at her with rapt attention and approving smiles. "More than *they* see? Can you see *me* at all? Am I only the wrapping on an empty package?"

Cale had the unmistakable feeling this was vitally important to her and she wasn't going to drop the subject until he'd given her a straight answer. "Are you asking if I see the little spitfire who squared off against me in that clearing not so long ago and refused to stir another step until she'd done the honorable and decent thing? Do I see the intelligent woman who's tried to absorb the survival skills I've taught her so she can become self-reliant?"

When she nodded, then glanced discreetly toward their table, silently indicating that the gentlemanly action was to pull out the chair for her, Cale complied. He also made a mental note to do so henceforth.

"Yup, I do, Magnolia Blossom," he said as he pulled out her chair. "You've got a will of iron and a heart of gold, but these gawking fools can't see the real you hidden beneath all that satin, all those ruffles. They look no further than your shapely figure and enchanting face. A damn shame, that.''

The smile she bestowed on him as she sank gracefully into the chair made him feel squishy inside. He'd pleased her. Well, how 'bout that.

''So you don't think I'm just window dressing, as my father claims?'' she asked earnestly.

''Hell no! The man must be an idiot to say such a thing,'' Cale said, scowling as he dropped into his chair.

That seemed to please her immensely, too. Cale was pretty sure he'd never understand the complicated workings of the female mind if his comment put such a radiant glow in her eyes and a satisfied smile on her lips—lips so soft and sensuous that he wanted to lean over and devour her. Forget the meal. He'd rather feast on Hanna's luscious mouth any ol' day.

Well, damn it, now he was being as shallow as her other male admirers, he realized.

''Elbows off the table,'' she murmured confidentially.

Cale self-consciously jerked down his arms and clamped his hands on his thighs. Apparently, she'd decided to use this opportunity to polish his gentlemanly manners. Fine. He knew that he was sadly lacking in that department. Hoping for self-improvement, he studied Hanna's sophisticated mannerisms and emulated them so he could pass himself off as a gentleman shopkeeper when they arrived in Texas.

''Did you get Julius settled in?'' she asked as she rearranged the silverware in the proper placement beside her napkin.

''Yeah…er, yes,'' he replied. ''Julius is going to have a helluva—''

''Dreadful,'' she corrected quietly. ''No swearing in the presence of ladies.''

"—dreadful hangover when he wakes up," Cale continued. "But he'll be fine in a few days."

Hanna glanced sideways to note Skeet had nudged open the door with his nose and trotted outside, then she frowned curiously. "Where's Pierce? Isn't he dining with us?"

"No, he's guarding the prisoners. I'll take his place after we eat. Opal is saving him a plate."

Hanna's gaze lifted and clung to his. "You'll be on guard duty all night?" She glanced sideways when Millie sauntered between the tables, filling coffee cups and flirting with the guests. Then Hanna stared directly at him. "Perhaps I should stand guard with you, in case any trouble arises."

Cale's lips quirked in a smile. He had the feeling Hanna wasn't referring to a possible jailbreak, but rather a probable visit from Millie. "You don't need to worry about me, Mags. I told you already. A deal's a deal."

"I trust you," she said without hesitation, then inclined her head ever so slightly toward the buxom brunette who was staring possessively at Cale. "It's *her* I don't trust. I know I said I didn't—"

He pressed his index finger to her lips, wishing it were his lips that were shushing her. "Forget it, Mags. I've got the situation under control."

Or so he thought. Millie sauntered over to fill his coffee cup, and made certain she brushed her full bosom against his shoulder. Hanna's gaze narrowed disapprovingly, though it didn't faze Millie, who smiled devilishly—then spilled coffee in Hanna's lap, accidentally on purpose.

"Oh, good gracious, how clumsy of me," Millie said, her tone not even remotely apologetic.

Hanna swallowed a shriek as hot coffee saturated her gown and petticoats. Two pair of feminine gazes locked and clashed. Millie looked so triumphant that Cale wanted to swat her fanny. Hanna looked to be about an inch away from murder, and he considered flinging himself between them before his new wife went for his former lover's jugular.

Damn! Cale had dealt with dozens of difficult situations before, but he'd never found himself between two women who looked as if they wanted to take each other apart with their nails and teeth!

# Chapter Ten

"I hope I didn't ruin your fancy dress," Millie jeered sarcastically.

To Hanna's credit, she recovered her composure. "This old thing? Don't give it another thought, *Mildred*," she said, purposely drawling out Millie's given name. She scored a direct hit with that. Millie glowered at her. "I was planning to tear this dress into rags soon, anyway. That is, unless you would like to have it as a hand-me-down."

Millie's face flamed with fury. "You prissy little b—"

Cale reacted instantly, aware of the mutinous glint in Millie's eyes. He applied pressure to her arm before she dumped the entire pot of coffee on Hanna's head.

"Hey, Millie, get over here. My cup's empty," one of the men called out.

"I'm not through with you, little princess," Millie said through gritted teeth as she jerked her arm from Cale's grasp.

"A pity, because I'm finished with you," Hanna said dismissively. "You may go now."

Cale bit back a grin while Millie silently fumed and stomped away. He had to admit that Hanna could portray the regal princess when the mood suited her.

"Impressive," he murmured.

"Thank you." Hanna blotted at the coffee stains.

"I take it that while men rely on six-shooters to settle differences, women rely on razor-sharp tongues."

Hanna nodded, ashamed that she'd stooped to Millie's level. However, she wasn't about to let that vicious-minded chit get the better of her while Cale was a witness. She did have her pride, after all.

Thankfully, the incident was forgotten when Opal Linden showed up, balancing two heaping plates of food in her hands. Hanna hadn't realized she was famished until she tasted the succulent meal.

When Hanna finished eating, Cale insisted on walking her back to the room before relieving Pierce. Hanna was reluctant to see him go, knowing Millie was lurking about, anxious to use her wiles on Cale and humiliate Hanna in the process.

Hanna was determined to ensure her new husband returned to their room when he completed his shift at the stockade. Although she knew nothing about seduction, she wanted it known that whatever Cale needed physically, she intended to provide, despite the previous terms of their bargain. The indisputable truth was that wanting Cale had become an intense need that Hanna was ready to explore.

"Make sure you keep the door l—"

Hanna didn't allow Cale to finish his warning. She reached up to pull his head to hers, then kissed him squarely on the mouth. Then, just in case the implication was lost on him, she said, "I'll be waiting for you tonight. There's something I want you to teach me. As my husband that instruction falls to you."

He stood there gaping at her as if she had tree limbs sprouting from her ears. He opened and shut his mouth a couple of times, but no words came out. This man who'd lectured her about expecting the unexpected had been struck speechless. Hanna rather liked knowing she'd stunned him to the bone.

Finally he found his tongue and frowned. "Look, Magnolia, if you're worried that it has to be *you,* just so it won't be *her* tonight, you can forget it," he said, his voice sounding strangled and not at all like that deep resonant baritone she'd come to associate with him. "We have a deal."

"The terms have changed since we last spoke of it."

Hanna noted that she had his complete and undivided attention. She wanted this man who was her husband to know that she was curious and willing to explore the passion he instilled in her. Millie's intrusion and threats had stiffened Hanna's resolve, and she wasn't going to back down, even if she was a mite apprehensive about what awaited her.

He stared at her in that unique, probing way of his for so long that she fidgeted from one foot to the other. "You're sure about this, Mags?" he asked eventually.

Hanna nodded, then unlocked the door. "I'll be waiting for you," she said. Then she closed the door in his face.

Cale braced both arms on the wall, sucked in a great gulp of air and tried to recover from shock. Hanna wanted him to teach her the intricacies of passion? And he was hesitant, why?

He glanced down to note that Skeet had returned and had come to heel. Cale hesitantly reached out to open the door for the dog. Hanna was standing in the middle of the room, looking like the devil's own temptation, despite the fading bruise on her cheek and the stain on her gown.

"I'll be back in three hours. Lock the door," he said before he turned and walked away.

He shouldn't even consider the prospect of bedding his new wife, he told himself on the way downstairs. He saw Millie sometimes when he was killing time between forays. But Hanna was...well, she *wasn't* about killing time and simply appeasing basic needs. Worse, he could bring an unwanted child into the world. Being one himself, he'd been very careful not to let that happen. Besides, Hanna was chasing long-held dreams of independence and unlimited freedom. She didn't want a child to slow her down. And certainly not a half-breed's child.

Cale dragged in a steadying breath and ambled toward the stockade. He had three hours to decide whether to accept his wife's unexpected invitation.

Halfway there Cale realized the decision had been made. He wanted Hanna—badly. Maybe even more than he wanted to see justice served on Otis Pryor. The intensity of that need shocked him, unsettled him.

Hopelessly distracted, Cale mumbled a response to Pierce's attempt at conversation during the changing of the guard. Cale sank down on the ground and spent the next three hours trying to figure out how a gentleman was supposed to handle the deflowering of his innocent bride to ensure *she* enjoyed the encounter. Now how was that possible when her husband was so eager to have her that he wasn't sure he possessed the tenderness and patience required?

Those next three hours were the longest, most uncertain and troubling of his life.

Dressed in a nightgown, Hanna lay in bed. She was a mass of jittery nerves. She reminded herself—about a hundred times—that she'd asked for this monumental night with Cale. True, she did want to consummate their marriage so her father couldn't have it annulled, but that wasn't the deciding factor. She also realized that her decision had nothing to do with wanting Cale in her bed just because she couldn't tolerate the prospect of Cale ending up in *Millie's* bed. No, Millie might have triggered the decision, but this was about what Hanna felt for Cale, what she wanted to share with him.

Resolved though she was, she knew she'd be a nervous wreck by the time Cale arrived. She'd been out of her element for over a week and now she really was treading deep water. She hadn't a clue how to pleasure a man, especially since she'd spent the past few years devising ways to *avoid* unwanted male attention.

The quiet rap echoed in the silence and Hanna tensed. Since Skeet hadn't growled a warning she was pretty sure it was a friendly caller, but Cale had instructed her never to open the door without demanding to know who was on the other side. And even then, to be prepared for the unexpected.

"Who's there?" she called out.

"Pierce Hayden," a male voice replied quietly.

Hanna bolted upright. "Is Julius all right? Is Cale? Is there some sort of trouble with the prisoners?"

"No, ma'am. Julius is resting. Just thought I'd let you know I'm on my way down to relieve your husband."

"Thank you," Hanna murmured.

Knowing Cale would arrive in a few minutes gave Hanna a worse case of the jitters than she already had. She reminded herself the intimate ordeal wouldn't take long— not according to her married friends. Then she'd be a wife and woman in the true sense of the words. All she had to do was endure the intimate invasion and pretend to enjoy the tryst—somewhat, at least.

The faint creak of the window sliding upward brought Hanna's head around. With her breath trapped in her throat, she watched the muscular hulk in buckskins glide agilely through the opening. Obviously Cale had remembered he didn't have a key and had chosen an alternate route.

He said not one word as he rose to full stature. Silhouetted by moonlight, he peeled off his shirt. Hanna sighed at the sheer masculine beauty poised before her. She'd seen this impressive muscular chest once before and she itched to get her hands on it. Whether or not she had an aptitude for art, she did know she had a fine appreciation for masterpieces. Cale Elliot was definitely a masterpiece of rugged and powerful beauty. She studied him admiringly and felt her apprehension drifting away in the cool breeze that flowed through the window.

Mesmerized, she watched Cale move silently toward her like a mystical warrior. She waited expectantly for him to shed his breeches and quickly conclude his husbandly duties. But he didn't move, just hovered beside the bed, looking down at her from the shadows. She wanted to rant at him to get on with it because the suspense was about to kill her.

Finally he spoke. "I'll ask you again. Are you sure about this, Magnolia? Now's the time to tell me if you've changed your mind."

His voice sounded rough, almost gruff—which didn't do a thing for the apprehension that returned full force. "I'm sure," she bleated.

When he reached down to doff his breeches, Hanna stared, wide-eyed, then gulped when she saw her first frontal view of a fully aroused man in the buff. Her startled gaze shot up to his shadowed face. His white teeth flashed and she heard the soft rumble of laughter.

"Absolute last chance," he said as he sank down on the edge of the bed.

He leaned over to kiss her tenderly, gently, as if he had all the time in the world. Even though Hanna knew it would be an impossible fit, which suggested serious discomfort on her part, she told herself this incredibly sweet kiss was worth the forthcoming pain. His sensuous lips skimmed unhurriedly over hers. Then he kissed her cheeks, her eyelids and her forehead in a way that touched her heart. The tension evaporated and she didn't object when he slowly drew her nightgown over her head and tossed it on the foot of the bed.

Hanna trembled when his hand slid around her waist, then glided up her rib cage to cup her breast. His thumb brushed her nipple and fire coiled in the pit of her belly. Her breath sighed out of her and she went boneless as he gently urged her to her back. Like her own shadow, he followed her down, his lips hovering over the aching peaks of her breasts.

"Oh…my," Hanna wheezed, marveling at the unexpected sensations shimmering through her.

She felt his smile against her skin and wondered what he found amusing. There was nothing funny about the tingling feelings he evoked in her as his hands and lips grazed her flesh, igniting scalding fires that burst through her bloodstream.

For a man who'd proved himself to be swiftly expedient—and was known for getting right to the point in conversation—Cale was certainly taking his sweet time in doing the deed. Oh certainly, she'd sensed and seen that there was more to this legendary bounty hunter than what the world perceived. And to be sure, he was hard-nosed and tough. But there was a gentler side to Cale Elliot that stirred her heart and touched her soul.

She suspected that he'd sensed her anxiety and uncertainty, and the dear, sweet man was trying to make this encounter as painless for her as possible. He'd accomplished that about three kisses and caresses ago, for she felt like molded clay in his skillful hands. He, she decided, was the artist in the family. He was sketching tenderness all over her—from breasts to hips and everywhere in between.

When his hand drifted down her belly, headed for more intimate places, her breath stalled in her chest. She tensed, uncertain and yet curious about what he planned to do next.

"Breathe, Hanna," he murmured as his lips skimmed over her bare hip. "I won't hurt you. I'd never hurt you."

She tried to breathe, really she did. But her ultrasensitive skin trembled like an earthquake as his hands, tongue and lips ventured lower, setting off all sorts of indescribable sensations. Desire, like a lightning bolt, shot into the very core of her being and left her body rumbling like thunder. Her breath came out in shallow spurts and muffled moans when his fingertips grazed her inner thigh and his thumb glided over the slick heat between her legs.

"Cale? What…ah…" Her voice gave out when he dragged his mouth over her and his tongue flicked out to tease her. Nothing had prepared her for the throbbing heat of erotic pleasure that shattered her inhibitions in less than a heartbeat. Shamelessly, she arched toward his mouth, then felt the gentle glide of his fingertips against her softest flesh. With each stroke of his fingers, need coiled tighter and tighter. When he intimately caressed her with the tip of his tongue, wild spasms of pleasure riveted her.

She clutched at his shoulders in frantic desperation and gasped for breath. What was he doing to her? She was coming unwound from inside out, and intense pleasure was expanding and spreading through her so rapidly that she feared she'd burst with it!

"No!" Hanna gasped when his hands and lips glided over her and a dozen more red-hot tremors of need bombarded her. "Do something!"

"I thought I was," he said, chuckling as she writhed beneath his hands and lips, begging for an end to the sweet torture. But Cale had waited three long hours for this one chance to touch Hanna intimately, to taste the liquid fire of desire he'd called from her. As much as he wanted her—and that went without saying—feeling her shimmering like hot rain on his lips and fingertips was beyond incredible. He'd never taken so much time with a woman, never dared such intimacy, never felt such an inexplicable need to give so much of himself to what had previously been brief, empty encounters to appease basic lust.

# Get FREE BOOKS and a FREE GIFT when you play the...

## LAS VEGAS GAME

*Just scratch off the gold box with a coin. Then check below to see the gifts you get!*

**YES!** I have scratched off the gold Box. Please send me my **2 FREE BOOKS** and **gift for which I qualify.** I understand that I am under no obligation to purchase any books as explained on the back of this card.

**349 HDL DRQQ**                    **246 HDL DRQ6**

FIRST NAME                    LAST NAME

ADDRESS

APT.#          CITY

STATE/PROV.          ZIP/POSTAL CODE

(H-H-12/02)

| 7 | 7 | 7 | Worth TWO FREE BOOKS plus a BONUS Mystery Gift! |
| | | | Worth TWO FREE BOOKS! |
| | | | TRY AGAIN! |

Visit us online at
**www.eHarlequin.com**

# BUSINESS REPLY MAIL

FIRST-CLASS MAIL    PERMIT NO. 717-003    BUFFALO, NY

POSTAGE WILL BE PAID BY ADDRESSEE

**HARLEQUIN READER SERVICE**
**3010 WALDEN AVE**
**PO BOX 1867**
**BUFFALO NY 14240-9952**

NO POSTAGE
NECESSARY
IF MAILED
IN THE
UNITED STATES

Lust he understood and accepted for what it was. This was different, because Hanna was different. She was his virgin wife. A woman who'd placed trust in him to protect her. A woman who knew nothing about passion and desire—except what *he* taught her.

"I want you," she panted, still clawing impatiently at him.

The woman was a wildcat and she was leaving her mark on his forearms. "You'll have me," he insisted, grinning as he'd never grinned before. "Patience, Mags, in due time—"

His voice shattered when her hand folded around his rigid flesh and she drew him toward her. He'd intended to get to that phase of lovemaking during the second lesson. Third, maybe. He hadn't wanted to rush through this unprecedented moment with Hanna, but when she took him in hand—literally—the need to possess her completely overwhelmed his barely restrained body.

"Please…please," she chanted breathlessly.

Cale fought the good fight for self-control and discovered the meaning of defeat. He surged over her, braced himself on his knees and drove into her like a wild man. When she groaned, he cursed himself soundly and repeatedly.

"You just couldn't wait, could you, Mags?" he said hoarsely. "I didn't want to hurt you and now I have."

"Hurt me?" She gyrated her hips, pushing him deeper into her velvety warmth. "I ached worse when you weren't inside me. Now I feel better."

The woman never failed to surprise and delight him, and he was a man who'd never liked to be surprised or ill prepared. But he was totally unprepared when Hanna arched toward him, then grabbed him by the hair on his head and brought his lips down hard upon hers. She kissed him as if she wanted him—as desperately as he wanted and needed her.

Cale's self-control deserted him completely. He held nothing back, giving all of himself to her pleasure—and his. He plunged and withdrew, caught up in the ageless rhythm that mindless passion demanded—and so did his uninhibited wife. Cale felt the coil of desire unraveling, felt the fervent sensations blazing through him like a river of molten fire.

Indescribable sensations swamped him as he drove into her, and she matched him thrust for desperate thrust. He felt her contracting around him, heard her muffled shriek against his chest and then he tumbled pell-mell into the kaleidoscopic abyss.

Shudder after helpless shudder wracked his body. He cursed himself mightily for not withdrawing from her immediately. As if he could have untangled himself from Hanna, he mused, dazed. She clung to him, her legs locked around his hips, her nails spiking the corded muscles of his back.

A smart man knew the difference between possessing and being possessed. A wise man knew when he was both. At that precise moment, while Cale was wrapped tightly in Hanna's embrace and he held her captive in his, Cale became a wise man indeed. He acknowledged that nothing had ever hit him with such overwhelming intensity. Nothing compared to, or had prepared him for, this unparalleled experience of passion that demanded the willing participation of mind, body and spirit. Making love with Hanna blew the stars around and turned his world upside down. It was as simple and as complicated as that.

In the aftermath of the total and complete destruction of his self-control and his ability to process thought, Cale collapsed and struggled to draw breath. He felt as if a train that went by the name of Hanna had hit him head-on.

Of course, he couldn't tell her that she'd just found her true calling in life. She could pitch the paint, knitting needles and writing supplies out the window because she excelled at lovemaking. It pleased him immensely to know that he alone had discovered her hidden talents.

"Well, I can tell you right now that I've either been purposely lied to or my friends have wed the wrong men. For the life of me I don't know why I spent three hours worrying myself into a nervous frenzy," Hanna declared.

She smiled impishly when Cale raised his tousled head, cocked a thick brow, stared dazedly at her and said, "Huh?"

"I was told that wifely duties were to be tolerated periodically. It was an outright lie. That was incredible." And it was. She'd never felt so weightless and free. It was the most incredible contradiction. While Cale pinned her down, his powerful body joined intimately with hers, she'd felt as if she could fly unrestrained. She had never experienced such exhilarating, mind-boggling pleasure in her life. But Cale obviously had...

The sudden thought burst her euphoric bubble and sent her crashing back to reality. "Get off me," she demanded.

"What?" he mumbled, obviously dumbfounded by her abrupt mood swing. "You weren't complaining a few minutes ago. I swear, you and your kind are the most confounding and unpredictable creatures on the planet."

"I said get off." She gave him a forceful shove to punctuate her demand. His comment upset her. As if she wasn't tormented enough by the disconcerting thought that was buzzing through her mind.

"What's wrong?" Cale asked as he withdrew, leaving her cold and empty and feeling even more like the naive fool that she obviously was.

Hanna clutched the sheet around her and rolled off the bed. Her emotions were cresting like storm-tossed waves on the sea. What had been uniquely and incredibly intimate one moment became humiliating in the face of reality. She'd reveled in newfound passion—until it dawned on her that what she'd shared with Cale was exactly the same as Millie Roberts had experienced with him, plenty of times before. That really hurt!

This was lusty, heart-pounding sex, she presumed. It was coupling for the sake of physical release. It had nothing whatsoever to do with love.

Not that she knew the first thing about love, of course, but she knew enough to know she'd just become a man's conquest. Nothing more. The thought crushed her self-esteem in one second flat.

"Hanna, come back to bed," Cale insisted as he grabbed the trailing end of the sheet.

"Not on your life!" she sputtered indignantly, then jerked the sheet from his grasp. "It wouldn't have mattered, would it?"

"Woman, I don't have the slightest idea what in the hell you're talking about," he muttered, exasperated. "One minute you nearly claw me to death and demand more and the next minute you can't get away from me fast enough!"

"Millie or me," she huffed. "For you, it was just the same. Any female would have served you just as well."

Cale went perfectly still. Uh-oh. He never claimed to be an authority on women, but he recognized an offended female when he saw one. He was definitely staring at one now. Her chin was tilted in a look of indignation. No doubt about it, her misconception was the direct result of her inexperience with men. Changing bed partners was the only way to rectify her erroneous conclusions, but Cale definitely wasn't in favor of *that!* He was pretty sure that the prospect of another man making love with Hanna would drive him insane.

"It wasn't the same at all, Mags," he told her truthfully. "You've got to believe me."

"Do I?" She expelled an unladylike snort and tossed her tangled blond hair in a gesture of annoyance. "Don't lie to me, Cale." There was a hitch in her voice that indicated she was close to tears. "I'd rather hear the hurtful truth than to know I can't count on your honesty in all matters.''

Frustrated, Cale levered himself onto the edge of the bed. He wished he could exchange places with Skeet and let him handle this awkward situation. ''So what do you plan to do? Look up Pierce, sleep with him and determine if I've lied to you?''

Her chin went airborne. ''Certainly not.''

''Why not?'' he grilled her, unsure why the answer to the question seemed so important to him.

''Because I…'' Her voice trailed off and she glared at him as if this was all his fault. Which he reckoned she thought it was.

''Even if it was the same—which it was *not*,'' he was quick to assure her, ''you're the one who said we had no hold over each other. You said we're free to do as we pleased, when we pleased, with whom we pleased. Are you changing the rules again…? Well, are you?''

Hanna turned her back on him, so confused and exasperated she wasn't sure she could trust herself to speak rationally. She was afraid her admiration and hero worship for this man who was her temporary husband, tutor and guide was evolving into love—or something very much like it. But that way led to disaster. Love spoke of vulnerability and restrictions.

She'd been confined and susceptible before. She'd loved her father and ached for his affection and acceptance in return. She'd loved her mother and brother and she'd lost them. Falling in love with Cale spelled heartache and disappointment. Besides, she'd waited years for the freedom to embrace the world and feed her hungry soul. If she let herself fall in love with Cale she'd be tormented by the knowledge that each time he stopped at Bennigan's Trading Post, Millie would take her place in his bed and share what Hanna had shared with him.

But how did you make that *not* matter to your heart?

How could you make your heart *not* love someone when you were already halfway there?

Hanna hadn't realized Cale had quietly dressed and left the room until she heard the window slide back into place. She turned to see his silhouette hovering outside momentarily before he vanished like a phantom in the night.

She plopped down on the bed and asked herself how she was supposed to face the man she'd made love with after she'd behaved like a jealous ninny and all but shouted him out of their room. And sweet mercy, how could such an incredible night in Cale's sinewy arms end on such a sour note?

Pierce stumbled to his feet and grabbed his pistol when Cale stalked toward him. "What are you doing back here? I told you I'd take the night watch."

"Go check on Julius," Cale snapped brusquely.

Pierce looked him up and down, then smiled. "Trouble in marital paradise, Chief?"

"Don't wanna talk about it," Cale mumbled.

"Millie, I suppose," Pierce speculated as he holstered his Colt. "Told ya she'd brew up trouble. It's never good to let a possessive and jealous woman near a man's wife."

"Didn't know you were such an expert on marriage," Cale grunted. "Been married a lot, have you?"

"Once," Pierce admitted. "She ran off with someone else while I was out here, making the world safe for humanity. Guess I was hunting the wrong criminal. If you ask me, wife-stealing ought to be an offense punishable by hanging, same as horse-thieving."

When Pierce ambled off, Cale plopped down in the grass and leaned against the rough-hewn wall of the stockade. How was it possible for heaven to turn into hell in one night? He and Hanna had been getting along well enough until she took it into her head that having sex with Millie and the intimacy he shared with Hanna were the same damn thing. What was he supposed to do to convince her otherwise? Send Pierce to have a turn with Hanna so she'd know the difference?

The thought soured Cale's already deteriorating mood. Anyone who thought a marriage of convenience wasn't *in*convenient and complicated needed to have his head examined. Not only did Cale have a disillusioned wife on his hands, but there was a strong possibility that her offended pride and anger would put her on the morning stage and send her rumbling off with the other passengers. Then where would he be in his quest to infiltrate Otis Pryor's stronghold and bring that bastard to justice?

*You shouldn't have walked out,* the voice of reason chastised him. *You should have stayed to reassure Hanna. Since when do you tiptoe around trouble?*

Since he'd encountered a woman who stirred up the kind of emotion he wasn't accustomed to dealing with.

Cale sighed audibly. Who would've thought that, by him *exceeding* Hanna's low expectations of passion, she'd leap to the worst of all possible conclusions?

He decided he'd been better off when he simply served as Hanna's trail guide and survival instructor. True, frustrated desire had gnawed at him until hell wouldn't have it, but he'd coped with it. The pleasure and satisfaction he'd found in Hanna's embrace had been phenomenal, and he longed to have the chance to spend every night in her arms, fulfilling his wildest fantasies. Now that he knew what he'd been missing it would drive him absolutely crazy.

Cale, who'd never found himself in the middle of a situation like this before, was having difficulty figuring out how to make things right between him and Hanna. How could he make her understand that what they'd shared was rare and unique?

Knowing that she was hurting and that she'd turned away from him tormented him no end. This was the first time he'd ever felt compelled to comfort and reassure anyone, and he'd failed miserably at it. He hadn't known what to say or do to put things back the way they were.

The inexpressible feelings that roiled inside him made his chest tighten uncomfortably. He felt twitchy, restless and dissatisfied. Indeed, Cale preferred to face down outlaws than to know Hanna was upset and disillusioned.

He'd spent three hours worrying for all the wrong reasons, he realized. He'd worried that he might hurt her. Worried that he wouldn't be gentle and attentive enough to pleasure his innocent bride.

And what really troubled him was that he'd somehow lost her trust. That was the one thing *he* had come to depend on.

Hanna had become his haven, his contact with normalcy in life—something outside the grueling rigors of his duties for Parker. Now he'd spoiled it.

Cale squeezed his eyes shut and swore foully. If he'd had a chance for a decent night's sleep it had been shot to hell. He had too much on his mind.

But maybe things wouldn't seem so grim and confusing in the morning, he tried to console himself.

Or maybe, he thought pessimistically, things would be worse.

## Chapter Eleven

Dressed in her ill-fitting buckskins, her hair tucked beneath her cap, Hanna descended the steps to see the stage passengers filing from the dining room to board the coach. She ignored Millie's lethal glare, then followed the travelers outside. Her footsteps faltered when she saw Cale poised beside the wagon, staring directly at her. His face was devoid of emotion as he glanced toward the waiting stage, then at her. His muscled body was rigid, as if braced for trouble.

Hanna veered away from the passengers, noticing as she did so that Cale breathed a small sigh of relief. He was trying not to give the slightest indication, but she presumed that he'd expected her to board the stage and leave him high and dry.

"What changed your mind?" he murmured when Hanna tossed her satchel in the back of their wagon.

She pivoted to face his searching gaze. "In the middle of the night, when I should have been sleeping instead of turning and tossing fitfully, I reminded myself that we made a bargain. I like to think I'm honorable enough to keep my word."

He looked her squarely in the eye and replied, "It wasn't the same, Mags. Not at all."

Which, of course, had nothing whatsoever to do with her comment. He had no idea how much she wanted to believe him, and there was no question that he seemed intent on convincing her that he'd meant what he said.

Abruptly, Cale swooped down and scooped her up in his brawny arms, then deposited her on the wagon seat. His touch triggered visions of their shared passion, and Hanna shivered helplessly in response.

Despite the number of men who'd courted her and her money, despite the confusion and uncertainty she'd suffered last night, it was *this* man who affected her on a dozen different levels. That was an indisputable, undeniable fact.

Hanna frowned pensively. Admittedly, she had a narrow frame of reference—a peephole, actually—when it came to passion. She wondered if Cale might have told her the truth. Could it be that he harbored a certain affection for her? Could their joining have been special for him, too? Could it be that even with her lack of experience she'd somehow touched something deep inside him? Was it possible that she had misjudged their passionate encounter because of her narrow field of reference? Had she overreacted the previous night?

"Now what's wrong?" he grumbled.

Hanna jerked her attention to Cale, who'd climbed up beside her to grab the reins. The man was so alert and attentive that nothing got past him. "I was just thinking."

"I'm not sure that's a good idea, Mags. It didn't help the situation last night." He gestured for Skeet to hop into the wagon bed. "What are you thinking about?"

Hanna didn't reply until Cale steered the wagon behind the stagecoach, which lurched off at a fast clip. "How many lovers have you had?" she asked flat out.

Cale nearly choked. "Damn, Magnolia Blossom. Why do we have to discuss *that* in order to get past last night?"

Her lips twitched when she noticed a blush creeping

across his bronzed face. She wasn't sure if she'd witnessed anything so endearing in her life. "Because I'm trying to puzzle something out."

"Well, puzzle something else out, if you don't mind," he mumbled, shifting awkwardly on the seat.

"I want an honest answer."

"Don't you usually?"

She watched the stage disappear around the bend before she glanced at Cale. "Less than a dozen?"

He cleared his throat, blushed again and stared straight ahead. "Considerably less," he replied.

The admission pacified her. "Fine, we'll leave it at that."

"Good. Can't tell ya how glad I am to hear it."

"And it *wasn't* like that with the rest of them? Truly?" She had to know because it mattered greatly.

"No, Magnolia, it wasn't," he said, staring straight at her, willing her to believe him.

She studied him for a long, pensive moment, then nodded and smiled. Cale nearly keeled off the seat in sheer relief. Within a matter of minutes they'd gotten past the hurdle that had kept him awake all night. Poof! Just like that and he was back in her good graces. Why? Because she *believed* in him. Because he'd never lied to her. Well, wasn't that something?

The tension drained away and Cale realized the sleepless night had plumb worn him out. He needed a nap to compensate.

"I checked on Julius this morning," she commented. "He seemed to be feeling considerably better, despite his horrendous headache."

Cale had checked on Julius, too, and was relieved to see the wound showed no signs of infection.

"Pierce dropped by to say his farewells," she added. "Nice men, those deputy marshals. I hope I'll have the opportunity to see them again someday."

Cale handed the reins to Hanna. "Keep a two-mile distance from the stage," he instructed.

"Why...?" Suddenly Hanna nodded thoughtfully and answered her own question. "Because if they meet with trouble we'll be close enough to assist, but far enough away to use the element of surprise."

Cale couldn't help himself: he dropped an impulsive kiss to her petal-soft lips. "You catch on quick, Mags. Good for you."

Impish amusement danced in her violet eyes as she watched him squirm between the supplies to make a nest to take a nap. "This journey has been a very enlightening experience all the way around." She glanced at the dog. "Come up here, Skeet. I'll talk your leg off while Cale catches up on his rest."

Wearing what he was sure was a goofy smile, Cale closed his eyes and slumped in exhaustion. He'd made peace with Hanna and all was right in his world again. He'd been physically weary before—lots of times. But the emotional turmoil that had hounded him throughout the night was ten times worse than anything in his past experiences.

Seeing Hanna hurt and upset really hit him where he lived. He *never* wanted that to happen again, because he was beginning to live for her endearing smiles. Without them, the sun didn't seem to shine as brightly. He wondered why that was, but fell asleep before he could puzzle it out.

Cale and Hanna followed the stage for two days without mishap. On the third evening, ominous clouds piled on the horizon at sunset, indicating a threatening storm was about to unleash its fury. Hanna cuddled up beside Cale on the wagon seat to ward off the chill. A cold blast of wind slapped her in the face, and lightning, like bony fingers, clawed at the gloomy clouds. Thunder crashed and the earth shook in response.

"The storm is about three miles away," Cale reported.

Hanna glanced inquisitively at him. "How do you know that?"

"I've lived in the wide-open spaces for years," he reminded her over the howling wind. "Indian cultures make a study of Mother Nature. For every five seconds between the flash of lightning and the roll of thunder, you can calculate a mile's distance between you and the storm."

Hanna watched lightning flare in the darkening sky, then counted to sixteen before she heard the grumble of thunder. She wondered why her studies in physics at finishing school hadn't revealed that useful information. It was definitely something she'd need to know during her travels.

Thus far, Cale had been a font of useful information, and she'd given him a few pointers in gentlemanly behavior during their southwestward trek. She definitely needed to begin her instructions on etiquette in earnest, because Cale had informed her they would reach Cromwell, Texas, by the end of the week.

When Cale suddenly jerked upright, Hanna felt heightened awareness sizzle through him. "What's wrong?"

"Listen," he said as he brought the wagon to a halt.

Hanna heard it then. The alarming sound indicated that trouble followed swiftly on the heels of a crash of thunder. Gunfire! The stagecoach! As if she'd read Cale's mind, she lunged for the reins at the exact moment he thrust them hurriedly at her. He bounded off the seat, clambered over the supplies and hopped onto his saddle horse, which was tied behind the wagon.

"Keep your distance while I find out what's going on ahead of us.... Skeet!"

"But—" Hanna protested when Cale, with his faithful dog at his heels, took off like an arrow.

Cale plunged into the dense underbrush beside the road

and disappeared just as another blinding flash of light gouged the clouds. Rain came down in torrents. Hanna looped the reins around the brake handle, then twisted on the seat to grab the canvas tarp. Hurriedly she covered their supplies and secured the tarp. By the time she retrieved the reins she was thoroughly soaked.

The horses trotted along, heads ducked in the driving rain. Hanna pulled the cap low on her forehead and squinted to see where she was going. Cale had told her to keep her distance from whatever calamity had befallen the stage passengers, but that didn't mean she couldn't top the hill and see for herself what was going on in the valley below.

She gasped in dismay when she did so and spotted the overturned coach beside the road—which was quickly turning into mud. From her vantage point she could see three masked riders circling the coach like vultures, exchanging gunfire with the stage driver and guard, who were crouched beside the wheels. Her first impulse was to race downhill and provide aid and comfort for the passengers trapped in the upended coach. But Cale's constant warnings had finally soaked in like the rain beating down on her.

She knew Cale was down there somewhere, lurking like a shadow, fearless in his intent to apprehend the robbers who'd attacked the stage. Her need to protect and assist Cale spurred her into action before she had time to reconsider. It was pure instinct that put her in motion and kept her there.

With a wild whoop that would've done any self-respecting Indian warrior proud, Hanna snapped the reins and sent the horses stampeding downhill. Despite the rumble of thunder, she gained the three thieves' attention as they converged to confiscate the strongbox that had tumbled into the grass. Hanna didn't cease yelling and squawking, just pulled the wagon to a halt and bounded to her feet to flap her arms in protest.

While Hanna was drawing attention to herself, Cale was cursing the air black-and-blue. Hadn't he taught that woman anything? It was her duty to remain safe while he concentrated on neutralizing the threat to the coach. Although he admired her courage in the face of danger, and her attempt to provide a distraction for him, he did not *need* a distraction. He'd handled three-to-one odds more times than he could count. Apparently she didn't trust him to do his job efficiently. Either that or she was a daredevil at heart and only now had the opportunity to expose that alarming trait.

"Skeet." Cale thrust his wet arm toward the masked bandit who circled north. The dog plunged through the thicket, took off at a dead run and made a flying leap at the rider. The startled horse reared, upending the bandit, who'd trained his pistol on Hanna. When the rider cartwheeled off his horse and hit the ground with a thud and a splash, Skeet attacked his gun hand.

Cale was already on the move to blindside the bandit who'd made the mistake of riding near his hiding place in the underbrush. Cale had the unsuspecting man disarmed and sprawled on his back in nothing flat. Gunfire zinged over his head and he reflexively dropped to the ground and rolled toward the protection of the upturned coach.

"Damn glad to see you, Elliot," the driver murmured as he took the last bandit's measure down the sight of his rifle.

Cale was glad to note that the stage driver was a fair shot. He winged the bandit's right arm, causing the man to teeter sideways. Cale vaulted to his feet the moment the bandit attempted to shift his pistol to his left hand. Before the hombre could fire off a shot, Cale jerked on his injured arm, sent him facedown on the road and left him howling in pain.

Cale cursed mightily when Hanna raced the wagon downhill, the wheels skidding precariously in the mud. He nearly suffered heart seizure before she regained control and prevented the speeding vehicle from overturning.

Leaving the driver and guard in charge of the captives, Cale headed straight for her, intent on biting her head off for refusing to follow his precise orders, and for scaring him witless.

"Thank God you're all right," she said as she bounded from the seat.

Before he could fire off one word of criticism, she gave him a swift kiss on the lips, then raced toward the coach to check on the passengers. Resigned to postponing his lecture on avoiding unnecessary risks that could get her damn fool head blown off, Cale tramped after her.

Two disheveled heads popped from the door as Hanna crouched atop the overturned coach. "Is everyone okay?" she asked.

"As good as can be expected," a thin, mustached passenger replied. "Here, take the child. She's frightened and she sustained a few bumps and bruises."

Hanna cuddled the whimpering three-year-old girl close and nuzzled her pale cheek. "Shh, it's okay, sweetheart. We'll have your mama out of there in a moment. Cale will see to it, don't you worry."

Cale found himself immobilized by the touching scene of Hanna—looking like a drowned rat, with her hair draped over her soggy shoulders like a mop—comforting the shaken child. Her innate kindness and concern for others never failed to impress him. The woman definitely had a heart of twenty-four karat gold.

Reminded of her previous comment about a man's value being measured by his service to others—or something to that effect—Cale hunkered on the stage and began to hoist up the passengers. One by one he pulled them out into the pouring rain and inspected them for injury. He wasn't quite sure what to do with the woman who flung her arms around his neck and thanked him about a dozen times for saving her and her little girl from certain death. While the woman clung to him he shot Hanna an uneasy glance, afraid she'd think he was enjoying being hugged by another female.

She grinned impishly at him. "It seems I've married a man whom other women just can't keep their hands off. I suppose I'll have to get used to it."

When the little girl wailed for her mama, the woman released Cale abruptly and gathered her distraught daughter into her sheltering arms. "I'm eternally indebted to you," she said over her shoulder. "My husband is stationed at Fort Griffin in Texas. We're on our way to rejoin him. If you ever pass by the fort you'll be most welcome in our home. Thank you so much for your help."

While Hanna assisted mother and daughter to the ground, Cale inspected the coach. Fortunately, there appeared to be no serious damage that would impede travel. After Cale restrained the prisoners, he assisted the driver, guard and passengers in uprighting the vehicle. Within fifteen minutes the entourage was under way to the small stage station located five miles south.

After Cale had tied the prisoners in the wagon bed, he climbed aboard and stared at Hanna from beneath jutting brows. "Don't ever do that again," he growled at her.

She cocked her head and met his thunderous scowl. "I was trying to provide a distraction," she pointed out.

"Don't care. You go around scaring ten years off my life every few days and I won't live long enough to reach Texas."

She touched his arm and smiled one of those magical smiles that had the power to boil him down to mush. Damn it, he was annoyed at her, but her touch always soothed the savage beast growling inside him.

"I do appreciate your concern, but it's not my nature to

sit back and watch when you need my help,'' she told him.
''We're in this together and you need to remember that.''

Cale sighed in resignation as he headed for the stage
station. He tried to recall if he'd ever won an argument
against this willful female he'd married. He was sorry to
say that he didn't think he had.

Hanna was well pleased with the outcome of their evening adventure. She'd aided in thwarting a stage holdup
and Cale hadn't bitten her head off—well, not completely.
Her need to be useful had been satisfied once again, and
she reminded herself that she'd done more living in a week
than she'd done in twenty years beneath her father's domineering control.

She'd also had time to give considerable thought to the
embarrassing tantrum she'd thrown at Bennigan's Trading
Post. She was more than a little annoyed at herself for
allowing her feelings to be hurt so easily. It was just that
she was hypersensitive about the intimacy she'd shared
with Cale. But perhaps the moment *had* been special for
him, too. After all, he'd never made love to a wife before.
That would make their night together different than his
nights with Millie and the other women who had shared
his bed.

Hanna told herself not to analyze that monumental night
to death. She should simply accept the erotic pleasure for
what it was. Cale had insisted that it *was* different for him,
and she should leave it at that. Besides, he wasn't the kind
of man who gushed sentimentality and offered permanent
commitments. He couldn't. Not in his dangerous line of
work. She could understand why he lived in the moment
and didn't look too far into the future. His world consisted
of day-to-day survival.

Scooping up her yarn and knitting needles, Hanna
headed downstairs to the stage station's dining hall to join
the passengers. Cale had left an hour earlier to ensure the

root cellar that served as an improvised jail for the bandits was secured. He'd also informed her that he needed to speak to one of his former colleagues who operated a ranch six miles west of the station. While Cale was making arrangements to have the bandits delivered to the deputy marshals at Bennigan's, Hanna decided to try her hand at knitting.

Mary Watkins, whose daughter Hanna had pulled from the overturned coach, had offered knitting instructions while the passengers lounged near the fireplace. Mary, Hanna noted, was exceptionally skilled at knitting. Her needles clacked and moved like extensions of her hands while she knitted a dainty shawl for her daughter, Elaina. Mary never slipped a stitch.

Hanna, however, had to apply profound concentration to learn the basic techniques that came so easily to Mary. The brown afghan Hanna was knitting for Skeet to use as a mat looked like Swiss cheese—with holes all over it. Hanna told herself she'd get better with practice. Skeet certainly wouldn't object to sleeping on the lopsided mat. Besides, it was the thought that counted, wasn't it?

Hanna was finally getting the hang of knitting when Elaina yawned and snuggled up to her mother. After Mary strode off to tuck the child in bed, Hanna worked with the needles until her fingers cramped and her eyes threatened to slam shut.

Cale still hadn't returned, even after the last of the stage passengers retired to their sleeping quarters. Determined to wait up for her husband, Hanna tucked away the needles and yarn and ventured outside for a breath of fresh air.

Fog enshrouded the station and barn. Steady drips plunked off the eaves as Hanna wandered aimlessly around the compound. She glanced sideways when she heard the clip-clop of hooves. Her heart all but melted when Cale, mounted on his pinto gelding, materialized from the fog in the glowing light cast by the lantern that hung outside the barn.

Even dripping wet the man was a magnificent sight to behold. To some, perhaps, he was the vulture of doom who rode for Parker. A dangerous man to be avoided. To Hanna, he was the epitome of what a man should be: strong, capable, fearless and reliable. She'd seen him in action often enough and he'd never failed to impress her. Rough-edged and rugged though he was, he'd been amazingly tender and gentle when he introduced her to passion.

Desire gnawed at Hanna as she clung to the shadows and watched Cale dismount, then lead his horse to the barn. She was astounded by her overwhelming need to be with him again. Suddenly it didn't matter whether their shared passion was the same or different than he'd experienced with other women. All that mattered was that she was compelled to be one with him, to revisit that incredible space out of time when she'd felt alive and free and totally uninhibited in his arms.

It dawned on Hanna as she walked toward the barn that freedom wasn't to be found in a particular place in a specific part of the country. It was a feeling that dwelled inside oneself. Cale Elliot had provided her with that unique feeling and she longed to return the favor. Somehow, she promised herself as she strode through the heavy fog, she was going to learn to pleasure her husband the same way he'd pleasured her. And she wasn't going to let pride and vanity get in her way again.

Hanna veered around the corner of the barn—and found herself hauled against the solid wall of a man's chest. This time the cold steel of a dagger lay against her throat before she had time to react.

"Damn it, Magnolia," an annoyed voice muttered next to her ear. "What are you doing out here? You should be in bed by now."

Cale released her immediately. She pivoted to face him

and glided her hands over his wet shirt. "You're right. I should be in bed," she told him saucily. "But I didn't want to go to bed without you in it."

She raised up on tiptoe to press her lips to his, and found herself hoisted off the ground, her feet dangling in midair. He kissed her hungrily, greedily, and she kissed him back with the same fervent impatience. Need plowed through her as he crushed her against his body and all but devoured her.

The gentleness he'd displayed the first time was nonexistent. But she realized she didn't mind all that much. His impatience indicated that he wanted her to the same mindless degree that she wanted him. If he decided to lay her down in the straw and take her, right where they were, she wouldn't have voiced a single complaint. But her hard-as-nails marshal of a husband suddenly transformed into a gentleman. He scooped her up in his arms and made a beeline for the station.

"Not out here. Not with you, Mags," he said in a raspy voice. "The first thing I'm buying, when we reach Cromwell, is the biggest, softest feather bed to be found. That's what you deserve."

Hanna snickered as he set her on the porch. "My, I have married well, haven't I? I have a husband who places my comfort above all else—"

She barely had time to complete the teasing comment before Cale clutched her hand and nearly dragged her up the steps in his haste for privacy. A blush exploded on her cheeks when the stage owner—a wiry little man with frizzy gray hair—glanced up from where he sat in his rocker, warming himself by the fire. He grinned wryly as his gaze bounced back and forth between her and Cale.

Hanna decided she didn't care if the proprietor knew why they were in an all-fired rush to reach their room. If her legs were longer *she* would have been the one tugging Cale up the steps.

Skeet, who'd followed at their heels, nearly got his hind section smashed when Cale hurriedly shut the bedroom door. The dog yelped and scurried to lie down at the foot of the bed. Hanna tugged impatiently at the lacing of Cale's shirt and he yanked *her* shirt over her head, making no attempt to conceal his pleasure at feasting his hungry eyes on her afterward.

"God, you're beautiful," he murmured huskily. "If that offends you, Mags, I'm sorry. But you are."

"From you, I'll take it as a compliment," she said as she pushed her breeches off her hips and let them drop into a pool at her ankles.

Cale looked his fill at this vision of unrivaled beauty. He wanted his hands on every inch of her satiny skin and he wanted his hands on her *now,* this very minute. He'd spent the past few days practicing honorable restraint, but he'd run clean out of willpower when she'd showed up in the barn and kissed him as if she were dying for a taste of him.

Damn, what this woman did to him should be declared illegal in all thirty-eight states of the nation. She assaulted his senses with her taste, her touch, her scent and the alluring sight of her luscious body. She robbed him of breath, repeatedly. She stole one corner after another of his carefully guarded heart, and she was absolute *murder* on his self-control. Definitely criminal, he decided.

"Teach me to pleasure you the way you pleasured me," she rasped as her nails raked over his bare chest. "Do you like this?"

Her sensuous lips whispered over his male nipples, and heat pulsed through every fiber of his being. Cale braced his back against the wall and dragged in an unsteady breath when her featherlight kisses trailed over his belly.

"Yeah, I like it, a lot," he managed to answer—just barely.

"What about this?"

Her splayed hand glided along the waistband of his breeches. When her fingers skimmed over the buckskin that covered his throbbing length Cale fought to drag air into his lungs. "Hanna…"

"Do you?" she persisted, caressing him boldly.

"Yeah, but—"

"I want my turn with you," she insisted when he tried to grab her adventurous hand. "I want you to know how it feels to be so hopelessly out of control that you don't care if there's a tomorrow or a day after. The same way I didn't care because I couldn't see beyond the pleasure of your touch."

He'd made her feel like that? Her honesty and the thoughts she expressed pleased him immensely. But he didn't have time to dwell on that because she'd released him from his breeches and folded her hand around his aroused flesh. Cale went weak in the knees when she measured him from base to tip with the pad of her thumb. When she knelt before him and her lips grazed his most sensitive flesh, he swallowed a howl of unholy torment. The woman was killing him—and he was savoring every moment of her intimate touch.

Over and over again, she stroked him, tasted him, teased him with teeth and tongue. Again he reminded himself that her hidden talents as a natural-born seductress were unequaled. Desire, hot and intense, pelted him like gunfire. His pulse hammered in his ears and his runaway heart slammed against his ribs—and stuck there.

"Enough, Hanna," he muttered between clenched teeth.

"Not nearly enough," she murmured against his aching flesh. "You're still standing. You're always the last man standing but, in only this, I want to see you fall."

His breath hitched when she took him into her mouth again and suckled him. He was dying here—one erotic moment at a time—and he had to stop her before his self-control abandoned him completely. He was clinging desperately to that thought when she urged him into the straight-back chair that he'd situated beside the door as reinforcement for the flimsy lock. Still holding him in her hand, she reached down to peel off his boots and breeches.

Cale glanced down to see her blond hair shimmering like moonbeams in the lantern light that filtered through the window. When she crouched between his legs and bent her head to tease him with lips and fingertips, hot chills shot up and down his spine. Need billowed like a wildfire inside him.

He wasn't going to last, and the thought of *not* having his hands on Hanna, *not* unleashing the passion he'd called from her that first night, was intolerable to him. If he didn't act now he was going to discover the full meaning of hopeless surrender, and that was something he'd never encountered in his life.

Cale twisted his hands in her hair and tugged her upward. Although she still held him in her hand, his mouth came down on hers in an all-consuming kiss that testified to his frantic need for her.

"I want you more than I want air to breathe," he groaned. "I need to touch you again, Hanna. Now."

He surged off the chair and nearly tripped over the clothes that were strewn about the floor. On wobbly legs he walked her backward to sit her on the edge of the bed. He sank between her knees, guiding them apart with a nudge of his shoulders. And when he touched her intimately, he found her hot and slick beneath his lips and fingertips.

He wasn't going to be satisfied until he pleasured her to the very limits of her sanity. He wanted her to be as achy and needy as he was. He wanted to hear his name on her lips, wanted to hear those desperate cries that assured him he held the same power over her that she held over him.

She could enslave him with her tenderness and her determination to pleasure him. She could bring him to his knees—quite literally—with wanting her. He'd never known such helplessness, such vulnerability, and he'd certainly never thought he'd like it so much. But when she seduced him and reduced him to a quivering mass of desire, he didn't care about anything except becoming one with her.

"Cale…" She gasped, and shivered with pleasure.

He smiled when she used those claws on him again, dragging him upward to capture his lips. They tasted each other's passion in a kiss that spoke of desperation, of an intimate knowledge they'd shared with no others. Groaning with impatience, Cale urged her toward the middle of the bed. He hovered over her, watching the shaft of golden lantern light stream across her passion-drugged face. She reminded him of a fantasy he'd conjured up from the fog. But she was flesh and blood and all alluring woman. She was here with him, wanting him as much as he wanted her, giving herself to him for this space of time, until the terms of their bargain were met. And until he released her to chase her rainbows, she would be his wife, his lover and his closest friend.

He sank into her, marveling at the incredible sense of rightness, savoring the remarkable pleasure of being inside her, surrounded by her shimmering warmth. She moved with him, as if they'd been lovers throughout eternity, as if they instinctively knew how to please and satisfy one another. He drove into her mindlessly, and she chanted his name while she clung to him, then convulsed around him. The echo of her pleasure resounded through his body, sending him spiraling in a wild freefall of passion.

Cale held her to him as uncontrollable shudders buffeted his body. He buried his face in the scented tendrils of her hair, then pressed his lips to her cheek. "It was never like this, Hanna. Believe that," he whispered raggedly.

She brushed her lips against his shoulder and he felt her smile against his flesh. "I believe you."

Her words touched him to the bottom of his soul.

In the past he'd acknowledged the begrudging respect other folks directed at him, because they feared him and his reputation. He'd accepted the isolation of being different and unwelcome in proper society. But he'd never before encountered Hanna's brand of unfaltering faith, and it humbled him. She made him feel wanted, worthy and special.

"You make me need you too much," he murmured hoarsely. "That's a dangerous thing, Hanna."

"You make me want you too much," she whispered back. "It's a dangerous thing, Cale. But I'm finding that I love living dangerously."

He smiled wryly. "You proved that with your daring heroics during the stage holdup. And they call *me* a daredevil?"

Cale rolled away, then gathered her close. He'd never spent an entire night with a woman before. Never wanted to. Was always driven by the need to move on, to maintain his lone-wolf lifestyle. But when Hanna burst into his life with her astounding proposition, she'd tugged at the tender emotion that had callused over in his heart five years ago. She made him want more from life, things he'd never considered within the realm of possibility. Things too dangerous to consider even now.

"Good night, husband," she murmured as she cuddled against him.

"Good night, wife."

Cale was sure he fell asleep with an idiotic smile on his lips. It was becoming a habit that he wasn't sure he wanted to break...until the day when he kept their bargain and let her go her own way.

# Chapter Twelve

At dawn, Hanna said her farewells to Mary Watkins, her young daughter and the other passengers. She and Cale left the stage station and headed south on a trail plagued by mud to reach the Red River ferry to Texas. The trek was slow going and far too rough for Hanna to work on the mat she was knitting for Skeet. Cale hadn't had much to say and Hanna sensed that he was concentrating on his upcoming encounter with Otis Pryor.

Hanna kept the chitchat to a minimum because she knew how important apprehending Pryor was to Cale. Her only comments centered around tidbits of information on gentlemanly behavior. Such as gallantly holding open doors for women, polite greetings and small talk that would convince the townsfolk of Cromwell that Cale Elliot was only what he appeared to be: a shopkeeper and gunsmith who was making a fresh start with his new bride.

"That must be the place," Cale said at last, dragging Hanna from her own pensive thoughts.

She glanced downhill to note the stone ranch house, barns and corrals and the startling number of saddle horses tethered to every available hitching post. Pryor's stronghold, Hanna mused as she scanned the place. Situated in a sprawling valley filled with grazing cattle, the ranch was surrounded by towering sandstone cliffs. She wondered how much of the livestock was stolen property and decided that most of it probably was. According to Cale, Otis Pryor was a leech who preyed on others' prosperity to get ahead in the world. For Cale's sake, Hanna intended to play this charade to the hilt and ensure justice was served, so he could avenge his family's senseless deaths.

Hanna stared east, surveying the small hamlet of Cromwell, which was set near a river lined with trees and heavy underbrush. This was to be her home for the next few weeks, she mused as Cale lifted her from the wagon so they could change into suitable clothing.

When Hanna's gaze strayed to Cale's bare chest, and thoughts of their splendorous nights together tried to intrude, she glanced away. She had to concentrate on using her proper upbringing and social skills to be quickly accepted in this frontier community. She didn't doubt her abilities because her father had groomed her to be the perfect hostess who knew just the right thing to say and how to behave, but she was concerned that she hadn't given Cale enough instruction to ensure he was comfortable with his role.

Her concern eased considerably when Cale donned a crisp linen shirt, black vest and trousers. She smiled in approval when he struck a dignified pose. Cale now looked the part of a gentleman shopkeeper.

"In honor of my half brother, Gray Cloud, I've decided to use Grayson McCloud as an alias," Cale announced as he fastened the buttons on the back of Hanna's lavender gown.

"Very fitting. I approve," she said as she smoothed the wrinkles from her dress.

As the wagon rolled into town, Hanna searched the main street for a vacant shop and was relieved to note there were two available spaces. One appeared to have living quarters upstairs. "That one," she said, pointing it out to Cale.

He nodded agreeably as he veered toward the town marshal's office to ask about renting or buying the space. Hanna took the opportunity to stroll the boardwalk that lined the town square and greet passersby while Cale talked to the marshal. The citizens she met seemed polite but restrained, and she speculated as to the cause of it.

Hanna suspected Otis Pryor was responsible for making the townsfolk cautious. Judging by the number of signs overhead—Pryor's General Store, Pryor's Livery, Pryor's Saloon—the bully and his brigade had taken control of this town. Hanna was left to wonder who had previously owned the shops and what had become of the former proprietors.

She gulped uneasily. Maybe she didn't want to know.

By the time Hanna returned to the wagon, Cale and the town marshal were standing on the boardwalk waiting for her. She pasted on a smile to greet the bewhiskered marshal, but she didn't like the looks of him, especially when she saw him spit tobacco juice on the boardwalk and she had to veer around it. She was certain Cale was correct when he said the law enforcement was in Pryor's pocket. This was one of his henchmen, no doubt.

"This is my wife, Hanna," Cale said in introduction. "Marshal Sam Vickers informed me that the shop is available for rent. He volunteered to contact the owner while we have lunch."

Hanna tried hard not to react to the Southern accent Cale had suddenly developed. She had the feeling he'd been paying close attention to the way she talked so he could adapt her manner of speech for his role as gentleman shopkeeper.

Offering her best smile to the scraggly looking marshal, Hanna held out her hand. "A pleasure to meet you, sir."

When Sam's lecherous gaze flooded over her, Hanna forced herself not to take offense. She wouldn't have walked out on the street alone after dark while this hooligan was on patrol. He looked as if he could cause more trouble than he would quell. Yes, this town definitely needed to be cleaned up and control returned to its citizens, she decided instantly. And she had married the man who could do exactly that.

Hanna stared after the supposed marshal when he mounted his horse and trotted northwest. "No question as to whom our new landlord is," she murmured.

Cale nodded grimly. "I'm telling you here and now, Mags—watch your step. I suspect Pryor has infiltrated this town and planted his men to insure that he maintains control."

"Men like Sam Vickers, for one. I figured that out quickly enough. Fortunately, we have a secret weapon," she said confidently.

"Yeah? What's that?" he asked as he escorted her toward the restaurant.

"You. I'm not going to mind delaying my journey west because it's going to be pure pleasure watching you give these citizens their town back and ridding this part of Texas of self-serving bullies like Otis Pryor."

Her confidence in him was flattering, but Cale had detected a strong whiff of trouble the moment he arrived in Cromwell. Otis Pryor had taken a foothold here and he'd be around personally to check out the new arrivals. Cale knew Hanna was smart enough not to reveal their ultimate purpose, but what worried him most was that leer the marshal directed at her. If Hanna came to harm because of this scheme Cale would never forgive himself.

He stopped abruptly and tugged her into his arms before she breezed into the restaurant. Violet eyes hedged with thick lashes lifted inquiringly to his. The need to protect Hanna hit Cale with the impact of a flying bullet.

"Promise me you'll be careful," he murmured. "Promise me you'll remember to expect the unexpected. Don't argue with me when I tell you to take Skeet with you when you venture out.''

She stared at him just as intently and said, "Promise me that you won't try to take on Pryor and his henchmen alone. Promise me that you'll let me do what I can to help.''

He couldn't make that promise because that was exactly what he planned to do. Once he'd monitored Pryor's activities he'd know where and how to strike—without Hanna's assistance.

His expression must have given him away because she blew out a breath, regarded him accusingly and said, "That's what I thought. Well, so much for promises, my dear husband. Shall we dine?''

Cale reached out to snag her arm, but she sailed inside to distribute her beguiling smile around the café. All eyes focused on her as she headed toward a corner table.

Another wave of protectiveness splashed over him as he followed in her wake. Cale had the unshakable feeling that he was going to need to be in two places at once while keeping surveillance on Pryor's activities. Someone needed to keep a sharp eye out for *Hanna*—if the hungry looks she instantly drew from this group of men were any indication.

Maybe he should put her on the next stage that came through Cromwell. He couldn't bear the thought of seeing her hurt. Watching it happen would be pure torment. If she was off chasing her rainbows, at least he could hope she was safe and sound. He wouldn't have to watch her be hurt and know he was personally responsible.

Cale pulled out a chair for Hanna, then plunked down across from her. He'd prided himself on making very few mistakes in life, but he was pretty sure that dragging her into this mess was going to haunt him for years to come.

Hanna was truly amazed at Cale's ability to restrain himself when Otis Pryor swaggered down the boardwalk beside Sam Vickers. The man was far more handsome than she expected—considering he was a murdering bully. Blond and blue-eyed, tall and lean, Otis Pryor could easily pass himself off as a respectable citizen in his expensive clothes. No wonder the townsfolk hadn't realized what trouble awaited them until Otis sank his fangs into this unsuspecting community.

"So, Sam tells me you're anxious to set up shop in Cromwell," Otis said as he came to a halt, cast Cale a quick glance and then focused his hawkish gaze on Hanna. "Otis Pryor at your service, ma'am."

She forced a bright smile for his benefit. "Nice to meet you, Mr. Pryor. My husband and I are recently married and we're hoping to settle here. After growing up in N'Awlins I'm eager to begin our life together in this quaint community."

"I wondered where that enchanting accent originated," Otis replied as he took her hand and gallantly pressed a kiss to her wrist. Hanna inwardly winced when a repulsive shiver slithered through her. "You have a charming wife, Mr. McCloud."

"My greatest treasure," Cale drawled as his gaze settled adoringly on Hanna. "I'm hoping we can come to terms with you quickly. My wife and I have had a long journey and I'm anxious to see her settled in."

"Of course, where are my manners," Otis said, then gestured toward the abandoned shop. "Come inside and see what you think of the place."

Hanna eyed Otis warily. Despite what he said—and how he said it—she knew his sense of honor and decency was nonexistent. This was not a man who spent his time fretting over the safety and comfort of others.

Somehow she would take his flaws and turn them against him. She'd seen the flicker of masculine interest in his deep blue eyes. She wasn't sure how she'd use it to aid Cale, but she vowed to find a way. For certain, she'd allow Otis to take her for granted and see her as no possible threat. But she'd been listening closely to Cale's constant instructions about using her wits and showing precaution. She was going to be of assistance in Cale's mission. She'd see to it.

"This shop will suit us perfectly while we get our business up and running," Hanna declared as she stepped into the establishment, which looked as if it had once served as a lawyer's office. Empty bookshelves lined the walls and large oak conference tables divided the room in half. "Why, it won't take long a-tall to convert this shop to suit our needs."

"A gunsmith, are you?" Otis eyed Cale speculatively.

Cale nodded, and drawled, "As was my father before me. I grew up dismantling and cleaning weapons. And I suppose you could say that I'm an avid hunter because I have always been fascinated with hunting a variety of game and using all manner of weapons."

Hanna knew, right there and then, that if Cale decided to switch from a professional gunfighter to a professional liar the transition wouldn't be difficult. He sounded so sincere that she almost believed that nonsense, and she knew better.

Otis regarded Cale for a long moment—sized him up was nearer the mark—then gestured toward the stairs. "Let me show you the living quarters."

Hanna studied the simple accommodations, which would require considerable elbow grease to make them livable. "I was hoping for something larger, but we'll make do for the time being." Hanna wanted to leave the impression with Otis that she was accustomed to better quarters, but she would work with what she had—temporarily. She smiled—just the slightest bit flirtatiously—at him. "We'll take good care of your property, sir. No need to fret about that."

"I'm sure you will, my dear." His teeth flashed and Hanna was instantly reminded of a slimy shark. "I can hardly turn down a lovely lady like you. I just don't have it in me to disappoint a beautiful woman. The place is yours."

When Otis named his price, Hanna muffled a gasp of outrage, but she managed not to call attention to herself. Without so much as a grimace Cale agreed to the astronomical rent and the transaction was over as quickly as it began. Cale asked for directions to Otis's ranch and promised to deliver the rent in person the following day.

The moment the two men closed the door behind them Hanna pivoted toward Cale. "Although I much prefer a larger place, we can manage here for a while," she said for the benefit of Otis and Sam, whom she predicted had their ears pressed to the other side of the door. "It's a start."

"Are you sure you'll be satisfied here, love?" Cale crooned in his newly acquired Southern drawl. "I'll be happy wherever you are. You know that, don't you?"

Hanna walked over to the window that overlooked the street to watch the blue-eyed sidewinder who went by the fictitious name of Otis Pryor exit from the shop and swing into the saddle to ride away. Their new accommodations offered a bird's-eye view of town, she noted with satisfaction. They had made a wise choice.

Her thoughts trailed off when Cale looped his arms around her waist and rested his chin on the top of her head. "This won't work," he said grimly. "I want you on the first stage out of town."

Hanna lurched around to face his determined expression. "I will do no such thing. A deal is a deal," she huffed.

Cale cupped her chin and met her defiant stare. "I've got years of experience under my belt," he reminded her sternly. "I sense real trouble here. I don't want you involved in it. I don't know how I'd react if you got hurt and I sure as hell don't want to find out the hard way. You can concoct the tale that your mother has suddenly taken ill and you're needed to care for her and your younger siblings. That won't raise suspicion, and you'll be free to go wherever you wish, without your father reeling you back to New Orleans like a landed fish."

Hanna planted her fists on her hips and stared him down like a gunfighter at twenty paces. First off, she wanted to help him bring down this murdering thief who'd destroyed Cale's family. Second, she wasn't ready to give Cale up. She'd mentally prepared herself to part company with him in a few weeks, but she wasn't ready to do so *now*. She hadn't had time to talk herself out of these tender feelings that mushroomed with each passing day.

And, of course, there was the phenomenal passion that she would never experience again. She intended to be married only once, and she already had the perfect husband, so there was no point in settling for a disappointing substitute. And lastly, her need to feel useful compelled her to help the citizens in town regain control of their community.

No, she definitely wasn't leaving until she was good and ready.

"I'm not leaving you alone in this hornet's nest of trouble and that's that," she told him in no uncertain terms. "I know I don't have your impressive skills, but I can be an asset to this investigation and I demand to be included."

"You could get hurt, Magnolia," he told her bluntly. "Or worse. *Dead* is worse. I want you to realize your dreams, starting *now*."

She didn't confide that he was becoming as important as her long-held dreams. She refused to clutter up his scheme by blurting out that if she wasn't in love with him already, then she was perilously close. He didn't want to hear that, didn't need that. And certainly, that wasn't part of her original plan to locate the perfect husband. But this rugged bounty hunter and marshal had turned out to be *too* perfect. Perfect enough to draw her interest, her admiration, her trust and her affection.

True, the qualities and traits she saw in him were in direct opposition to the portrait society usually painted of him, but she cared deeply for Cale. He'd complicated her plans and tangled up her dreams, but she couldn't help the way she felt about him.

"No, you're stuck with me, so you better get used to the idea, my dear husband," she insisted. "I'm going downstairs to start unloading the wagon. You can stay here and argue with the wall, if you wish, but I have work to do." Head held at a determined angle, Hanna veered around him and marched across the room.

"Stop right there," Cale commanded in his best marshal voice.

Hanna didn't even glance back or break stride. She sailed from the room and heard Cale mutter, "Stubborn woman," before she closed the door behind her.

Cale worked side by side with Hanna to unload their supplies and spiffy up the shop. For now, he'd given up on persuading her to leave town. But the discussion wasn't over, not by a long shot. This situation was potentially lethal and Cale refused to let Hanna be injured if things turned sour. And there was a strong possibility that they might. Otis Pryor definitely had a hired army at his beck and call, plus he had informants strategically placed around town to keep constant surveillance.

"I don't see the need for this," Cale grumbled when Hanna, with writing tablet in hand, tugged him out the door and down the boardwalk.

"I do," she insisted. "I'm the social expert here. This is my forte. We need to meet and greet our business associates and form an alliance of sorts. It's called social connections. Now paste on a smile and mind your manners.''

Cale marshaled the semblance of a smile and tried to remember the gentlemanly nuances Hanna had rattled off during their trek to Cromwell. She took the lead, winning over the proprietors in every shop they entered.

Cale could easily visualize Hanna flitting around a formal soiree, making friends left and right. She had the charm and the knack. He also noted how differently people in Cromwell responded to him, simply because of his association with this bewitching female. She opened doors for him that were usually closed and locked. For once his reputation hadn't preceded him, and his change in appearance and behavior would allow him to make an attempt to fit into society.

Each time Hanna exited a shop, she jotted down the proprietor's name and any background information she'd gleaned—such as a wife's name, number of children and previous residences. According to Hanna, the easiest way to win friends and fit into society was to show an interest in all things important in someone else's life. By the time they made the rounds she had several pages of notes and had placed an ad in the newspaper, announcing the opening of their new shop.

While Hanna industriously set the upstairs to rights, Cale made a discreet exit from town to survey Pryor's headquarters. He'd tried to leave Skeet for Hanna's protection, but she insisted that he was the one riding into a viper's nest and needed an extra pair of eyes and ears.

Using the cover of the trees along the river, Cale made the two-mile jaunt, then retrieved his spyglass to pinpoint the location of each posted lookout station—and there were several of them. He also noted the evidence of caverns in the sandstone cliffs that towered over the ranch headquarters. Pryor had certainly picked an impregnable fortress to defend against intruders.

Frowning curiously, Cale watched four men—heavily armed and dressed in chaps—gallop south. Off to rustle cattle, was Cale's guess. Judging by the size of the herd of young calves that were pinned at one end of the pasture, Pryor was making preparations for a cattle drive to the nearest railhead. Apparently he planned to steal more livestock to sell for straight profit.

Cale moved from one hiding place to the next to keep close tabs on the goings-on at the ranch. He noted the excessive amount of whiskey bottles that were passed around during the changing of the guards. No doubt Pryor had taken over the local saloon to provide an endless supply of liquor to his men. Cale made a mental note to thank Hanna for dragging him all over town to acquaint himself with the locals, because he recognized the scroungy-looking bartender from the saloon who was presently driving a wagonload of liquor to the ranch. Definitely one of Pryor's informants, he mused.

While Cale kept watch, the four rustlers returned, herding two dozen calves, which were hurriedly pinned in the corral. More whiskey bottles changed hands.

A wry smile pursed Cale's lips as he and Skeet circled around to take a closer look at the two-story ranch house. Cale planned to send Hanna to the local apothecary for laudanum to spike these renegades' drinks. Otis would think his hired guns were falling asleep on the job. Nothing like internal conflict to undermine the workings of an outlaw gang.

Cale waited until after dark—immediately after the recent changing of the guard—to make his move. With the stealth and cunning he'd learned from the old Cherokee warriors, he slithered through the grass toward the corral gate. When the guards sank into their drunken stupor, Cale reached up to unlatch the gate, allowing the cattle to wander off to graze. Pryor and his men would have to make a mad scramble the following morning to regather their livestock and drive them to the railhead.

The timing couldn't be better, Cale thought. There wouldn't be as many men on guard for the next week. That would lessen the odds against him.

Two hours later Cale was walking up the steps to rejoin Hanna. He tapped a quiet signal on the door, then waited for her to let him in. When the door swung open Cale's eyes nearly popped from their sockets. Hanna had arranged and decorated their living quarters and purchased linens and a quilt for the bed. Frilly curtains covered the windows. The crude furniture had been polished to a shine. The place looked like a real home.

*Home.* The word never had any meaning to Cale—until now.

"Where the devil have you been so long?" Hanna fussed at him. "I was on the verge of setting off to track you down."

He smiled at her anxious expression. He rather liked the way she fretted about his welfare. It was definitely a first and it made him feel wanted, needed. "It's good to see you again, too, dear," he said wryly.

Hanna's breath came out in a huff and her amethyst gaze narrowed on him. "What took you so long?"

"Scouting requires considerable time." He cast another approving glance at the living area. "This place looks great, Mags. You really knocked yourself out."

"I had to do something to occupy my time while worrying about your safety." She snatched up the lopsided mass of brown yarn and shook it in his face. "And I have discovered that I don't have any talent whatsoever for knitting. This was supposed to be a mat for Skeet."

Cale swallowed a chuckle. Hanna had obviously wasted time and money on yarn and knitting needles. He kept telling her that she excelled in people skills, but she never wanted to hear that. She was searching for other talents in her never-ending quest to find herself.

"Well?" she demanded, casting her knitting in the trash. "What did you find out during your long hours of skulking and snooping?"

His amusement vanished in a heartbeat. "Pryor has surrounded himself with a legion of hired guns who rustle cattle in their spare time…. What are you doing?" he asked when she reached for her tablet and pen.

"Keeping a journal that will serve as evidence for Pryor's illegal activities," she said as she hastily jotted the time, date and brief account of tonight's findings. She cast him a somber glance. "Just in case neither of us is around to point an accusing finger at the scoundrel, we'll have documented notes for his trial."

"And that's another thing," Cale said as he came to loom over her. "You need to leave, the sooner the better."

Hanna thrust up her hand in a deterring gesture. "Don't start. I told you this afternoon that I'm staying to the end— bitter or otherwise—because we made a pact."

Cale knelt before her, forcing her to meet his gaze. "Damn it, Mags, you have a future awaiting you, and the incoming stage can take you wherever you want to go. You could stay with Mary Watkins at Fort Griffin until you decide on your destination. This is *my* personal battle. You've laid the groundwork with your presence. It's enough."

She took his callused hands in hers and got that determined look in her eyes that he'd come to recognize. She said, "For an intelligent man you can be deliberately obtuse sometimes. I plan to stay because I *want* to stay and help you deliver justice for your family. My father never let me be useful. I *need* to matter. I *need* to make a difference. It feeds my soul."

Another corner of Cale's heart crumbled like a rock slide. He'd come to understand her, knew what motivated her and drove her. He knew what inspired and moved her. He wanted to provide what she needed, but he was still torn between giving her what she wanted and this awful sense of impending doom that lurked in the back of his mind. Keeping her safe and protected had become vital to him because she'd become an important part of his life. She mattered to him—too damn much for his own good.

When she leaned forward to kiss him tenderly, as if he mattered greatly to her, too, Cale lost the ability to reason. Wanting her had become such a constant thing that one kiss sent desire twisting through him like a tornado. He tugged her into his arms and filled his hands with her luscious body. She yielded instantly to him and Cale struggled to his feet, determined to christen their bed instead of taking her in a heated rush on the floor.

They tumbled together, tangled in each other's arms, impatient to be rid of the barriers of clothing that separated them. Cale sighed in masculine appreciation when he finally got his hands on her silky flesh and heard her quiet moans of pleasure.

When passion overtook him, he came to her, marveling at the satisfaction he derived from being surrounded by her, buried deep inside her. Being with her like this made him wonder how he could possibly exist when she went her own way. Life without her would never be the same, because she had changed him. She'd touched his carefully guarded emotions.

The uneasy thought that his life would become empty, and that loneliness would become his constant companion, prompted him to clutch Hanna desperately to him. Cale savored each rapturous sensation, each heady moment of pleasure in her arms. And as always, her shimmering release sent him plummeting over the edge into oblivion.

In the aftermath of mind-numbing passion, Cale nestled against Hanna and made a solemn vow that no matter what else happened, no matter what personal sacrifices he had to make, Hanna would remain safe to embrace her future. He would not permit *her* to become the sacrifice he had to make to avenge his brother and sister-in-law's deaths. That was one promise he vowed to keep, he mused as he fell asleep with Hanna cocooned protectively in his arms.

Walter Malloy glanced up from the ledger on his desk when the butler announced the arrival of a guest. He eased back in his chair as his deceased wife's attorney entered the room. Walter didn't care much for the straitlaced old goat, who was a stickler for rules and legal regulations.

"What are you doing here?" Walter said impolitely.

He was in no mood to be sociable when the last two telegrams he'd received from the Pinkerton detectives could do no more than report where Hanna *had been,* not where she *was.* He failed to see how his citified daughter could elude a passel of men who were hailed as the best detectives and bloodhounds in the country.

Without invitation Benjamin Caldwell stoically seated himself in the chair across from Walter's desk. Typical, thought Walter. The aging lawyer was definitely on a mission and refused to be deterred, no matter how unwelcome he might be.

"I have a legal duty to inform you that your daughter has met the requirements of the trust fund Clarissa left to her," Benjamin announced as he adjusted his spectacles and glanced down at the document in his lap.

A sense of impending doom settled over Walter and he slumped in his chair. He had the unmistakable feeling that Clarissa's by-the-book lawyer was informing him *after* the fact that Hanna had taken control of her inheritance.

"As requested, I have wired the funds to your daughter," Benjamin continued in his no-nonsense voice. He folded the document and rose from the chair. "You have been officially informed, Malloy. My work here is done."

"Wait!" Walter shouted when the lawyer spun around

and strode off. "Where is she? Where did you send the funds?"

Benjamin looked down his nose at Walter. "To Texas."

"It's a big state. Be more specific," Walter demanded.

Benjamin smiled faintly. "Under the law, Malloy, I have conveyed all the information necessary. Miss Hanna requested that I keep an official copy of the wedding certificate filed in my office…just in case. Good night, Malloy."

Walter gnashed his teeth as the attorney made his regal exit. He was one of the few men Walter had never been able to maneuver or control. Well, at least Walter knew Hanna was somewhere in Texas. That was a start.

Bolting to his feet, he breezed out the door to have his carriage readied. He intended to send off a message—even if he had to drag the telegraph agent out of bed—to inform the Pinkertons to stop dallying around in Indian Territory and hightail it to Texas. Now that Hanna had control of her inheritance she could be blazing a path to who knew where! He had to find her, to bring her home, and he was running out of time before Louis Beauchamp backed out of their shipping merger.

Damnation, if a man wanted something done right he had to do it himself. And that's what he'd do, Walter decided. If he wanted Hanna back then he'd turn Texas upside down to find her.

# Chapter Thirteen

Hanna hiked off down the street to purchase another supply of the sedatives Cale had requested, while he added more weapons to his displays at the shop. She was well pleased with his scheme to leave Pryor's guards asleep on their watch, and his clever plot to sabotage the outlaws' trail drive.

Stealth and cunning always served Cale well, she reminded herself with a smile. She'd previously noticed that, despite his formidable reputation with weapons, her husband wasn't bloodthirsty or trigger-happy. No, he disarmed and incapacitated criminals without relying exclusively on deadly gunplay. But she suspected that, when it came to a last resort, Cale would indeed be the last man standing in a firefight. She sincerely hoped that apprehending Pryor wouldn't come to that because the odds weighed heavily against Cale.

The unnerving thought sent Hanna across the street to the telegraph office. Impulsively, she decided to contact Julius Tanner, who would still be convalescing at Bennigan's Trading Post. If it was remotely possible for Julius and Pierce to lend a hand in Cromwell, Cale could use the help. Since he would never ask for assistance, she had to take matters into her own hands.

Hanna smiled at red-haired Arliss Fenton, the telegraph agent she'd introduced herself to earlier in the week. "I'd like to send a message," she requested politely.

"Certainly, ma'am." The young agent glanced cautiously toward the door, then said confidentially, "I don't know what message you plan to send, but keep in mind that the town marshal reads all telegrams before I'm allowed to send them."

Hanna wasn't surprised by the news and she was grateful for the information. Keeping that in mind, she wrote: "My dear brothers, my husband and I need help setting up shop in Cromwell. Could you return the favor my husband did for you recently? Love, Hanna."

She handed her message to Arliss and was startled when he handed a telegram back to her.

"This came in a few minutes ago," he reported, smiling warmly. "The marshal hasn't seen it yet."

Hanna quickly read the message from Benjamin Caldwell. The attorney had informed her that her trust fund had been sent to the local bank. Now she had the financial means to control her destiny.

To her dismay, Hanna realized that she wasn't quite as thrilled with the news as she'd anticipated. Her dreams had altered since she'd begun her exodus to her personal promised land. Leaving Cale behind wasn't going to be easy, not easy a-tall.

Hanna bid Arliss good day, then headed to the bank to open an account and deposit her trust fund. Once she'd made the necessary transactions she headed for the apothecary shop to pick up more laudanum. When she returned to the gunsmith shop she was pleased to note Cale was waiting on two customers.

Smiling wryly, Hanna watched her handsome husband portray the gentleman shopkeeper. He could be polite and sociable when the mood suited him. Now the mood suited because he was on a mission of utmost importance, and he'd vowed to do whatever was necessary to build a case against Pryor.

"Hanna, glad you're back," Cale said as he glanced over his customers' heads. "These good people were telling me about the fandango scheduled for this weekend. It's become an annual festivity, so I'm told."

"I'll look forward to it." Hanna smiled brightly at the two men, owners of the bakery and barbershop, respectively.

"There will be plenty of food, music and dancing in the town square," the barber reported, then shifted uneasily. "Sometimes things get a bit rowdy around midnight, but we do our best to avoid trouble."

In other words, thought Hanna, Pryor's brigands drank heavily and posed problems for the citizens. Hmm. Perhaps she needed to purchase more laudanum for the occasion.

"Now, gentlemen, perhaps you would like some instruction on the use and care of your new pistols," Cale offered, jostling Hanna from her pensive musings.

While Cale assisted his customers, Hanna went upstairs. Cale had told her to go about her daily business affairs and establish a predictable routine. He'd made it clear that Pryor's spies and informants were keeping close tabs on the new arrivals, and it was important to do nothing that might arouse suspicion.

With that in mind, Hanna set up her easel and canvas. Her vantage point from the window provided a scenic view of the tree-lined river, rolling hills and horses grazing in the distance. Gathering paints and brushes, Hanna applied splash-and-dash sweeping motions to fill in the background. She used her charcoal pencil to sketch in the trees, then tried her hand at drawing a herd of grazing horses.

After two hours her landscape painting had begun to take shape. She stepped back to appraise the results. Her shoulders slumped and disappointment swamped her. Obviously oil wasn't her medium, either. Her horses resembled long-necked coyotes. The rolling hills appeared flat and the trees looked more like scraggly bushes.

Blast it, did she have no hidden talents whatsoever? Thus far, her quest of self-discovery indicated there was nothing to discover. She couldn't draw, couldn't paint and couldn't knit. Her attempt to write detailed notes for the investigation were too descriptive and probably contained far more pages than Judge Parker preferred to read.

Frustrated, she spun around, surprised to see Cale hovering inside the doorway, scrutinizing her painting. She didn't ask for his honest opinion because she wasn't in the mood to hear the discouraging truth aloud.

When his lips twitched and his dark eyes twinkled, Hanna lost her temper. "This is not amusing," she muttered.

"Of course not," he said in mock seriousness. "Maybe with a little more work—"

"Waste of time," she interrupted as she snatched up the canvas and turned it against the wall. "After we have lunch I'll try my hand at designing a gown with the fabric I brought from Fort Smith. Or perhaps I can make you a colorful vest."

He made a muffled sound that could have meant anything, then said, "One of Pryor's men came in before I closed for lunch. He had his eye on a new rifle."

"Good." Hanna breezed across the room. "Make sure you remove the firing mechanism if he decides to make the purchase. I prefer to see him shoot blanks."

Cale followed Hanna down the steps, noting the frustrated pelting of her feet. He'd hoped she'd find a talent with oils to satisfy her craving. Unfortunately, she was as bad with oils as she was with charcoal pencils and knitting needles. He could only hope she had a gift for stitchery, because she was running out of hidden-talent options.

Throughout lunch Hanna didn't have much to say,

which was unusual. She'd always been a font of chitchat. Oh certainly, she spread her endearing smile around the café in her ongoing attempt to ensure the McClouds were accepted as part of the community. But she was discouraged. Cale could see it in the lack of sparkle in her eyes. He had to do something to cheer her up, he decided.

"I received a telegram from my attorney," Hanna told him as they ambled back to the gun shop. "My trust fund has arrived."

Cale halted in his tracks when an uneasy feeling settled over him. "When did you contact your attorney?"

"At Bennigan's. I asked Benjamin Caldwell to send the funds to Cromwell. Why?" she questioned.

"Damn, Mags, you left a paper trail," Cale muttered.

The color drained from her face. "Dear God, what have I done? If the Pinkertons find out where I am and come charging into town to apprehend me, I might jeopardize your... Oh, Lord!"

When she swayed on her feet Cale grabbed her elbow and steered her into the shop. "It's okay," he said reassuringly. But it wasn't okay. Having her father or the Pinkertons come thundering into town would definitely complicate his investigation and scare off Pryor. Damnation, why hadn't he thought to caution her to wait a couple of weeks before making contact with her lawyer? Timing was essential here.

"No, it's not okay a-tall," Hanna said bleakly. "It gets worse."

Cale stilled, watching the last bit of color seep from her face. "How much worse?"

Hanna fidgeted, muttered an unladylike curse half under her breath, then reluctantly met his probing gaze. "I sent a message to Bennigan's this morning, asking for Julius's and Pierce's help with this investigation."

*"What?"* Cale exploded before he could stop himself.

Hanna flinched. "I thought you needed help against the lopsided odds."

"Help?" he repeated stupidly.

"Arliss Fenton warned me that the town marshal reads all outgoing and incoming telegrams, so I made it sound as if I was asking my brothers to come help us set up shop."

Cale wanted to scold her for jeopardizing the investigation, and yet he wanted to hold her close because she looked utterly miserable and guilty. He decided to do both at once. He roped his arm around her waist, pulled her flush against him, dropped a kiss on her lips and said, "Damn it, Mags, do you realize how complicated this situation could get if your father's detectives and two deputy marshals descend on Cromwell simultaneously? Pryor is cautious by habit and he'll know something is afoot. Scores of innocent people could be caught in the crossfire."

Big shiny tears dribbled from her eyes and her lower lip quivered. "I—I'm s-so s-sorry," she said brokenly. "I can't seem to do anything right. I'm nothing but useless window dressing, just as my father claims."

When she howled in dismay Cale cuddled her closer. "No, you're not. You've got lots of impressive qualities." A sudden idea dawned on him and he abruptly set her away from him. "Wait here, Mags. I'll be right back."

Cale bounded up the steps two at a time to grab Hanna's writing tablet and pencil. Reversing direction, he leaped down the steps to fetch a shiny new shotgun from the display table.

Tears streaming unchecked down her cheeks, Hanna stared at him. "If you're planning to shoot me and put me out of my misery, I won't object. But what's the tablet for? So I can write my last will and testament?"

Cale locked the front door, grabbed her hand and towed her toward the back exit. "Skeet, stay," he ordered the dog, who was sprawled beneath the display table. If anyone decided to break in and steal the weapons, Skeet would have something to say in the matter.

"Where are we going?" Hanna asked as Cale scurried down the alley, then headed for the trees that lined the river.

"You're going to take target practice," he replied.

"Not a wise idea," she murmured as she wiped her tears on the sleeve of her gown. "I might accidentally shoot you."

Cale squatted on his haunches to hastily draw a bull's-eye on the paper, then strode over to attach it to a tree. He was certain that no one—even a novice with weapons like Hanna—could miss the target with the wide-scatter pattern of a shotgun. If nothing else, she could blow her frustration to smithereens. There was nothing like blasting an object to bits to make you feel better, he mused as he strode back to her.

Cale briefly explained the procedure of balancing and bracing the weapon against her shoulder and steadying her legs to counter the kick of the shotgun. He showed her how to take aim down the sight and focus on her target.

Sniffling, Hanna followed his precise instructions, then, before Cale could rattle off another comment, she pulled the trigger.

The kick of the shotgun knocked her off her feet. Yelping, she landed on her backside in the grass. Cale swooped down to hoist her upright.

"I told you to be prepared for the kick," he said as he brushed twigs from her gown.

"I didn't realize the weapon would kick with the force of a mule," she grumbled as she rubbed her throbbing shoulder.

"Next time I'll stand behind you for additional support. Once you get accustomed to..." His voice fizzled out when he glanced at what was left of the paper target. "Well, I'll be damned."

"No doubt you will, thanks to me and my stupidity," she mumbled. "I've spoiled everything in this investigation."

Cale thrust his arm toward the demolished bull's-eye. "Look at that, will you?"

Hanna's eyes widened in disbelief when she saw the battered target. "I did that all by myself?"

Grinning in response to her pleased expression, Cale drew another target and placed it on a branch. "This time back up a few paces," he requested.

Hanna backed up, lifted the weapon, braced herself for the inevitable kick and stared down the barrel. Cale positioned himself directly behind her so she wouldn't knock herself off her feet again.

The discharging shotgun propelled Hanna against him, but he barely noticed that her elbow slammed into his solar plexus. He was too busy gaping at the tattered target. Jaw sagging, he glanced down at Hanna. This was definitely more than beginner's luck. Hanna had a natural eye. Of all the hidden potential she had hoped to discover, who would've thought she was a natural sharpshooter?

Cale took the shotgun from her hands and reached for the pistol he kept tucked at the small of his back. "Okay, Miz Crackshot, let's see how you do with small firearms. Different arm position, different sighting. Now pay attention here."

Hanna listened with absolute concentration while Cale instructed her to hold the weapon waist-high, using the invisible line from her shoulder to the target to ensure accuracy. He showed her how to cock the trigger and squeeze in one fluid motion.

While Hanna waited eagerly, Cale sketched another target and hung it on the tree. "This requires more concentration for accuracy, Mags," he told her. "You're working with a bullet, not a spray of buckshot. Now then, whenever you're ready, take aim and fire. Keep the pistol parallel to the ground. That's good.''

The report of the pistol broke the silence. He squinted at the target, then his eyes popped. In disbelief his gaze leaped to Hanna. True, he'd drawn a large bull's-eye, but still…!

Cale threw back his head and laughed in delight. His dainty little bride, who'd been sheltered and stifled all her life, who couldn't knit, couldn't paint, sing or draw, had an amazing knack with weapons. Who would've thought it?

Cale was still chuckling when Hanna threw herself into his arms, and he had to grab the pistol barrel before it clanked against his skull. "Watch where you're pointing that thing, woman."

"Sorry." She practically squeezed the stuffing out of him, then said, "I'm going to love you forever for giving me back my pride and self-confidence. This is wonderful! Now that I know I have an aptitude for weapons you can teach me all about them and I can mind the shop so you can devote your time to monitoring Pryor's activities. Now that I've bungled everything, time is of the essence."

And then she kissed him, and Cale forgot about target practice, the investigation, an irate father hot on their heels, the Pinkertons and two deputy marshals who might walk into an ambush, and the tempting stack of money that had arrived to finance Hanna's dreams of adventure in the West. The only thing on his mind was the woman who'd become so entangled in his life that letting her go would be like amputating his arms and legs.

Cale kissed her back and his hands wandered at will, mapping her lush curves and swells. When the pistol dropped from her hand and thumped on his boot, Cale gave himself a mental shake and set her away from him.

"We need to get back to the shop," he rasped.

Hanna nodded, then rearranged the bodice of her gown where his hands had been prowling moments before. "Right. I have scads of things to learn about weapons."

"And starting now, since you can shoot, I want you to carry a derringer strapped to your thigh and a dagger in your boot. I'll rest easier knowing you're armed."

As Cale and Hanna walked hand in hand to town, her words echoed in his mind. *I'm going to love you forever.* She hadn't meant it literally, of course. She'd only meant that she was grateful that he'd discovered her hidden talent. Regardless, the words rattled him. He wasn't the kind of man who deserved a woman like Hanna. He couldn't match her social status, her pedigree, and he wasn't accepted and respected in most communities because of his lack of breeding and his profession.

He glanced discreetly at Hanna, noting the pleased smile on her face, the confident set of her shoulders. He'd bolstered her self-esteem and given her a useful purpose. He should be satisfied with having an impact on her life— temporarily.

It had to be enough. He'd never expected much from life, and this wasn't the time to start wanting more. He and Hanna had made a deal and he'd keep it. Despite all these alien feelings that sometimes got in his way, this was still a charade and he couldn't let himself forget that.

Otis Pryor stared at the approaching horseman, wondering if Sam Vickers was riding out to the ranch to report more bad news. The past few days hadn't gone well, and Otis was in no mood for more complications. He'd ranted and raved at his negligent guards for not securing the corral gate after they'd added the stolen livestock to the herd before the trail drive. It had taken four hours and considerable manpower to regather the herd and begin the drive to the Texas and Pacific Railroad depot at Fort Worth. With half of his men absent, Otis felt twitchy and vulnerable. He preferred feelings of absolute power and dominance over potential threats.

To make matters worse, something had been niggling him since he'd met the newcomers in town. There was something in Grayson McCloud's dark, penetrating gaze that seemed unnervingly familiar. Otis swore he'd never laid eyes on the gunsmith before, but the expression around McCloud's eyes and mouth reminded him of another bronzed face that belonged to a knife-wielding Indian who'd viciously attacked when Otis had latched on to his pretty squaw. The incident had nearly cost Otis his life.

Injured and bleeding, Otis and his men had headed south to Texas and never returned to Indian Territory. It had taken six months to recover from that crazed Indian's attack. And Otis had suffered excruciating pain each time he moved.

*Fearless,* Otis thought suddenly. That was the similarity in expression between that vicious Indian and Grayson McCloud. That's what bothered him about the new gunsmith. Yet it was McCloud's beguiling wife that occupied Otis's thoughts most every night. She was exactly the kind of attractive trophy he needed at his side while he ruled this region of Texas. Incomparably beautiful and obviously well bred, Hanna McCloud could bring him the cultured respectability that would complement his acquired land, vast cattle herds and wealth.

The only thing standing between the woman Otis decided he wanted to reign by his side was the man with no fear of anything—save one. A diabolical smile pursed Otis's lips. Grayson McCloud's greatest treasure was also his greatest weakness.

"What are you grinning about, boss?" Sam Vickers asked as he dismounted from his lathered horse. "Last time I saw you, you were pitching a fit and cursing because the men keep leaving the corral gates open and cattle keep scattering to kingdom come."

Otis momentarily discarded his erotic thoughts of having Hanna McCloud in his bed. "What are you doing out here?" he asked. "I told you to keep close tabs on the McClouds."

"Have been." Sam spat a stream of tobacco, wiped his mouth on his grimy sleeve, then retrieved the telegrams from his pocket. "But I came across a couple of interesting messages I thought you'd like to see—pronto."

Otis frowned curiously as he unfolded the messages. His brows shot up when he noted that Hanna had inherited a trust fund. How much? He didn't know. The message didn't say. But judging from Hanna's polished manners and sophistication he suspected she'd come from considerable wealth. The second correspondence, from Hanna to her brothers in Indian Territory, caused him to frown warily.

"Bennigan's Trading Post?" Otis mused aloud. "I swore Hanna said they'd come from New Orleans. What are her brothers doing there?"

"Dunno." Sam spat tobacco juice as he leisurely propped himself against his sweaty horse. "I just thought you'd like to know she's called in family. Four newcomers in town at once will be more difficult to keep up with. Especially with half your men headed to Fort Worth."

Otis was getting another bad feeling. He needed to act quickly to counter any potential threats to his control over the town. He never questioned these uneasy feelings, for they'd kept him one step ahead of the law for years.

"Get back to town and keep watching the gun shop," Otis ordered.

"Not much to see, except customers tramping in and out," Sam reported. "After lunch I looked through the window to see McCloud hugging his wife." He grinned wickedly. "I've seen him do that twice already. That chit must really be something in bed."

The comment reinforced Otis's craving to have Hanna

at his beck and call. He did indeed have plans to make and he needed to make them now. He also needed to ensure Hanna's brothers didn't live long enough to complicate the situation.

Millie Roberts glanced out the window to see three well-dressed riders dismount in front of Bennigan's Trading Post. She didn't recognize the men, but she'd seen their counterparts around here before. Pinkertons. This was one of their favorite stops while investigating high-profile cases for the government or their wealthy clients. Millie saw Julius Tanner scowl when he, too, spotted the new arrivals.

"What the hell are they doing here?" Julius grumbled as he stretched his stiff leg beneath the dining table.

"Don't know who they'd be tracking," Pierce Hayden replied between bites of Opal's delicious food.

Millie refilled the marshals' coffee cups, but her attention was glued to the three men who filed into the dining hall to survey the local patrons and stage passengers. When one of the men—the tall good-looking one—glanced in her direction, she flashed him a seductive smile. Millie struck her best pose—chest thrust out, one hip cocked—as the three men headed straight toward her.

To her dismay the Pinkertons were more interested in the badges pinned to Julius's and Pierce's shirts.

"We're looking for information, gentlemen," Agent Richard Sykes—the handsome one—said without preamble. "Have you seen Marshal Cale Elliot lately?"

"Or his wife?" Agent Gilmore added. "Blonde? Extremely attractive?"

Julius propped his elbows on the table, then shrugged noncommittally. "What do you boys want with Elliot?"

"This has more to do with his new wife," Agent Williams said impatiently. "Her father posted a thousand dollar reward for information that will lead us to her."

A thousand dollars! Millie's head spun like a cyclone.

With that kind of money she could make a fresh start in civilized society. She was wasting away in this wilderness, and she certainly had no loyalty to Cale after he'd betrayed her by marrying that prissy bitch.

"Cale and Hanna Elliot were here last week," Millie blurted out. "For a thousand dollars, I'll tell you anything you want to know."

"Damn it, Millie," Julius growled at her.

She ignored Julius and shook loose from his firm grasp on her arm. If he thought clamping hold of her was going to prevent her from offering information, then he thought wrong.

Agent Sykes perked up immediately. "You've seen them? In person? Did they have that man-eating mutt with them?"

"Millie…" Pierce said warningly.

She ignored that, too, and nodded. "Definitely in person and with the dog," she confirmed. "They spent the night here, and then followed the southbound stage that was headed to Texas." She went on, despite the marshals' glares that branded her a traitor. What did she care what they thought? She was getting herself a ticket out of this backwoods post and she was latching on to it with both hands. "Word came back from down the line that Elliot foiled a stage holdup." She gestured toward the stockade. "The three bandits were delivered yesterday. These marshals are planning to head back to their base camp with their prisoners, first thing in the morning."

The Pinkertons glared down at the uncooperative marshals and the marshals glared right back. Clearly, there was professional rivalry between these two groups of law officials. Not that she cared about their obvious hostility. All she wanted was the reward for her information.

Before Millie could think of something else to add to her report, Elmer Linden lumbered to the table and thrust his beefy arm toward Julius.

"Got a strange message here, Julius. See if you can make sense of it." Elmer pivoted toward the new arrivals. "Pinkertons, right? Which one of you is Richard Sykes? Got a message for you, too."

Without the slightest change of expression, Julius read the telegram, then handed it to Pierce, who showed no reaction in turn. Agent Sykes, however, read his own missive, then scowled.

Millie had no idea what was going on, but all she wanted was the solemn promise that she'd receive reward money. She stared pointedly at Agent Sykes. "I cooperated fully and I demand to be paid."

Richard Sykes fished into his vest pocket to retrieve the crisp banknotes. He counted them into Millie's hot little hand and her fist closed up like an oyster around its pearl. She was free at last! Free to begin a new life, and she didn't have to latch on to a man to find security.

Millie plunked down the coffeepot and wheeled toward Elmer. "I quit. I plan to be on the stage that leaves within the hour."

While Elmer sputtered in disbelief, Millie barreled toward her cramped living quarters behind the trading post to pack her bags. It would serve that prissy blonde right when the Pinkertons caught up with her and dragged her back to her father. As for Cale, he deserved to lose his fancy meal ticket. Millie had known there had to be a specific reason why Cale had up and married that woman, who was impossibly wrong for him.

It was all about money, Millie mused. Wasn't it always?

Grinning triumphantly, she tucked the banknotes in her chemise and gathered her meager belongings.

Julius Tanner swore under his breath when Agent Sykes waved the telegram under his nose. "So, what do you want me to do, Sykes? Read the damn thing for you?"

Agent Sykes glowered at Julius, then spared Pierce a

condescending glance when he had the audacity to snicker. "Hanna Malloy is in Texas. We've just had that confirmed by her father. Now then, would you care to tell us exactly where to find her?"

*"Malloy?"* Pierce hooted, eyes bulging. "The shipping magnate Malloy? *That* Malloy?"

"The one and only," Agent Williams confirmed. He stared curiously at the telegram Pierce had wadded up in his fist. "We showed our missive to you. Perhaps you'd like to show yours to us."

"Whatever gave you that idea?" Julius smirked. "It's got nothing to do with your investigation."

"No?" Agent Sykes said dubiously. "Why don't I believe that?"

"I dunno, why don't you?" Julius countered sarcastically.

The rejoinder earned him three annoyed glowers. Arrogant bunch, thought Julius. So full of themselves that it was a wonder they weren't floating sky-high like balloons. Always thought they were a step above deputy marshals. Well-dressed in their dandified suits and derby hats. Well-paid. Well, tough. Julius's and Pierce's allegiance was to Cale Elliot. The man had saved their bacon recently and patched up Julius when he was bleeding all over the place.

"There is still considerable reward money left," Agent Sykes said, baiting them. "I know exactly how much you gentlemen make to risk your life for Judge Parker, and it isn't much. You could live a life of leisure on what Walter Malloy will pay for your information and cooperation."

Julius didn't so much as blink. Millie might have sold out Cale, but he and Pierce wouldn't do it. Nope. According to Hanna's peculiar missive, Cale needed assistance, and he was sure as hell going to get it. These pompous Pinkertons weren't going to turn them against one of their own kind.

"If you must know, that telegram was from my baby

sister," Julius said. "It's personal. Now why don't you boys back off and let me and Pierce eat our meal in peace? We've got prisoners to cart back to the base camp...for damn little pay, don'tcha know."

The Pinkertons stared at him, but Julius ignored them and gobbled his meal. He and Pierce had arrangements to make if they were going to hotfoot it to Cromwell, Texas, to offer backup for whatever calamity had befallen the newlyweds.

"Hanna *Malloy?*" Julius shook his head in disbelief after the Pinkertons strutted off. "A half-breed Cherokee bounty hunter and deputy marshal married to a shipping heiress?"

"Boggles the mind, don't it?" Pierce murmured.

Sure 'nuff did. Yet, oddly enough, after seeing Hanna and Cale together, discovering how attentive they were to each other, Julius thought it was kinda touching. Romantic, even.

No matter what had motivated them to get hitched in a rush, there was something between them. Julius would be damned if he'd see that spoiled and severed by Hanna's bribe-wielding father and a few hoity-toity Pinkertons.

"You send off a telegram to have the other marshals swing down to pick up our prisoners," Julius murmured quietly to Pierce. "I'll make a big production of limping upstairs to take a nap, then I'll grab our saddlebags. I'll take the short way down from the window and we'll be Texas bound."

"You got it, partner." Pierce smiled conspiratorially. "But we don't have Judge Parker's permission to go haring off to Texas."

"Do we need it?" Julius asked in feigned ignorance. "Don't recall anything about that in the code manual. Must've missed that part."

Pierce grinned as he rose to his feet. "We better split up to give the Pinkertons a run for their money. I'll meet you at the Red River ferry at dawn. Make sure you shake those bloodhounds off your heels before we rendezvous."

# Chapter Fourteen

Cale was amazed at how quickly and eagerly Hanna absorbed knowledge about the various weapons he'd bought to stock the shop. She insisted on knowing the advantages, disadvantages and purposes of every variety of pistol, rifle and shotgun so she could convey the information to potential customers.

The men who came to browse were reluctant to allow Hanna to wait on them. But it only took a few minutes for them to realize she'd become a weapons expert. Her astounding abilities freed up time for Cale to make discreet inquiries around town about Otis Pryor's initial arrival. At first the townsfolk were reluctant to divulge information. It was obvious that they feared for their lives and their businesses.

Arliss Fenton, the telegraph agent, was more courageous than most. He chafed at having private telegrams screened by Marshal Vickers and Otis Pryor. Arliss suggested an evening rendezvous so he could speak freely about the goings-on in Cromwell.

While Hanna was recording the information Cale had relayed to her, he ventured off to meet Arliss near the river. The red-haired young man confirmed Otis's arrival in town five years earlier, in addition to four scraggly looking scoundrels—Sam Vickers, for one—who demanded that shopkeepers pay monthly fees for protection against the criminal elements—namely themselves.

According to Arliss, several town founders had loudly protested the strong-arm tactics—and then mysteriously disappeared. Otis's men took over the vacated businesses and within a year Otis had supposedly purchased the prosperous ranch and equipped it with several hundred head of cattle and horses. The former owner and his wife, Otis claimed, had decided to move west to be near their married son and grandchild.

Cale didn't believe that for a moment. And neither did Arliss, obviously. The former owners had likely been victimized, the same way Cale's half brother and sister-in-law had. What Otis Pryor wanted he simply took by force. He had acquired the manpower to see that his will was done.

"In case you haven't noticed," Arliss said quietly, then glanced around when he heard a bird chirp in the distance, "the town marshal has been keeping close watch on you. He's been in my office twice a day to see if your wife has sent other messages."

Cale inwardly grimaced. He had been afraid that Hanna's missives had raised the wrong eyebrows. What he didn't need was for Otis to be on the alert for possible trouble.

"I appreciate your assistance, Arliss," Cale said gratefully. "It's always best to know your potential enemies so you can be prepared for trouble."

Arliss's young face scrunched up in a scowl. "My father owned the shop you've rented. He tried to bring legal charges against Otis." There was a long pause before he added, "My father hasn't been seen or heard from in almost three years, and my mother still hasn't recovered from her grief. I don't know if you plan to do anything about our resident devil and his ghouls, but I'll do whatever necessary to assist you."

Arliss looked him straight in the eye. "And by the way, if you're nothing more than a shopkeeper I will eat my hat—whole."

Cale chuckled at his newfound ally. "Perhaps I'm just a concerned citizen who wants to ensure peace in this town where I've decided to settle down."

"A concerned citizen who is giving his lovely wife shooting lessons?"

Cale's smile turned upside down.

Arliss waved his hand dismissively. "Not to worry. You've timed the lessons well. The town marshal is usually disgustingly drunk by eight o'clock, and so are Pryor's other spies and informants. I've followed you to the river twice, but I kept my distance from your sharp-eyed dog. No one else knows you've been taking target practice and I'm not planning to tell another living soul."

That came as a relief. Cale was glad to know this young man, who had his own score to settle with Otis Pryor and his goons, was guarding his back.

"You should know that the barber and baker will also do what they can for you, but they aren't particularly skilled with weapons, either," Arliss imparted.

"So I discovered when they purchased pistols. I should have sold them shotguns." Cale stared somberly at Arliss. "I'll do all I can to remove the threat Otis poses, but I have one request of you."

Arliss came to immediate attention. "Name it, my friend."

"If anything happens to me, I'm counting on you to see that Hanna gets on the westbound stage."

Arliss clasped Cale's hand firmly and met his gaze directly. "You have my word on that. It's obvious that you have the same kind of love and devotion for Hanna that my father had for my mother."

Cale was still standing there with his jaw scraping his chest when Arliss skulked off into the underbrush. Good gad, Cale was a better actor than he thought if he'd convinced that attentive young whelp that he was hopelessly in love. True, he'd let himself think differently, act differently when he'd crossed over into husband territory. He'd also taken great pains in portraying the devoted husband in public, and he'd let himself get caught up in his role in the charade. But this was only make-believe and there were definite time limits.

He might be suffering the most incredible case of lust he'd ever experienced—which he obviously was—but he couldn't be *in love* with Hanna. He wasn't even sure he was capable of love, having seen so little evidence of it in his life. He could be Hanna's lover, her confidant, her protector and friend. But he couldn't actually *love* her because they had no future. He'd come to care about her and she'd come to depend on him. But Hanna wanted to chase her dreams and he had to let her be what she was meant to be. Furthermore, Cale had made a commitment—the incarceration of Otis Pryor and his band of murdering thieves. That's all he'd lived for these past five years.

Had Cale given Hanna the impression that he was in love with her? Had she drawn the same conclusions as Arliss had because he *did* treat her differently than any other woman he'd known?

Cale decided it was time for him to pull back and regroup. He had to put these unproductive and conflicting emotions that had Hanna's name attached to them under lock and key—where they should've been in the first place. It was time to focus on his promise to avenge his brother's death; he couldn't allow himself to become distracted from his life's purpose.

Hounded by Arliss's observations and conclusions, Cale hiked back to town to retrieve his horse. He had bottles of whiskey to spike with sleeping potion. He needed to keep Otis rattled and off balance, and that meant ensuring the night watchmen were asleep at their posts when a few more cattle strayed from their pastures.

Resolutely, Cale trotted away from town to undermine the workings of Pryor's ranch. *In love? Impossible!* He couldn't let himself be that foolish. It wouldn't do him or Hanna a bit of good. This was temporary, he reminded himself again. Any feelings he and Hanna had for each other had to end the moment the terms of their bargain were met.

Hanna stirred drowsily when she heard the bed creak, and felt the warm presence slide in beside her. She'd waited up as long as she could, but exhaustion had overtaken her and she'd crawled into bed. Cale said not one word as he settled next to her. He didn't loop his arm over her hip or press a featherlight kiss to the curve of her neck, as he'd made a habit of doing lately.

She turned toward him, seeking the closeness they'd shared each night. "I trust you haven't been out this late because you're seeing another woman," she murmured teasingly as her hand drifted across the wide expanse of his chest.

"No, go back to sleep. I didn't mean to wake you."

There was something in his voice, a quality she couldn't decipher, that alarmed her. Her eyes shot open and her wandering hand stilled on his chest. "What's wrong?"

"Nothing's wrong. It's been a long tiring night is all."

Hanna didn't believe him. She could feel the return of the emotional distance that had become nonexistent this past week. He'd made love with her every night, and suddenly this big brawny hulk of man was too tired? Well, they'd see about that, she decided as her hand ventured over the washboard muscles of his belly.

Cale grabbed her hand. "Hanna, don't," he said, pulling away.

He was rejecting her? Why? Dear God, had he tired of

her already? The thought crushed her, devastated her. She knew he didn't love her, but she knew he desired her, cared about her in his own way. What in heaven's name had happened?

Hanna scooted sideways to provide him with more bed space, then wrapped her arms around herself as if to ward off the hurt. She squeezed her eyes shut and told herself to go to sleep. But she kept asking herself what she'd done or said to make Cale withdraw from her.

They'd been so close, had been through so much together. They were comrades fighting a battle to serve justice. And then wham, he didn't want her physically and had become emotionally remote. Was this another of the many lessons he was trying to teach her? Well, she didn't get it.

Three hours later, while listening to Cale's methodic breathing, Hanna still didn't get it. She did, however, realize that she'd come full circle—from feeling rejected to determined acceptance. Whatever the reason for Cale's sudden lack of interest, it was better this way, she told herself.

The simple truth of the matter was that Cale was now using her as her father had. She'd become his conversation piece, his social window dressing while he laid his trap for Otis Pryor, and he didn't want her help. She was, in fact, his cover to infiltrate Pryor's kingdom and sabotage his army.

When this investigation was concluded Cale would return to Fort Smith to see Otis Pryor stand trial. She would take her inheritance and head west to enjoy limitless freedom. Any leftover feelings for Cale would be unnecessary emotion that would weigh her down. *He,* obviously, wouldn't be hindered by any ties to her when he left.

A tear trickled down Hanna's cheek as she accepted the reality of this charade she was playing with Cale. And it was definitely a charade. She'd just let herself get caught up in playing house with him. This wasn't real and neither were her feelings for him—or so she tried to tell herself.

Hanna squeezed back more tears and reminded herself that she'd been rejected and unloved by her father, too. She really should be getting used to it by now.

Otis Pryor was positively livid! He stood on the front porch of his ranch house and didn't see a single head of livestock. The empty water tank indicated the windmill had malfunctioned, and none of his men had checked on it. Of all the guards who were supposed to be standing watch on the sandstone peaks, only three were at their positions. The rest were sprawled on the ground, sleeping off their drunken stupor.

It was one thing for him to drink himself unconscious, but he paid these worthless bastards good money and gave them perks to watch his back. How dare they neglect their duties!

Wheeling around, Otis stormed into the house to grab a shotgun from the gun case that stood beside the front door. He stamped back outside to shoot off several rounds of ammunition. On the canyon rim, his guards staggered to their feet to answer his signal.

When the men congregated around him, Otis vented his fury by employing every profanity in his vocabulary. When he finished raking his bleary-eyed men over live coals, his arm shot northwest. "Take your sorry asses down to the river and soak your heads!" he bellowed. "Then round up your horses and find my straying cattle!"

The scraggly group of men wobbled off, leaving Otis to curse their incompetence. They'd gotten lazy and lax because there were no longer threats from neighboring ranchers and townsfolk. The bullying tactics Otis had used had worked *too* well. His men had no challenge to keep them alert and sober. Now they countered their boredom and lack of excitement by turning to the bottle. He knew that for a fact because he was bored and restless himself.

Otis blew out a frustrated breath. He needed a diversion, a challenge. The thought put a devilish smile on his lips. Perhaps it was time to focus his attention on Hanna McCloud. Charming the new bride away from her husband would be an intriguing challenge. Taking a woman that belonged to another man had always given him a thrilling sense of accomplishment. Otis knew he had the kind of good looks women appreciated, and now he had the lure of wealth to go with it. He could be gallant and charming if he felt like it. Indeed, pouring on the charm had worked well for him over the years.

Ah yes, he mused as he returned to the house to make himself presentable. Stealing a man's lovely wife out from under his nose was as gratifying as stealing cattle, horses and stagecoach strongboxes. Appeasing his lust with the harlots in Cromwell had lost its appeal. He was ready to focus on acquiring the kind of woman who would complement his new status in society. That woman was Hanna McCloud. And once Otis set his mind to what he wanted he was determined to acquire it—one way or another.

In order to keep her mind occupied, Hanna dismantled several pistols on display at the shop, then quickly reassembled them. She'd learned the name and function of each part and she could rattle them off without fail. That served to reassure skeptical male customers who were hesitant to make purchases on her recommendation.

A few days earlier she had been bursting with enthusiasm because she'd discovered her aptitude with weapons. Now that she and Cale were barely speaking, and he made excuses not to be alone with her—most especially in the privacy of their living quarters—her sense of self-satisfaction had taken a nosedive.

Cale rarely bothered to glance in her direction or make

direct eye contact. She was reminded of the way her father
had treated her the past few years, and she wanted to rail
at Cale because of it. He'd obviously grown bored and
disinterested and totally focused on the primary objective
of this stint in Cromwell. Repeatedly, Hanna told herself
that it didn't matter, that she'd soon be on her way and
he'd become a bittersweet memory that she could outrun
when she headed west.

Hanna glanced sideways when the shop door swung
open. She inwardly winced when Otis Pryor sauntered in.
He was decked out in expensive finery and wearing a
charming smile. He reminded her of the scores of men her
father had paraded past her in recent years.

"Good morning, Hanna. You're looking lovely, as always," he murmured.

No, she wasn't. She hadn't been sleeping well because
of this emotional estrangement from Cale. Nonetheless,
she flashed a smile and let Otis think his empty flattery
was getting to her.

"Why, thank you, Mr. Pryor. How kind of you to say
that."

"Otis," he corrected, sending her another charming
grin.

Hanna decided she liked it better when snakes-in-the-
grass slithered on their slimy bellies rather than stood upright, smiling pleasantly at her. But two could play this
game, she decided.

"Very well, Otis it is." She batted her eyes at him and
pivoted, just so, granting him a view of her profile. Men
seemed to like that—shallow insincere creatures that they
were. "What brings you into town this morning…? Oh
dear, did my husband forget our rent payment? We've
been so busy getting settled that it probably slipped his
mind."

"No, your husband brought out the cash payment earlier

this week,'' Otis reported. He glanced curiously toward the back storeroom. ''Where is Grayson this morning?''

He'd left at the crack of dawn to undermine the workings of Pryor's ranch. Releasing cattle from pastures, tampering with whiskey bottles, sabotaging windmills and discreetly slicing saddle cinches and reins had been on his list of things to do. But, of course, Hanna wasn't about to tell Otis that his doom was impending.

''Actually,'' she replied, prefabricating as she went along, ''Grayson is a bit under the weather. I insisted he stay abed. Something he ate must not have agreed with him and he was nauseous most of the night.''

''Sorry to hear that.''

Sure he was. Hanna smiled sweetly. ''I'll convey your concern.''

Otis reached into the pocket of his gold brocade vest to fish out his ornately decorated timepiece. The status symbol reminded her of the pocket watch her father carried so he could impress members of high society.

''Since Grayson isn't feeling well perhaps you'd allow me to escort you to lunch,'' Otis suggested.

Hanna turned up the radiance on her smile. ''That's kind of you. I would appreciate the companionship at lunch.'' She glanced toward the stairs. ''Perhaps I should inform Grayson.''

''Why bother the poor man?'' Otis said smoothly. ''Let him sleep. After all, the annual fandango is tomorrow night and I'm sure he'll want to be in better health so he can accompany his lovely wife. I do envy him that, my dear.''

Another flirtation. Another flicker of blatant interest in those sea-blue eyes. Hanna might not know all the survival techniques she needed, but she definitely knew how to play these social games. Otis was making his interest known, as many men had done before him.

Hanna batted her lashes and smiled at the devious

scoundrel. "Really, Otis, all this flattery will leave my head spinning."

"Flattery? Ah, my lovely Hanna, I only speak the truth. You are the most beguiling woman I've ever met."

She trilled a laugh for his benefit. She was sure he would try to come up with something more original if he knew she'd heard such empty compliments a few hundred times before and had been unimpressed by it.

Cale, on the other hand, would never have stooped to such manipulative tactics…. Hanna forced aside the thought and concentrated on outcharming Otis. "Let me fetch my purse from the storage room, and I can close for lunch."

"No need to fetch your purse, sweet Hanna," Otis cooed. "Lunch is on me."

"I'd dearly love to see that," Hanna said under her breath.

"Pardon, my dear?"

"I said that is kind of you, but unnecessary."

"Nonsense. A man likes to treat a beautiful woman to a meal. I insist."

And what, as if she didn't know, did he expect as payment for this meal? Hanna returned his smile. "Very well then, but I still need my key and it's in my purse." Swinging her hips in a manner that would've done Millie Roberts proud, Hanna entered the storeroom. She swallowed a surprised yelp when she saw Cale looming by the back exit like a shadow. As always, the sight of him stirred suppressed emotions, and she had to concentrate to maintain her composure. He didn't speak, just studied her with those penetrating obsidian eyes that probed into her heart and nearly broke it in two.

"Hanna, my dear, is something wrong?" Otis called out.

She jerked to attention, her gaze still glued to Cale's

ruggedly handsome face. "No, just checking to ensure I have my key," she called back.

When she turned and left the storeroom, Cale swallowed a salty curse. The moment he'd seen Pryor mount up and ride toward town, Cale had followed him. From the look of things Otis Pryor wasn't satisfied with stealing his neighbors' livestock and keeping the citizens of Cromwell under his thumb. Now he'd set his greedy eyes on Hanna.

Damnation, Cale should have put Hanna on a westbound stage. Now she was determined to aid his cause and was playing along with Pryor's pursuit. An amorous and intimate pursuit, obviously. Otis was a master at getting his way, by hook or by crook. The bastard.

Cale slumped against the wall, muttered sourly, then reached over to let Skeet in the door. Cale had eavesdropped on the entire conversation and had heard the deceptive charm oozing from Otis's voice. Possessive annoyance fizzed through him. He'd taught Hanna to take care of herself, but he still wanted to take Otis apart with his bare hands for flirting with his wife.

That kind of thinking was unproductive, Cale reminded himself. Hanna had no interest in Pryor. She was trying to do Cale a favor by keeping Otis occupied, and encouraging his obvious scheme of seduction. But if that murdering scoundrel laid a hand on her... Cale sucked in a steadying breath and willfully cast aside that repulsive prospect so he could concentrate on the matter at hand.

The sooner he disabled Pryor's ranch operation and dissolved the theft ring, the sooner Hanna would be out of harm's way. Cale had to trust her to take care of herself and provide a distraction, while he focused his time and energy on this investigation.

Cale was building a case, establishing dates and times matching the man's illegally acquired prosperity with the mysterious disappearance of local citizens who'd resisted his takeover. There could be no loopholes, and Cale intended to be on hand to give his recommendations to Judge Parker when Otis Pryor and his band of murdering cutthroats went to trial.

Let them all hang—twice. Three times would be even better.

Forcing himself not to dwell on Hanna joining Otis for lunch, Cale made a discreet exit. Now was the time to sneak into Otis's stronghold and have a look around the house. Pryor had sent most of his men to round up livestock, repair broken fences and malfunctioning windmills. Cale needed to confiscate the land deeds and bills of sale that were likely stashed in the man's home office. Cale preferred not to slip into the house in broad daylight, but he'd managed similar feats before and he was going to take advantage of the opportunity Hanna had provided by keeping Otis occupied.

With Skeet at his heels, Cale headed for the ranch, wondering if this empty feeling around his heart was going to plague him for the rest of his life. Funny, he'd distanced himself from the rest of the world for years, but the distance he'd purposely placed between Hanna and himself— for her benefit as well as his own—felt unnatural, uncomfortable.

"Get used to it," he ordered himself. Hanna wasn't his to keep, and he'd known that from the onset.

Pierce Hayden paced back and forth beside the Red River, which separated Indian Territory from Texas. Impatiently, he checked his watch—again. Julius was four hours late. Had those pesky Pinkertons overtaken him? Had his injured leg made it difficult to spend so many hours in the saddle? Pierce blew out a frustrated breath, then halted in his tracks when he heard a thrashing in the underbrush.

"Damn leg." Julius scowled as he hobbled from the bushes, leading his horse.

"What the hell took you so long?" Pierce asked.

"Blasted Pinkertons," Julius muttered. He wiped a smudge of dirt from his whiskered face, then plunked down on a tree stump to take a load off his leg. "Made it out of the upstairs window dandy fine, but that Sykes character—the pretty boy of the Pinkerton trio—saw me ride off. Before I knew it those bloodhounds were on my trail."

When Pierce glanced around uneasily, Julius waved off his concern. "Not to worry. I lost 'em by doubling back and brushing away my tracks. They cost me a few hours and I had them running in circles, but I'm guessing they'll be here shortly. After all, there are only a few safe places to cross the Red and that trio has enough reward money to shell out for information that they'll persuade folks to point them in our direction." Julius heaved himself to his feet, expelled a weary sigh and said, "C'mon, partner, we've got Pinkertons breathing down our necks. We've got to reach Cromwell and give the Big Chief fair warning that his father-in-law wants Hanna back, pronto."

"Sure wish I knew what that's all about," Pierce murmured as he mounted up. "And no telling what kind of trouble Cale's in if Hanna's sending an SOS."

Julius unpinned his badge and crammed it in his shirt pocket. "Yup, don't sound too good. Elliot doesn't usually require anybody's help when he's on a foray. He must've gotten himself mixed up with a whole nest of vicious varmints."

Pierce snickered. "It'd serve those Pinkertons right to find themselves on *our* side when we reach Cromwell. I'm curious to know if they're as good in a showdown as they seem to think they are."

While Julius and Pierce thundered off to catch the ferry, Agent Richard Sykes monitored their progress through his high-powered field glasses. "They'll lead us right to Hanna Malloy," he said confidently.

"Ignorant fools," Agent Gilmore scoffed as he swung into the saddle. "Who do those yahoos think they're dealing with here?"

"It's going to be a pleasure humiliating those bungling marshals," Agent Williams said as he trotted his horse toward the departing ferry.

# *Chapter Fifteen*

While Hanna dressed for the fandango, she could hear Cale moving quietly around the room. She was careful not to let her gaze stray toward him while he dressed because she needed no reminders of that swarthy masculine body she'd once had her hands all over, at any time she pleased. The peaceful camaraderie and immense pleasure they'd shared had been replaced by a strained existence, where two people living in each other's pockets tried not to encroach on one another's private space.

So many times during the past few days Hanna had wanted to reach out to touch Cale, but she'd held back at the last moment. So many times she'd awakened in the night to find her arm or leg draped over him and had forced herself to inch way.

Not so long ago he'd been her closest friend, her lover. Now he was a stranger who'd built an emotional wall to separate them.

And while Cale had been pushing her away, Otis Pryor had been doing his damnedest to get up close and personal. He'd showed up the previous evening to escort her to supper, and had found all sorts of excuses to touch her. Hanna had endured it, and even behaved as if she approved, but she'd had to force herself not to wince or withdraw.

Otis had returned again this morning, insisting that he wanted to formally introduce her to the group of women responsible for organizing the fandango and setting up the refreshment tables. During the introductions Otis had kept a possessive hand on the small of her back and stood too close for her comfort. He'd been subtly staking his claim and drawing the speculative glances of the other women. No doubt he wanted word to get back to Cale that he had a rival for his wife's affection.

Otis had been persistent about giving Hanna a tour of his home. And, naturally, he'd insisted that she join him for a home-cooked meal prepared by his servant. Otis had cornered Hanna before she could exit the door and had crowded her against the wall.

"Do you have the slightest idea what you do to me, sweet Hanna?" he'd murmured against her neck.

When his arousal pressed against her thigh she'd felt as if she'd betrayed the memories of the passion she'd shared with only one man. Her first reaction had been to shove Otis away, but she'd reminded herself that it was more beneficial to the cause to play along.

She hadn't wanted the scoundrel to see her as the slightest threat because there might come a time when she needed him to take her for granted so he'd let down his guard. Taking him by surprise at an opportune moment was a vital weapon she needed at her disposal.

When Otis had leaned down to kiss her it had taken every ounce of self-control not to spit in his face. Otis repulsed her, while Cale had the ability to melt her down to shivering desire. It had taken tremendous acting ability for Hanna to pretend to enjoy Otis's kiss when she'd craved the sensuous feel of Cale's mouth upon hers.

"We could go upstairs, Hanna," he'd whispered against her cheek.

"I'm still married, you know," she'd reminded him,

forcing herself to peer into those blue eyes that flared with primal lust.

"Some marriages simply aren't meant to be," he'd told her huskily. "I want you in my bed. I can lay the world at your feet. You should be surrounded by wealth and luxury, not wasting away at that shop in town, married to a man who doesn't fully appreciate you."

"I do miss the wealth and luxury I grew up with," she replied. When he'd tried to kiss her again Hanna had ducked under his arm and latched on to the doorknob. "I really should go. Unfortunately, I have responsibilities at the shop."

To her relief, Otis had backed off, then accompanied her to town. Although Hanna hadn't openly encouraged his advances, neither had she discouraged them. She'd allowed him to think she was contemplating his offer. Little did the man know that offers of wealth and status didn't impress her. She'd had the world at her fingertips, but had left it all behind to chase her own dreams....

"Are you ready, Mags?"

Cale's question jostled her back to the present. Hanna cast one last look in the mirror to ensure the coil of hair she'd pinned atop her head was secured and wouldn't come tumbling down in disarray while she was dancing. "Ready as I'll ever be," she murmured, dreading another encounter with Otis.

Although Cale bowed gallantly, then offered his arm— as she'd instructed—there was no smile on his rugged features. His expression was astonishingly intense. "Did you enjoy this afternoon's kiss at Pryor's ranch?"

Stunned, Hanna gaped at him. "You were there?" she croaked. "How?"

"Did you?" he persisted. His expression was now carefully devoid of emotion.

She tilted her chin and met his gaze directly. Other women might employ jealousy to force a commitment from the man who'd captured her interest, but Hanna refused to sink to that petty level. Even though Cale's interest in her had withered away, she had no intention of punishing him for hurting her. It wasn't his fault that he didn't love her. After all, she expected nothing less than honesty from him, and she would offer nothing less than honesty in return.

"Kissing devious sidewinders is not my idea of enjoyment," she told him. "But if there comes a time when I can turn his lust against him, then you can be positively certain that I will. Otis is your archenemy, therefore, mine as well. Does that answer your question satisfactorily?"

"I didn't like watching him kiss you," he snapped gruffly.

"I didn't like kissing him, either. He is despicable and repulsive, so I presume we both endured an unpleasant afternoon."

The faintest hint of a smile pursed his lips as he leaned his head deliberately toward hers. Ah, what a difference the right man made when it came to kissing, she mused as she willed his lips to touch down on hers. She wanted Cale to erase the repugnant memory of kissing a snake, but his sensuous mouth hovered just shy of her lips. She was tempted to grab him by the lapels of his expensive black jacket and yank him to her.

"The man is a snake, to be sure," he rasped as he stared at her mouth. "But he has the kind of charisma that I don't have."

She could feel the heat of Cale's body. She could feel her own response. "You have more than your fair share of charisma, dear husband," she whispered, wanting his mouth on hers so badly she could almost taste him. "You've just grown tired of tossing it in my direction."

"Mags, I—"

She didn't let him finish because she wasn't sure she wanted to hear what he had to say. He'd probably break her heart. "Just hush up and kiss me one last time," she demanded as she grabbed his jacket lapels and brought his mouth those last few inches to hers.

Hanna kissed him for all she was worth, for all the times the past few days that she'd wanted his kisses and he hadn't offered. If this was to be their last kiss then it was going to have to last her a lifetime, because she knew she'd never let another man this close again.

The scent, feel and taste of Cale would be forever emblazoned in her memory, branded on her heart. When she was with him she felt as if she was everything she'd ever hoped to be. And he alone held the power to hurt her or pleasure her. He could send her spiraling to rapturous pinnacles or plunging into depths of despair. He'd touched her soul and made her feel whole and alive, and she was never going to be the same again.

She knew he didn't return the depths of her feelings, but, fool that she was, she loved him nonetheless. There was no talking herself out of it. No matter how many times Cale backed away and turned himself into the lone wolf he'd been when they'd first met, she was going to go on loving him.

When he finally abandoned that infuriating restraint she'd encountered the past few days and kissed her senseless, Hanna knew what heaven was like without actually dying first. His tongue swept into her mouth as he hooked his arm around her waist and pulled her full length against him. He kissed her as if he wanted to devour her whole, and she felt him grow hard against her.

He still desired her. At least there was still that. Even knowing he didn't love her, she savored this last kiss and gave all of herself to him, hoping he understood what she didn't have the nerve to translate into words.

When there was no more air left in her lungs, Hanna was forced to break the steamy kiss. Hang the fandango! She wanted to rip off Cale's citified clothes and have her way with him for the last time. Dancing with the male citizens of Cromwell—and Otis, no doubt—wouldn't be half as much fun as making love with Cale.

Before he could circle back to whatever he'd tried to say—before she interrupted him with a hungry kiss—Hanna grabbed his hand and opened the door.

"Hanna—"

"For a man who disapproves of conversation that lasts more than a minute, you've started talking entirely too much," she interrupted as she tugged him down the steps.

"Mags, I—"

"Cale, *do* hush up," she demanded. "There are only two things that prevent you from being the perfect husband. You don't know when to keep your mouth shut."

"And the second?" he asked, chuckling.

"Let's tackle first things first, shall we?" she said as she led him onto the street.

Several times during their leisurely stroll to the town square Cale considered dragging Hanna to a halt and assuring her that it wasn't lack of interest that prompted him to keep his distance from her. As long as he drew breath he'd desire her, want her. But he'd never make it out of Cromwell with his heart intact if he didn't maintain this emotional detachment and let her believe the worst.

This was for the best, he reminded himself. What did he possibly have to offer Hanna after they completed this assignment? Money? She had plenty of her own. A home? He didn't have one to share with her. Respectability? Hell, he didn't have that, either. He'd given up all *his* personal dreams five years ago to avenge his brother's death, but *her* dreams were still ahead of her, shimmering on the western horizon. He had to set her free when this investigation was concluded.

And it was very close to its conclusion now.

Cale had collected the evidence he needed to confront

Otis Pryor. He'd confiscated the land deeds and the former owners' will. As predicted, there had been no exchange of money or property titles that indicated Pryor had legally obtained the land. Furthermore, there were no bills of sale for the hundreds of cattle that Pryor claimed to own. In short, everything Pryor had was stolen.

Tomorrow night, while the guards were asleep at their posts, Cale intended to lure that murdering bastard away from the house, slap him in irons and then gather up his small army. He'd make preparations to haul Pryor and company to Fort Smith to stand trial.

Hanna would be out of harm's way, because Cale had already purchased a ticket and he intended to put her on the morning stage—kicking and screaming, if that's the only way she'd go. But she *would* be long gone when Cale made the arrests.

Music and laughter wafted on the evening air as Cale and Hanna approached the square. Lanterns hung overhead, spotlighting the refreshment tables, the dance area and the group of local musicians. Citizens had turned out in full force to celebrate the founding of their community. Women were decked out in finery, but none of them remotely compared to Hanna's stunning beauty. She was the belle of the ball, just as she'd likely been while she was rubbing shoulders with the aristocracy in New Orleans.

Cale glanced sideways, noting how her hair shone like moonbeams in the light. He yearned to reach over and loosen that sophisticated braid atop her head so he could run his fingers through those silky strands. The locket she always wore around her neck like some sort of talisman glowed in the golden light and called attention to the slender column of her throat. Her pale blue satin gown accentuated her perfect figure, and his fingers itched to map her luscious curves and swells.

Indeed, Hanna was a bewitching sight to behold, and every male in attendance turned to stare as she walked by.

Hell, Cale could almost hear the collective sigh of male approval as she strolled toward the dance area.

Cale had never learned to dance and he wasn't about to make a fool of himself in front of Hanna. When she tugged on his hand he shook his head. "I don't know how," he admitted.

"You don't know—" She clamped her mouth shut and stared at him. "Why didn't you tell me? As light and agile as you are on your feet, it wouldn't have taken long a-tall for me to teach you. Heavens, it isn't like you haven't taught me one lesson after another. Even things I wish I hadn't learned—" She snapped her mouth shut so fast she bit her tongue. "Ouch."

"Things like what?" he couldn't help but ask when he noticed the rueful expression on her face.

"Never mind." She stared at the air over his right shoulder. "Well, then, I suppose we should mix and mingle with the crowd and sample the refreshments."

"What things?" he insisted, refusing to be distracted.

She tossed him a sugarcoated smile. "None of your business. Ah, there's Mrs. Hensley. I met her this morning. I think I'll have a chat with her. Excuse me."

When Hanna buzzed off, Cale glanced around uncertainly. Talk about feeling out of place! He wasn't a party goer. He had, however, interrupted one or two necktie parties—hosted by criminals who'd made some innocent victim their guest of honor—during his forays for Parker. But those didn't count.

If nothing else, this fandango reinforced Cale's conviction that no matter how much he enjoyed Hanna's companionship and her presence in his life, they didn't suit each other. He could don the fancy trappings of a gentleman shopkeeper, but he was still a half-breed bounty hunter who was better adapted to life in the wilderness than in society. He couldn't dance. He wasn't a master of conversation—idle or otherwise—and the only thing he knew about fashion was what the tailor who'd sold him this suit had told him.

Cale's train of thought derailed when he saw Otis Pryor. The rancher was dressed fit to kill—and the evidence Cale had collected certainly indicated he'd done it several times since his arrival in Cromwell. He was also stalking Hanna. Cale gritted his teeth when the well-dressed bastard took her arm and drew her toward the dance area. Watching Otis pull Hanna close was as tormenting as watching the man kiss her that afternoon. Cale's stomach churned as if he'd ingested rancid bacon.

Hanna was absolutely, positively going to be on that morning stage, he promised himself. He wanted her as far from Otis as she could get. The man was staring at her as if he wanted to gobble her up. Otis's veneer of gentlemanly patience was wearing thin, Cale predicted. Being a man himself, he could sense Otis's desire to take his budding "friendship" with Hanna to an intimate level.

Over Cale's dead body!

He was so thoroughly distracted, watching Otis spin Hanna in circles, that he hadn't noticed several of Otis's men sneaking up behind him. Suddenly Cale felt a pistol barrel boring into his spine, smelled the foul order of trouble crowding in on him.

"Easy, friend," Sam Vickers growled from directly behind him. He patted Cale's back, then reached beneath his jacket to grab the concealed pistol. "Make one move to resist and your lovely wife will become our target. I've received an anonymous tip that your inventory of weapons is stolen property. I'll need to see your bill of sale and ask you a few questions."

Same song, tenth verse, Cale mused. According to his findings—and Arliss Fenton's helpful information—former store owners had been accused of theft before their inventory was confiscated and they mysteriously disappeared. Cale had the unshakable feeling that not only did

Otis Pryor and his henchmen want to stock their arsenal with his weapons, but Otis had decided that claiming Hanna as his own would be a damned sight easier if Cale was conveniently out of the way.

When Sam Vickers grabbed his arm, every instinct inside Cale screamed to attack, but he noticed the pistol aimed directly at Hanna, and counted dozens of innocent citizens who could be injured if the shot was fired. Damn it to hell!

"C'mon, McCloud. You're under arrest," Sam sneered. "Move it."

While the band played a lively tune and the townsfolk danced and chatted, Cale allowed himself to be led away from Hanna and the other citizens, and ushered into the shadows on the street. He swore foully when he took a head count and noted the gunman who'd targeted Hanna had remained behind to ensure Cale's cooperation.

Cale waited until the men frog-marched him far enough from the dance area that the potential sniper couldn't see what was going on. Suddenly, Cale wheeled around, kicking Sam's pistol from his hand and simultaneously plowing his fist into the nearest bearded jaw. Muted curses erupted around him as he attacked his would-be assailants with a vengeance.

Suddenly he heard the pounding of feet and saw shadowy figures racing from the alley like wraiths surging from the bowels of hell. The abrupt blow to the back of his head left him staggering. A doubled fist—equipped with brass knuckles—plowed into his solar plexus, and Cale's knees threatened to buckle beneath him.

He reminded himself that he'd been pummeled before— for being a half-breed, for being a deputy that criminals wanted off their trail. He could take a punch and endure the pain.

Snarling, he launched himself at the man directly in front of him. By the time they landed in the dirt Cale had already retrieved the dagger tucked in his shirtsleeve and slashed the gunman's wrist. The man squealed in pain and lashed out, but Cale rolled away and regained his feet.

"Damn, who *are* you?" Sam scowled as he darted away from the slashing dagger.

"The curse of your life, Vickers," Cale growled. By sheer will alone he kept on his feet to square off against the five men who'd formed a semicircle around him. He could smell the blood oozing from the wound on the back of his head, but he refused to be distracted. "Call off your sniper or eat this knife. Your choice."

Vickers smirked as he shifted in front of one of the other men. "Apparently you're short on brains if you haven't figured out that you aren't calling the shots here, McCloud. Just try to use that knife and see where it gets you." He nodded slightly to the man standing behind him. "Smitty, go tell Harlan to keep his pistol trained on McCloud's lovely wife until I tell him otherwise."

Cale swore under his breath when the henchman Vickers had been shielding turned and darted off. He glanced discreetly at the six-shooter that had fallen from his victim's bleeding hand and now lay four feet away. Damn it, he really needed that pistol. Certainly, he had another knife tucked in his boot, but he could do a lot more damage with a loaded pistol. And double damn it, these men were trying to use Hanna as leverage over him. Her life or his. Hell, that was no choice at all, but he doubted his assailants understood the full measure of extremes that Cale would dare to go to give Hanna a sporting chance.

"Skeet!" Cale called suddenly.

"Expecting your mutt to come to your rescue?" Vickers chuckled wickedly. "Sorry, McCloud. No help from that quarter. Guess it's you against all of us. This all boils down to whether you want to keep your wife alive—"

Cale hurled the knife, noting the look of surprise on Sam Vickers's whiskered face when he glanced down at the lethal wound on his chest. Shocked amazement registered on the other henchmen's faces, immobilizing them for a split second. It was all the time Cale needed to dive for the discarded pistol and get off a couple of shots before the gunmen could react.

He dropped two men before he felt a bullet graze his shoulder. He rolled and fired off two rapid shots, and two more assailants pitched forward in the dirt.

Screams erupted in the town square, and Cale hoped to hell that the sniper couldn't get off a shot at Hanna while people were scattering in all directions. He hoped Hanna had the presence of mind to run for her life before Otis got his filthy hands on her. He prayed that she remembered the tricks of the trade he'd taught her....

From out of nowhere, another blow landed on the back of Cale's head. Damn, Otis had posted his men in every nook and cranny in town, Cale figured, as intense pain exploded in his skull. His stomach rolled and stars flashed before his eyes. He staggered, braced himself, then lurched around to clip his attacker in the jaw, but his strength was fading fast.

Cale felt as if the world was caving in around him. His knees folded when someone blindsided him with a blow to the ribs, forcing out his breath in an agonized whoosh. He had the unmistakable feeling his life was about to end, but he hoped to hell that Hanna's didn't. Cale hadn't asked the Indian's or the white man's God for anything, but he was damn sure asking now. Let Hanna survive this ordeal so she could chase her own dreams!

His only regret was that he hadn't had the courage to tell her that he loved her when he had the chance. He hadn't wanted to admit it to himself, wasn't pleased that young Arliss Fenton had seen right through him. Granted, Cale hadn't wanted to love Hanna, but it seemed there were some things that a man just couldn't overcome. The heart, he'd discovered, had a mind of its own.

Cale had kept his feelings to himself because he'd known she'd leave him eventually. Taking that knowledge with her wouldn't have done either of them any good. But now he wondered if maybe he'd been wrong about hiding his affection.

Maybe he should have told her the truth. After all, the woman always expected and demanded the truth from him. And now she'd never know how he felt, and he was going to die on this dusty street in his failed attempt to see his brother's killer brought to justice.

Damn, Cale thought sickly, life just wasn't fair. He'd always known that, but this was one time he really hated being right.

The image of Hanna's face flashed in his dazed mind. He couldn't give up! He couldn't leave Hanna to battle Pryor by herself. He had to get back on his feet, to keep moving. He'd made a promise not to let her get hurt.

"Hell! What does it take to keep this man down?"

The voice sounded as if it came to him through a winding tunnel, and Cale struggled from his hands and knees to his feet. Before he could push himself fully upright another blow sent him sprawling. Darkness swirled and he slumped in the dirt.

Alarmed by nearby gunfire, Hanna wheeled around. Frantically, she searched for Cale in the scattering crowd. Where the devil was he? Knowing him, he was in the thick of things, defying the odds. Blast it, he better not get himself killed or she'd never forgive him. Even if he couldn't love her the way she loved him, she needed the assurance that he was out there somewhere in the world.

The instant Hanna tried to dash off to investigate, Otis snaked his arm around her. "Easy, honey," he breathed. "You're coming with me."

"No!" She ground her heel in the toe of his boot, elbowed him in the midsection, then launched herself away from him.

"You little hellcat," Otis snarled as he lunged at her. His fists clenched in her hair, jerking her backward until her body collided with his. "I said you're coming with me."

Hannah struggled in protest while he dragged her backward. To her dismay, three of Otis's henchmen closed around them. She squirmed, fighting for release, defying the threat of having her hair pulled out by the roots. She ignored the pistol that Otis crammed into the side of her throat, and fought for freedom. *Never make it easy for your captor,* Cale had lectured her. *Never let him know you're afraid.*

Otis yelped when Hanna's nails scored his cheek and she bit into his gun hand—practically daring him to do his worst. But she was counting on the fact that he wouldn't pull the trigger with so many witnesses on hand to directly connect him to her death.

"Do you want your husband to live?" Otis snarled against her ear. "You keep fighting me and I promise he'll be a dead man."

The growled threat caused Hanna to hesitate. She realized her mistake a moment too late. She could almost see Cale scowling at her, hear him scolding her for refusing to stay focused on escape. Her hesitation granted Otis the chance to lever her arm behind her back. He held it at such a painful angle that she could only gasp in agony. Before she could grit her teeth against the pain and renew her struggles, two of Pryor's men secured her wrists behind her back with a strand of rope, then stuffed a gag in her mouth.

*Pick your battles, Mags. Choose the one you have the best chance at winning,* Cale had told her the last night he'd given her target practice.

Hanna ceased resisting immediately.

"Wise choice, my dear." Otis chuckled victoriously as he propelled her across the street to his waiting carriage.

It dawned on Hanna that Otis had arrived in a carriage rather than on horseback because he'd picked tonight to whisk her away from Cale. Otis had struck before Cale had the chance to spring his trap.

This was her fault. Otis had disposed of Cale because she'd let him think she was interested in him. Now Cale was suffering because her plan had backfired in her face.

Her very soul shriveled inside her when she glanced sideways to see Cale lying facedown in the street. Lantern light glinted off his raven hair. Blood dribbled over the side of his ashen face. And then suddenly, he tried to climb to his feet, but two shadowy figures leaped from the alley to club him over the head.

He collapsed, unmoving. Hanna tried to scream his name, and nearly choked on the gag. When she instinctively lurched toward Cale, Otis jerked her roughly against his chest.

"Your choice, my dear," Pryor growled at her. "Do you want him to survive the beating or shall I have my men finish the deed?"

Wide-eyed, panting for breath, Hanna surveyed the grisly scene. Five of Otis's men lay crumpled in the dirt. Five more had converged on Cale. She knew what Cale would have done if the situation were reversed. He would have dropped to his knees unexpectedly, forcing Otis off balance. He would have made a grab for the pistol so he could take out as many of his enemies as possible while they were frozen in surprise.

But Hanna wasn't big enough, strong enough or skilled enough to topple Otis and fire a pistol repeatedly with the kind of accuracy this situation demanded. All she could do was promise her cooperation in exchange for Cale's life.

"Make up your mind," Otis said impatiently. "Do you want him alive?"

She nodded. Her gaze remained transfixed on Cale's motionless body. She prayed that he wasn't so badly injured that he couldn't fight his way out of another confrontation. If he didn't survive, then her reasons for living would become meaningless. She simply could not stand there and witness his execution.

Hanna cursed when Otis spun her around to hoist her into the carriage. There on the boardwalk, in front of the gun shop, Skeet lay lifelessly on his side. A chunk of raw meat lay a few feet away. No doubt Skeet had been baited, then attacked when he sniffed at the food.

Oh God, not Skeet, too. Cale needed him. The dog was Cale's extra pair of eyes and ears. He was a fearless warrior in his own right, but he'd been rendered as helpless as his master.

Otis snickered when he noticed where Hanna's gaze had strayed. "I took care of that mangy mutt myself," he told her. "So don't expect him to come to your rescue, either."

Otis shoved her into the carriage, then plunked down beside her. He hauled her up against him so she couldn't give him a fierce kick in the groin or stuff her heel in his chin to vent her fury and frustration.

If her hands were free she'd clasp the gold locket to center herself, to find the sense of strength and peace that it usually provided. Instead, she focused on the image of Cale that rose in her mind's eye. He'd become her true touchstone, and she would draw strength from his strength. And most assuredly, she would find a way to make Otis Pryor pay for his past and present sins—or she'd die trying.

# Chapter Sixteen

Arliss Fenton stopped short when he saw Otis force Hanna into the carriage, then whisk her off into the night. He'd tried to reach Grayson, but five burly henchmen had dragged him into the alley. Arliss stood there, feeling helpless and frustrated. He wondered how many of Cromwell's citizens were willing to risk their lives to form a posse. Damn few, he figured. They'd known this kind of brutality before, and too many of them had been personally affected by it. Otis Pryor always won because his overwhelming manpower of ruthless criminals was there to back him up.

Arliss thought of his mother sitting home alone, still mourning her husband. He remembered the tormented rage he'd endured, knowing he wasn't capable of avenging his father's senseless death. He thought of Grayson and Hanna, who'd been torn apart because Otis had decided he wanted Hanna for his own.

Well, he wasn't going to let them down the way he had his father. Somewhere in this town of frightened citizens there had to be someone willing to help him fight for justice.

Arliss drew himself up and walked across the shadowy street to where five men had fallen in an attempt to bring down one incredibly brave man. He shoved his heel against Sam Vickers's shoulder and rolled him to his back. Teeth gritted, Arliss doubled at the waist to pluck up the badge that was supposed to represent law and order. For sure, this evil bastard wouldn't need it where he was going. And good riddance to him.

Arliss was still standing in the middle of the street when the stage rolled into town. The jangle of harnesses and pounding hooves died into silence when the driver halted ten feet away. It was either that or mow Arliss down, because he refused to move.

While the driver surveyed the grim scene, one well-dressed passenger bounded to the ground, glanced around and shouted, "What the hell is going on in this godforsaken little town?"

Arliss was in no mood to answer the demanding gent, who behaved as if his sudden arrival was as important as that of the president of these United States. Arliss pivoted toward the gun shop to fetch weapons and ammunition, wondering if he'd have to take on Prior's renegades all by himself. No other townsfolk had poked their heads through the doorways of their homes to join him in the street.

"Hold it right there, boy!" the passenger snapped. "I came here to find my daughter, and don't you dare walk away from me until you tell me where she is!"

It was that Southern drawl, not the shouted demand, that caught Arliss's attention. He wheeled and squinted at the gent, who had puffed up like a toad.

"Your daughter?" Arliss parroted.

"Hanna," he barked. "Where the devil is my daughter and where are those blasted Pinkertons? If they think I intend to pay them exorbitant fees when I'm the one who located her, then they've got another think coming!"

"Pinkertons?" he repeated, dumbfounded. There were Pinkertons coming to the rescue? Arliss breathed a gigantic sigh of relief. Well, hallelujah! Maybe he wouldn't have

to take on Pryor's heavily armed brigands—minus five—
by himself, after all.

Walter Malloy was travel weary and concerned about
his daughter. He'd had to bribe Benjamin Caldwell's sec-
retary to acquire the information about Hanna's whereabouts, but he'd discovered what he'd wanted to know.
Walter had boarded the first stage west to retrieve her.
Now that he was here, his concern for Hanna's safety rose
by alarming degrees.

He stomped forward, casting a repulsed glance at the
casualties lying in the street. Then he focused all his frustration on the skinny red-haired man who was blinking like
a disturbed owl.

"Speak up! You have to do better than to repeat what
I've said. Damn it all, man, I want to know where Hanna
is and I want to know right now!"

The drumming of approaching hooves prompted Walter
to glance past the young man, who'd provided no assistance whatsoever. Walter's gaze narrowed in irritation
when he spotted two riders being pursued by three men in
dignified suits.

"Well, the troops have finally arrived," he said, then
snorted. He flicked his wrist, shooing Arliss on his way.
"Run along. Now I'll get some results. I damn well
better."

The stage driver clambered over the top of the coach to
unfasten Walter's luggage, and dumped it unceremoni-
ously in the dirt. Rather than waylaying overnight, as
scheduled, he hurriedly returned to his seat and took off
in a cloud of dust to avoid future disaster in town.

Swearing, Walter traipsed over to retrieve his baggage,
hauling it onto the boardwalk. "Uncivilized heathen," he
muttered at the driver's departing back.

The instant the two riders and the Pinkertons dismounted, Walter stepped up to them. "Where have you

been? Chasing your own tails? We've got dead bodies lying around and my daughter is nowhere to be seen. I want
her located and I want her loaded up beside me on the
next stage.''

"Mr. Malloy, sir,'' Agent Richard Sykes said respect-
fully. "I'm—''

"I know what you are,'' Walter interrupted sharply.
"You're damn sorry at what you're highly paid to do. If
I ran my shipping business the same slipshod way you
handle your investigations I'd be broke. Now get on with
what I've paid you to do! And where are the other three
agents I requested for this case? I've been shortchanged,
damn it!''

While Walter Malloy was jumping down the Pinkertons'
throats—a sight that pleased Julius Tanner to no end—the
deputy marshal limped toward the young man with carrot-
colored hair, who was still standing in the street. "Evening, son. I'm Deputy Marshal Julius Tanner and this is
my partner, Pierce Hayden.''

"Julius Tanner?'' Recognition dawned on Arliss's face.
"You're the man Hanna sent the telegram to, aren't you?''

"None other,'' Julius affirmed. "While that bombastic
gent rips the Pinkertons to shreds, why don't you tell us
where we can find Deputy Marshal Cale Elliot and his
wife?''

"Deputy Marshal Elliot? He is using the name Grayson
McCloud. I knew he was more than a gunsmith.'' Arliss
gestured toward the downed men. "This is Cale's handi-
work, but the other five men got the best of him. I can tell
you, though, he didn't go down easily.''

Julius grimaced. "Is he dead?''

"Not yet,'' Arliss said grimly, "but if Otis Pryor has
his way, and he has for five years, Cale Elliot will be dead
soon.''

"Where's Hanna?'' Pierce questioned worriedly.

"Otis Pryor tied her up and hauled her off in his carriage. My guess is that he's taken her to his stronghold, which is surrounded by armed guards.''

"What about Skeet?" Julius questioned.

"I was about to look for him when the stage arrived and Hanna's father started firing questions and shouting demands.'' Arliss spun on his heels and headed for the shop. "I was going to borrow Cale's ammunition and weapons and try to rouse a posse, but I wasn't expecting any volunteers. Folks around here are terrified of Pryor. And with good reason.''

Julius and Pierce followed the young man down the street. Julius cursed mightily when he saw Skeet laid out on the boardwalk like a misplaced doormat.

Since Julius's leg was stiff, Pierce squatted down to examine the badly beaten and bloody dog. "Hey, boy. You still with us?''

The dog whined and his eyes fluttered open. His belly swelled and contracted, as if he was struggling to draw a pained breath.

"Got any idea how we're going to locate the Elliots?" Julius asked Pierce.

Pierce heaved a sigh as he patted the injured dog. "I was sort of hoping we could count on ol' Skeet to lead us to them. But I'm not sure Skeet's got a good leg left to stand on.''

Cursing the fact that they'd arrived about an hour too late to provide backup, Julius hobbled around the dog. "Kick down the door, son. We need all the hardware and ammunition we can carry.''

After six hard kicks, the locked door splintered and swung open. Once inside, Julius grabbed enough firepower for an all-out war. "Leave it to Cale to purchase only the best weapons money can buy," he murmured. "I hope I get the chance to thank him for it.''

Hurriedly, the three men stuffed ammunition in every

available pocket and grabbed a rifle. Arliss picked up a shotgun, since he wasn't much of a marksman.

"You think we ought to ask the Pinkertons for help?" Julius asked Pierce.

"Hell, teaming up with those pompous asses ain't my idea of fun," Pierce grumbled. "But yeah, I suppose we better. Might as well see if they're worth their salt in a fight. I'll go ask—" Pierce stopped in midsentence when he glanced toward the door. "Well, damn, I guess outright dying is all that'll keep that dog down."

Julius gaped at the battered dog that stood in the doorway, favoring his right front leg and wobbling unsteadily on both hind legs. The lawman smiled wryly as he stared at Skeet in open admiration. "Remind you of someone else you know?"

"Yep," Pierce said. "The Big Chief. I gave him up for dead twice when all odds were against him, but I'm betting on him now."

Laden down with ordnance, Julius limped outside and grinned when he realized the raging Walter Malloy was still giving the Pinkertons hell. No doubt, the three agents would leap at the chance to take action rather than listen to Malloy rip a few more strips off their hides. The way Malloy was going at it, there wouldn't be enough left of their hides to make rugs.

Cale regained consciousness—or at least he hoped this surreal state of awareness didn't mean he'd crossed over to the other side. Considering the pain thrumming in rhythm with his pulse, he figured he was more or less alive.

Dead, he was sure, would feel better than this.

It was impossible to tell where he hurt the worst. His head maybe—if he had to choose. If he didn't have a concussion it'd surprise the hell out of him. His belly was pitching and rolling, and he was almost afraid to open his eyes because he was pretty sure he'd be seeing double.

The sound of laughter and the scent of whiskey penetrated Cale's dazed senses. There were guards in the near distance, but since his ears were ringing like a school bell it was impossible to tell how far away. Cale risked a quick peek and discovered only one eyelid was functioning—at half-mast. He couldn't see his own hand in front of his face. Not that it mattered, because his hands were tied behind his back and his bruised cheek was resting on a cold stone floor.

Near as he could tell he was sprawled in one of the caves that served as lookout posts for Pryor's ranch. Cale had the unshakable feeling that the only reason he was still alive was because Pryor was using him as leverage against Hanna, ensuring she did whatever he told her to do.

Hanna... Her name rolled through Cale's mind like a whisper. Hair like shiny moonbeams. The face of an angel. The body of a siren. *His wife.*

The unholy fear of what cruelties might befall Hanna at Pryor's hands gave Cale the incentive to attempt to move. Sure enough, though, every muscle in his body screamed in protest. He grabbed a shallow breath, feeling the excessive strain on his ribs.

Well hell, he mused sickly. He needed to lie here for a few minutes until he convinced his battered body that it needed to move—for Hanna's sake. Time was of the essence and he *had* to find her.

Cale realized the dagger was still in his boot, and thanked whatever powers that be that the guards had neglected to check for concealed weapons. They must've concluded that the knife that had sent Sam Vickers straight to hell was the only one Cale had on him.

Teeth clenched against the pain, Cale contorted his abused body to retrieve the dagger. He nicked his thumb while cutting the rope from his wrist, but he got the job done. Slicing a finger was the least of his problems at the moment.

Marshaling his strength, he fought his way to his hands and knees. The darkness in the cave teetered sideways and he cursed the dizzy sensations spinning around his head. No matter how bad he felt he was going to fight his way from this hellhole and locate Hanna. She had rainbows to chase, and he'd be damned if he'd be the reason her life was cut short. This was all his fault. It might take his last dying breath to get it done, but he'd find her and apologize for putting her through hell.

Cale inhaled a cathartic breath and focused on the images of his half brother, sister-in-law and Hanna—most especially Hanna. He'd loved them, every one, and he'd never gotten around to saying so. It had taken a few brain-scrambling blows to get his feelings in proper perspective, but he had his head on straight now—sort of.

On hands and knees, Cale crawled toward the mouth of the cave to determine the odds against him. Three to one. Okay, more realistically it was three to one-third. But if he could calculate fractions, then he still had enough mental capability to figure out how to get the hell out of here.

Cale squinted toward the three men, who were propped against the sandstone cliff, passing around a whiskey bottle. He had a toast of his own that he'd like to share with them, and it looked as if the timing was about as good as it was ever going to get. Relying on sheer will—and a body that moved sluggishly—Cale quickly devised a plan then put it into action.

The moment Otis shoveled Hanna through his front door she spun to face his leering smile. How to play this situation to her advantage? she mused. She wanted to spit in his face, claw out his eyes and hold a pistol to his head until he told her where his men were holding Cale captive. Unfortunately, her hostility wasn't going to help Cale's chances of survival. She had to make Otis let his guard down so he'd untie her.

The handy little derringer that Cale had encouraged her to strap to her thigh wouldn't do her any good until her hands were free. Worse, with Otis standing there, looking at her as if he wanted to gobble her alive, she couldn't grab the dagger tucked in her kid boot to cut herself free. She desperately needed time alone.

"Now then," Otis said as he swaggered up to trail his index finger over her cheek. "Your inconvenience of a husband is out of our way and it's time you took me up on the invitation I offered earlier." His gaze drifted to the staircase, as if she didn't understand what he implied.

"And if I promise to join you in bed, are you planning to spare my husband's life? Although you successfully managed to turn my head, my conscience forbids me from permanently disposing of the man I rashly married for no other reason than to escape my domineering father's control. I will not see Grayson McCloud die, just to ensure I'm not eternally damned for adultery. Surely you realize that I'm not quite *that* ruthless."

Otis smiled faintly as he visually undressed her with his licentious gaze. "A woman of principles. I do admire that, my dear. So what shall we do with that inconvenient husband of yours?"

"Send him away," she suggested. "After the beating your men gave him and the lack of interest I've shown the past few days I doubt he'll feel compelled to retrieve me."

"You think not?" Otis studied her dubiously. "And what of your touching display to escape me so you could run to him while he lay defeated in the street?"

Hanna knew she had to sound convincing if she was going to trick Otis into believing she posed no physical threat and had no sincere interest in Cale. "And how would it have looked to the citizens of Cromwell if I hadn't shown compassion to my husband?" she argued, looking down her nose at him as haughtily as she knew how.

Hanna could portray her father's daughter if needed. It

was easy for his words to come pouring from her mouth—
she'd certainly heard them so often that she'd memorized
them. "You see, Otis, I've discovered that nothing is quite
so important as the *perception* society has of you. Your
worth and importance are judged by that perception. My
image in town can only be redeemed if the townsfolk believe I didn't willingly abandon Grayson to enjoy the ma-
terial benefits *you* can offer that *he* cannot."

Otis frowned pensively. No doubt he was trying to decide if he believed her.

"Our liaison won't be satisfactory for either of us if you
don't realize that keeping up appearances is vitally important to me. I will not walk the streets of Cromwell and
have people looking down on me as if I'm a traitor and a
harlot who changed loyalty because you're more prosperous than my husband. You should be aware that I'm loyal
to my image as well as interested in the luxuries you can
provide. Make no mistake about that.

"Now then," she added, staring pointedly at him. "Am
I going upstairs with you willingly or are you going to
have a fight on your hands to consummate this liaison?"

Hanna had the feeling she was talking over Otis's head
and that he was having difficulty keeping up with her ra-
tionalizations and conclusions. The man's intelligence was
noticeably inferior to Cale's, she noted. She'd have to remember to use that to her advantage, too.

"Well?" she prompted when he stood there, attempting
to digest all she'd said. "Untie my hands."

"I think," he said eventually, "that I'm not going to be
hasty in deciding how loyal you are to me."

"Probably wise," she replied with a nonchalant shrug.
"I'll be testing you, too, of course. The next match I make
won't be as hasty as the first, on that you can depend. But
as I said, Grayson McCloud served his purpose well
enough."

When she twirled around, he snatched her arm and

reeled her back to him. "Where do you think you're going?"

"To see to my needs, and it would be much easier if my hands weren't tied behind my back. I trust you have accommodations upstairs?"

He studied her indecisively. "I don't think I trust you, my dear Hanna."

"And I'm beginning to wonder if I didn't make an error in judgment by trading my husband for you. Perhaps I let your wealth and influence in Cromwell sway me too hastily. Is there someone else around here who approaches your power and position? Perhaps I should look further before I decide where to place my allegiance."

"No," he said fiercely. "You're going to belong to me."

She sniffed superciliously. "Then give me good reason to stay, Otis. And *please* make it something besides a tumble in bed. From past experience I've discovered that most men aren't exceptionally good lovers. That leaves only the promise of wealth and influential position that commands respect and ensures preferential treatment."

Hanna bit back a wicked grin when Otis puffed up in indignation. Criticizing a man's skills in the boudoir was obviously the quickest way to offend him.

"If you haven't been satisfied in bed then you've obviously been sleeping with the wrong men, Hanna," he insisted arrogantly.

Ah good, she'd definitely trounced on his male pride. She'd turn that against him, too. "Well, that remains to be seen. Now are you going to untie me or must I perform acrobatics to see to my needs?"

After a moment he strode behind her to untie her hands, then breathed down her neck. "Give me only one reason to distrust you, my dear, and I'll make you damn sorry."

"*Dreadfully* sorry," she corrected flippantly. "Your manners need some work, Otis. A gentleman doesn't swear in the presence of a lady. I've had to give the same lesson to my husband.''

"You're not quite the woman I first thought you were," he said, appraising her carefully.

"You aren't the charming gentleman you led me to believe you were, either. I guess that makes us even," she countered as she rubbed her wrists to revive the circulation in her hands. "Now, I need a moment of privacy. I don't have to go outside to find it, do I?''

He gestured toward the stairs without taking his eyes off her. "I'll be up to join you in a few minutes."

The comment hung heavily in the air and Hanna battled to keep her repulsion from showing. "I hope it will be pleasant. I've had my fill of a man whose only concern was to satisfy his own needs." With that, Hanna sauntered toward the stairs, ensuring she had his undivided attention. Otis, she vowed, wasn't going to get the reception he anticipated. She turned on the landing to stare quizzically at him. "Which way to our room?''

"Second door on the left," he told her, flashing a lecherous grin. "I took the liberty of buying you lingerie to celebrate our first evening together.''

She arched her brow and made herself return his smile. "Ah, my first gift from you. Thank you, Otis. It's a start, but I'll be expecting more.''

Hanna forced herself to walk regally up the remainder of the steps rather than making a mad dash to the bedroom to lock and barricade the door. She'd picked a battle she thought she might be able to win. Now she had to find a way to catch Otis off guard and use him as her pawn and hostage.

Once inside the room, Hanna sagged against the door, then dragged in a steadying breath. It was the first time in her life that she wanted to thank her father for his arrogance and his habit of bowling over individuals to ensure his will was done. She hadn't asked for Otis's cooperation, she'd demanded it, as if it were her natural-born right.

*Think!* Hanna railed silently. She had only a few minutes to decide how to handle Otis and devise a way to get past the armed guards posted around the house.

Her gaze swung to the bed, which had been turned down in preparation for Otis's seductive tryst. She frowned disapprovingly when she spied the skimpy red corset that looked as if it had been designed for a madam in a house of ill repute. Indecent though the garment was, Hanna decided that stuffing herself into it would serve to keep Otis distracted.

This was definitely the site of another battle she could win. Her armor might be no more than lacy lingerie, but she'd have a dagger in her boot and a derringer tucked behind her back when Otis walked in—with other things on his mind besides defending himself against her. The tables were definitely going to turn, she promised herself fiercely.

Hurriedly, Hanna peeled off her respectable satin gown and wormed into the skintight corset that was cut so low her breasts all but spilled from the bloodred lace. The garment hugged her waist like a second skin and barely covered her hips. Pleated ruffles that rode indecently high on her thighs adorned the seductive getup. Although her sense of modesty objected, Hanna was desperate and determined. At least she didn't have to disrobe for that disgusting bastard, she consoled herself.

A sense of panic threatened her composure when she heard footfalls in the hall. She had to act calm and self-assured. She *had* to outsmart Otis, because Cale's life hung in the balance.

Julius had to give Skeet credit. The poor beast belonged in an animal infirmary, but he hobbled and whimpered through the two-mile jaunt to Pryor's ranch. Arliss Fenton used the time to fill Julius and Pierce in on the criminal activity in Cromwell. Julius didn't have a clue what Cale's or Hanna's interest was in Pryor. But the bastard had sure 'nuff invited Julius's and Pierce's wrath by preying on the newlyweds.

As for the Pinkertons, they were unusually quiet. Licking their wounds, no doubt. Walter Malloy was still dressing them down, and then threatening to see them dismissed from their positions at the agency.

Julius couldn't let that one alone. Grinning devilishly, he glanced over his shoulder and said, "If you boys lose your cushy jobs I'll put in a good word for you to Judge Parker. Pay's lousy. Accommodations stink. But you don't have to get trussed up in those dapper suits and prissy hats to chase criminals."

Having been stripped of their arrogance and dignity, thanks to Malloy's verbal thrashing, the agents actually grinned at Julius's taunt. Well hell, he was starting to like these Pinkertons.

Julius's thoughts trailed off and he became instantly alert when he heard the sound of a horse scrabbling down the slope. In the darkness he couldn't spot a mount or rider, but he drew his pistol, just to be on the safe side.

Ordinarily, Skeet was quick to growl or snarl a warning, but the poor mutt just hobbled torturously along the narrow path.

"There are caves up ahead," Arliss murmured quietly. "Maybe that's where Pryor stashed Cale."

"I don't know why we're wasting precious time looking for that worthless half-breed when my daughter's life is in perilous danger," Walter grumbled. "If she isn't up here I'll never let you Pinkertons hear the end of it."

Julius was pretty sure Malloy wasn't going to let *anybody* hear the end of *anything*. But despite Malloy's annoying qualities, it was obvious that he was desperate to have his daughter back.

"Wait here," Pierce murmured when he spotted a dark crevice in the sandstone cliff.

With both his pistols drawn and cocked, Pierce inched toward the cave, then disappeared inside. Julius's shoulders slumped in disappointment when Pierce didn't fire a single shot. A moment later, the deputy stepped outside and stared down the hill toward the ranch house.

"Well?" Walter Malloy demanded impatiently.

Pierce returned to his horse and mounted up. "From the look of things, Cale was here and gone."

"And how can you tell that?" Walter asked, then smirked. "Leave you a note, did he?"

Pierce stared down the cocky gent. "No, sir, but you can add three more to the head count of men who tangled with Marshal Elliot—and lost. That's eight so far."

"But I saw him in the street," Arliss choked out. "Pryor's men nearly beat him to a pulp and shot him. How could he possibly have managed to take down three more men in his condition?"

Julius reined his horse around and took great satisfaction in saying, "We don't call Cale Elliot the last man standing for nothing. The devil himself would think twice about taking him on half-dead." Julius fixed his somber gaze on Walter Malloy. "Sir, in between your ranting and raving, you might ought to send up a prayer of thanks that Cale Elliot is on your daughter's side."

"Yes, well…" Walter shifted in the saddle, clearly unwilling to give an inch. He frowned curiously as he stared into the distance. "Now where's that mangled mutt headed?"

"My guess is the house," Pierce answered grimly. "If that's where Skeet's headed then that's where Cale's headed, which means that's probably where Hanna is being held."

"Then what the blazes are we waiting for?" Walter demanded. "You Pinkertons get down there and earn your wages. I want my daughter back!"

Agent Sykes tilted his head toward the silhouettes of guards that patrolled the house. "That fortress is heavily protected, Mr. Malloy."

"I don't care how many men are standing guard. I have to find my daughter!" Walter wheeled his horse around and clattered downhill.

Pierce glanced grimly at Julius as the procession headed toward the ranch house. Julius had the twitchy feeling that all hell was about to break loose, and he prayed nonstop that Hanna wouldn't be caught in the middle. Walter Malloy would see to it that heads rolled if his daughter came to harm.

# Chapter Seventeen

When the door swung open Hanna struck a seductive pose on the far side of the bedroom. She forced herself to smile invitingly as Otis's gaze ran over her in lusty approval.

"You were definitely worth the wait," he purred as he shed his brocade vest and unbuttoned his shirt.

"More importantly," she said, "I hope you won't prove to be the same disappointment my husband was. I found his impatience tiresome."

Hanna watched Otis cast aside his shirt, and found herself comparing the man's chest to Cale's. There was no contest. Even if Otis wasn't a treacherous murderer he wouldn't have appealed to Hanna, because she had eyes for only one man—and he desperately needed her help.

When Otis reached down to unfasten his breeches, Hanna pulled the derringer from behind her back and aimed it directly at his private parts. "No need for that, Otis. I've had a change of heart."

His look of surprise transformed into a vicious glower. But then he smirked at the pistol she had trained on him. "And you expect me to believe you'd pull the trigger?"

"I really don't care what you believe," she told him. "I've changed my mind. Call it fickle female whim, if you wish, but it dawned on me that now you've gotten my husband out of my way, I have control over my trust fund and I don't need the security a man can provide.''

His smirk became a growl as he stalked toward her. ''We're through playing games,'' he snarled at her.

''No, we're not,'' she snapped, all pretended arrogance forgotten. ''You're going to lead me out of this house and past your guards. If you don't, then you'll be dead and I'll find my own way out—''

Suddenly Otis lunged at her, and Hanna was left with no choice but to assure him that she meant business. She squeezed the trigger and fired at his thigh, knowing she'd alert the guards and would soon have another fight on her hands.

''You little bitch!'' Otis yelped as he grabbed his wounded leg.

He tried to backhand her, but Hanna bounded over the bed and dashed from the room. She could hear Otis spewing profanity as he gave chase on his injured leg. Hanna flew down the steps, hoping against hope that she could reach the shotgun Otis kept in the gun case beside the front door before his guards barreled into the house.

She thanked her lucky stars that Otis had locked the front door when they'd arrived. It was all that kept the guards from bursting inside and apprehending her before she could grab the shotgun and ensure it was loaded. She glanced back to see Otis hobbling down the steps, a pistol clamped in his hand. Hurriedly, she swung the shotgun toward him and took his measure.

Stalemate.

Glass shattered as the door burst open and five armed men charged inside.

''Shoot her!'' Otis roared furiously.

''Not a good idea.''

Hanna gasped in surprise when she heard Cale's gravelly voice coming from the head of the steps. She nearly dropped the shotgun when she saw him leaning heavily on the banister. One eye was completely swollen shut. The other one wasn't much better. The sleeve of his jacket was stained with blood and he was covered with dirt. How he managed to hold himself upright was completely beyond Hanna. But the rifle in his hand never wavered from its target—the back of Otis's head.

Damn the man! Hanna silently fumed. He knew his sudden appearance would draw the guards' attention away from her. The five rifles that had zeroed in on her immediately swung toward Cale. Meanwhile, Hanna held Otis at gunpoint, while he aimed the pistol at her chest. Sweet mercy! She didn't see how any of them were going to get out of here alive when bullets and buckshot started flying.

"Mags, if even one of those guards so much as looks as if he's about to fire, I want you to blow Pryor's head off," Cale ordered. "Whatever else happens, he's going to die first. Understand?"

"Absolutely," she confirmed.

"Shoot her—" Otis screeched furiously.

"Better not," Cale interrupted. "Then I'll be the one who blows your head off. Like I said, Otis, no matter what else goes down, you're a dead man. That's a promise."

Hanna heard a familiar growl and a startled yelp that indicated Skeet had arrived on the scene. His unsuspecting victim—the guard who stood in the doorway—slammed into the gunman beside him. It was all the distraction Cale needed to leap down the steps and plow into Otis. When Cale hammered the butt of his rifle against Otis's skull, the rancher slumped on the floor.

Hanna swung her shotgun toward the guards, who'd been distracted by Skeet's attack. The sound of approaching riders sent the gunmen racing outside—undoubtedly anticipating that their cohorts had arrived to lend support. The thought of more gunmen arriving sent Hanna into panic. Once they had regrouped, she fully expected them to lay siege to the house.

Her alarmed gaze flew to Cale when he tried to stagger to his feet. She dashed frantically toward him to lend support, knowing that he needed immediate medical attention—not another battle against overpowering odds with thugs cannoning through the front door.

Hanna braced herself to hoist Cale upright. He sagged so heavily against her that she feared they'd both topple to the floor. She leaned against the balustrade and kept her shotgun trained on the open door, anticipating a firefight any second.

Two shots erupted outside and Cale clutched her shoulder. "Back door," he said through clenched teeth. "Get the hell out of here, Mags."

"Not without you." She wrapped her free arm around his waist to shove him ahead of her.

"Damn it, Mags, do what I tell you," he growled at her.

"Damn it, Cale, do what I tell *you*," she snapped back at him. "I—"

Too late, Hanna realized Otis had regained consciousness and closed his hand around the pistol that lay at his fingertips. Cale tried to react swiftly, but he'd had to use his rifle as a makeshift crutch to hold himself upright. Hanna couldn't bring her shotgun into firing position—one-handed—in time to get off a shot.

"No!" she shrieked when Cale shifted to shield her with his body.

Skeet tried to pounce, but Otis got off a shot before the dog went for his throat. Hanna screeched in terror when Cale swayed on his feet, then staggered toward Otis.

Jaws clamped around Otis's neck, and Skeet refused to let go, even when Otis turned the pistol on him. Cale dived toward man and dog, knocking Otis's arm sideways to misdirect the bullet, which slammed into the wall. Cale jerked the weapon from Otis's grasp.

"You're under arrest, you son of a bitch. You murdered Gray Cloud and his wife five years ago. He was my brother," Cale growled in pained breaths. "I'm Cale Elliot, and Judge Parker is going to hang you high."

Otis's eyes widened in recognition of Cale's legendary reputation as he lay pinned beneath Skeet's powerful jaws. Then Cale teetered sideways and passed out, knocking Skeet to the floor. Otis heaved himself up to grab the pistol in Cale's hand.

In a flash, Hanna pounced on Otis. She pounded the butt of the shotgun against his temple while tears of fury and despair streamed down her cheeks. Otis tried to go for her throat, but he only managed to rip the locket from her neck. Her talisman skidded across the floor to land beside Cale's shoulder.

"Good gawd!" Walter Malloy yelped as he barreled into the house on Julius's and Pierce's heels.

The last person Hanna expected—or wanted—to see in the middle of this showdown was her father. But there he was, gaping at her in disbelief while, garbed in her scanty red garment, she pounded on Otis venting her anguish.

She wanted to crawl over to Cale and determine his condition, but she was worried that he might have died to protect her, just as he'd promised he'd do—if need be—when they'd struck off on this overland journey.

Her heart caved in at the prospect of losing Cale forever, and she collapsed beside Skeet in a sobbing heap. The dog whined and sank gingerly beside her, as if to offer consolation. Her heart told her to dash to Cale's side. But her head warned her that if she examined his injuries and found them fatal she'd have to deal with the horrendous grief of losing him.

Despite her torment, she forced herself to crawl to Cale and check his pulse. He was alive, thank goodness. But he'd taken another shot in the arm. She tore a piece of fabric from his shirt to wrap around the wound.

"For God's sake, girl!" Walter roared. "Put some clothes over that obscene getup! I'm appalled that your worthless husband has you dressing like a second-rate prostitute!"

Hanna lifted her head and pushed her hair away from her face to glance in her father's direction. It was difficult to see him through the scalding tears in her eyes. "This wasn't my husband's idea. He definitely wouldn't approve. It was *his* idea," she said, gesturing toward Otis's sprawled form.

"Then he deserves to be shot, the lecherous scoundrel!" Walter huffed.

"I already shot him once," Hanna sobbed.

"Well," Walter huffed, glowering at Otis's unconscious form. "Someone should shoot him again!"

When Julius limped over to assist Hanna to her feet, she threw her arms around his neck and held on for dear life. In the aftermath of one traumatic incident after another, Hanna's composure disintegrated. She cried on Julius's shoulder while he patted her comfortingly. It didn't escape her that she'd gone to Julius instead of her father for consolation. Neither did it escape her that Walter had arrived to drag her back to New Orleans to pawn her off on Louis Beauchamp—of the titled pedigree Beauchamps of France. The despairing thought provoked another round of sobs that were surely soaking the collar of Julius's shirt.

"Mags?"

Hanna went stock-still, then peered around Julius's shoulder. Relieved that Cale had regained consciousness, she sank to her knees beside him. "You shouldn't have taken that bullet for me—" Her voice broke when his hand folded weakly over her trembling fingertips.

"The next time I tell you to get out while the getting's

good you goddamn better not disobey me," he wheezed hoarsely.

Carefully, she eased him to his back and cupped his bruised and swollen face in her hands. He stared at her with a steely one-eyed squint. "Okay," she murmured brokenly. "Maybe. Depends on whether you're coming with me or staying to fight."

"Hey, you Pinkertons," Pierce called out when the three agents came through the door—after capturing and restraining Pryor's men. "Make yourselves useful and help me get Cale upstairs to bed. He took another shot in the arm and needs to be patched up. Any of you know a damn thing about doctoring?"

"I do," Agent Sykes replied.

"Good," Pierce said. "Usually it's the Chief who patches everyone else up."

The men formed a circle around Cale, waiting impatiently for Hanna to release him—which she didn't look interested in doing any time soon.

"Ma'am," Agent Sykes prompted. "We really need to check his wounds. He's lost a lot of blood."

Reluctantly Hanna withdrew. She picked up her locket and tucked it in Cale's hand. The locket had given her inner strength and moral support when she needed it, and she prayed the symbolic love surrounding the heirloom locket would protect Cale.

She knew she was personally responsible for bringing him pain and agony, and she longed to beg his forgiveness. But Pierce and the Pinkertons were waiting to carry Cale away, leaving her to deal with her father. Not a pleasant prospect.

Hanna drew herself up with dignity—as much dignity as she could muster when dressed like a parlor madam who entertained men for a living. Resolutely, she turned to confront her father, who looked weary, bewildered and angry all at once.

"I'm not going home with you," she told him flat out.

He just kept staring at her with an odd look on his face that she couldn't decipher.

"I mean it, Father. I love my husband and I'm staying here," Hanna insisted, swiping at her tears.

Julius glanced up from where he'd crouched—injured leg outstretched—to bind up Otis's wrists and ankles. He tossed Hanna a wink and an encouraging grin. "Damn straight she loves her husband, Malloy. It looks as if you owe Cale Elliot your daughter's life. Told ya they didn't come any better than him."

Pierce appeared at the top of the staircase. "Hanna, Cale is asking for you."

Hanna bounded toward the steps. "Father, give Julius a hand in dragging Otis outside."

Walter blinked, startled.

"Right now," she demanded. "There are criminals to be locked in jail and a townful of citizens to be reassured that their lives can finally return to normal. Now make yourself useful."

She didn't look back, but heard her father sputtering and Julius snickering. It was time her father realized that Hanna had become her own woman—if he hadn't figured that out already. Furthermore, it would take an act of God, plus an act of Congress, to convince her to return to New Orleans. She'd outgrown the restrictions of polite society, outgrown Walter's attempt to stifle her independent spirit. She'd been to hell and back tonight and she'd been purged by fire. And by damned, no one could stop her from living up to her potential now!

Cale winced in pain when Agent Sykes dug the bullet from the meaty flesh of his left arm. Pierce had poured whiskey down Cale's gullet in preparation for primitive surgery, but it still hurt like a son of a bitch. Cale willed himself to remain conscious long enough to speak to

Hanna. He wanted her gone from here—first thing in the morning. They'd made a deal and she was free to leave.

And he was *never* going to forgive himself for nearly getting her molested and murdered!

He hadn't been in all that good a shape to begin with, and damn it, he'd nearly suffered a seizure when he'd looked down the steps to see Hanna squared off against Otis and his gunmen, wearing that wildly provocative red corset that was the devil's own distraction.

"Hurry it up, Sykes. I don't have all night," Cale said through gritted teeth.

Sykes nodded mutely as he retrieved the bullet and then swabbed the wound with whiskey.

Despite the burning pain pulsing in his arm, Cale knew the exact instant that Hanna stepped into the room. Her presence was as palpable to him as the wind. He wanted these men gone so he could speak privately with her. Plus he didn't want the men gawking at her in that body-hugging red garment that advertised her every swell and curve to its best advantage.

"Give Hanna your jacket," Cale told Agent Williams. "And then get out." He didn't have to portray the gentleman anymore and he didn't feel up to pleasantries. If he offended the Pinkertons that was just too damn bad.

As soon as Agent Sykes bandaged Cale's arm, the men cleared out. Cale squinted up at Hanna's alluring image. He would've smiled in masculine appreciation if his face hadn't been so sore and swollen. She looked incredibly beautiful, even with her hair tumbling in disarray and that oversize jacket hitting her at midthigh.

Although she'd assured her father that Cale would disapprove of this seductive getup, Cale had felt the jolt of awareness the moment he'd seen her in it—and so, he suspected, had the gunmen who'd been ordered to shoot her. In fact, that saucy getup could very well have saved her life.

He'd been so proud of Hanna when she'd taken on those criminals so courageously—though it went without saying that she'd scared him half to death when she did it. But she was really something. She wasn't the same woman who'd come to call on him in Fort Smith. She'd tested her weaknesses and fortified her strength of character since then. Hers had been a journey of self-examination and self-discovery and she'd come out shining like the brightest star in the galaxy. Damn, he was going to miss her something terrible when she left.

And now that he knew he was going to survive this ordeal he decided *not* to confess his feelings for her. He'd considered it during a moment of weakness and desperation—when faced with the likelihood of dying. But now that he'd survived and had given the matter further consideration, he knew it would be easier to say goodbye without those three words standing between them and complicating her departure.

Plus, while he'd been lurking outside the bedroom window, trying to muster the energy to burst inside to overtake Otis, he'd heard Hanna tell Otis that Cale was too impatient in the heat of passion and that he'd only served her purpose temporarily. He wanted to believe that she'd only said those things for Otis's benefit, but he couldn't quite convince himself of that.

All things considered, it was best for Cale to let Hanna go so she could follow her long-awaited dreams.

"Agent Sykes thinks you'll be fine after you've had time to rest and recuperate," Hanna said as she carefully eased down on the side of the bed. She leaned over to press a kiss to the one place on his forehead that wasn't bruised. "I'm so pleased that you could keep your vow of bringing your family's killer to justice. Thanks to you, Otis will never hurt another living soul again."

"Without your help I couldn't have gotten close to Pryor. Thanks, Magnolia," he rasped.

She smiled radiantly at him and he nearly went blind. "You're more than welcome, Cale." Her smile suddenly fizzled out and she blinked rapidly to stifle the tears that swam in her eyes. "But if not for me, you wouldn't have been beaten and shot. This is all my fault and I'm so terribly sorry!"

Despite her best efforts, tears dribbled down her cheeks. Cale reached over to wipe them away with the pad of his thumb. "No, it was *my* fault you nearly got killed in that showdown," he contradicted. "I'm the one who's sorry."

Grimacing, he reached for the stage ticket he'd tucked in the pocket of his trousers, then handed it to Hanna. "I have one more promise to keep," he whispered raggedly. "I'm setting you free, with my gratitude for your assistance. This is a ticket all the way to California, if that's how far you want to go. Now you can go wherever you want and do whatever your heart desires. Have a good life, Magnolia Blossom. You've more than earned it."

She looked at him as though he'd backhanded her. "That's it? After all we've been through together, all you have to say is thanks for the help and have a good life?"

"What do you want me to say?" He couldn't blurt out that he loved her so much it was killing him to let her go. He was *not* going to say it. She did not need to know that. He wasn't the kind of man she needed or deserved, and he cared too much about her to allow her to settle for less than the best.

"I'd feel better if you said you'd miss me," she muttered, staring at the far wall rather than at him.

"I'll miss you," he acknowledged.

She bolted off the bed as if she'd been sitting on a scorpion, then turned her back on him. His gaze drifted over the bare curve of her legs, and Cale found himself wishing… Well, there was no sense wishing that he could make love with her one last time because that wasn't possible after he'd had the hell beaten out of him. Not to mention being plugged in the arm by bullets.

"Take care of yourself, Mags," he whispered, aching to reach out to touch her, but knowing that would make their parting even more difficult for him.

"You, too, Cale." She stared at the stage ticket in her hand, then glanced over her shoulder at him. Tears glistened in her violet eyes—each teardrop like a spike driven into his empty heart. "If you decide to marry in the future, contact my attorney, Benjamin Caldwell, in New Orleans. I'll make certain he knows where I can be reached."

"Same goes, Mags. Send your message to Fort Smith, in care of Judge Parker." Cale held out his hand to her. "Here, take your locket."

She shook her head and a few more silver-blond tendrils tumbled around her shoulders. "You keep my good-luck charm, Cale. It's my parting gift to you."

And then she was gone and he heard her choked sobs wafting back to him as she dashed down the hall.

Cale flicked open the locket—and stopped breathing. My God! He couldn't bear to stare at that tiny portrait. It hurt more than being shot and taking a thrashing. Swearing, he snapped the locket shut, closed his good eye and shifted gingerly on the bed to find a more comfortable position.

Five minutes later his good eye popped open when an epiphany hit him like a fist in the face—and he knew exactly what *that* felt like. Cale levered himself up on his elbow, then pushed himself upright on the edge of the bed. He glanced down to see Skeet sprawled on the floor, looking as bad as Cale felt.

"Julius? Pierce?" he called out.

A moment later Arliss Fenton poked his head around the doorjamb. "Julius and Pierce took the prisoners to town," he reported. "I volunteered to stay here in case you needed me."

"I need a horse. A carriage would be better," Cale said.

Arliss gaped at him. "You can't be serious!"

"Damn serious," he insisted.

"You've been beaten and shot and you need to rest," Arliss reminded him.

"I'll rest when I'm dead," Cale snapped crankily.

"You *will* be dead if you don't rest," Arliss countered, frowning disapprovingly.

Cale met the young man's unyielding stare. "You can either help me outside or watch me get there by myself."

When Cale surged onto his wobbly legs, Arliss rushed forward to lend support. Despite Arliss's objections—and he had plenty of them—Cale staggered down the steps. He clung to the balustrade to take a needed breather while Arliss brought the carriage up to the front porch.

With the young man's begrudging assistance, Cale clambered into the vehicle, waited for Skeet to join him and then sprawled on the seat during the ride to town. He had one more piece of business to conduct before Hanna caught the morning stage. By damned, nothing was going to stand in the way of the pursuit of Hanna's hopes and dreams.

Walter Malloy bolted straight up in his hotel room bed when the door suddenly banged against the wall. A hulking silhouette, almost larger than life, filled the entrance.

"Light the lantern, Malloy. We're gonna talk."

It was that blasted bounty hunter, Walter mused as he begrudgingly obeyed the growled request. The man had been shot down and beaten up, yet he just kept coming. Although Walter didn't approve of this marriage between Cale Elliot and Hanna, he couldn't help but admire the man's determination and fortitude. If nothing else, Walter was beyond grateful that Elliot possessed the selfless courage to step in front of a speeding bullet to save Hanna's life.

When golden light flickered across the room, Walter peered at the battered bounty hunter and said, "Ten thousand dollars to divorce my daughter. I'll handle the paperwork."

Elliot had the audacity to laugh right in Walter's face. "You're a real piece of work, Malloy."

"Same goes for you, Elliot." Walter watched Cale shuffle across the room to park himself, uninvited, in the chair. "What do you want? I'm tired and it's been a harrowing night. If you had a lick of sense left after having your head bashed in you'd be in bed, too."

"While we're waiting for Arliss to fetch Hanna I want you to know—and I'm only going to say this once, Malloy—that if you do anything to prevent Hanna from heading west tomorrow to follow her own dreams, I'll be all over you like a bad rash. If she ain't happy, then I ain't happy. Remember that," he said ominously.

"Twenty thousand dollars," Walter stated, without batting an eye.

"You can go straight to hell and take your money with you," Cale growled at him.

Walter glanced up when Hanna, dressed in a conservative calico gown, ambled into the room. It was obvious that she'd been crying because her eyes were red and puffy. No doubt the aftermath of her horrendous ordeal had caught up with her, and she'd come crashing down from the emotional tidal wave she'd been riding.

Hanna's curious gaze bounced from Walter to Cale. "What's going on?"

"We have one more thing to get squared away before you leave town, Mags." Cale reached into his pocket to retrieve the gold locket, then tossed it to Walter. "Open it." When Walter merely clutched it tightly in his fist and glowered defiantly, Cale repeated the curt command. "I said open it."

While Hanna stared quizzically at him, Cale focused on

the bleak expression that suddenly claimed Malloy's wrinkled features. And, just like that, Cale's suspicions were confirmed. "It's time to tell Hanna why you've pushed her away from you these past few years. It's time to explain why looking at her is so difficult for you. Go on, tell her, Malloy, or I'll do it for you."

"Cale, please—" Hanna tried to object.

Cale held up his hand, demanding her silence. He kept his piercing gaze fixed on Malloy. The color drained from the older man's face and his shoulders slumped. But, damn the man, he refused to admit why he couldn't bear to do more than spare his bewitching daughter a passing glance. Well, fine; Cale would take care of the matter himself.

"Mags, do you remember me telling you that my own mother sent me away because I was a daily reminder of the nightmare that brought me into the world? She couldn't look at me without seeing the man who molested her."

Hanna nodded. "I remember, but I fail to see—"

"We have more in common than I thought," Cale interrupted as he stared Malloy down. "In your case, I think looking at you and seeing the spitting image of your mother was painful for an entirely different reason. Wasn't it, Malloy?"

The reason for the rift between father and daughter had become vividly clear to Cale an hour earlier, when he'd opened the locket to see Hanna's startling likeness staring back at him. The sight of the delicate, fair-haired woman standing beside a young boy had hit Cale like a body blow and had robbed him of breath. He'd been staring at Clarissa Malloy, but all Cale had been able to see was Hanna. No doubt Walter had been tormented the same way, only in reverse.

Malloy's head dropped, his chin resting on his chest. He squeezed the locket in his fist and after a long moment nodded his head. "I loved her so much," he whispered on a hitched breath. "She was my life. With each passing year, Hanna, you became more like your mother when I looked at you. You already had her delicate features, her smile and her eyes. You blossomed into the beautiful young woman that Clarissa had been. It was a painful reminder of what I'd lost. Every day of my empty life was staring back at me. I wanted to mold you into her. She was so delicate, refined, soft-spoken and gentle. She was the contrasting half of my soul that made me a better man. Without her…''

His voice shattered as he lifted misty eyes to Hanna. "I'm sorry, child. I had no right to try to make you into someone you're not, for my own personal whim. When I saw you tonight, every inch a bold, courageous woman facing dangerous odds, I finally saw you for who you are and what you're meant to be. Someone very different from your mother. But every bit as exceptional in your own right.''

"Oh, Papa." Hanna was in his arms in a flash, holding him to her, and Malloy was clutching her desperately, his eyes glistening with tears of regret. "If you'd only told me what there was about me that tormented you so much I would have understood.''

Cale swallowed the lump in his throat and reminded himself that sentimentality had no place in the hellish world where he resided. Unnoticed, he rose from the chair to take his leave. He didn't need to hang around during this tearful reconciliation that had been so long in coming. Father and daughter needed time alone, and he needed to be horizontal in a bed. The energy and strength he'd drawn on to make the trip into town was rapidly abandoning him, and standing upright was becoming an arduous chore.

When Cale stepped into the hall to prop himself wearily against the wall, Arliss was there to lend a supporting arm. "That was a nice thing you did.'' He guided Cale down the hall to a vacant room. "I took the liberty of renting a room, because you definitely need to rest…right now.''

Cale couldn't argue with that. He was totally exhausted and he hurt all over. Even worse, he had this hollow, empty feeling in his heart. He knew that—like Walter Malloy, who used bluff and bluster to counter a love that continued to haunt him—*he* was doomed to the same tormenting fate. He loved Hanna so much he ached with it. He'd taken a bullet for her. He would have died for her if it had come to that. He wanted to ensure that all her dreams came true, even if those dreams didn't include him.

With Arliss's help Cale shed his shirt and stretched out in bed. He was asleep in less than three minutes. But sometime during the night he felt moisture on his lips and tongue, and reflexively swallowed. He thought he caught a whiff of Hanna's unique scent and felt a featherlight kiss skimming his brow. Or maybe it was just a lifelike fantasy swirling around him. He couldn't be sure. But he was certain that same fantasy would remain with him all the lonely days of his life.

# Chapter Eighteen

"Well, Papa? What do you think?" From atop the wagon seat, Hanna smiled admiringly at the ranch house that had become her new home.

"Are you sure this is what you want?" Walter asked as he critically surveyed the valley. "This is definitely *not* New Orleans. It's the middle of nowhere."

"I don't want New Orleans," she countered, then smiled indulgently at him.

Ah, what a difference three days had made in her relationship with her father. They'd come to an understanding once she'd realized why he'd kept an emotional distance between them the past few years. It touched her deeply that her father harbored such strong, unfaltering affection for Clarissa. For all his bombastic bluster Walter Malloy was a passionate man who loved deeply and had turned to business to fill the empty gap in his life.

*And isn't that what you're doing, too?* Hanna asked herself. She was looking for a place to transfer her unrequited love for Cale. She was searching for another purpose in her life. This recently abandoned ranch near Cromwell was going to be the place where she could make a difference. It wasn't so far away from New Orleans that she and her father couldn't visit one another regularly, and she could find plenty of noble causes to support in Cromwell.

Two days earlier, Hanna had asked Arliss to send a telegram to the son of the former owners of the ranch that Pryor had overtaken. Yesterday, Hanna had received word that the ranch was hers for the generous purchase price she'd offered. She had every intention of making something honest and good from this place that had become the devil's playground.

In addition, she'd purchased the gun shop property from Arliss and intended to oversee the business—with the help of an assistant. Weaponry, after all, appeared to be her hidden talent. She'd become something of a heroine, an inspiration to the other women in town, after her participation in the battle that had brought an end to Pryor's reign of terror.

Cromwell was going to become Hanna's new hometown, and she knew she needed to look no further to find her niche in this world.

"This place will need considerable work," Walter commented. "That furniture has got to go. I'll have the proper furnishings delivered after I return to New Orleans."

When Hanna tossed him a warning glance, he blew out a breath. "Oh all right, do it your way," he said, relenting.

She leaned over to press a kiss to his cheek. "Thank you, Papa. I'm glad you're beginning to realize that I'm in control of my life these days."

"And I'm stuck with the annoying task of informing Louis Beauchamp that you don't want to marry him." Walter rubbed his temples and scowled. "The mere prospect of listening to him issue more threats gives me a headache."

"I've no doubt that you can handle that pompous aristocrat," she said confidently. "You've managed to handle everyone else."

"Except you and that fire-breathing husband of yours," he grumbled. "Just what *are* you going to do about him?"

The question wiped the teasing smile off Hanna's lips. She stared into the distance, trying to compose herself, trying not to let her hurt and longing show.

"You already admitted that you're in love with that big brute," Walter reminded her. "What are you going to do about it?"

"We had a bargain and we both kept our end of it," Hanna said as she guided the wagon of supplies to her new home.

"And you're not your father's daughter if you're going to give up what you want that easily," Walter declared. "*Bribe* the man to stay. It works for me."

Hanna chuckled and her father grinned playfully.

"And furthermore," Walter continued, "how am I going to get grandchildren to spoil and pamper if you're *married* without actually *being* married in the true sense of the word?"

The prospect of never having children of her own to love caused Hanna's smile to wobble. The vision of a son with coal-black hair and eyes the color of midnight leaped to mind. Well, not all dreams were meant to come true, she reminded herself. She'd have to settle for making a home on this ranch and overseeing the gun shop.

"I suppose I could offer to pay the man to get you with child, in between his forays in Indian Territory," Walter said.

"Papa!" Hanna gaped at him, scandalized.

"Oh, for heaven sake, don't look at me like that," Walter grumbled. "The man will obviously do anything you ask of him. You've kept him drugged with laudanum for three days so he'll stay off his feet long enough to recover from the bullet he took for you. I can't imagine that sleeping with a beautiful woman who is legally his wife would be an appalling imposition."

"We will have no more discussion on the subject," Hanna declared as she brought the wagon to a halt beside the front porch. "You promised to help me stock the house, not overrun my life. I'm holding you to that promise."

Although Walter mumbled and grumbled and objected to the fact that Hanna hadn't hired someone to tackle the task of moving into the house, he toted one box after another inside.

Hanna was relieved that her father had dropped the sensitive subject of her husband and their permanent separation. She desperately needed time to accept the fact that Cale wanted no future with her.

Cale Elliot didn't love her. He was an honest man and he would have said so in plain English if he did. She'd always been able to count on Cale to be truthful with her.

She, like her father, obviously fell in love only once, and nothing could alter or diminish those soul-deep feelings. Well, at least her father had had several years with Clarissa. Unfortunately, Hanna had been granted only a little more than a month with Cale. Maybe their short time together would make forgetting him easier—but she had serious doubts about that.

Hanna drew a steadying breath and glanced around her new home on the outskirts of civilization. She was committed to making this ranch prosper and bringing about improvement in Cromwell. This was her life now and she would fill it with newfound friends, noble causes and community activities. She'd find dozens of projects to occupy her days and nights after the one great love of her life recovered from his injuries and rode away to resume his duties for Parker.

Cale would take her heart with him when he left. She couldn't imagine how she would function without it. Without *him.*

* * *

Cale groaned as he came slowly awake. His lashes fluttered up and he was pleased to note that both eyelids were functioning normally. Damn, what an amazing difference one night's sleep had made! He glanced at his arm to note a fresh bandage had been applied to the gunshot wound. A pasty salve covered the nick left by the first bullet he hadn't quite dodged during the fiasco in the street.

He glanced toward the blaring light that shone in the window and felt a huge sense of loss settle over him. He knew Hanna was long gone and he'd never see her again. The thought caused a knot to coil in his growling belly.

Cale knew he'd done the right thing by letting Hanna go, but he missed her like crazy already. Well, he'd just have to keep himself occupied. He'd haul Pryor and company to Fort Smith, then he'd head out with another pocketful of bench warrants to clean up Indian Territory. That's what he did, after all. That's what he was good at. Good *for*.

The creak of the hotel room door put Cale on instant alert. He reflexively reached for his pistol, but it wasn't on his hip or under his pillow. Well, damn. If the intruder pounced, Cale would have to rely on hand-to-hand combat, and he wasn't up to that yet. His body still pulsed and ached in places he'd forgotten he had.

To his vast relief, Arliss Fenton's red head appeared around the side of the door. "Good morning," Arliss greeted him cheerfully. "I'm sending in some young lads to fill the tub so you can bathe and shave."

Cale appreciated the considerate gesture. He waited for the procession of boys to file in and out, and then he eased into the steamy tub. Feeling much better, he dressed in the clean clothes someone had laid over the back of the chair.

A few minutes later Arliss returned, carrying a breakfast tray. Cale's eyes popped when he noticed the town marshal badge pinned to Arliss's chest. "When did that happen?"

"The townsfolk appointed me as their interim marshal,"

Arliss said proudly. "Although I don't have the same hero status as you and Hanna, I was sworn in by Julius and Pierce. They claimed that, since I was the only man in town willing to stand up against Pryor, the job should be mine."

Cale stared at the badge, which had been polished to a shine. Once again it was a prestigious symbol of law and order. "The townsfolk made a wise choice."

Arliss grinned as he set the tray on Cale's lap. "Thank you. Luckily, there'll be no criminal activities now that Otis Pryor and his henchmen have been toted off to Fort Smith. I don't have to divide too much of my time between the telegraph and marshal's offices."

"What?" Cale howled in disbelief. "Who hauled off Pryor's gang? Julius and Pierce? Damn it, that was to be my job."

He needed that preoccupation to keep his mind off Hanna, so he wouldn't spend every waking hour wondering where she was, how much trouble she'd get herself into without him around to protect her, and how many men were standing in line to take his place in her bed.

"Julius and Pierce are still in town. It was the Pinkertons who volunteered to transport the prisoners to Fort Smith. They will be sending your reward money to Cromwell," the red-haired marshal said. Then he winked. "According to Julius and Pierce you're going to make a bundle on the bounties."

"I don't want the money," Cale grumbled before he dived into the crisp bacon and fluffy biscuits. Damn, he was famished. You'd think he hadn't eaten in a week.

"The reward money is yours, nonetheless," Arliss replied as he crossed his arms over his narrow chest and propped himself leisurely against the wall.

"Did you see that Hanna got on the morning stage without her father demanding that she return to New Orleans?" Cale asked. His gaze narrowed warily when Arliss shifted uneasily from one booted foot to the other. Cale slammed down his fork. "Damn it, Arliss, I only asked one favor of you."

He nodded his head. "Yes, you did, and technically I didn't renege. You said, and I quote, 'If anything happens to me, see that Hanna is on the westbound stage.'"

"Well, something *did* happen to me," Cale all but shouted in frustration. "I got the hell beaten out of me and I got shot twice last night!"

A wry grin pursed Arliss's lips and his hazel eyes twinkled. "Actually, it wasn't last night. It was six days ago."

"Six!" Cale erupted in disbelief. "I slept six days away?"

"Well yes, with the aid of the laudanum Hanna poured down your throat to make sure you stayed in bed long enough to recuperate. She also shaved and bathed you regularly and changed your bandages."

Cale muttered under his breath. His wife, Mrs. Defiance Personified, hadn't boarded the stage to chase her dreams. She'd sneaked in to sedate him the same way he'd sedated Pryor's guards. He'd created a monster when he'd taught Hanna the tricks of his trade.

"And where is my dear wife now?" Cale demanded grouchily.

Arliss scratched his chin and his lips quirked. "Can't say for certain."

"You're the new marshal. You're supposed to keep track of what's going on around here. If Hanna's father refused—"

Arliss waved his hand for silence. "No need to fret about Malloy. Last I noticed, Hanna had him marching to the beat of *her* drum."

"And where, I'd like to know, is she presently beating her new drum?" he asked irritably.

"Well, Rip van Winkle—"

"Never heard of him," Cale growled impatiently.

"Rip is a fictitious character who falls asleep for twenty years and wakes up to find that the world has changed," Arliss supplied helpfully.

Cale's gaze narrowed sourly. Arliss's cheery attitude was wasted on him. "And what has changed so drastically around here while I was drugged?"

Arliss ticked off the changes on his fingers. "First off, I'm marshal, as I mentioned. Second, Julius and Pierce recently returned from purchasing a cattle herd for Hanna."

Cale's jaw sagged on its hinges. "Hanna has decided to become a cattle baroness?"

"Uh-huh. Third, she's purchased Pryor's ranch and is keeping the gun shop. She hired an attendant, a young man desperately in need of work to support his pregnant wife. Hanna rented the living quarters above the shop to them."

Arliss stroked his chin thoughtfully. "Let's see, what else has she been up to? Oh yes, she appointed Mrs. Hensley as president of the Cromwell Beautification Club and ordered scads of flowers to decorate the boardwalks and town square. Plus she got her father to donate funds to improve the school."

"Why?" Cale asked incredulously.

"Because she's settling down here and she wants to take an active role in improving our community."

Cale was dumbfounded. Why had Hanna decided to put down roots here when her dream had been to venture west and see all there was to see and experience all that life offered?

"Oh yes, and you'll be relieved to know that Skeet is feeling much better, too," Arliss reported. "Hanna sedated him so he wouldn't be following her around like a devoted guard dog."

Hearing footsteps in the hall, Cale glanced toward the door. He nodded a curt greeting when Pierce and Julius trooped inside.

"Well, you look a damn sight better than the last time I saw you, Big Chief," Julius said, grinning. "Thought you might need assistance getting out to the ranch to settle in."

Puzzled, Cale stared at the rugged-looking deputy marshal. "Who said anything about settling in at the ranch?"

"We just assumed," Pierce commented. "After all, that's where your wife is."

"You assumed wrong. I'm headed for Fort Smith, as soon as I collect my horse, my dog and my gear."

Julius stared owl-eyed at him. "What?"

"You heard me." Cale set aside the empty tray and tested his legs. Good. They were functioning better than the last time he'd stood up on them.

"Well, I think I speak for everyone here when I say are you out of your mind?" Julius cried. "You love Hanna and she loves you. You've done your duty for Parker for years. It's time to get on with your life."

"That *is* my life," Cale countered. "It's what I do."

His colleagues didn't understand, Cale mused as he awkwardly pulled on his boots and tried not to strain his arm and ribs. Hanna had needed him to guide and tutor her, but now that she'd come into her own she didn't need to be hampered by the stigma that would always be attached to him. Sooner or later the folks in town would find out who and what he was and would avoid association with him. Besides, if he were out of the picture, some well-deserving gentleman would come along to catch Hanna's eye. Eventually she'd remarry. Cale was just a passing phase of her life, that was all.

"Well, are you at least going to tell her goodbye before you ride off?" Pierce asked.

"I already did. Last night…er, six nights ago," he corrected.

Julius stared him down. "Damn it, man, don't you realize what you're giving up?"

Of course he realized. He loved Hanna. He would always love her. And he'd always be a half-breed who'd been made to feel less than human, unacceptable and unworthy of respect in society. His only saving grace was that he was handy with firearms, knives and his fists. He could fight battles that other folks weren't capable of fighting for themselves. He'd been trained as a warrior whose only value and contribution to society was to clean up a territory where criminals ran rampant.

And what Julius said about Hanna loving him wasn't true. Sure, she'd suffered a severe case of hero worship as she tried to emulate his survival skills. She was also grateful that he'd made it possible for her to escape her father's control. And, of course, she'd gotten caught up in the newness of passion that flared between them. But all that didn't add up to love. Not the kind he felt for her, leastwise, and he couldn't settle for less, loving her the way he did.

Besides, if she really loved him, she would've said so, because she was an honest woman who meant what she said. And she *hadn't* said she loved him. Well, except for that one time that she'd been so overcome with delight when she'd discovered her aptitude for weapons. But that was just a turn of a phrase and she hadn't meant it in the literal sense.

Cale jerked to attention when the door banged open and Walter Malloy barged in uninvited and unannounced. "Leave now," he said, dismissing the other three men in the room. "I want to talk to Elliot alone."

When the men filed out, Walter peeled several large banknotes from the roll in his fist and tossed them on the bed.

Cale glared at his father-in-law. "The answer is still no way in hell, Malloy," he growled. "I intend to stay married to Hanna as long as she wishes it. There isn't enough money in the Federal Treasury to buy me off so stop wasting my time."

Walter waved him off with an expansive gesture. "Forget the divorce. I'm fine with the marriage."

Cale's mouth dropped open wide enough for a pigeon to roost. "Why? Since when?"

"Since when? Since a few days ago. Why? Because of your legendary reputation in these parts. It provides my daughter with protection. Folks realize that if they mess with Hanna they'll have to answer to you. Your name is chaperon enough."

Bumfuzzled, Cale stared at the offered money, then at Malloy. "What is it you want that you're willing to pay extravagantly to obtain?" he asked suspiciously.

"A grandchild," Malloy announced, shocking Cale speechless. "I bungled my attempts to raise Hanna and I want the chance to redeem myself. In addition, I have accumulated a fortune and I intend to see it passed down to another heir."

"You want to hire me to—" Cale felt his throat close up. Malloy had managed to take him by complete surprise.

"Exactly," the shipping magnate said in a businesslike tone. "You *are* Hanna's lawfully wedded husband, after all. It's your duty to provide me with a grandchild. I'm not getting any younger, you know, and I want you to hurry up about it."

"But I'm half—"

Malloy cut him off with an impatient flick of his wrist. "I've decided it's of no consequence to my future grandson. He'll be a quarter Cherokee, a quarter French and half mixed-heritage American. I've decided that's not a bad lineage and it will provide him with plenty of important social connections. Besides, the boy will be so disgustingly wealthy that no one would dare offend him. Well?"

"Malloy," Cale said when he finally recovered his powers of speech, "you're an arrogant, high-handed ass."

"Call the pot black, why don't you?" he retaliated sarcastically. "My daughter loves you."

So everyone kept trying to convince him, Cale mused. He still thought it was wishful thinking and an attempt at matchmaking.

"Though why she thinks she loves you is completely beyond me. It's not that she's desperate," Walter continued. "After all, she could have any man she wants. You're offensive and plain spoken—"

"Now who's calling the kettle black?" Cale interrupted just as sarcastically.

"Fine, we're both asses, but if you don't have enough sense to ride out to Hanna's ranch, a place she purchased just to keep herself occupied so she won't miss you when you leave, then maybe *I* should club you over the head myself!" Malloy bellowed. "You wrung the truth out of me when you tossed that blasted locket at me. I've been lonely and miserable for years and took it out on my own child. Now, do you love my daughter or not? And, damn it, don't you dare lie to me, Elliot."

Cale heaved an audible sigh, looked Malloy straight in the eye and said, "Yeah, I do, whether that's the best thing for her or not."

"Well, at least we agree on something." Malloy's arm shot toward the door. "But regardless, I want you to get out there and tell her how you feel or you'll end up just like me. I lost the love of my life and mourned for years. If I had it to do over again I wouldn't waste a single minute of a single day that I could have spent with Clarissa," he said earnestly. "If you love Hanna, then surely you have the courage to tell her so. You seem to have the gumption to do everything else!"

Cale wasn't so sure it was the right thing to do, and doubted Malloy fully understood the dynamics of the relationship. But maybe the man was right. Maybe Cale did owe himself a chance to chase the forbidden dream of loving and being loved in return.

Malloy opened the door. "Now, go!"

Cale strode down the hall, feeling more uncertain and unsure of himself than he ever had in his life. He'd never said those three words to anyone before, and the thought of laying his heart on the line made him feel like he was walking into a gun battle without a weapon.

Hanna loved him? Cale still couldn't make himself believe that, but he reckoned he'd just have to ride out to the ranch and find out for himself.

Hanna's gaze shifted from the three teenage boys she'd hired to erect a picket fence around the house to the lone rider who topped the rise and began his descent into the valley.

Cale… Her heart stalled in her chest and then hammered furiously against her ribs. He reminded her of a magnificent centaur, moving in perfect rhythm with his horse. His white linen shirt was a sharp contrast to his bronzed features. His black breeches clung to his muscular thighs, and staring at him took her breath away. She felt a stab of intense longing that went straight to her heart.

She'd have to guard her feelings carefully and restrain her instinctive responses when she confronted him, she warned herself. She couldn't let him know that she was slowly dying inside because he couldn't return her love.

There had been a time not so long ago Hanna had discarded all inhibition and simply been herself around him. But now there were too many conflicting emotions roiling inside her, and untangling them was impossible. She'd just have to guard her tongue and treat him as no more than a friend, not the lover she wanted to keep for the rest of her life.

Of course, Hanna doubted this was a friendly visit. More than likely Cale was riding out to rake her over the coals for sedating him. But she'd done it for his own good. Now he had the strength and stamina to race off to testify at Pryor's trial in Fort Smith.

She also recalled that the last thing Cale had said to her was "Board the stage and find your dreams." She'd defied his command, of course. She was a woman of independent means now and she'd acquired the self-confidence to stand up for what she wanted.

Hanna stood her ground when Cale rode up to her, then stared her down. She studied him pensively, then said, "You look much better. Well rested."

"Better be," he replied as he dismounted. "Somebody knocked me out with laudanum for six days and took control of my life without my permission or consent."

She hadn't thought he'd take it well.

He cut her a quick glance, then watched the boys hammer the picket boards on the new fence. "I guess that's how you felt when your father tried to tell you what to do and when you should do it. No wonder you rebelled, Magnolia. It's damn frustrating to be at someone else's mercy."

"Yes, it is," she agreed. "But after seeing you wobbling around, wounded and bleeding all over yourself, I decided you needed mandatory rest. So…" She shrugged, then glanced away, hesitant to meet his gaze for more than a moment. "Did you come to say goodbye?" *If you did then please make it quick and painless. Seeing you reminds me that some dreams aren't meant to be.*

He shifted awkwardly from one foot to the other. "Actually, I came to make sure you are happy and that this is truly where you want to be."

Hanna nodded and smiled. "I'm satisfied here."

Those probing onyx eyes bore down on her, searching for the secrets in her soul. "That's not what I asked, Mags. Are you *happy?*"

*No, because you aren't here with me and I love you like crazy, damn it!* "Of course I'm happy," she said instead. "You engineered a reconciliation with my father and my life is now my own. I have what I've always wanted. And you have what you want. Justice. I imagine your sense of satisfaction is overwhelming.''

What was overwhelming was Cale's obsessive need to reach out and touch Hanna, to hold her close to his heart, to breathe her in and remember those incredible days and nights when all felt right in his world, when he was truly at peace with himself.

*Go on, say it, you big coward. Tell her how you feel. Find out if she really does love you and if she wants to make this a true marriage, not just a temporary bargain that's over and done.*

''Hanna, I—''

''Don't!'' She pressed her fingertips to his lips and tears instantly filled her violet eyes. ''Just go. Please. Don't make this harder than it is. Don't you know it's killing me to have you here, knowing you're going away and won't be back?''

He drew her fingertips from his lips and held her hand in his. He stared at her while shiny tears slid down her flushed cheeks. ''You want me to stay? Why's that, Mags?''

She swatted his chest, stamped her foot and blurted out, ''Blast it, Cale, I love you, that's why! There, I've said it. I can't even remember what it felt like not to love you.'' Her free arm swept outward in an all-encompassing gesture. ''This is just busy work. I completely understand why my father immersed himself in business after losing my mother and brother. He was trying to outrun the ache of lost love and recover from the kind of wound that never heals.''

''I love you, too, Hanna,'' Cale said quietly, humbled by her courage to speak from her heart while he kept dillydallying and testing the waters—just in case Malloy, Arliss and the deputy marshals were mistaken about her feelings for him. He hadn't been sure enough of *himself* to believe, not until he heard the words from *her* lips.

Her misty violet eyes shot open and her jaw dropped. "What did you say?"

"I said I love you, too." It was easier to say the unfamiliar words the second time. Cale thought maybe, with regular practice, he'd get even better at it.

Despite her tears, a radiant smile encompassed her face. "Oh my God! You do? Truly?" She flung her arms around his neck and squeezed the stuffing out of him.

"Yeah, I truly do." He winced and added, "Ouch."

"Sorry." Hanna quickly withdrew. She grabbed his hand and towed him toward the house, away from the curious gazes of her young laborers. "Let me show you what I've done with the place. If you don't approve, of course we'll change it because—"

"Magnolia Blossom," he interrupted, grinning like an absolute idiot who was so deeply in love that he was practically floating on air.

"I want this to be our home," she continued, ignoring his attempt to interject a comment.

"Mags—"

"My father suggested importing furniture," she said, speaking over him, "but I insisted on practical comfort first and foremost. So…what do you think?"

Cale halted inside the front door, marveling at the drastic changes. The colorful new drapes were flung open to provide a grand view of the wide-open spaces. A dozen vases of riotous wildflowers graced the spacious room. Overstuffed couches and chairs had been arranged around the sandstone hearth, where Skeet lay napping on a pallet that Hanna obviously hadn't made herself. It looked too good to be one of her knitting projects.

"The place looks grand," he said approvingly.

"Come on, I want you to see what I've done with the master bedroom," she insisted, leading him upstairs.

Cale screeched to a halt and stared at the extra-wide bed, which was covered with a fluffy, down-filled comforter.

"Now that's a bed," he said approvingly, and remembered he'd once told Hanna that the first thing he wanted to purchase when they settled into the loft over the gun shop was a big featherbed. Unfortunately, investigating Otis Pryor's criminal activities had occupied all of his time.

He jerked upright when the realization of what Hanna had done fully soaked in. She'd purchased *his* dream and furnished it with him in mind. This was the ranch he hadn't been able to share with his half brother. This wasn't *Hanna's* dream. It was *his!*

"Why'd you do this?" he asked, his searching gaze fixed on her.

Her lashes swept up and she smiled at him. "Because I thought if you ever stopped through here, in between your forays for Parker, it might feel like the home you always wanted and never had. Even if you couldn't stay forever I wanted you to realize you were always welcome here."

He leaned down to brush his lips over hers in a gentle kiss. No one had ever gone to such extremes for him. No one had ever taken his wants and needs into consideration. Only Hanna, who made it a habit of placing others' needs before her own.

God, she humbled him, awed him. And at the same time she made him feel important enough to merit this kind of preferential treatment. Yet the deep-seated voice of unworthiness kept whispering that he'd done nothing to deserve her and wasn't entitled to this chance at happiness.

When her arms glided gingerly up his chest and around his neck, mindful of his injured arm and bruises too numerous to mention, Cale buried his face in the waterfall of silver-blond hair. He savored the unforgettable scent of her, marveled at the satisfaction he derived from holding her in his arms.

"I want you to stay with me always," she whispered.

He smiled ruefully. "In a perfect world I could stay

right here and we could love each other. Society might eventually accept it.''

''Society can go hang,'' she countered, holding on to him fiercely. ''And *because* we love each other it *is* a perfect world. You are my dream come true.''

''I never figured to be anyone's dream come true, Mags. When people treat you like you're only half-human and second rate all your life, you start thinking maybe you are, that maybe you don't deserve to wish for the same dreams that other folks chase. I was afraid to tell you how I felt because I thought you'd be better off without me.''

''Oh, Cale, I'd like to round up all those people who made you believe you were unworthy and undeserving and take after them with a shotgun. You're the most remarkable man I've ever met.''

''When your own mother looks at you as if you are her worst nightmare revisited it's hard not to think you don't really belong anywhere except in the wilds with the other inhuman creatures of nature,'' he murmured, admitting to his long-harbored insecurities for the first time in his life.

Cale held on tightly, amazed at all the deeply buried feelings and thoughts that suddenly bubbled up like a geyser, as if he couldn't make a fresh new start with Hanna until she knew him completely.

She was crying now, bleeding tears for him. And that's when he knew beyond all doubt that he truly had her heart. She cared about him the same way he cared about her— cared so much that she'd been willing to live out his dream for him, even when he'd been afraid to let himself believe in all those magical possibilities.

Cale felt tears clouding his own eyes—an unprecedented occurrence that would have humiliated him if anyone but Hanna had witnessed it. But she was the other half of his soul, the pure light that drew him from the darkness and shadows. He was no longer inferior, no longer just an accident of birth cast out in the world to live and die, unwanted and unloved.

He *mattered* because Hanna cared. *She* made him special, worthy.

"Well, that's a damn good start."

Hanna and Cale sprang apart at the sound of Malloy's booming voice rolling through the bedroom.

"Try knocking next time," Cale said, and scowled. "And when you come for future visits, I insist on at least a week's warning."

Malloy stared at him pointedly. "Do we have a deal or not, Elliot?" he demanded.

Hanna gasped in outrage as her gaze bounced between Cale and her father. "Did you bribe him to come here, Papa?"

"Don't go getting all wounded and defensive, little girl," Malloy said, undaunted by Hanna's disapproving glare. "I didn't bribe the man to come out here. I only bribed him to give me a grandchild…or three."

Her mouth fell open. "I swear to goodness, Papa, your audacity never ceases to amaze me. One minute I think we've reconciled and the next instant you're trying to dictate my life all over again."

Smiling, Cale leaned close to Hanna. "Surely you know me better than to believe I'd take a bribe, Mags."

"Well, I should certainly hope not!" she huffed.

"I was planning to give him a grandchild…or three…for free," he added confidentially as his wandering hand settled familiarly on her hip, giving her a playful squeeze. "I'm committed to doing the incredibly pleasurable deed as many times as it takes to produce results."

While Hanna blushed profusely, Malloy strutted over to press a kiss to her brow. "I'm headed to New Orleans in a few hours, now that I'm assured I have everything going my way out here in the outback of society. But I will return. You can depend on it."

"I was afraid of that," Cale said in mock regret. Truth be told, Malloy was starting to grow on him—in an exasperating sort of way.

"Be happy," Walter murmured fondly. "I do love you, though I'm years too late in saying it." His graying brows flattened over his narrowed gaze as he focused his stern attention on Cale. "And as for you, Elliot, you better make my little girl happy or I'll become a permanent fixture in this house to ensure that you do!"

When Malloy sauntered out the door, Hanna plucked at the buttons on Cale's shirt. "I don't suppose you feel up to practicing making babies yet."

The prospect of getting naked with Hanna caused desire to slam through him with astonishing speed. He hadn't been sure he'd recovered enough after the strenuous physical exertion from six days' past, but apparently he had because her suggestion got an instant rise out of him.

He grinned as he led her to the bed. "With the right incentive I could be persuaded," he assured her wickedly.

"And what incentive might that be?" she asked as she helped him shed his shirt.

"What happened to that obscene little passion-red garment you assured your father that I wouldn't approve of?"

She arched an amused brow. "You liked it, did you?"

"On you, Mags, I loved it." He waggled his brows suggestively. "I've even had a few fantasies about it during my laudanum-induced dreams."

She smiled saucily at him. "Well, I wouldn't want to disappoint you, my dear husband. After all, I live to please you." She sauntered to the dresser to pluck up the outrageously seductive garment, then stepped behind the dressing screen.

He had never undressed so quickly in his life. Although he looked like a walking bruise, he'd been thoroughly assured that Hanna loved him for who he was deep down inside. The way he looked on the outside wasn't what mattered most to his wife.

Cale was lying in bed, waiting in eager anticipation, when Hanna reappeared in that skimpy little creation that made him want to throw back his head and howl. Damn, she was bewitching and seductive.

And her heart belonged to him. He hadn't had to earn her respect and affection and loyalty. She offered it unconditionally, and Cale had never understood what that meant until Hanna came into his life like a refreshing breath of air.

When she approached the bed, doing her amusing imitation of Millie Roberts's drumroll saunter, Cale made a visual feast of her. She definitely had his undivided attention and his everlasting affection. When she leaned over him, her breasts came dangerously close to spilling from that scrap of red lace. Cale groaned aloud.

"You like, Mr. Big Tough Deputy Marshal?" she purred provocatively.

"I *love*," he murmured as he pulled the pins from her hair and let the silky strands cascade over his hand. "It's my first time in love. I never understood what love was about until you barged into my life to propose marriage."

Hanna eased down beside him and swept her hand lightly over his chest. Her dewy lips grazed his shoulder, then his neck. "I was searching for the perfect husband and I found him in you," she whispered.

"You said there were two things that prevented me from being the perfect husband," he reminded her huskily. His hand drifted over the lush swells of her breasts, feeling her immediate response. "One—learn when to keep your trap shut. What was the other?"

"Two—love me forever," she told him as she stared deeply into his eyes. "The second is vastly more important than the first. Your love is all I need to make me happy."

"Then I guess that makes me absolutely perfect for you,

Magnolia Blossom,'' he drawled, mimicking her Southern accent. ''No one's ever gonna love you the way I do. Starting now. Until long past forever.''

And then he made love to his wife with a gentle reverence that only she called from him. He whispered his love over every inch of her responsive body, giving all that he was—the very best of what he was—to her forevermore.

He came to Hanna eagerly, breathlessly, urgently. He became a vital part of her and she became the most vital part of him. Hanna made him believe that, of all the men who walked the face of the earth, he was the shining example of the perfect husband. He knew when to be silent and he knew how to love her with every beat of his heart, and to the depths of his soul.

Call it fate. Call it destiny, Cale mused as he and Hanna tumbled over the edge of rapturous oblivion. But it was meant to be. Because only now, only with Hanna, did he fully understand and accept who he was. He *was*, he thought as he lay spent and secure in his wife's loving arms, the perfect husband for Hanna.

And that was all that truly mattered in life.

\* \* \* \* \*

# SAVOR THE BREATHTAKING ROMANCES AND THRILLING ADVENTURES OF THE OLD WEST WITH HARLEQUIN HISTORICALS

## On sale March 2003

### TEMPTING A TEXAN by Carolyn Davidson

A wealthy Texas businessman is ambitious, demanding and in no rush to get to the altar. But when a beautiful woman arrives with a child she claims is his niece, he must decide between wealth and love....

### THE ANGEL OF DEVIL'S CAMP by Lynna Banning

When a Southern belle goes to Oregon to start a new life, the last thing she expects is to have her heart captured by a stubborn Yankee!

## On sale April 2003

### McKINNON'S BRIDE by Sharon Harlow

While traveling with her children, a young widow falls in love with the kind rancher who opens his home and his heart to her family....

### ADAM'S PROMISE by Julianne MacLean

A ruggedly handsome Canadian finds unexpected love when his fiancée arrives and he discovers she's not the woman he thought he was marrying!

**Harlequin Historicals®**
Historical Romantic Adventure!

# From Regency Ballrooms to Medieval Castles, fall in love with these stirring tales from Harlequin Historicals

## On sale March 2003

### THE SILVER LORD by Miranda Jarrett

Don't miss the first of **The Lordly Claremonts** trilogy!
Despite their being on opposite sides of the law,
a spinster with a secret smuggling habit can't resist
a handsome navy captain!

### FALCON'S DESIRE by Denise Lynn

A woman bent on revenge holds captive the man
accused of killing her intended—and discovers
a love beyond her wildest dreams!

## On sale April 2003

### LADY ALLERTON'S WAGER by Nicola Cornick

A woman masquerading as a cyprian challenges a
dashing earl to a wager—with the stake being an island
he owns against her favors!

### HIGHLAND SWORD by Ruth Langan

Be sure to read this first installment in the
**Mystical Highlands** series about three sisters
and the handsome Highlanders they bewitch!

Harlequin Historicals®
Historical Romantic Adventure!